A LIFE WRAPPED IN LIES

SEARCHING FOR TRUTH

GWEN STOKES

Fiction
A Life Wrapped in Lies - Searching for the Truth

All rights are reserved. No part of this book may be used or reproduced in any manner without the copyright owner's written permission, except for quotations in book reviews.

Copyright © 2025 Gwen Stokes

ISBN: 978-1-959811-68-8 (Paperback)
ISBN: 978-1-959811-69-5 (eBook)

Library of Congress Control Number: 2024919551

First Edition

Cover Design: Christine Pentagonias
Interior & E-book Design: Amit Dey
Editor: A.E. Williams
Author Photo Credit: Praxi Branford Of Alexstar Images L.L.C.

Website: www.wordeee.com
Twitter.com/wordeeeupdates
Facebook: facebook.com/Wordeee/
e-mail: contact@wordeee.com

Published by Wordeee in the United States, New York, New York 20

A LIFE WRAPPED IN LIES

Dedication

For my brother, sister, and father, whose absences are felt but whose spirits remain ever near. And for my mother, brother, and nieces, whose strength, love, and quiet brilliance continue to guide me. This book began as a bridge to someone I missed beyond words. In time, it became a lifeline; an intimate thread connecting memory to hope, grief to grace. May you find as much meaning in these pages as I found solace in bringing them to life.

1

Thank God It's Friday

The flight from Los Angeles to Philadelphia is excruciating. My mind replays the argument with Phil Kaplan, CEO of my biggest account. Phil, in his drunken rage, crossed the line. Not only had he thrown a major league temper tantrum, but he also kicked me out of his office. As the head of a major Hollywood studio, he's practically untouchable. How will this affect me? No one will bat an eye at his behavior, and he knows it. Despite my fifteen years at EPN (Entertainment Placement Network) and my involvement in major product placement campaigns for blockbuster films, I can't help but worry about how Jack, my sales manager, will react when he hears what happened. If he finds out about Phil, I might not have a job on Monday. Right now, all I can think is, "*Thank God it's Friday.*"

As soon as we land, I'm heading straight home. I'm exhausted, physically and mentally. I have no energy to explain what happened with Phil, especially to Jack. To make matters worse, the guy sitting next to me in 3A won't stop talking. I regret exchanging business cards.

"Sienna K. Lewis, it's a pleasure to meet you."

"Likewise." I nod, slipping my AirPods in. I'm too tired for conversation. The moment the plane doors open, I bolt.

The traffic leaving the airport is horrendous. The man in front of me slams hard on his brakes as a car cuts in front of him to avoid the construction a few hundred feet away. I brake hard, swearing at city officials. Why is there construction on the busiest highway in the city on a Friday evening? I curse myself for not staying over in LA. It would have been nice to visit with Gloria, one of my girlfriends from college.

I crawl along in traffic, dreaming of my silken sheets. But first, I have to pick up Millie, my dog. I groan lovingly. *When will I ever get home?* Stuck in traffic, my eye catches a huge billboard displaying the 76ers' new rookie player. *Welcome to Philly, Osei Wharton, it's an Osay Jawn.* Clever way to teach the city how to pronounce his name. I hope he can play, but if he can't, the ladies of Philly won't complain. He's gorgeous.

To pass the time in traffic, I check my voicemail. Jack's left a message. He can wait until Monday. The next one is from Gloria, a top plastic surgeon to Hollywood's elite, and one of the four women I cherish the most. No matter how much I press, she will not divulge the names of her clients. Too busy with our lives, we seldom get together anymore, but just thinking of Taylor, Rainey, Gloria, and Dee warms my heart. We met over twenty years ago as freshmen. Dee, we met in our sophomore year, and we've been loving and supporting each other ever since. I push the message button.

"*Sese, I know damn well you didn't come to LA and not see me. Why'd I have to hear about your trip from Rainey? Call me!*"

"Do you want to reply?" the car monitor asks.

I press no. I know she's upset, but she can wait until tomorrow.

She'll understand why I left without seeing her when I explain the incident with Phil.

I pick up Millie, my beloved Bouvier and protector, and it feels good to walk into my home. I can finally breathe. And clearly, Millie feels the same; her tail hasn't stopped wagging.

Monday morning comes far too soon. I check my calendar. Of course, Jack has scheduled a 9:30 am meeting. After eight years of working together, Jack and I still struggle to communicate. I wonder how we made it work all these years. I dread telling him about what happened with Phil, though I suspect he already knows. I brace for the worst, the account taken away, or even being fired. Taking a deep breath, I walk into Jack's office.

"How did you do it?" Jack's all smiles.

"Do what?"

"Sweet talk Phil's hard ass in renewing for three more years. You're my hero."

I try to hide my shock, maintaining a calm façade. "What can I say, I have the Midas touch."

EPN represents several hundred brands from toothpaste to high-end luxury items from modest mid-size vehicles to expensive sports cars. While Jack reviews the contract with his assistant, I replay my uncomfortable meeting with Phil.

The meeting started as usual, with us reviewing his new project. Our top priority was finding ways to enhance the scenes in his latest movie with products viewers used in their everyday lives. If a car is needed, we ask what make and model would best fit the character's lifestyle and personality. When we met that morning, it was clear Phil had already been drinking. Every suggestion I made seemed to irritate him.

"Why should I have any of the products you're suggesting? Clearly, you don't understand the characters; your suggestions are all wrong," he yelled.

I tried to explain my rationale, but he wasn't listening. Sensing he was about to explode, to lighten the mood, I made the mistake of asking about his wife. Phil's wife is much younger than he is. Everyone, but Phil, knows she married him for his money.

"How dare you ask me about my personal life? I hate doing business with you and your company. A bunch of amateurs," he lashed out at me, then paused as another thought crossed his mind. "How did you know my wife and I are having issues? What have you heard? What gossip are you spreading about me?"

The more I tried to calm him down, the angrier he became. He lost control and threw the storyboard we were working on across the room.

"Phil, have you lost your mind?" I looked up, startled.

He then grabbed the phone from his desk and threw it at the wall, narrowly missing me. I calmly picked up my belongings and headed for the door. As I was leaving, security guards suddenly appeared. Phil asked them to escort me out of the building. The people in the office stared at me as if I had stolen something, mostly avoiding making eye contact. I was angry and embarrassed: I wanted nothing to do with him ever again!

Jack interrupts my thoughts. "Sienna, are you okay?"

"I'm fine, just jet-lagged."

After reviewing the products with Jack to satisfy Phil's contract, I head to my office to digest what had just happened. A large arrangement of roses is sitting on my desk. I pull out the card. *Please forgive me, Phil.* Next to the bouquet is a FedEx envelope with a five-thousand-dollar Saks gift card. *Guilt has its perks,* I thought as I picked up the phone to call Phil. I want him to apologize to me personally. I get his voicemail. Refusing to leave a voicemail, I dial his assistant, Valerie.

"Hello Valerie, is Phil available?"

"Hi, Sienna. Are you okay? Did you receive the flowers and the gift card?"

"Yes, thank you."

"Phil will be in within the hour Sienna," she pleads, "please be patient. He's going through a brutal divorce, and his wife is taking him to the cleaners. And things are tense. What happened to you happens almost daily now. We're all walking on eggshells around him. We never know when he'll explode."

"Thank you for the flowers and the gift card."

"Sienna, I didn't send them. Phil did. He adores you."

"Thanks, Valerie. Let him know I called."

The multi-year deal with Phil gives me some breathing room at work. In this business, you're as good as your last sale, and the incident with Phil was a stark reminder not to get too comfortable with one three-year, multimillion-dollar contract. This could've been a disaster. My goal is to close another major deal, which means a trip to New York.

2

Counting Stars

The trip to New York is a resounding success. I close another multimillion-dollar deal, and I'm on fire. But all the traveling has taken its toll, and I'm in serious need of a break. I call Jack to share the win and ask for a vacation. He agrees to a three-week break, on one condition: I stay somewhat plugged in. I promise to work remotely if needed.

I'm heading to my happy place. Excited, I text my girls to see if they can take a few days off to join me on Martha's Vineyard, and to my delight, they all say yes. The next day, I book the ferry, load Millie into the car, and head to my sanctuary. One perk of owning a vacation home is that there's no need to pack clothes. I have to bring the essentials: Scotch, beer, Soju, and plenty of wine. I'll spend the first week alone, catching up on my reading and taking long, meditative walks on the beach with Millie. Work interruptions are few, and I'm finally getting the break I need. I can't wait to see my girls.

On Monday of my second week, I'm busy picking up the girls from the airport and the ferry. Gloria's the first to arrive, already complaining about her flight and how I went to LA without seeing her. She'll forgive me. She loves the Vineyard. Many of her clients vacation here, and she is always on the lookout for new referrals. Plus, her father-in-law has a place on the island, so she knows it well.

"Hello, gorgeous, stop complaining. I've missed you," I say, my eyes appreciating her always magnificent style. How are Jackson and the boys doing?"

"They're fine. Jackson isn't too happy about watching the twins for a week by himself, but he knows I need to unwind and relax."

I give her a big hug. Gloria has been married to Jackson, a now successful film executive, ever since he laid eyes on her in college. He'd come to visit her roommate, she opened the door, and they've been inseparable since.

"Yes, relaxing is definitely part of the plan," I say. "The next few days will be all about sunrises and sunsets, Luther, Jill Scott, Gregory Porter, Anita Baker, and when we're ready to let loose, Michael Jackson, Whitney, and Prince."

"I can't wait!" Gloria exclaims.

Dee was next to arrive. We didn't meet her until sophomore year, but we bonded fast, mostly because she could cook, and we were always starving. From then on she's been feeding us ever since. Often mistaken for Vanessa Williams on the streets of New York, she's now a celebrity chef with a top-rated, internationally syndicated show. Her excellent skill means we'll feast like queens for the next week. As she struggles with her luggage, Gloria gets out to help.

"My God, Dee, did you pack a body in here?" Gloria laughs, kissing her on the cheek.

"It's spices, and everything I need to feed you all for a week."

"In that case, I'll lift with joy."

"It's been too long," Dee says, sliding into the back seat and kissing my cheek.

On the way home, we stop by the Edgartown Seafood Market to buy lobsters and the freshest seafood the island has to offer. Dee is going to make her famous lobster *Fra Diavolo* for dinner. It's a delicious mix of sweet and spicy tomato sauce over homemade pasta and fresh lobster. She has a knack for making everything taste so soulful and rich.

"Dee, how is Marie?" Gloria asks.

Dee groans. "Apart from the fact that the girl is dating a white guy from Scotland, and Lord knows you don't get much whiter than that, she's fine. She's thriving at Princeton and never misses a social cause to champion."

"Well, you raised Marie to have her own mind, and it turns out, she's got enough opinions for three," Gloria says with a smile.

The car announces a text. It's Rainey, the self-proclaimed voice of reason in our group, who has missed her flight, so she'll arrive tomorrow. There's a sigh of relief. Rainey isn't her real name, but the one I gave her because she rains on everyone else's parade. Quick to give advice but one never to take it, we all know that before we leave the Vineyard, at least one of us will have argued with her. As annoying as Rainey can be, she's dear to all our hearts.

A few hours later, I'm on my way to pick up Taylor from the Ferry in Oak Bluffs. Of all the girls, she's my best friend and closest confidant. An investment banker and the cheapest person I know. Taylor didn't disappoint. To save money on airfare, she flew into Boston, took the Peter Pan Bus to Woods Hole, and the ferry to Martha's Vineyard. She doesn't consider that time is money. Taylor is Taylor, and we never miss a chance to tease her about being cheap. Honestly, I wouldn't be shocked if her bank account rivals the GDP of a small country.

"Hey, Love." I'm over the moon to see her, and I give her a giant hug, but all she sees is my new car.

"Sese! You bought a Porsche Cayenne! Seriously? I could have invested what you spent on this car and made you a few hundred thousand dollars. Don't you have better things to do with your money?"

"Just take care of the money you already have of mine. Really, Taylor, I haven't seen you in forever, and all you want to do is yell at me for buying a Porsche?"

"At least it's a hybrid," she replies sarcastically.

"How can you keep a straight face and ask clients to trust you with their money when you're such a cheap ass?"

"That is precisely why they give me their money. Honestly, Sese, you are such a dumb ass. People love a banker who knows the value of a dollar."

Taylor and I have a steadfast ritual whenever she hits the island. First stop, Farm Neck Golf Club Café. She claims it's for the drinks at the bar, but the real reason is to see the golf players starting from the first tee. Her hope is to see Barack Obama. He summers on the Vineyard and plays here often, though all of these years, we've yet to see him swing a club. Regardless, we raise a glass to Barack and Michelle. We head to the house, listening to the *Love Jones* soundtrack and mellowing out before we get there. She's relieved to hear Rainey won't be arriving until tomorrow. A little peace and quiet before the storm never hurts.

Dee has prepared dinner, and we dine while watching the most beautiful sunset. We listen to the sound of Senge, short for Sengekontacket, steps away from my screened-in porch. We watch as gulls drop clams and oysters on the rocks, then swoop down to gobble them up. At nightfall, we're mesmerized by the stars. As we get deeper into our drinks, we start to count them.

"Will we ever finish counting all the stars?" Taylor asks, gazing up at the sky.

Gloria chuckles, "If you think we've been close, you're not just drunk but you're delusional."

Dee smiles and says, "Taylor, as long as we're counting them together, that's all that matters."

I raise my glass. "Here's to counting stars."

The next morning, I pick Rainey up from the airport. She's on her phone, blows me an air kiss like she's royalty, and tosses her luggage into the back seat without missing a word of her donor pitch. Rainey, the CEO of a nonprofit, is always fundraising.

When we arrive at the house, she steps out of the car, points to her luggage, and walks away. I glance sideways at her, then at her bags, and keep walking. Her majesty has arrived. Taylor comes out to greet us. Rainey gives her a little wave, as if she were indeed royalty, points to her luggage, and mouths the word "please." Taylor blows her an air kiss and takes Rainey's bags inside.

By noon, Rainey has worked everyone's last nerve, and we all want to give her a knuckle sandwich. Everyone except me heads to the beach. I, on the other hand, head to the golf course.

3

To Tee or Not to Tee

I have a 1:40 P.M. tee time at Farm Neck Golf Club in Oak Bluffs, one of the top-ranked courses in the Northeast. I love playing here. The course fits my eye: not overly difficult, but far from easy. All eighteen holes wind through tree-lined fairways, with scenic views and impressive glimpses of Vineyard Sound and the Pond.

Today I'm paired with two guys, one from New Jersey and another from DC, neither of whom is thrilled to be playing with a woman. Their stony expressions and sidelong glances make it clear enough. No greeting, no small talk, just silence. It's fine by me; it makes winning even sweeter.

On the third hole, I birdied a difficult par 5. This is when they realize I can play, and they don't have a snowball's chance in hell of beating me. They finally relax and start discussing hockey, baseball, and basketball, intentionally excluding me from their conversation.

By the eighth hole, their conversation turns to the 76ers and their new draft pick, Osei Wharton. They're seriously man-crushing, calling him a mix of Allen Iverson and Dr. J rolled into one, a pure, unadulterated talent.

As we're teeing from the tee box on the ninth hole, who but Barack Obama is finishing up on the eighteenth green! I grab my phone, take a photo, and text it to Taylor.

She responds immediately, *"I'm heartbroken,"* followed by several crying emojis. I wave at the President as he speeds by in his golf cart, surrounded by Secret Service.

After a satisfying round of golf, I head back to the house to join the girls. We play backgammon and drink, laughter echoing late into the night. The game draws us into deeper conversation and easy contentment.

The next morning, I wake to the smell of coffee, cinnamon, and the melodic drumbeat of rain. When it rains at the Vineyard, time stands still, demanding relaxation. Dee has made the morning even more perfect with French toast bread pudding, herb-baked eggs, and apple turkey sausage. We have breakfast on the screened-in porch enjoying the view of the pond and watching the ships glide across Vineyard Sound. We sip on mimosas and catch up on everything that can't be shared over the phone, texts, or on social media. It's comforting to see that we're not just living well but loving well.

The next day is a beautiful beach day, fresh with the scent of rain as we make our way to the Inkwell. The Inkwell is a beach in Oak Bluffs frequented by African Americans since the nineteenth century. The name was given to the beach because of the skin color of the beachgoers and has become a source of pride among the folks who frequent it. Ridiculously small, it's very rocky in places, but the water is beautiful, calm, and peaceful. If you want a good spot, however, you have to get there early. We spend the day reminiscing about our first visits to the Vineyard, lost in stories and laughter.

We watch the sunset and linger at the Inkwell well into the evening. Queen Rainey is perched on a bench above the beach, holding court. Being there feels like visiting an old friend, comforting and timeless. Later, Dee prepares a fantastic dinner, and just like that, our cherished ritual picks up where it left off. It's a rhythm we'll continue over the next few days.

On our last morning on the Vineyard, preparing our minds to go back to our daily lives, we make plans to return in August. Gloria and Dee are the first to leave. Taylor and Rainey decide to ride back with me. I'll drop them both in Manhattan. Rainey isn't thrilled to share the backseat with Millie, and the feeling is mutual. When Rainey is upset, she makes it her mission to spoil the atmosphere for everyone else. To get under our skin, she leans in with that condescending tone we've come to dread, and asks, "Why don't you two have any children?"

Taylor and I exchange a look and say in unison, "Marie," Dee's lovely but very opinionated daughter.

"Marie is the baby Rosemary had with the devil," Taylor says.

I nod, "That child is the best birth control ever."

Rainey chuckles, nodding in agreement. Taylor and I are single with no children. We both wanted husbands but no children, or was it the other way around? Either way, we succeeded at not having husbands and definitely not having children.

By the time we reach Providence, Rhode Island, everyone, including Millie, is asleep. Too quiet, I put in my AirPods and listened to *The Emperor of Ocean Park* by Stephen L. Carter, a favorite of mine. The novel, an intriguing story about the affluence and privilege of the people who summer on the Vineyard, is always delightful. I listen to it often, especially when leaving the Vineyard, reaffirming my love for the island.

4

The Element of Surprise

I drop Taylor and Rainey off in the city and make my way to Philly. I'm excited I've another week of vacation before having to think about anything to do with work. I'm making a mental note of the things I need to get done around the house. The car phone rings. It's Rainey. I just dropped her off on the Upper West Side of Manhattan forty minutes earlier.

"Damn, Rainey, do you miss me already?"

"I have some juicy gossip. I know you haven't heard it yet."

"I'm sure I haven't, so tell me."

"I heard Bruce's wife is asking for a divorce. He's an emotional wreck because he never saw it coming."

Rainey is never diplomatic. She knows how long it took me to get over Bruce. Bruce and I met in college and lived together for a few years in New York. When we broke up, he married someone else almost immediately. I have no interest in discussing my ex and his soon-to-be ex-wife with Rainey.

"I'm sorry to hear it," I say. "I need to focus on the road. Traffic is horrible, and the Lincoln Tunnel needs my full attention."

"Don't give me that bull. Your car has hands-free calling."

"Goodbye, Rainey, I love you."

Just thinking about that man makes my blood boil, and a wave of heat consumes my body. I grip the steering wheel tightly. Dropping this tidbit on me is Rainey's revenge for having to ride in the back with Millie.

I don't want to think about Bruce and his divorce problems. As much as I try to pretend otherwise, my heart feels the jolt at the mention of my first and only love. God looks out for drunks and fools, and Bruce is no exception. To distract myself, I pull up my playlist, determined to relax and groove my way home.

I arrive home planning to do nothing for the next few days. But you know what they say about well-made plans have a way of unraveling. It all starts with the doorbell ringing. I check the security cameras and see a tall young man, well over six feet tall, standing at the front door. His baseball cap is pulled low, and he shifts nervously, staring into the monitor.

"Hello," I say.

"Hello, I'm looking for Sienna Lewis."

"Yes, I'm Sienna Lewis. How can I help you?"

He says nothing.

"How can I help you?" I ask again.

"I can come back if this isn't a convenient time," he says.

"Excuse me, convenient time for what, exactly? What's this about?"

He doesn't say a word, just turns and walks away.

I watch the camera as he pauses, glances back at the door, hesitates, then finally leaves. I consider calling the police. But what would I say? Someone I couldn't identify rang my doorbell and left. The encounter bothers me for the rest of the day. He knew my name, so this wasn't a random visit.

The week passes by quickly, and in the blink of an eye, I'm back at work.

Jack needs me to fly to London to sort out a situation that a colleague mishandled. I agree, but only on the condition that I receive sixty percent of the commission. If I'm going to clean up someone else's mistake, it should come with fair compensation.

5

London is Calling.

I love London. I'm here to see Rhett Nelson, my rebound love and the owner of the production company, who swears he moved here because I broke his heart. We've remained close friends. He is extremely handsome, tall, lean, yet muscular. Think Tom Cullen with a beard so magnificent it deserves its own social media page.

I head straight to his office from Heathrow.

"My love." He greets me with a kiss. "You look fantastic."

"And so do you," I reply.

"Sese, it seems I only see you when there is a crisis."

"How bad is it?" I ask.

"The worst," he groans, leading me to his office. We review the storyboard and immediately agree that the current products are all wrong. We quickly pivot to new products that fit the storyline, resonate directly with the audience and align with the film's goals. After hours of work, we agree that a solution won't happen tonight. Knowing I love the London jazz scene, Rhett suggests dinner and live music as the perfect reset.

We go straight to Vortex, one of London's premier jazz clubs. The hostess can't take her eyes off Rhett. That's nothing new. She frowns when he places his arm around my waist. We end the night at Ronnie Scott's, my all-time favorite jazz spot. It's just before midnight when we arrive. The quartet on stage is extraordinary, and the energy is electric. We find a table close to the stage and order drinks. My stomach growls loudly, reminding me that I haven't eaten all day.

"I think it's time for Ronnie's famous veggie burger," Rhett says, signaling a server. "One veggie burger for her and fish and chips for me."

We stay until closing. When we step outside, dawn is beginning to stretch across the sky. I feel guilty for keeping Rhett out all night.

"Sienna, I have an extra ticket for the 76ers and the Celtics exhibition game at The O2 Arena tonight. Care to join me?"

"I'd love to, but I can't accept the ticket."

"Why not?"

"Because you're my client. I entertain you, not the other way around."

He frowns and sticks out his bottom lip like a sulking child. He knows I can't say no when he acts like a two-year-old. I look into his beautiful blue eyes and feel myself giving in.

"Fine, I'll go, but it's work, not a date."

"Understood. I've been telling Jack I want you back on my account. Maybe if we spend more time together, we can rekindle..."

"Rhett." I stop him. "You'll find your person, someone better than me, who isn't flawed and will accept all your love."

Instead of taking a taxi, I walk the mile back to the hotel to enjoy the crisp breeze.

After a few hours of sleep, I'm in Rhett's office early. We work diligently until we finally land on a solution.

"Why don't we let Jack sweat it out a few more hours?" Rhett suggests.

I agree and head back to the hotel to freshen up and watch a Korean drama on Netflix. One day, I'll find the kind of love that exists in those beautifully addictive dramas. A few hours later, I meet Rhett at the entrance of The O2 Arena. I'm instantly in awe. This place is amazing. It feels like Madison Square Garden on steroids. The corridors are lined with high-end shops and Michelin-starred restaurants: Japanese, Chinese, Italian, French, and Mexican.

"I want sushi," I say.

Rhett grins, "You'll love the food in the suite."

"Will there be sushi?"

"Probably not."

I grab his arm playfully. "Whatever is served had better be good."

The arena is buzzing with excitement, and I'm feeling the energy—the type that only exists at a live sporting event. It vibrates through the air, through my bones. We're in a suite with ten others, all friends of Rhett. They are Celtics fans, which means Rhett and I become the loudest, most unapologetic 76ers fans in the suite. I settle in with a cold Scottish ale and the best-grilled shrimp tacos I've ever tasted. I'm not missing the sushi at all. Tonight is Osei Wharton's debut, the 76ers' newest phenom, the same player the men on the Vineyard couldn't stop raving about. From the tip-off, it's clear the kid is special and absolutely locked in. His movements are sharp and deliberate. He reads the court like a veteran. He sees the game seconds before everyone else. He glides past defenders as if he owns the floor. I love this feeling, the rush, the anticipation of willing my team to win.

Rhett leans forward, rattling off his stats with childlike excitement. The entire stadium feels it too. The crowd rises with every play, breath held, hearts thumping, waiting for the next flash of brilliance. Osei has captured them, every fan rising to their feet, voices uniting in a single chant.

"Osei! Osei! Osei!"

The kid is six foot seven, a hundred and ninety-five pounds of pure energy. An energy that is shaking the rafters. Then it happens. The breakthrough moment. A breathtaking steal, lightning-fast drive, and a slam dunk. The crowd erupts. The sound is like thunder. And for the moment, everyone is swept away.

I'm feeling pleasantly buzzed from the ale, not to mention a couple of drams of Scotch. After the game, I hurriedly say goodbye to Rhett. If I linger in this state, we end up being a couple, even if only for one night.

After hugging Rhett goodbye, I head to Ronnie Scott's. I leave tomorrow, but first, I want one last jazz set. About thirty minutes in, the club is packed, standing room only. I notice a group of towering guys at the bar just as the server sets a drink in front of me.

"I didn't order this."

"Compliments of one of the basketball players," he says, nodding toward the bar.

I glance over and offer a polite nod in thanks. *I'm old enough to be their mother. Why is one of them buying me a drink?*

"Whatever he's having," I say. "Put it on my tab."

The waiter smirks. "I think he is drinking milk."

I laugh. "Looks like they all should be drinking milk."

He nods and grins as he walks away.

Back at the hotel, something feels off, though I can't quite put my finger on what. A faint uneasiness settles over me. I should be exhausted, but sleep refuses to come, even though I need to rest before my early morning flight back to Philadelphia.

6

What Can I Say

As I crawl along the Schuylkill Expressway, a billboard of Osei Wharton catches my eye. Philadelphia's latest obsession is the 76ers' second coming of Allen Iverson. That's when I realized why he looked so familiar in London. I'd seen his face plastered across Philly billboards.

On Monday morning, fresh off saving the London account. HR informs me that my assistant has been reassigned to another account manager, and the search was on for someone with senior-level experience. Fortunately, I keep a running list of top-tier talent, and by the end of the week, I hire Chloe Donovan away from a competitor. Chloe, a Hampton University graduate currently pursuing her MBA at Drexel, brings a deep knowledge of accounts I have been targeting and an infectious drive to succeed. She's sharp, ambitious, and from day one, we clicked. As the only African American assistant in the company, Chloe is determined to carve out her place, and she's already making waves.

My desk phone buzzes.

"Sienna, Taylor is on line one for you," Chloe says.

"Hello, Taylor. What's up?"

"Hey, Sese. I was just reviewing your account, and I think there are some stock moves you should make. Can you come to New York and hang out while we review your portfolio?"

"Taylor, I'm tired of traveling. Can you come to Philly?"

She arrives two days later. We review my portfolio and make the changes she recommends. I convince her to stay for the weekend. Our conversations are easy; we aren't pressed to discuss politics, relationships, or work. Instead, we cook, play music, and simply exist. At twilight, my favorite time of the day, we sit on the porch, watching the sky turn a soft, glowing red. It feels like a Miles Davis kind of night.

"I could sleep out here," Taylor says, as the mellow sound of Muted Miles floats from the outdoor speakers.

"I have," I reply with a smile.

Remembering my gift from crazy Phil, I decide to go shopping on Sunday morning, and I invite Taylor to come along.

"I'm not going shopping with you," she groans. "Sese, you spend too much money on clothes and shoes. I can't sit back and watch you spend so frivolously."

"I honestly don't know how we're even friends," I say. "And yet, you're my best friend. It was a gift, five grand," I add, waving the Saks Gift Card in her face. "If you come with me, I'll give you a thousand to spend."

"Give me ten minutes," she says, "I'll be ready."

"So, you're not cheap when it's someone else's money."

"You got that right!"

At Saks, the lower lot is full, a rare sight for a Sunday. Inside, every department buzzes with young women. It is unusually busy for a Sunday morning.

"What is going on?" I ask a sales associate. "Is there a designer trunk show today?"

"No, a few 76ers players are here shopping, and it was posted on social media. Within ten minutes, the store was flooded," he replies.

You can't miss seeing the players. They tower over everyone around them. I suddenly lose interest in shopping. I am not in the mood to fight through crowds. I turn to tell Taylor I want to leave, but she's gone. In the blink of an eye, she vanished. I find her in the shoe department, drooling over a pair of designer kitten heel slingback pumps. Eyeing the condition of the shoes she's wearing, it's time for a new pair. I sit on the nearest bench, slip in my AirPods, and let her enjoy her shopping spree.

She nudges me. "Do you know that young man over at the perfume counter? He's staring at you."

"I'm sure he's looking at all these pretty young girls trying to get his attention."

"No. He's staring at you!"

I glance over and lock eyes with the 76ers' second coming of Allen Iverson, Osei Wharton.

"That's Osei Wharton," I say. "His face is plastered on billboards all over town. He's supposed to be the next Allen Iverson. Rhett took me to see him play in London."

Taylor raises an eyebrow. "So, why is he staring at you?"

"What can I say? 'Cause I'm pretty."

I pay for Taylor's shoes, and we leave Saks. We swing by our favorite sushi spot and grab takeout. We eat on the deck, enjoying it with sake. Afterward, I drop Taylor at 30th Street Station.

Back home, I crawl into bed, ready to binge on Korean dramas, where conflicts and confusion are resolved with style. I'm in love with half of the leading men and in awe of the talented female leads. But I can't keep my eyes open. I turn off the TV and lower the blackout curtains.

7

I'm Not a Dangerous Person

Millie is frantic at the front door, all teeth and fury. I check the cameras, and everything inside me goes still. The young man from before. Only this time, I recognize the face the city can't stop talking about.

Osei Wharton.

What is he doing here?

I press the microphone, "Hello, aren't you Osei Wharton?"

"Yes, ma'am."

"How may I help you?"

"I'd like to speak with you. It's personal."

"Personal?"

"It'll only take a few minutes of your time."

My pulse quickens. I hesitate, then say, "Give me a second. I'll be right down."

I open the door, and Millie immediately does her I like you routine. She nudges up against Osei's leg and drops her favorite stuffed animal at his feet. This gesture is reserved for family and friends. It's not Osei Wharton towering over me in the foyer that leaves me speechless; it's her reaction to him that truly surprises me.

"How may I help you?"

He glances around nervously, not saying anything.

"Mr. Wharton. How can I help you?" I ask again, my voice sharper now.

"Call me Osei. You can't…" he trails off.

"If I can't help you, then why are you here? You're making me extremely nervous."

"Look, I'm not a dangerous person." He slowly extends his hand.

I reluctantly shake it.

"I just want to meet my mother," he says quietly.

I blink, "Do I know your mother?"

"You're my mother," he says, tears threatening.

I'm dumbfounded.

"Please don't cry."

I stare at this incredibly handsome, vulnerable young man, searching for the words to tell him I'm not his mother.

"Me? I..."

Before I can finish, Osei abruptly cuts me off.

"Yes, you are," he says quietly, but with force.

This is going to be a long conversation. I inhale, steadying myself. "Would you like a glass of water?" I ask, hoping to ease the tension.

"Yes, thank you."

I hand him a glass of water and make myself a cup of coffee. We sit across from each other in silence. My heart races as I search for questions I don't know how to ask.

"You have a very lovely home," he says finally. "I'm a fan of mid-century modern homes."

Before I can ask him how he knows that, he adds, "I majored in architecture with a minor in engineering at UNC."

He's recovered his composure; the vulnerability is gone. Confidence settling in its place.

"That's nice." I manage. "Osei, what makes you think I'm your mother?"

"What makes you think you aren't?" His voice is firm. "Don't we have the same eyes?"

I look at him closely. And for the first time, really look. *His eyes—they're my eyes! How could this be?*

"I'll tell you one thing for certain," I say, keeping my voice steady. "I've never given birth to anyone. And if I had, I would never give my child up for adoption."

He reaches into his pocket and unfolds several sheets of paper. Worn, creased, handled a thousand times. He places them gently in front of me.

A birth certificate and adoption papers.

Mother, Sienna K. Lewis

Father, Bruce Le Blanc

The room tilts. I grip the paper, unable to breathe.

"This can't be real," I whisper, my voice trembling. "I swear to you, I'm not your mother. And there's no way Bruce is your father. We're not your parents."

I look him dead in the eyes. "How long have you had these documents? And where did you get them?"

"Since I was twelve. From my former guardian who took care of me at the orphanage."

"How old are you now?"

"I'm twenty-two."

"If you had proof that I was your mother all this time, why did you wait so many years to contact me?"

He gives me a severe look. "I didn't know if I wanted to meet you. Clearly, you didn't want to know or meet me."

With as much indignation as I can muster, I say, "That's because I'm not your mother."

"Once the 76ers drafted me and I had money, I hired a private detective to investigate you."

"You did what? Are you kidding me?"

"Is it unusual to want to know why your parents abandoned you?"

"But we're not your parents. We didn't abandon you! I'd like to see that detective's report."

Ignoring my words, he says, "Okay. I was impressed with the information he provided, and so I wanted to meet you. I had many offers, but I wanted to become a 76er and gain fame, so you'd regret abandoning me. So, you are one of the reasons I'm here. After moving to Philly, I could then seriously think about meeting you."

"Look, Osei. I..."

"Since I've been in Philly,"—he cuts me off—"I've driven by your home a thousand times. I've seen you walking your dog, working in your garden, and relaxing on your deck. Wondering if you ever thought of me."

"So you've been stalking me," I say, half-teasing, half-accusing. The laugh that slips out surprises me, easing the tension hanging between us. "I wish I had better news for you, but I'm not your mother."

Suspicion shows in his eyes, "Would you take a DNA test to prove that?"

"Of course," I reply, steadying my voice. "But I assure you, I'm not your mother."

"Where do you live?" I ask.

"Bala Cynwyd," he says, watching my reaction.

"That's only five minutes from here."

"Yeah. I know. Most of my teammates live in New Jersey, and they suggested I do the same, but I wanted to be close to you. I live across the street from your office."

I look him in the eyes. "You are starting to scare me. Osei, I'm not your mother."

He points to the paper in my hand. "How can you say that? Here's the proof."

I look into his eyes, which are moist again.

"Osei, please listen to me. I'm not your mother, but I promise I'll help you find her."

He drops his head. "Why can't you just accept me and be my mom? I'm so tired of being on this planet all alone." The tears fall this time, and before me is a twelve-year-old kid who desperately wanted to find his mother.

My heart is moved in every direction, and I take his hand. "Until we find your birth parents. I'm adopting you. Please stop crying. I'll be your mom until we find her."

Drying tears from his face, he says. "I hope you're my mom, but either way, I can stop stalking you."

"You'd better." I squeezed his hand.

There's a long, uncomfortable pause between us.

"Osei, when were you born?"

"December 30, 1999."

I smile as I remember what I was doing on December 30, 1999, and it wasn't giving birth. Bruce and I had decided at the last minute to leave Manhattan and drive to Philadelphia to celebrate the New Year with Gloria and Jackson, who were in Philly visiting Jackson's father.

"I can't believe you don't know when my birthday is."

"If I were your mother, I'd celebrate your birthday and celebrate you every day, because God gave you to me."

I can tell for the first time he might be thinking I was telling the truth. To lighten the mood, I say, "Are you aware you share a birthday with Tiger Woods and LeBron James?"

"Yes, I just hope to reach their level one day."

"Something tells me you will be."

We exchange phone numbers.

"Can I call you every day?"

I place my hand on his shoulder. "Call me whenever you need to talk."

Saying goodbye to Osei feels more awkward than the shock of seeing him on my doorstep forty-five minutes earlier.

Millie settles at my feet, but I can't settle with her. Someone used my identity, and the question of who and why won't let me sleep. Something about this is deeply wrong, and I need answers.

8

DNA Anyone?

Still reeling from Osei's revelation and the guilt of disappointing him, I'm grateful the Christmas season is near. I need the distraction. The holidays are always my busiest and most festive time of year. I love entertaining, and Christmas gives me the perfect excuse.

It's a time to reflect, to be thankful for family, friends, and the blessings life brings. I'll fill the house and yard with thousands of twinkling white lights. My Christmas tree is never less than twelve feet tall and will shine with delicate and commemorative ornaments collected over the years. For the next few weeks, I'll throw myself into preparing for my annual Everything Chocolate holiday dinner. I'm determined to help Osei...but that will have to wait until I find my footing.

The days blur in a whirlwind of activities. The Everything Chocolate holiday dinner is my traditional event where I invite friends to indulge in chocolate-inspired dishes. A decadent gathering where every dish celebrates chocolate. I picture Osei alone for the holidays, and for a moment, I consider inviting him.

But no. Not yet. Until I fully understand what I'm dealing with, I need to be careful about how much access I give him in my life. I don't want to hurt him further, and having him here would not be good for either of us.

A sharp ring slices through the silence, making my heart skip a beat, interrupting my thoughts.

I answer, and it's Osei.

"Hey, Sese. What's up?"

Sese? I take the phone from my ear, and I intentionally pause. "Sienna, are you there?"

I bring the phone slowly back. "Sienna is here," I say evenly, "But Sese is not. How do you know that name? Sese is a name only people very close to me use."

"I'm sorry," he says quickly. "I meant no disrespect. Your nickname was included in the file I received from the private detective. "

"How are you doing?" I ask him.

"I'm fine. I was wondering when you'll be available to take the DNA test."

I again take the phone away from my ear. This time, I curse under my breath. "Osei, is this necessary? I'm truly not your mother."

"Yes," he says. "It's necessary."

"But I'm not your mother! Once this is confirmed, are you going to be alright?"

"Why wouldn't I be?" His voice softens. "As long as you keep your promise to help me find my birth mother."

"Okay, but I'm not doing some sketchy online or a Maury-type DNA test."

"I'd never ask you to. Given who I am, I can't take that kind of risk. I've already asked one of the team doctors to handle it. "

Two days later, we meet at the stadium. The doctor swabs our cheeks and tells us the results will be ready in three to five days. Osei unexpectedly tears up. All of a sudden, he's a twelve-year-old again.

My chest tightens. I try to stay guarded, but seeing him fight tears splinters my defenses.

I touch his arm, hesitant.

"Osei...one step at a time. Whatever the truth is, you won't face it alone."

When the test is done, Osei gives me a tour of the facility. It's not The O2 Arena, but it's impressive, nevertheless. NBA sanctuaries smell like hard work and ambition, sweat and dreams baked into the polished floors.

We grab lunch at the Cadillac Grille and order Caesar salads with grilled shrimp and tall glasses of lemonade. I study him, not as a stranger, but as a question that refuses to fade. The high cheekbones. The jawline. The slightly slanted eyes that seem to hold the weight of the world. If I'm being honest, there's a resemblance. Our face shape. Our eyes are mirrors of each other.

I watch him as he talks, wondering how he made it all alone. No doubt by his sheer will and determination. I find myself admiring his tenacity and drive.

"Osei, what or who gave you the drive to succeed?"

He looks directly into my eyes, unblinking.

"I longed for the day to make you proud," he continues, "I was six months old when I was placed at Wharton. I moved in with Albert and Hannah Becker, the director, and his wife when I was five or so. I went to a private school in town, while the other kids attended public school. The Beckers were from Germany, and they introduced me to everyone as their grandson. I didn't know they weren't my grandparents until Mr. Albert died."

He pauses, jaws tightening.

"Mr. Albert died of a heart attack when I was six, and everything changed. Ms. Hannah packed up and moved back to Germany to be with her family. She told me she needed a fresh start. I just didn't realize that a fresh start didn't include me."

My heart cracks a little.

"When Mr. Albert died," he says, "he left a trust for me."

"That was very generous of him."

"Maybe." His tone sharpens. "But as I got older, I resented that trust."

"Why?"

"Because I always wondered if that trust was the reason I was never adopted."

"Who managed your trust?"

"After Dr. Becker died, his replacement was Dr. Samuelson. The trust was earmarked for my college education."

"And how old were you when you received the trust?"

"Eighteen, but I received a full academic scholarship from UNC and didn't need the money, so I invested the money in Amazon and Berkshire Hathaway stocks instead. As of now, it's valued well over a million dollars." He catches the look on my face. "Yes, I have a financial advisor."

"Good. If not, I was going to introduce you to the person who manages my portfolio. But that's not why I looked at you like that. I just assumed you went to college on an athletic scholarship, not an academic one."

"You aren't alone. Most people can't believe I'm a scholar. I love learning, and I was always at the top of my class. I attended UNC on an academic scholarship," he repeats proudly.

"How did you cope with your new surroundings when Ms. Hannah left?" I ask.

"Not very well," he says, voice flat. "I don't remember being happy. I stopped making friends because they always left. Sometimes they even came back."

"Came back? Why would they come back?"

"If it didn't work out, they were sent back. They never came back the same."

"Wow, there's an adoption return policy. Who knew?"

He shrugs. "I made friends with the kids I attended private school with." His shoulders sag with sadness. "Can we change the subject?"

I nod, shifting the mood. "Has anyone ever told you that you look like Tyson Beckford, only taller?"

He laughs. "More like Mike Tyson. Who's Tyson Beckford?"

I Google Tyson Beckford images. "He was a supermodel known for the work he did with Ralph Lauren's Polo brand in the '90s."

He studies the photos, and the radiant grin spreads across his face. "I can see that."

We finish lunch, and he walks me to my car.

"Sienna, can I give you a hug?"

"Yes, you can have a ten-second hug."

"Why ten seconds?"

"Anything longer would be uncomfortable, and anything shorter is worthless."

He laughs, then bends and pulls me into a hug. In that moment, my heart aches for a boy who never got held enough.

"Thank you. I'll let you know when I have the DNA results."

As I leave the stadium, my thoughts shift unwillingly to Bruce. His name is on that birth certificate, too. We've barely spoken in twenty years, just polite nods at charity events, and I hate the idea of calling him. But I can't risk Osei reaching him first. I may not be his mother, but Bruce could be his father. And that thought sends a chill down my spine.

9

Hello, My Friend

Bruce, who himself had a period of abandonment before his grandparents rescued him, I feel, would have compassion for Osei, but I'll keep Osei's identity a secret. Now a college professor at NYU, the last time I saw him was about five years ago at a mutual friend's get-together. *We were both standing at the bar waiting for drinks. When the bartender handed me mine, Bruce said, "I see you're still drinking scotch."*

If my memory serves me correctly, I was not friendly and was very sarcastic when he spoke to me. *I'd glared at him and then rolled my eyes before saying, "You forfeited the right to know anything about me. Why do you care?" Not waiting for a response, I walked away.*

The rest of the evening, he stayed on one side of the room with his wife, who seemed to have drunk an entire bottle of scotch, and I stayed on the other side of the room alone.

The only number I have for Bruce my mistake his office. My heart races as I dial, praying it goes to voicemail. But then, he answers.

"Hello, my friend," he says.

"This is Sienna."

"I know. How are you?"

"I'm well. How did you know it was me, and since when have we been friends?"

"Since always. I have your cell number."

"I've never called you or given you my cell number. How do you have it?"

I don't want to argue, so I let it go.

"Never mind. I wasn't expecting you to pick up. I was going to leave a message. I'm in traffic, and it's not the best time."

"Okay," he says, unfazed. "Pretend I didn't answer and leave the message."

I can't help but chuckle. He still has that dry sense of humor. I play along.

"Hello Bruce, this is Sienna. I need to speak with you. It's urgent. Talk soon."

"Call me when you get home," he says.

"I will. Should take about twenty minutes."

Once again, I'm stuck in traffic, but this time I'm not complaining. I use the time to think about how I'm going to tell Bruce about Osei. Finally, at home, I pour myself a glass of wine, and I call Bruce.

He answers on the first ring.

"Talk to me. Are you okay? I've been on pins and needles waiting for you to call."

"I'm doing well. How about you?" I ask him, and regret it because I know about his pending divorce.

"I'm fine."

"You are not fine. The only reason you would call me is if the world were ending."

"Are you sure about that?"

"I'm sure I wouldn't be the first person on your list to call."

"You're right, but this isn't the time for small talk. A young man showed up at my door, Bruce. He had paperwork and official-looking documents, claiming that I'm his mother... and that you're his father."

There's a pause.

"Are you there?"

"What did you just say?"

I start to repeat, but he cuts me off.

"He says that we're his parents. And what did you tell him?"

"I told him I'm not his mother. Are you his father?" I ask. "Bruce, are you his father?" I ask again.

"He was born in Virginia and left at an orphanage not far from our alma mater."

"Why did he reach out to you and not to me?"

"He lives in Philadelphia, minutes away from me, and it's possible the mother may not have told the father she was pregnant. Is there any chance you could be his father?" I press.

Bruce's tone sharpens; he's agitated. "No. Why would you even ask that? You were the only one I was with."

"Shouldn't you count the one-night stands?" I say, dripping with sarcasm.

"Sese, there was only you, and you know it. How did you leave it with him?"

"I agreed to help him find his birth mother."

"Why would you do that?"

"Why do you think? Because someone falsely used my identity, and I need to find out who that person is."

"I have to come to Philly next week for work. Can we discuss this further then?"

"Bruce, at some point, I'd like you to meet him. He's a good kid."

"I don't know why. Nothing will come of it."

"He's truly a lovely person."

"I'm sure you're right. But I still don't think I need to meet him. Sese, I'm not his father."

"I understand. It's a lot to process. I've known for a while, and I'm still struggling. In a week, I doubt I'll know any more than I do now. Plus, work is insane, and I'm preparing for my annual Everything Chocolate dinner. Let's meet in the New Year."

"I've heard about that dinner. Can I come?"

Without thinking, I blurt out, "Hell no!"

Bruce laughs, and I can't help but join him. His voice, his warmth, it transports me back in time. A wave of sadness hits.

We agree to meet in the second week of January. Time and place still TBD.

10

Everything Chocolate

The Everything Chocolate dinner is known for being elegant and fun, and Dee's cooking is the jewel in the crown. She's putting together the Christmas dinner menu. I check in to see how she's doing. Before we even get to the menu, Dee launches into the latest Marie drama, though this time, it's all excitement. Marie's heading to Oxford, and Dee has already hired a realtor to find her a flat. Dee adores London. Her cooking show is a hit there, and she's besties with some of England's top chefs. If the chance came, she'd move there in a heartbeat. Now, she gets to live vicariously through Marie.

The funny thing is, the Everything Chocolate theme was Marie's idea. She came up with it when she was just ten years old. A chocolate lover as a child, she worshipped Jacques Torres, aka Mr. Chocolate, and she was the only child in his master's class. Marie had been spending the weekend with me in Philly, having her favorite macaroni and cheese and drinking hot chocolate, when the genius idea struck.

I was talking to her mom, discussing the menu for my first Christmas dinner party, when she said, "Auntie Sese, why don't you make all the dishes using chocolate?"

From the mind of a ten-year-old, the elegant Everything Chocolate holiday party was born. This year, the menu will consist of lobster risotto drizzled with a white chocolate cream sauce, cocoa-rubbed diver scallops, chocolate-chipotle sirloin steak, and cocoa-rubbed baby back ribs.

"I need to give more thought to the vegetables and desserts," Dee says, "I'll email you my thoughts on those later."

To continue the chocolate theme, I suggest white knight martinis, vodka, and white chocolate, as well as tall, dark, and handsome made with chocolate and vodka.

"Oh, by the way, when was the last time you spoke with Rainey?" Dee asks.

"We talked last week," I reply.

"Did she mention Bruce's divorce?"

"Of course, she did, and I'm wondering why she hasn't called with an update."

"She's in Brentwood. She talked Gloria and Jackson into letting her use their backyard for a casino night fundraiser, raising over two million. Pretty impressive. I need to send her flowers and a check," Dee says.

"I'm sorry, did you say Gloria gave Rainey two million dollars?"

"Sienna Lewis, are you listening? You're not hearing a word I'm saying."

"I have a couple of issues I'm wrestling with, but nothing for you to worry about."

"Is Jack giving you a hard time?" she asks, reminding me of my manager.

"Yes, but nothing I can't manage."

We say our goodbyes. I'm dying to tell her and the girls about Osei, but I can't.

When life throws me something this heavy, Taylor and Dee are my first calls. But not this time. The thought that one of them might be Osei's birth mother is unbearable. This is a path that Osei and I have to walk alone, at least for now. It breaks my heart just thinking that one of them could betray me.

With two weeks until the dinner, I focus on the things I can control and that need my immediate attention. Dee and I have a handle on the menu. I'll hire the wait staff and the bartender, and Dee will bring a couple of people to assist her with the food preparations. The festive evening will mark the beginning of our holiday season.

But I can't get my mind off Osei. Where would I start with this search, and could I do this all by myself? I have to pull myself together and not let doubt creep in, but it's proving difficult.

The phone jolts to life, vibrating so hard it nearly falls off the table. It's Osei.

"Hey, Sienna. Are you busy?"

"I'm making last-minute arrangements for my Christmas party."

"Am I invited?"

"I'll think about it, but explaining you at my Christmas party won't be easy."

"I'm not holding my breath. Anyway, I've had the DNA results for a while."

"And?"

"Inconclusive."

"How can that be, and why are you just now telling me?"

"The team doctor said the sample was compromised. Some kind of cross-contamination. I was trying to process it."

A chill runs through me. Inconclusive feels worse than yes or no.

"Osei, I don't understand. I think I should speak to the doctor directly. Let me know when we can schedule to take the test again."

"There's no need. I know you're not my mother."

"Really?"

"Yes. If you were my mother and had abandoned me, you wouldn't want to take the test again."

In his mind, I'd been his mother since he was twelve. I can only imagine his disappointment.

"Osei, are you okay?"

"Yes, I'm okay."

"It's still early. Do you want to come over for a cup of hot chocolate?"

"Sure."

My heart is bursting with sadness. Who could have abandoned this amazing and beautiful child? At that moment, I doubled down on my promise to help him find his parents.

Osei arrives, and Millie greets him with her favorite stuffed animal. They play while I make the hot chocolate.

"Did I tell you I have a dog?"

"No, what kind of dog do you have?"

"Rottweiler."

"Male or female?"

"Female," he says.

"What's her name?"

"Millie."

"Wait, are you serious?" I ask, stunned.

"Yes, she's staying with my friend Mason in North Carolina. He's bringing her here next weekend. Can I bring her over sometime?"

"Of course. Why did you name your dog Millie?"

"At the orphanage, there was a stray dog I named Millie. At night, I would sneak her into my bed. I'd get in trouble because I smelled like a dog when I woke up."

I hand him his hot chocolate.

He takes a sip. "Wow, I have never tasted hot chocolate this good."

"It's a secret family recipe."

I immediately regret saying that, feeling the uncomfortable sting of the words lingering in the air, and I turn away from him, not knowing what to say next.

Feeling the need to change the topic, I say, "Osei, tell me more about your friend, Mason."

"Are you seriously not going to give me the hot chocolate recipe?"

"Only if you can keep it a secret."

"I promise."

I open the kitchen cabinet and hand him the Godiva hot cocoa canister.

He grins, eyes lighting up. "You never fail to surprise me."

"I've known Mason since I was nine years old. We played in the same youth basketball league. He now lives in Chapel Hill and is working on his master's in biomedical engineering at UNC. He's my best friend. In fact, he's my only friend."

Before I could ask him why he only has one friend, he says, "I have a tough time trusting people, but Mason was determined to be my friend. He would follow me around, telling me he wanted to play ball like me. I was good on the courts even back then. We even had sleepovers at the orphanage."

"Wait-what, who would allow their child to spend the night in an orphanage?"

"His father is an admiral in the Navy and was stationed in Norfolk. Nobody bothered Mason or me. He's engaged to be married in the spring of next year. Would you like to see a photo of him and his fiancée?"

He takes out his phone and shows me a picture of a very tall and handsome guy with a blonde man bun and a very tall, strikingly beautiful Black girl.

He chuckles. "You thought Mason was Black, didn't you?"

"I didn't really think about it."

He smirks. "Well, he thinks he is and considers himself racially fluid."

"Interesting, didn't see that coming. Osei, are you sure about the DNA test?"

"Yes. Like I said earlier, the fact that you want to take another test confirms for me you aren't my mother." His mood suddenly changes.

Standing up, he says, "But I still wish you were. I'd better get going. We have a game against the Nets tomorrow night. I'll call you when I get back."

I walk him to his car and wish him well. Watching as he hurriedly drives away, I pat Millie on her head and say, "I don't know about you, but he's growing on me."

The coolness of the night air is enticing underneath a bright full moon. Millie and I go on an evening walk. The evening breeze helps clear my head, but the moment is cut short by the sound of my phone ringing. It's Gloria.

"Hubby and the boys are going skiing in Aspen," she says excitedly. "I'm coming to the Everything Chocolate Christmas dinner solo, and I don't have to be a wife or a mother."

"You can at least try to contain your happiness. I'm sure your husband and the twins are disappointed to know you're glad they aren't coming with you."

"Hey, family," she yells, "I'm going on vacation without you, and I'm so happy."

I hear one of the twins in the background say, "Whatever."

"By the way, I loved the invitations. Did you make them yourself?"

"No, not exactly. I borrowed the idea from a chic boutique in London. They had brown velvet boxes shaped like Christmas trees and ornaments hanging from the ceiling. They weren't for sale, but I begged the owner to let me buy a few. I had them gold-stitched and personalized as keepsake ornaments for each guest."

"Either way, I'm impressed."

"Can I tell you, Rainey and her fundraiser were a pain in the ass," Gloria sighed. She told me about Bruce. Have you spoken to him?"

"No, and I don't plan to."

I hang up, and I feel bad about having lied. I do plan to talk to him, just not about his divorce.

11

Single Ladies

The day before the Christmas dinner, Dee and her team arrive to help with the food prep and decorations. They start with stringing Christmas lights on the trees outside. On the walkway, battery-operated luminaries are placed to cast a warm, soft, and welcoming glow. Inside, the stairway is decorated with Florida pine garlands accented with olive leaves intertwined with small white lights.

Later that evening, Dee and I picked up Gloria from the airport.

Dee sees her first and says, "Is she a vampire? She never ages."

Gloria has always looked much younger than she is. The tallest of us, in her bare feet, she's six feet tall. Towering over everyone in a pair of designer six-inch heels, people stare in awe because she truly looks like a movie star.

"Hello, gorgeous. How was your flight?" Dee asks as Gloria gets into the car.

"I don't know. I took a sleeping pill and slept the entire way." She hugs me tightly. "This is the gorgeous one."

I turn and kiss her on the cheek. "Thank you. How are you doing?"

"I'm exhausted. Between Rainey and work, I'm worn out. All I want to do is relax," Gloria says.

"Don't worry. After the party, we're going to relax. Remember those Christmases when we'd all get together? We would have to clean the house, cook, and clean the house again," I say.

"I don't miss being poor," Dee grimaces.

"We were never poor. To quote Benny, 'Having been poor is no shame, but being ashamed of it is,' I reply."

"Who's Benny?" Dee asks.

"Benjamin Franklin," Gloria says sarcastically.

"Did he say that before or after he freed his slaves?" Dee shoots back.

"I can't win with you two," I say, laughing.

The car phone buzzes, cutting through our laughter. It's Taylor. I put her on the speaker.

"Hey, Taylor. What's up?"

"Please save me," she whispers.

"Save you from what? Where are you and why are you whispering?" I ask.

"I'm at 30th Street Station."

"I was expecting you and Rainey later tonight."

"We took an early train to help with the setup," Taylor says.

"Why do you need saving?" Gloria chimes in.

"Rainey ran into a couple of guys who donate to her organization on the train, and now she's planning to have drinks with them. I can't..."

Interrupting her, Gloria says, clearly annoyed, "You're on your own. We're not getting caught up in Rainey's politics."

"We're ten minutes away," I say. "Exit on the Thirty-third Street side. It's the opposite side of Michael."

"Who is Michael?" Taylor asks.

"The Statue of Archangel Michael."

"Oh my. It truly is magnificent," she says of the towering statue of Archangel Michael standing with his wings raised high, lifting a soul to heaven. The intricate details of his wings glisten under the soft glow of the lights.

"You really never noticed it before?" I asked.

"Wow! I can't believe I've never noticed him before now."

"We're almost there. See you in a few," I say.

"You're asking for trouble," Dee says.

We arrive to see Taylor and Rainey talking to two men. I pull up next to them. "Ladies, your carriage has arrived." I pop open the hatch, and Taylor hurriedly throws in her luggage and gets in the backseat with Gloria. Rainey finishes her conversation and hugs the taller of the two men.

"Move over, wimpy," she says to Taylor,

"Rainey, did you get their contact information? The guy in the blue overcoat has potential." I admiringly say.

"I have it. He asked me to give it to Taylor," Rainey replies, then turns to her. "That man is fine."

I catch a glimpse of him as he crosses in front of us. Something about him pulls at a distant memory. "Doesn't he look familiar?" I ask, narrowing my eyes, trying to place his face. Dee leans forward, watching him disappear into the crowd.

"Yes," Dee says, "but I can't quite place him."

We sit in silence for a moment, both searching our memories.

"Whoever he is," she adds with a smirk, "he's absolutely gorgeous."

Taylor rolls her eyes at Rainey and says, "You know what you can do with his number."

"Forget about men, we're here to relax and enjoy ourselves," Gloria chimes in.

"Amen," Taylor says.

The Christmas lights twinkle like tiny stars as we pull up, casting an almost magical glow over the house. It looks like a postcard beaming with warmth and the Holiday Spirit.

"This is breathtaking," Rainey says.

"I hope my guests will have the same reaction," I respond.

"Oh, they will. Let's go inside. I've prepared samplers of everything for us to try tonight," Dee says.

I throw an arm around Taylor and Gloria, pulling them close. "I need help evaluating the adult beverages."

Gloria grins, eyes sparkling. "Now *that's* the kind of tasting I'm qualified for."

The scent hits me first, rich, decadent, irresistible. It's Everything Chocolate Day, and the spread is outrageous. Lobster risotto topped with cocoa-rubbed diver scallops. A chocolate-chipotle sirloin steak that sizzles just right. Baby back ribs with a smoky cocoa crust, glistening beneath warm lights in polished stainless steel buffet warmers. At the bar, the white knight martinis gleam like crystal magic, while the tall, dark, and handsome cocktails sit ready to cast their hypnotic spell.

The girls, dressed to the nines, are glowing and dancing like the night belongs to them. Seeing them so happy, it feels like the clock has struck midnight, and it's about to be Christmas morning, and I'm the kid with the biggest gift under the tree.

Taylor taps me on the shoulder, her eyes lit up. "Sese," she says, grinning. "This is insane. You've outdone yourself yet again."

To my surprise, Jack and his wife are the first to arrive. I'd sent him and Jia an invitation, but didn't think they would come. They haven't in the past. I walk over to and hug Jia, who looks stunning in a simple black dress.

"Merry Christmas, Sienna," Jia says, taking my hand. "Is my husband taking good care of you? You know I'll scold him if he's not."

"Yes, he's taking good care of me," I say, as I walk them over to the buffet. "I hope you'll enjoy the food. All the dishes are made with chocolate."

"I'm going to have to steal this idea," Jia playfully says, taking a bite of the cocoa-rubbed baby back ribs. "How decadent. I've never tasted ribs made with chocolate. Jack, you have to try these."

"Sienna," Jia says, "please email me the recipe."

"Sure, no problem."

"If you don't, she'll bug me until you do," Jack says.

By 9:00 pm the house is electric, music thumping, laughter spilling out into the chilly night air, and the party is in full swing. Pulsing with life, the glittering outfits, clinking glasses, and impromptu dance battles create a perfect evening. We lose track of time, swept up in the rhythm, the joy, the chaos, and we don't stop until the sky hints of the dawning morning. With hoarse laughter and glitter in our hair, we finally bid our guest good night. After the last guest leaves and the music fades, the girls and I slip into our favorite tradition. Still in our dresses, we kick off our heels and collapse into my oversized king bed. We laugh and rehash the night before, drifting off in a tangle of silk sheets and leftover confetti.

Still half asleep, even as the sun is high, the smell of coffee finally lures us from our cocoon. Dee and Gloria are missing. I head downstairs where one is making smoothies, and the other is brewing coffee.

"I hope the blender didn't wake you," Gloria says.

"No. Blame it on the coffee," I soulfully moan.

Dee hands me a cup, and I melt. "This is so delicious."

"Compliments of my friend Arjun. He picked up the beans while he was in Colombia," Dee says.

"Please let him know how grateful we are."

"Isn't he that gorgeous Indian guy with a cooking show that airs after yours?" Rainey asks, coming into the kitchen.

"Yes," Dee says.

"I love his show," Taylor chimes in, following her.

"Dee, you should ask him out on a date," Rainey teases.

Dee sighs. "He's out of my league."

"Have you looked in a mirror lately?" I ask.

"Stop being so self-deprecating. I hate it when unbelievably beautiful people downplay their attractiveness," Rainey says, rolling her eyes.

For once, Rainey is right. Dee is slender with an hourglass figure and a face that could start and stop a war. Her blue-gray eyes are spellbinding, the kind that make you stare a second too long.

I smirk and ask, "How many times a week do strangers mistake you for Vanessa Williams?"

"I look like Halle Berry," Dee says.

"You wish," Rainey quips.

"Where's Gloria?" I ask.

"She had a smoothie and went back to sleep," Taylor says.

"I'm going to join her," I say, yawning.

"Thank God for blackout curtains. I'm right behind you," Taylor says.

This holiday for us was relaxing and carefree, making it especially hard to say goodbye to one another. Gloria is the last to leave. On the ride to the airport, she notices a billboard displaying the 76ers' new player, Osei Wharton. Pointing to the billboard, she says, "The twins love him. Their grandfather has converted them to 76ers fans."

"I saw him play when I was in London working with Rhett, and I thoroughly enjoyed watching him."

"How's Rhett doing? Does he still want to marry you?"

"He's fine. And no, he doesn't want to marry me."

"Seriously, I'll never understand why you let him get away."

"The timing wasn't right."

"Timing, my ass. You were never available for him or anyone else. You're a lost cause."

"Gloria, really, this will be the last time I'll see you for a while. Can we talk about something else?"

"Sure. Why don't we talk about why you're meeting Bruce in Manhattan?"

"How do you know about that?"

"Bruce mentioned it to Jackson."

"Of course, he did."

"You know they're best friends."

"I'll keep that in mind moving forward."

Wanting to steer the conversation elsewhere, I say, "So, how's the facial serum line coming? When do we get the grand launch?"

"After doing the research, it seems like everyone, and their mother, has a cosmetic line. Did you know there are over fifty celebrity beauty brands? And that's not even counting the expert lines being launched by professionals like me? I'm going to have to think of another way to make my millions."

We pull up to the Terminal, and I step out to hug her and to help with her luggage. Before she disappears inside the revolving doors, she turns and yells back at me. "I'll call you when I get home, and we can talk about why you're making plans to go see Bruce."

12

Two Dangerous Men

I don't make any plans to celebrate New Year's Eve. Before I drift off to sleep, I reflect on the year and give thanks. It was truly a good one, and I'm grateful for all I've accomplished.

At 12:01 A.M., I'm groping for my chiming cell. It's Osei. Millie has taken up residence on my bed and seems annoyed with me for answering the phone. I give her a gentle pat on the head.

"Did I wake you?" Osei asks.

"Yes, you did."

"I want to be the first person you speak to in the New Year."

"Where are you?"

"At a teammate's place in New Jersey."

"Happy New Year, Osei. This is going to be a fantastic year for you. Drive carefully coming home."

I hear someone ask him who he's talking to, and he responds, "My mom."

"Osei, what are you saying? Please don't say that."

"Sese, didn't you say you would be my mom until we found my birth parents? So, I'm officially recruiting you as my mom. Are you still meeting with Bruce in New York next week?"

"It's Sienna to you and, yes, at Nobu. Why?"

"No particular reason."

"Happy New Year, Sese." He ignores my correction and hangs up the phone.

I roll over and say to Millie, "This is going to be an interesting year."

Bruce and I meet in Manhattan the second week in January. We have dinner reservations at Nobu 57 in Midtown. It's perfect for a relaxed conversation, stylish but not too intimate. I arrive early, take a seat at the bar, and order a drink for some much-needed liquid courage. It's been years since we've had a cordial face-to-face, and my nerves are kicking in.

Someone behind me asks, "Is this seat taken?"

I wouldn't mistake that voice anywhere; still I say, "Yes. I'm waiting for someone."

"I'm hoping that someone is me. I know I've changed, but I must say, you still look good."

"Thanks." I turn to look at him. *He hasn't changed a bit; he's still gorgeous.*

He waves to the bartender and says, "I'll have what she's drinking."

Taking the seat next to me, Bruce says, "Scotch, hmmm. If my memory serves me right, you only drink scotch when you need a little liquid courage."

"That's no longer true. I actually prefer scotch to wine these days."

"I heard your Everything Chocolate dinner party was a success. Perhaps one of these days, you'll invite me."

I give him a coquettish smile. *What are you doing? Don't flirt with this man!*

"Perhaps, how are you doing?" I ask.

"Other than my daughter moving out of the house, my dog dying, and my wife divorcing me to be with a woman, I'm doing fine."

I turn to him, doing my best to look genuinely remorseful.

"Sese, I know you want to laugh."

In that moment, laughter erupts from deep inside me. I laugh until my sides ache, not with sorrow, but from satisfaction.

Once I compose myself, I say, "I'm sorry about your dog."

"After all I told you, you're sorry my dog died?"

"I'm sorry you're having a rough time. Why did your daughter move out?"

"My daughter didn't move out, she ran away."

I stare at him incredulously, a storm of questions swirling inside me, but the words are caught in my throat.

"Sese, it's a long story, which I'll share with you one day. She's doing well and is in her second year at Columbia."

The hostess lets us know our table is ready. As she leads us to a corner table, I glance around, reminded of how much I love this restaurant. The server brings the menus, and Bruce suggests I order for both of us. The waiter takes our drink order: sake for me and Oban Neat for Bruce. For dinner, I chose the crispy rice with tuna and Unagi sushi, and for Bruce, the Chilean sea bass with black bean miso for Bruce.

"So, Sese, what's going on? Talk to me. Have you had any more conversations with the young man?"

Sitting face-to-face with Bruce. I'm nervous, my heart is pounding. I take a deep breath to steady myself, then get straight to the point.

"Bruce, when we were together, were you with anyone other than me?"

He gives me a puzzled, but heartfelt look. "Are you asking me *again* if I was intimate with anyone other than you?"

I nod slowly.

"Hell no. I already told you! There was no one else."

"A few months ago, a beautiful young man knocked on my door." I begin, telling the story of Osei while deliberately leaving out his name.

"Beautiful?" he says. "Not handsome." There's utter amazement on his face.

"Yes, beautiful, and sensitive. If it wasn't for the documentation stating that I was his mother, and that you were his father..."

"Sese, are you sure this isn't some sort of scam?" Bruce interrupts.

"Definitely not."

"Maybe it's time to involve the police. Next thing you know, he'll have some heartbreaking sob story and ask to borrow money."

"It's not like that. He doesn't need our money, alright? What he needs is to find his family, and I've committed to helping him."

"You need to think logically. And don't get attached to this kid. Scratch that, it's obvious you already have." Bruce takes a sip of his drink, eyeing me closely. "What's he like?" he asks. "And what is it about him that makes you so determined to help?"

"He's intelligent, confident, and most of all loving. Someone we both would be proud to have as our son. Look, I may or may not need your help, but if I do, can I count on you?"

"For what? Neither of us is his parents. Sese, you are not his mother."

That's not the answer I was looking for, but before I can answer, the restaurant all of a sudden becomes noisy. People were clapping and talking all at once.

"It must be someone famous," Bruce says.

"I don't care how famous they are; people here don't usually care. That's why the famous come here."

"Wow, check this out," Bruce says, nodding toward the commotion.

"It's a few of the Knicks, and I think some of the 76ers players as well. Wait, isn't that Osei Wharton?" he excitedly says.

I turn and look directly into Osei's face. I should never have told him I was meeting Bruce here. I excuse myself and go over to him. Through clenched teeth, I ask, "What are you doing here?"

"It's not what you think. I was forced to come here. Those guys over there lost," he says, pointing to the Knicks players. "They're treating us to dinner." He grins.

"Cut it out! Why are you here? We agreed you wouldn't meet Bruce." I give him the don't-lie-to-me look.

"Okay," he says. "I want to see my potential father, and I'm worried about you."

My heart skips. I want to send him straight back to his table, but the hope in his eyes stops me. I should be furious, but somehow his timing is so ridiculous it's almost perfect.

"Since you are here, you might as well meet him, but don't you dare ask him any questions."

We're walking over to Bruce when Osei says, "Hold on a second." He goes over to the table where his friends are seated, says a few words, and walks back over to me.

Bruce is standing when we get to the table. I introduce him to Osei.

"Osei Wharton needs no introduction," Bruce extends his hand. "How do you two know each other?" he asks.

"Well, Osei endorses one of the products my company represents, and we met while he was filming the commercial. I'm also helping him with his public speaking."

I ignore the look Osei gives me.

Osei orders the Wagyu steak, and he and Bruce immediately start to talk about basketball. I glance from one to the other, checking to see if there's any resemblance. Each man is handsome and attractive, but they bear no resemblance to each other. The thought surprises me, and I catch myself studying Osei's features, once again noticing the similarities in our expressions.

"Curfew time," Osei announces an hour later, and pushes back his chair. "I have to get back to the hotel."

"Nice to have met you." Bruce shakes Osei's hand again.

I walk him outside, and we have our ten-second hug.

"I'll see you when I get back from this road trip."

"Stay safe and healthy, and call me when you can."

When I get back to the table, Bruce has ordered another round of drinks.

"He's genuinely a very nice young man," he says.

"And that's exactly the reason you and I are going to help him find his birth mother."

Bruce stares at me, completely stunned. "Osei Wharton is the young man claiming we're his parents?"

"Yes, and he needs our help."

"Sese. I can see why he could think that you're his mother. He really does look like you."

"I know. Will you help me find his birth mother and the woman who used our identities? I wanted to believe I could handle this on my own, but I can't."

"Have you involved the Fantastic Four?" He asks, using his nickname for the girls.

I shake my head, "No."

"Why? Because one of them could be Osei's mother," he says, answering his own question.

I say nothing, overwhelmed by the thought that one of them *could* be Osei's mother. My heart aches with the guilt even thinking it.

The server comes over and informs us that Osei had paid the bill.

Bruce and I wait for the valet to bring my car around.
I text Osei: Thank you for dinner.
He immediately texted back: *You are welcome. I like Bruce a lot.*
My car arrives, and Bruce says, "Nice ride."
I'd forgotten what a car enthusiast he was and his passion for cars. In college, he was a complete gearhead working on cars for students, while occasionally working in auto repair shops to make extra money. He excitedly begins to tell me about the 1965 Mustang he and a friend are restoring. Once he starts talking about cars, you'd better buckle up and hang on for the ride. We are driving down Seventh Avenue when I realize that I have no idea where I'm taking him.

"Where do you live?" I ask.
"Jersey City, you can drop me at the nearest train."
"Jersey City is on the way for me. If you want, I can give you a ride."
"Thank you."
"Are you going to help me?"
"Sese, I don't see how I can."
A text comes through from Osei on the car display. The message reads,

Osei: Sese. Thank you for all you are doing.
Me: *You are welcome. I'll see you soon.*
"I thought I was the only person allowed to call you Sese."

"He's not allowed to call me Sese to my face. He knows that only my close friends call me Sese. As a matter of fact, you can no longer call me Sese."

"Oh, I see. I guess I have to earn the right to call you Sese again."

"That won't be an easy road for you, my friend." Remembering our painful past, I say nothing for a while. Bruce, sensing my mood, changes the subject.

"I remember you told me he was raised at Wharton. Sese, I used to work there part-time in the kitchen," he says.

"Now I remember. Was there anyone else from the school who worked there?"

"Not that I recall. Only me. If I were you, I'd start with the director and his wife."

"The director died, and his wife moved back to Germany," I reply.

"Wait, Ms. Hannah moved to Germany?" he asks, surprised.

"You know her?"

"Yes, and so do you."

"I don't remember her."

"She ran the cafeteria, and you two had a brief but memorable encounter. The infamous Oatmeal War."

"When I started a petition for steel-cut oatmeal over regular. Yeah, I remember now. So that's her?"

He laughs. "You only got twenty signatures because she hired students to work in the cafeteria and at Wharton. No one wanted to risk their job by signing your petition."

"Yeah, I surely lost that war," I say, pulling up to a nice high-rise building with a splendid view of Manhattan. "Wow, why would anyone live in the city when you have this type of view from Jersey?"

"Are you happy?" Bruce asks out of nowhere.

I look up at him and see that his eyes are filled with sadness. "What prompted that question?" I ask.

"I just can't remember the last time I was happy, and I was wondering if you're happy."

"I'm as happy as happy can be."

"Are you alone?" he asks.

"Yes. I'm alone, but I'm not lonely. I stay busy with work and various hobbies."

"I'm sure one or more of those hobbies includes high net worth individuals," he mischievously says.

"Get out."

"Let me know how I can help you and Osei. I'm around if you need me."

"I think that you've given us our first lead."

"What lead?" he says with a puzzled look.

"Ms. Hannah Becker. She had access to a lot of young, vulnerable women."

We say our goodbyes, and I make my way back to the Turnpike.

I mull over Ms. Hannah all the way home, deciding to connect with Taylor to see if she remembered Hannah Becker.

"Wasn't she the lady in the cafeteria?" she replied to my question.

"Yes."

"There were rumors of her helping pregnant girls."

"Helping how?" I ask.

"I think with abortions, but mostly adoptions."

"Are you serious? How did I not know that?"

"Because you never needed her services."

"And you did?" I ask.

"No, but why are you asking about her?"

"I read an article when I was in London," I lie. "It mentioned how instrumental she was in starting the organic gardening movement. It caught my eye because her passion was fueled by her alliance with local growers in Virginia. I was simply curious."

"When are you coming for a visit?" I ask, changing the subject.

"I just saw you at your holiday dinner. I can't believe you miss me already."

"Of course, I miss you. You're my best friend."

"I bet you say the same thing to Dee, Rainey, and Gloria."

"No, if I were to say that to either of them, they would absolutely not believe me."

"Sese, you missed your calling. You should have gone into politics."

"Goodbye. Love and hugs."

13

Ms. Hannah

Saturday morning, Millie and I are preparing for our morning walk, when Osei—back from a four-city road tour—arrives. He joins us on the trail to plan the next steps in our search. As we walk along, several deer nonchalantly cross in front of us. Millie is pulling hard on her leash, wanting to give chase.

Wide-eyed, like a kid on Christmas, Osei says, "Sese, did you see that? That was cool."

"It's cool until you hit one with your car."

"Does that happen very often?"

"Often enough."

The trail is used by walkers, runners, and people riding their mountain bikes over its rocky and very steep terrain. We hurriedly move out of the way of a couple of guys speeding by.

"How often do you walk here?"

"At least three times a week. It's good exercise."

"How often do you run?" I ask.

"Every day indoors, but I prefer running outside. I can run here and not be bothered by people wanting my autographs or wanting to run with me," he says.

Walk complete, we head back to my place to begin the journey toward Osei's truth. I place a cup of hot chocolate in front of Osei, and I take a sip of my coffee.

"Osei, I'd like to start with Ms. Hannah. How much do you know about her?"

"Why would we start with her?"

I tell him what Bruce and Taylor told me about Ms. Hannah helping young girls who became pregnant.

"Help how?" Osei asks, eyes wide with innocence.

"With adoptions and or abortions," I say quietly.

"Are you serious?"

"I am. Think about it. She even had access to the medical facilities at the orphanage. Maybe she assisted your birth mother with your birth."

"But she thinks you're my mother."

"She has to know I'm not. When was the last time you spoke to Ms. Hannah?"

"A few months ago."

"If she gave you those papers, I am sure she may be hiding something, or she really thinks I'm your mother. We need to find out, but be careful when you call."

"Actually, I called to tell her I had met you."

"What was her reaction?"

"She was excited and asked that I send her a picture of the two of us together. You might be mistaken."

"When was the last time you saw her?"

"Six months ago, when I was in Germany to celebrate her sixtieth birthday."

"I think Ms. Hannah could lead us to your parents."

Osei gives me a puzzled look. "I doubt it. She was the one who led me to you?"

"Do you think she'll speak to us?"

"For sure. We could do a conference call with her."

"Let's go to Germany. I'd rather see her face-to-face. Osei, don't mention that you know I'm not your mom and that you're still searching for your birth mother to Ms. Hannah."

"Why not?"

"We need her to believe you've already found her. If she suspects otherwise, she might shut down."

"Or she might help."

"I have a feeling Ms. Hannah knows I'm not your birth mother. The million-dollar question is, Why is she pretending I am?"

"Okay, good point. I won't say anything."

Osei leaves. I call Rainey and recount the same story I shared with Taylor to see what, if anything, she knows about Ms. Hannah. As usual, she has her own agenda.

"By the way, how was your dinner with Bruce?" she asks.

"How did you know we had dinner together?"

"I have informants everywhere. So, what did you and Bruce have to say to each other?"

"None of your business."

"Is it true?" She's laughing so hard, it's difficult for her to ask the question.

"Is what true?"

"Is it true his wife left him for a woman?"

"Rainey, why is that so funny?"

"We're talking about Mr. Casanova, the tall drink of water—the man who left you for a woman who likes women. Rather ironic, don't you think?"

"We didn't talk about his divorce." *We talked about everything but that.* I move the conversation back to Ms. Hannah.

"Are you sure you don't remember Ms. Hannah? Her husband ran the Wharton Orphanage."

"Yes, and so do you."

"How would I know her?"

"She oversaw the cafeteria. Don't you remember your petition to have steel-cut oatmeal served instead of regular oatmeal?"

"Yes, the oatmeal battle, which was my one and only interaction with her. I'm not sure I even knew her name."

"I'm sure you didn't. Since you did not need to work to pay for tuition, books, clothes, or food. There was no need for you to know her."

"Rainey, isn't this the pot calling the kettle black. When did you ever have to work to pay for tuition?"

My father, ambassador to the Republic of Côte d'Ivoire, gave me a cosmopolitan upbringing and financial stability. My parents and I traveled the world, but when it came time for school, I settled in with my grandparents, both college professors, in Philadelphia. Rainey's background was equally privileged. Her parents were successful doctors. She grew up in Manhattan's Upper East Side and attended the Dalton School.

"Why are we talking about Ms. Hannah anyway?" Rainey, easily bored with topics that are not about her, had a harsher tone than necessary. And this conversation is going nowhere. Changing the subject again, I say, "Okay. I was just wondering. Anyway, how have you been?"

"We can now add additional staff and upgrade our computers," she says, passionately recounting her successful fundraising efforts in LA.

"Rainey, hold on. I'm getting another call." I switch lines.

"Hello."

"Hey, Sese, I'm in Philly. Can I stop by?" Bruce asks.

"Hold on. I click back to Rainey.

"I need to take this call. I'll call you next week. Take care, love, and hugs."

14

Trouble Doesn't Live Here

"Bruce, why are you in Philly?"
"I had a meeting at the University of Pennsylvania. I'm leaving there now. Do you live close to the University?"
I don't answer. "Is this a good time?" Bruce asks.
"It's okay. I'll text you my address."

Fifteen minutes later, he's ringing my doorbell.
Millie greets him with her loud and fierce, what-the-hell-do-you-want bark.
The minute he steps into the foyer, she does an about-face and greets him like she does Osei.
"Wow! She's a beautiful dog."
"Miss Millie, thank you," I reply.

We settle in front of the fireplace with a glass of wine. The silence between us is uncomfortable, broken only by the soft crackle of the fire. The warmth from the flames barely thaws the chill that settles between us.
"Why are you really here?" I ask, breaking the silence.
"Any luck finding Osei's birth mother?" he replies, dodging my question.
"No, not yet," I say, then ask again, "Why are you here?"
He looks down, then up at me, a little shy. "I want to see you."
He stands, glancing at a painting. "Oh, by the way, I ran into Rainey and her husband after you dropped me off. They were

visiting someone in my building. Her husband seems nice. How does she get all these nice guys to marry her?"

"It's a mystery." I didn't mention that she and I were just talking about him.

"Osei and I are making plans to visit Ms. Hannah in Germany to ask her some questions about Osei's stay at Wharton."

"Why Germany? I thought she lived in DC"

"Are you sure? Osei told me she moved back to Germany shortly after her husband died. Why would she lie to him?"

"I saw her in DC a year or so ago at an educational conference. I remember her mentioning that she worked at Georgetown University. I was surprised she remembered me and found it strange she even asked about you."

"Maybe she asked about me because you and I dated in college, and I was the oatmeal troublemaker."

"I don't think that was it," he says. "But anything is possible."

"Why would she ask you about me then? Do you think it was because of Osei?"

"Maybe, but I don't know for sure."

I wonder if Osei knows she lived in DC I'll ask him the next time he and I talk.

"How often do you two talk?"

"At least three to four times a week. He was here earlier. We hiked the trail behind my property. So, how are you doing?" I ask.

"Better than expected."

"Why is that?"

"I have something money can't buy."

I give him a puzzled look.

"I have peace of mind, and I'm enjoying the solitude."

"Were you not happy?"

"I was happy a long time ago. At some point, we stopped loving each other, and it became clear we were leading separate lives."

"So, you woke up one day, and the love was just gone?" I say, dripping with sarcasm.

"That pretty much sums it up. Anyway, I think I'd better leave before I get into trouble," he awkwardly says.

"Please don't worry yourself. There's not a snowball's chance in hell you'll get into that type of trouble here."

He laughs so hard, it becomes infectious, and I quickly join in. On the ride to the train station, the conversation between us is flowing a bit more freely. There's an ease which wasn't there before, as if the weight of earlier tensions has lifted.

"Would you like tickets to the 76ers/Knicks' game?" I ask.

"Are you serious? Of course."

"How many would you like?"

"Two, I'd like to invite a colleague."

"Consider it done. I'll let Osei know."

Monday morning rolls around too quickly. I'm on my way to a breakfast meeting with clients when Osei FaceTimes me.

"Good morning, Mama Se. Are you busy? Can we talk?"

"Osei, what's with all the names?"

"I'm trying to find one we're both comfortable with."

"Osei, this isn't a work in progress, and I'm only comfortable with you calling me Sienna."

"Okay, okay, I apologize."

"Did you know Ms. Hannah lived in DC after Dr. Becker died?"

"No, she told me she moved to Germany."

"Bruce ran into her in DC a few years back, and she told him she was working at Georgetown University. What's even more strange is that she asked him about me. I barely saw Ms. Hannah when I was in school. Are you sure she lives in Germany?"

"Yes. I'm sure."

"We need to go to Germany," I say, my voice firm, the urgency of the situation pressing on me.

"I'll have a week off at the end of the month," Osei says.

"I'll have my assistant book the flights."

"Don't bother."

"Why?" I ask.

"I have a membership with a private jet company. Do you want to leave on a Sunday or Monday?"

"Sunday would work. Speaking of Sunday, Bruce would like two tickets for your game against the Knicks on Sunday."

"Okay. Let him know I can leave the tickets at the will-call for him, or I can email them to him."

"Will call is fine," I jokingly say, "Make sure he's sitting in the nosebleed section."

I text Bruce: *Osei will leave the tickets for you at the will-call window.*

On Sunday afternoon, I receive a call from Bruce. I can hear the excitement in his voice. "Hey, Sese, I just arrived at Madison Square Garden. You won't believe the tickets Osei gave me. They're courtside!" he exclaims.

"I suggested the nosebleed section." I tease. "Bruce, why are you calling me? Shouldn't you be enjoying the game?"

"I just had to call. These seats are on the visitors' side, and I'm looking across at Spike Lee and Jay-Z. This is turning out to be a night to remember. I'll die a happy man if the Knicks win the game tonight."

"Enjoy yourself." I am already picturing Bruce's amused reaction. "Osei told me you're having dinner after the game at Nobu's."

"Yes, I'm a little nervous being alone with him."

"Don't be, he's a very kind and gentle person, and you'll enjoy your time with him."

I have ESPN on in the background as I work. Osei had a phenomenal game, but his hard work didn't pay off. Bruce's prayers were answered when the Knicks won. It's after midnight, and I haven't heard from either one of them. As I reach for the water pitcher, the phone rings, startling me and knocking it over, spilling water across the bedside table and onto the floor.

I answer, trying to come off as cool and collected. "Hello Bruce, is everything okay?"

"Yes, more than okay. I had a wonderful time with Osei tonight."

"What did you talk about?"

"To start, he was surprised that I didn't ask him questions about us being his parents."

"Why didn't you?"

"I don't ask questions I already know the answers to. I know two things. I'm not his father, and you aren't his mother. To be honest with you, I told him things that I don't dare say out loud. The life we lived in Brooklyn, about being young and thinking love would conquer everything. Me, wanting a family, and you wanting a career. How we drifted apart. The scotch I drank offered me the courage to share my innermost thoughts."

"I'm not sure I'm comfortable with this level of sharing."

"He's so easy to talk to. Seeing for myself his quiet warmth, I now understand why you described him as being sensitive and beautiful. "

"How did he respond?" I ask.

"He sees you as a very nurturing person and wants you to accept him as a part of your family."

"I've told him several times, until we find his birth parents, I'll be his mom."

"Sese, talking with Osei tonight opened a scar I thought was well healed. I have missed you every day for the past twenty years."

"Let's just leave that conversation alone."

Ignoring me, he says, "I was angry with you for not trusting me and for not wanting to have our child. But I can't remember when I started being angry because you weren't there. I prayed every day for a second chance with you."

"Why did it take you all this time to recognize you had made a mistake?"

"I couldn't leave my daughter. She needed me, and taking care of her helped me to escape the misery I was feeling."

"Bruce, I need to sleep. Good night."

"Sese. What about us?"

"Bruce, there is no us. Good night."

15

That Evil Woman

Two days before we were to leave for Germany, Osei says to me, "I've been thinking. If you and Bruce are not my parents, don't you think Ms. Hannah would be hard-pressed to lie if you were both there?"

"Well," I stammer. "Not...."

"Just think about it," he says, cutting me off.

"I'm not asking him, so you'll have to."

"No problem," he says.

On Monday morning, we meet Bruce at Philadelphia Atlantic Aviation. A wide grin on his face, he gives Osei a man-slap greeting and a hug before hurrying over to greet me. As we board the Bombardier Global 6000, the flight attendant greets us warmly. I find a comfortable place, and once seated and buckled in, I cover up with a nice throw blanket. The attendant offers us drinks and reviews our menu choice. I ask for tea with lemon, and Bruce and Osei settle in plush leather seats with a drink. Talking and laughing, they seem like old friends. Once at cruising altitude, the jet's hum lulls me into much-needed sleep.

Upon arrival, a car is waiting for us. With all the traveling for my job, I've been to Germany on a few occasions, mainly Stuttgart and Munich, to the Porsche and Mercedes headquarters. A fairytale-like country, Germany can claim world dominance in the luxury automotive market. This time we were landing in Berlin, the classical music capital, and the site of the horrors of World War II.

A waiting car whisks us off to Leipzig, where Ms. Hannah lives, about an hour and a half out of Berlin. She's only expecting Osei and me. We're hoping that Bruce's presence will throw her off guard. An hour plus later, the car turns down a beautiful street and into a large gate with the words PRIVATE PROPERTY written in big red letters. Our driver presses the intercom, announcing our arrival, and the gate slowly opens. At the end of the driveway is a picturesque white brick house, covered in ivy. We press the bell on the ornately carved front doors.

A woman in a maid's uniform invites us in and shows us to a luxurious living room. I'm completely floored when Ms. Hannah enters. She wasn't what I was expecting.

"Osei," she says heading over to embrace him. "It's so good to see you again." If she's disturbed by Bruce's presence, she does not let on.

"Sienna," she kisses me on both cheeks. "You are still beautiful."

This isn't the woman I had conjured in my mind as a typical fräulein who runs an orphanage. Decked out in designer wear from head to toe, the petite woman with flowing blonde hair didn't look forty, much less sixty. Finally, she greets Bruce.

"Bruce, you are as handsome as ever. I'm happy to see you again," she nods to the maid, who disappears and returns with a tray of tea and traditional Lebkuchen cookies.

I clear my throat and say, "Osei has such good memories of you. Why didn't you take him with you when you left Virginia?"

She looks lovingly at Osei.

"It was an extremely hard decision. He was the apple of our eyes, and my husband adored him, but I didn't think my family would understand. After Albert's death, I was so distraught. I had every intention of going to get him after I had figured out what to do, but by then the new director of the orphanage had fallen in love with him." She again looks lovingly at Osei. "I thought it better for him to grow up in his own country. I kept in touch with the director and even went back to see Osei a few years later when I had gathered myself."

"She came to one of my games," Osei says proudly.

"That's right. When you were about twelve. I knew then you'd be the star you are now."

"Yes. It was my twelfth birthday. You bought me a birthday present. A pair of Air Jordans."

Bruce spoke for the first time. "Osei told us you gave him his birth and adoption papers."

"I did. I found them after my husband died. How does it feel to have such a successful son?"

The woman belongs in Hollywood! She knew damn well Bruce and I were not Osei's parents. No matter how much we tried, it was obvious she was not going to budge. She claimed over and over that she only found the papers after her husband died and thought Osei should have them."

"We're here to thank you for helping us find our son," Bruce says.

Her smile suddenly tightened, and I thought her lips would bleed. What Bruce says catches her off guard.

"It was simply the right thing to do," she says, steadying herself.

As we say goodbye, she suddenly says, "Sienna, how is your friend Dee? I remember her from the kitchen, and now she's a big-time Chef, I hear."

I'm shocked to hear myself say, "Dee is fine."

The car takes us to the Ritz Carlton in Berlin, and we leave Ms. Hannah behind, no further ahead than when we arrived.

But now, we know for sure that Ms. Hannah was not who she pretends to be. On the flight back home, I replay every second of our meeting with Ms. Hannah in my mind and concluded that Ms. Hannah is a very opportunistic and conniving woman. It is clear I need to have an ironclad plan the next time we meet her.

The moment I set foot into the house, I called Dee.

"Dee, how do you know a woman called Ms. Hannah?"

"Why are you asking about that evil woman?"

"Evil? Everyone I speak to says she's a nice lady."

"There's nothing nice about that woman. I worked in the cafeteria for a semester, and I can tell you there is nothing nice about that woman."

"You called it your prison sentence! And you always brought us hot cinnamon buns to go with the dinners you cooked! Did Ms. Hannah make them?"

"Hell no. She was a slave master. She used all of us because she knew we needed to work to stay in school. She was racist as hell and delighted in separating the staff by color. If you were light-skinned, you got the good jobs, helping to prepare menus, setting up food stations, and working the cash registers. If you were brown or dark brown, you washed dishes, mopped floors, and unloaded the food truck deliveries."

"Dee, unfortunately, Black people face that kind of discrimination all the time. Did she treat you differently because of the way you look?"

"Hell no! I wouldn't let her. I wore my Blackness like armor, and I wasn't about to bow to Ms. Hannah or anyone else, for that matter. It took me years to realize that while some people clung to her narrow views, others saw the world through an entirely different lens."

"What made you say she was evil?"

"Girls went to Ms. Hannah for help to either get rid of their babies or to put them up for adoption?"

"Are you serious?" I pretend not to know that fact.

"Her husband was the Director of the orphanage, for God's sake, and she had access to the entire facility."

"Why didn't I know about this?" I double down on my own deception.

"I never told anyone about it because if I did, I'd have to tell my story."

The wheels in my head are turning fast. I'm beginning to feel dizzy. *Could Dee be Osei's birth mother?*

"The reason I met you in my sophomore year was because I was pregnant my freshman year."

"Dee…"

I was working in the cafeteria when I found out. I was desperate. I couldn't go to my parents."

"Why not?"

"I couldn't stand to see the disappointment in their eyes, and I didn't know who the baby's father was. Sese, I was raped."

"Dee, why didn't you go to the police or your parents? It wasn't your fault?"

"Did you know I was my high school homecoming queen?"

"No, you never told me."

"I crowned the new queen and slipped away early. On the road home my car broke down. Some boys I thought I knew from school stopped to help, or so I believed. I woke in the woods to threats I could not risk testing. Weeks later, when cafeteria smells made me sick, Ms. Hannah approached me and promised a way out, a light in a night I thought would never end."

"So, you had an abortion?"

"No," she says. "When I told Ms. Hannah I had been raped by a group of white boys, she was elated, and I could see the wheels turning in her head."

"Why?"

"Because she could broker a mixed-race baby in Europe for a lot of money. I told my parents I had been given a scholarship to study abroad. Ms. Hannah took care of the rest."

"What else was there to take care of?"

"The school stuff, grades, and attendance."

"How was she able to fake your grades?"

"She had contacts throughout the administration and bursar offices."

"What happened to your baby?"

She paused before answering. "My baby was stillborn."

"Oh my God, Dee. I'm so sorry."

After a few more seconds of silence, she says, "That evil woman was going to sell my baby and use what happened to me as a means of extortion."

"Extortion? What do you mean? I don't understand. What could a college student have that she would want?"

"Sienna, I wasn't going to be a college student forever. That evil woman preys on others while making a fortune off their misery."

"Did she contact you after you became famous?"

"Yes."

"Did she demand money from you?"

"Yes."

"How much did you give her?"

"Not a dime, but that didn't stop her from threatening me."

Now I knew what Ms. Hannah wanted me to find out about her through Dee. This confirms, without a doubt, that she is an evil woman. How would I ever break this news to Osei?

"Dee, I need to explain why I asked about Ms. Hannah." I tell her about Osei and our involvement with her.

"She asked about you when I was leaving."

"That doesn't surprise me one bit."

"Sienna, what are you going to do?"

"I'm going to help Osei find his birth mother. Will you help me?"

"You can count me in. Please keep in mind, Ms. Hannah is an extremely dangerous person."

I reach out to Osei to fill him in on what I've learned about Ms. Hannah. I tried several times to reach him, but the calls went directly to voicemail, so I left him a message. I phone Bruce and tell him about my conversation with Dee, and what she told me about Ms. Hannah and the Wharton Orphanage. I don't tell him her story.

"I could tell that woman was a terrible person."

"I'm sure of it, but I don't know how to break the news to Osei."

Once again, I wasn't able to reach him, so I left another message.

"Hey, Osei. This is Sienna. I'm heading to LA, and I haven't heard from you. I'm starting to worry. Call me."

16

I'm Telling You What I Know

After an uneventful meeting with Phil, who repeatedly apologized for his tantrum, I text Gloria: *Meeting you and the boys in front of the hotel at 3:00 P.M.* I'm spending the next two days with Gloria and her family before heading home.

"Auntie Sese, we've missed you," the twins say in unison as I get in the car.

"I've missed you guys more."

"We wanted to pick you up...but..."

"They're bugging us to buy them a car," Gloria interjects.

"Not a car, Mom. Two cars."

"I stand corrected," Gloria says.

"Mom, you and Dad have never treated us like we were the same.

"We're different," Jason says.

Justin finishes his sentence, "And that's why we need our own car."

"That's right," Jason chimes in. "We need two cars. Don't you agree, Auntie Sese?"

I turn to look at them and I say, "I agree you are two different people, but when I look at you, I see the same face."

Gloria gives me a high five.

"Hey, Auntie Sese, when we come to Philly, will you take us to see the 76ers play? We love the new rookie, Osei Wharton."

"What is it about his game you like?" I ask.

"He has the ball IQ of Kobe and LeBron and the speed of Allen Iverson and Russell Westbrook," Jason replies.

The boys, who'd started playing basketball as toddlers because their father and grandfather are fanatical fans, knew everything about the game.

"Sure, I'll take you all to a game. Gloria, are you planning to come to Philly soon?"

"No, but Jackson and the boys will be there in three weeks."

"Is everything okay with your father-in-law?"

"We'll talk later," she says.

Gloria and her family live in Brentwood, a suburb of Los Angeles, in a three-story mid-century contemporary home with five bedrooms and six bathrooms. We drop off my bag, and the boys join their father, Jackson, who is grilling salmon in the backyard. Gloria and I head to the kitchen to make pasta and kale salads to go with the salmon, and she whips up a pitcher of sangria.

Jackson graduated two years ahead of us. Since their sunset wedding in the campus chapel two years after they met, through the good times and the bad, they have been each other's Rock of Gibraltar. When you are in their company, you can feel the love between the two of them. As one of Hollywood's leading casting directors, Jackson carries weight to match Gloria's. They're one of Hollywood's power couples. We take the salads and sangria outside and join Jackson and the boys.

"Mom, can we pass on the grown-up healthy food? We're going to get burgers and fries at In-N-Out," Justin says.

Jackson throws the keys to him.

"We'll see you later, Auntie Sese," Justin says.

"Bring me back a burger. I'll need it after all this healthy food," Jackson says.

"Don't you dare bring back a burger for your dad. If you do, you'll be grounded for a week," Gloria says to the boys.

Looking at them as they walk away, I say, "Gloria, you don't have babies anymore."

"I miss my babies, but I have one left," she says, as she winks at Jackson, and he'll never grow up."

Jackson playfully gives her the evil eye, then says to me, "I hear Bruce is getting a divorce."

"Let me guess. You heard that from Radio Rainey," I say.

"Of course, we did," Gloria says.

"She told us we should make sure you're not planning to reconnect with him, and that you had dinner with him," Jackson says, eyebrows raised.

"Wow, Radio Rainey dropping the 411 on me."

"Since Bruce is my best friend, we already knew about the divorce and the dinner, but it's always entertaining to hear Rainey's perspective," Jackson chuckles.

"She adds so much more drama," Gloria says.

"Yes, she does. I had dinner with him, and there's nothing more or nothing less about it."

"Would it be so bad if you two got back together? He can be your first and your last love," Jackson asks.

I punch him in the shoulder and look at Gloria, expecting her to object. Instead, she says, "I agree. What would be bad about you two rekindling the spark you once had?"

"You both are crazy."

"I know Bruce better than most. Sese, you don't know how many times he has called me drunk, wanting to know how you're doing, saying he made a mistake," Jackson says.

"So, he was content to be miserable rather than ending his mistake sooner. I find that hard to believe." I give Jackson a look, suggesting I want to change the subject and say, "Gloria, can you pass the kale salad? I'm famished."

"You can change the subject, but I'm telling you what I know," Jackson says.

After dinner, Gloria and I decide to take a late-night swim.

"Do you still love him?" she asks.

"Honestly, I don't know. When I saw him, there were no fireworks, but he still looks good."

"He was always good-looking," Gloria says.

"He hurt me, and my wounded heart is still not healed properly. I can't trust him with my emotions. So, as far as I'm concerned, all we can do is to be friends."

"Sese, that was twenty years ago! Don't you think you hurt him as well?"

"I suppose I did, and because of that pain, we can never be together."

"What if he wants more?" Gloria asks.

"Well, I can't give him more." Again, I'm feeling uncomfortable, and I need to change the subject. "Hey, Gloria, do you remember Ms. Hannah Becker?"

"The name sounds familiar. Why? Should I remember her?"

"I read an interesting article about her. In the article, our alma mater was mentioned. She oversaw food service and helped launch the school's organic farm."

Seeing that Gloria didn't know anything about Ms. Hannah. I move on.

"Why are Jackson and the boys coming to Philly?"

"Jackson's father is in poor health, and he wants to see the boys. His doctors aren't optimistic about him surviving the cancer this time. Jackson has to meet with his father's attorney since he's in charge of his estate. We haven't told the boys any of this."

"I'm so sorry. I'll make a point to check in on Dr. McCall from time to time."

"Jackson would appreciate it."

"How is Jackson's stepmother doing?"

"She's good. She now lives year-round in Oak Bluffs. She and Dr. McCall live separate lives."

"Is she aware?"

"Yeah. She and Jackson are pretty close. He likes her a lot because she wasn't a step-monster to him. He speaks with her weekly, and the boys love her as well."

17

*Pain May Endure for A Night,
but Joy Comes in the Morning*

I arrive in Philadelphia on the red-eye at 7:30 A.M. and head straight to the office. The breakfast meeting with Jack is a good one. My sales are up twenty percent over last year. Chloe follows me into my office.

"Sienna, a doctor from the Sixers, has been trying to reach you. He wants you to get in touch with him ASAP. She hands me a note with his number.

I dial the number Chloe gave me. The phone rings, each ring adding to my anxiety, making my heart race with every second.

"Hello, this is Doctor Ross."

"Dr. Ross, this is Sienna Lewis, and I'm returning your call."

"Ms. Lewis, how are you? Thanks…"

"I'm fine, Dr. Ross. Is Osei okay?"

"I'm not sure. His agent is out of the country, and Osei has you listed as his contact person."

"Dr. Ross, is Osei okay?" I nervously ask again.

"That's what I'm trying to find out. Have you spoken to him?"

"I've been trying to reach him for over a week."

"He had the flu eight days ago, but he should have recovered by now. I didn't know who else to call. I haven't reported this to the team management yet, but I'll have to soon. I'm hoping you can go check on him."

"When did he list me as next of kin?"

"Since he signed with the 76ers last year," Dr. Ross replies.

Stunned by this revelation, I drive to Osei's place and ring the doorbell. No answer. I try his cell phone. Still no answer. He has an electronic lock, and so I input his birthday: Access denied. I gamble and enter my birthday, and the door opens! I can't believe it. *This boy is absolutely insane.* I step into a large foyer, which opens to an even larger space void of any furniture. The kitchen gleams with expensive stainless-steel appliances. To the right of the kitchen is a spiral staircase, and I cautiously make my way up it. Unlike the open floor plan downstairs, this level has individual rooms. I open the first door, it's an unfurnished bedroom, as are the next three doors I open. At the end of the hall are frosted glass double doors. I knock, but no answer. Opening the door, I step inside and see what I think is Osei asleep in the bed. I immediately stop in my tracks, hearing a low growling noise coming from the side of the bed. I want to run, but my instincts tell me to stay put.

Softly, I say, "Hey, Millie. You're a good girl. Where's Osei?"

"I'm here," Osei answers and lifts himself slowly onto his elbows.

I go over and sit next to him, and I immediately place my hand on his forehead. "Osei, are you sick?"

"I was, but I'm recovering."

I get up and say, "Have you eaten? I'm going to make you some chicken noodle soup."

He grabs my hand and says, "I'm not hungry. I ate earlier."

Sitting down on the bed and taking in its massive size. "I've never seen a bed this big. How did you even get it up here?"

He gestures toward the windows. "With a crane."

Millie jumps onto the bed, snuggling against Osei.

I walk over to the windows to open the floor-to-ceiling blackout curtains, and as I reach to open them, the curtains begin to slide apart. I turn to see Osei with a remote in his hand.

"You have been holed up like this for a week?"

"I don't know. I lost track of the days."

"What is going on with you? Did you get the messages Dr. Ross and I left? Why haven't you returned our calls?"

"I'm not sure. I can't seem to get out of bed."

"Has this ever happened to you before?"

"No."

"Osei, I apologize if I've contributed to you being in this state of mind. What can I do to help you?"

"Be my mother."

"I promised you I'd be your mother until we find your birth mother."

"I don't think we're going to find her."

"Osei, don't say that."

"I was listening to Ms. Hannah and for the first time, I saw her in a different light. A six-year-old does not forget abandonment, and the way she told the story about why she left me was not how it happened."

"What do you remember?"

"I think I'd blocked it out. I remember the argument she had with the new director about my trust. I couldn't hear every word, but I remember her insisting that she should manage my trust."

Curious, I sit straight up. "What else do you remember?"

"She didn't seem too sad when Mr. Albert died. I think my child mind wanted to forget that. She had a look on her face when she was talking to you, which jogged my memory."

"Osei, what can I do to help you?"

"For now, and forever, you are my mother."

"Osei, why did you place me as your contact on your paperwork at work?"

"Because I had no one else to name. I want to think I'm not alone, that if people knew about me, they would love and care for me. My heart aches for my family. Why isn't there someone looking for me?"

I hug him tightly, stroking his broad shoulders. "You'll find your family. Now clean yourself up and come downstairs. I'm going to make you some hot chocolate in that ridiculously expensive kitchen of yours."

After speaking with Dr. Ross, Osei joins me in the kitchen.

"Did Doctor Ross ask you to check on me?"

"Yes, he's very worried."

"Mark is in Italy," Osei says.

"Not anymore. He's cut his vacation short, to come back and check on you."

"I'll get in touch and apologize."

Mark is Osei's agent and confidant. He has been by Osei's side since the 76ers drafted him.

"Is everything alright? Did they ask why you've been MIA?"

"Yeah, but I didn't go into detail."

"What are you going to tell them?"

"I don't know."

"First, we need to come up with a believable alibi for you to give them tomorrow."

Osei and I both agree he'll offer a version of the truth; he was still recovering from the flu, and the cold medicine was making him extremely drowsy.

I tell Osei what I discovered about Ms. Hannah—she abused and extorted young pregnant women.

"Do you think Ms. Hannah extorted my birth parents?" Osei asks.

"If they became rich or famous, I'm sure she did or is continuing to do so."

"A leopard can't change its spots. I bet we'll hear from Ms. Hannah soon enough. I have a plan to see if she knows anything about your birth parents. I want to flesh it out a bit more before I share it with you."

I look at my watch. "Oh no, Osei, I have an important client call in ten minutes. I have to go."

"Sese. I'll call you later. I'm feeling much better, don't worry about me."

By the time I make it home, everything has been handled to my client's satisfaction. I grab Millie's leash, and we head out for a walk. I put in my earbuds and begin listening to Luther's "So Amazing." Unfortunately, I'm interrupted.

"Hello, Rainey."

"Hey, Sese, what are you doing?"

"I'm walking, Millie."

"Taylor and I are coming to Philly this weekend. We need to talk."

"About what?"

I know it will be about Bruce, but I don't say anything. Instead, I say, "You guys are always welcome. I have another call coming in. I have to go. Text me the details of your arrival."

"Hello, Jack. What's up? Aren't you on vacation?" I ask.

"We leave tomorrow. I want to be the first to congratulate you."

"Congratulate me? For what?"

"You're being promoted to senior vice president."

"Are you serious?"

"You're doing an excellent job, and it should be rewarded."

"Thank you. I very much appreciate the promotion. Have a relaxing vacation."

I'm excited about the promotion, but I can't stop thinking about Osei and finding him all alone in a dark room. It's a clear sign of depression. If the search for his birth parents was bringing him this much pain, I wonder if we should continue. If I'm being honest, this search could bring us both pain.

I check on Osei before getting into bed.

"Hey, Sienna."

"How are you doing?"

"Are you still worrying about me?"

"Yes, I'm very worried about you. Why did you lock yourself in your apartment for a week?"

"Don't worry, it won't happen again. I just needed to feel the misery that has been building up inside of me my whole life, the misery I pretended wasn't there. I let it wash over me, the hurt of being abandoned, not knowing by whom, or why, but I'm done with it now. I won't carry this pain anymore. Instead, I'm going to truly live and find joy and happiness, my path is clear, and my journey will be free of pain."

"What triggered this spiritual and mental cleansing?"

"Being selected to play in an all-star game is a major accomplishment for me, so I needed to purge all the pain before all-star weekend."

"And you're going to start that journey by having a nice place to come home to. We're going shopping."

"I hate shopping," he says.

"I'll shop—using your credit card, of course. I'm going to decorate and furnish your apartment. You need to have a home where you can actually relax and unwind after games and travel. Are you renting, or do you own the apartment?"

"It's mine."

"Good, I'm going to turn your place into a home."

"Thank you. Can you be my guest at the game Friday night?"

"Sure, I have friends coming to visit this weekend. I'll make sure they come on Saturday."

"I'm so excited. I often dream of you being at my games."

"Okay, it's a date. I'll see you Friday night."

I text Rainey and Taylor.

—Come Saturday morning instead of Friday evening. Something came up—

Friday night, I get to the stadium early to pick up my ticket at will-call. I open the envelope to find a ticket and a note from Osei.

Sese,

This ticket is for the owner's suite. Don't have dinner. There will be food there. My agent, Mark, will be there, and he'll introduce you to everyone.

Love, Osei.

I show my ticket to the attendant, and he takes me to a private elevator. The doors open, and the attendant inside greets me with a warm smile.

"My name is Anna," she says, "and you are the guest of…"

"Osei Wharton."

"We love your son," she gushes. "He told me his mother would be attending the game tonight, but you don't look old enough to have a son Osei's age."

I want to tell Anna I'm not Osei's mother. But instead, I say, "Thank you for the compliment. I'm very flattered."

The elevator opens, and I step into the owner's suite, where Osei's agent, Mark Rosenfeld, greets me. He introduces me to everyone, including the wives and girlfriends of the players, all in designer clothes and flaunting huge diamond rings.

Mark gestures toward the men in expensive suits and whispers, "These guys are advertisers. Big sponsors for the team."

The room buzzes with excitement as everyone eagerly awaits Osei's performance. On a large table in the center of the suite sits an ice sculpture of Osei dribbling a basketball, with champagne cascading over it like a fountain.

"Impressive, isn't it?" Mark asks.

"Yes, but why?"

"Osei will take the 76ers to the championship and bring the Larry O'Brien Championship trophy to Philly."

"Are you serious? The team is expecting a championship from Osei this year?"

"No one is expecting him to do that this year. The plan is to build a team around him to help him win a championship."

Osei has a good night and has a triple-double, and the Sixers win. Everyone is expecting Osei to visit the suite after the game. Not wanting to be a distraction, I decide to leave. Mark told me that he and I will be staying at the Four Seasons tonight.

I text Osei: *I'll meet you at the bar in the Four Seasons.* When Osei arrives, people start clapping and calling his name. He waves at everyone as he makes his way over to me.

He gives me a hug, smiling, says, "You scored more points than I did tonight."

"What are you talking about?"

"Mark told me you were impressive. When I got to the suite, everyone was talking about you—how beautiful you are, and wanted to know more about you."

"I wasn't aware I was impressing anyone. I had a good time, and the food was spectacular, not to mention the selection of scotch. I asked the bartender to give me a sampling of them all. It's a wonder I'm able to stand."

"No worries. I'll drive you home."

Osei takes my hand. "Thank you for being you, and thank you for coming. I needed you to be there tonight."

"I sign a contract tomorrow with Caldwell Sterling and Co., one of the largest sports accounting firms in the world, and I want them to see I have someone who cares about me."

As we leave the bar, Osei turns to me. "Sienna, can you be there tomorrow morning when I sign my new contract? The company's brand centers on the belief that financial guidance is rooted in family values, so it matters that I show them I have one."

"I have friends visiting. I have to pick them up from the train station at eleven-thirty tomorrow. What time is the signing, and where?"

"It's at 9:00 A.M., and it's here at the Four Seasons. Sienna, for now, you are the only family I have, and I want to share this moment with my family."

"Osei, but—"

Before I could finish speaking, he gave me another hug and runs back into the hotel.

"Hey, where are you going?" I yell. "You're driving me home."

"It's cold. I'm going to grab my coat—be right back."

While waiting for Osei to return, I text Rainey: *Confirming your arrival at 11:45 A.M.. Exit through the doors opposite the Angel of the Resurrection.*

The next morning, I'm on edge and thoroughly stressed about what to wear to Osei's contract signing. I decided on black jeans, my Chanel car coat, and Rockstud Valentino straps. I text Osei that I'm on my way and I'll see him in fifteen minutes. When I arrive, I see him walking through the revolving doors, grinning from ear to ear.

"Good morning, Osei. What's with you?"

"Other than signing a multimillion-dollar deal? Nothing."

"I guess that's something to be excited about. What do you need me to do or say during the signing?"

"Nothing, just be my mom."

I cheerfully say, "I can do that," and loop my arm through his.

We enter the suite, and we're greeted by the owner of the team, Osei's agent, and a host of other people. There's an elaborate breakfast buffet, but my nerves steal my appetite.

A very ornate table anchors the room. Osei sits first, then Mark, both gesturing for me to join. I take the seat beside Osei, and I instinctively take his hand. The contract is laid out before us, page after page. When it is finally done, Osei has secured a five-year, fifty-million-dollar contract.

One of the guys across the table asks Osei what he's going to do now, and Osei turns and says, "I'm taking Sese to Disneyland."

I give him the I know you didn't just call me Sese look, as someone whispers, "Is that what he calls his mother?"

Keeping my voice low, "Osei, how are you going to celebrate?"

"I'm going home to hang out with Millie."

He reaches into his coat pocket and hands me a bag. As I go to open it, he grabs my hand. "Don't open it now. Wait until you get home," he says.

18

Sushi is Soul Food

I look at the clock, and it's eleven thirty. I put the bag Osei gave me in the car's center console. I arrive at 30th Street Station in time to see Rainey and Taylor coming out of the revolving doors. I open the hatch for them to put in their luggage. Rainey gets in the front seat—she nearly knocks Taylor's coffee out of her hand, reaching for the door handle.

"Are you hungry?"

They both say, "Hell yeah."

"Sushi or soul food," I ask.

"Sushi is soul food," Rainey says.

Taylor puts their return tickets in the center console for safekeeping. "What's this?" she asks, pulling out the bag Osei had given me.

"It's a gift from a friend."

"Oh, so Bruce is giving you gifts now. Why would you even accept a gift from him?" Rainey asks, eyebrows raised.

"It's not from Bruce. It's from a new, younger admirer."

Taylor opens the box and screams. Rainey jumps and hits her head, and I almost drive off the Ben Franklin Bridge.

"Taylor, what is wrong with you? You scared the hell out of me," I yell.

She turns the box around, and the canary yellow diamond ring shines so brightly it blinds me and takes my breath.

Rainey screams louder.

"Would you not do that? You're going to make me have an accident. What's all the fuss about? You both have enormous diamond rings." Inside, I'm shocked, but I don't let on.

A Life Wrapped in Lies

Rainey takes the ring from Taylor. "Yes, but they didn't cost $225,000."

"How do you know how much it costs?" I ask.

Without a word, Rainey holds up the price tag in my face.

I nearly swerve off the road. "You're kidding, right?"

My Apple Pay announces a call from an unknown number. Rainey presses the answer button.

"Hey, Sienna. Have you opened your gift yet?" Osei asks. I'm glad I didn't put his real name in my phone.

"I did, and we'll discuss it later." I press the end button.

"Who the hell was that?" Rainey asks.

"Someone who I plan on giving this ring back to."

"Are you insane? You'll do no such thing," Taylor says.

We arrive at the restaurant, and I'm bombarded with a million questions.

"Can I please eat in peace? I'm not going to discuss who gave me the ring because I'm returning it, conversation over."

As we make our way back to my house, Rainey says, "I'm glad Bruce didn't give you the ring."

"If Bruce did give her the ring, why would that be a bad thing?" Taylor asks.

Defiantly, Rainey says, "Because it's Bruce, the person who broke her heart and stomped on it, that's why."

Before bed, we have our favorite nightcap, boozy hot chocolate made with vodka, and whipped cream drizzled with chocolate sauce. Right after, Rainey heads to bed. Taylor and I sit by the fireplace, watching the flames dance.

"Rainey is not sleeping," Taylor says, holding up her phone. "She just sent a group text to me, Dee, and Gloria about your ring."

"I'm surprised it took her this long to spread the news."

Taylor reads the text from Dee: *WTF? Who gave Sese a six-carat emerald-cut canary yellow diamond ring? Call me now!*

"When you call her, tell her it's eight-carat."

"How do you know?"

"Six is too small, ten is too big. Give my best to Dee. I'll see you in the morning."

Before going to bed, I call Osei.

"Sienna, did you like the ring? I want to thank you for helping these last few months."

"Osei, I can't accept it."

"Why not?"

"It's too expensive and unnecessary."

"How do you know what it costs?"

"Because the price tag was still on it."

"I can't believe this. Are you kidding? She actually left the price tag on the ring, after I specifically asked for a gift receipt. She was too busy trying to get me to take her out to do her job properly.

Oh well," he says, "I'm still not taking it back. I'm going to love you as my mom."

"Why?" I ask softly, "Why are you going to love me?"

"I have never had anyone support me who didn't have an ulterior motive. So, I've decided to love you."

Ignoring the love comment, I say, "Okay, I'll keep the ring, but please don't buy me any more gifts. Good night, Osei." I hang up before he can respond.

I have a text from Dee.

I look at the clock and decide that it's not too late to call her.

I wake up early Sunday morning to make breakfast for Taylor and Rainey. Believing the ring is from him, I know Rainey will use time to vent about Bruce and what she thinks is going on between him and me. As always, she never disappoints.

"Sese, please don't fall in love with Bruce. He wasn't good for you in the past, and he won't be good for you now," Rainey says.

Before I can respond, Taylor says, "Why can't she love him?"

"Does Taylor know you tried to kill yourself, but instead, you killed your baby?" Rainey yells at me, visibly upset.

I am mortified she would say such a thing! Even for Rainey, this is unacceptable.

"Yes, I know."

"The fact that you'd bring that up at all is utterly despicable. Where is your sensitivity?" Taylor yells.

Somewhat recovered, I open my mouth to calm Taylor. The situation is spiraling out of control, but before I can say a word, Taylor turns with a fury I've never seen in her and slaps Rainey hard across the face. Rainey reels back, stunned.

"Why are you always such a busybody? I bet you never told Sese you had a crush on Bruce and went out with him before he met her. Did you tell her that? Maybe you hate Bruce because he left YOU!" Taylor screams.

Rainey holds her cheek and eyes wide with shock. She looks from me to Taylor.

Unfiltered as ever, Rainey doesn't realize how much her words hurt. Her gaze is distant, yet regretful.

"Rainey. It's okay. Bruce told me he took you out on a couple of dates."

"Why didn't you ever mention it to me?"

"Why would I. That was in the past. I cherished you as much as I loved Bruce back then. So, can we stop now? I want to be clear: I loved Bruce because he was the first person who loved me unconditionally, but I'm also totally and eternally in love with you. Let's move on."

I take their hands. "Can we kiss and make up, please?"

The ride to the train station is quiet and awkward. "Are you guys going to be okay?" I ask as they're getting out of the car.

"Taylor knows I hate her."

Taylor links arms with Rainey. "That's too bad because I'm totally and eternally in love with you."

"Unrequited love is my kind of love," Rainey says.

I drive away with a sense of peace, knowing they'll be alright.

Once home, Millie and I go for a walk. Halfway down the trail, we see Osei and his dog, Millie 2.0.

"How are you doing?" he asks.

"This has been a very wacky weekend. Seeing you is a pleasant surprise."

"Sese, will you make me some hot chocolate when we get back to your place?"

I flash my new diamond ring in his face. "Why the hell am I wearing an eight-carat diamond ring hiking?"

"Because you can," he says.

19

Chicken Noodle Soup

Monday morning, I awake to a fever and a pounding headache. I can barely muster the strength to pick up my phone to email my assistant Chloe and Jack, to let them know I'm not feeling well, but available if there's an emergency. I find my last bit of strength to text Rainey and Taylor to take the necessary precautions to keep themselves from getting sick as well.

Drifting in and out of sleep, I'm startled by Millie barking and the doorbell ringing. I turn on the security cameras to see Osei coming in the front door.

"Osei, how did you know I was at home?"

"I called your office, and your assistant told me you were out sick. Are you okay? How are you feeling?"

"Not very well. Please stay away. I don't want you to get sick."

"No way, I'll take care of you like you took care of me. Plus, I need to talk to you about Ms. Hannah. Are you up to that?"

"What about Ms. Hannah?"

"She called me this morning."

"And?"

"She went into a lot of nonsense about why she left and how she loves me. She even volunteered to be by my side to help me navigate my new contract. I told her the contract was signed, and you were there at the signing, and she lost it."

"What do you mean, lost it?"

"She went berserk, screaming that you were after my money and demanding to know why I'd allow you access to my personal business. Did I forget that you abandoned me?"

"Are you serious?"

"Yes, and she suggested I should do a DNA test. I told her I had, and the DNA test proved you are my mother. She kept insisting that you were after my money and that I shouldn't trust you. She also told me she wanted to introduce me to some people who could 'help' manage my finances. I told her my finances were just fine and that I didn't need any introductions. Sienna, to be honest, was downright scary."

"Osei, she knows I'm not your mother, and I'm betting she knows who your birth mother is. She can't contradict herself, so she has to portray me as a gold digger who abandoned you. We can use this to our advantage. We need to learn everything we can about her. I'll give Bruce a call. I'm betting Ms. Hannah is a seasoned criminal, and you need to limit your contact with her until we have a clear plan." I look into his beautiful eyes. "Osei, we can stop here. We don't have to go any further."

"Are you kidding? I started this, and I involved you. It's only right that we finish it together. I'll bring you a cup of tea, it'll help you to feel a little better."

I wake up several hours later, and Osei has dozed off in a chair next to me.

"Osei, can you get me a glass of water. I'm burning up," I ask.

"Sure."

He hands me a glass of water, but my hands are too shaky to hold it. "Sese, I need to take you to the hospital."

"That's not necessary. Please hand me my cell phone. I'll call my doctor and explain my symptoms and how I'm feeling."

The doctor diagnoses me with the flu, which has developed into a bronchial infection. He prescribes medicine that arrives in half an hour. I take it and go back to bed. I awaken to find a note from Osei and a thermos filled with green tea and honey.

Sese,

I walked and fed Millie. I'll call you tomorrow. I'll be on the road until Friday. I called Bruce and asked him to check on you.

Love you,

Osei

    I have missed calls from Osei, Bruce, Dee, and a text from my housekeeper to let me know she has made a pot of chicken noodle soup. I drag myself downstairs, take a few spoonsful, and go back to bed.
    "Hey, Sese," Bruce says. "I hear you're under the weather."
    "A little better now," I tell him about Osei's conversation with Ms. Hannah.

    "I'm sure Ms. Hannah didn't think you and Osei would bond the way you have. You were supposed to reject him and leave him vulnerable. She would then swoop in and be the shoulder he needed and help him manage his multimillion-dollar contract."
    "She certainly knows who Osei's parents are," I say, coughing.
    "You have a plan to get information out of her?"
    "My only plan for now is to feel better."
    "I can help with that! You know I make the best chicken noodle soup on the East Coast."
    "I remember, but my housekeeper makes the second-best chicken noodle soup on the East Coast, and I have a pot on the stove. Bruce, I need to say goodbye. I don't feel good. I'll talk to you later."

My last thought as I drift into a drug-induced sleep is about the last time Bruce made me chicken noodle soup. We were living together in Brooklyn. I got sick during the snowstorm of the century. Bruce walked in over twelve feet of snow to the grocery store to get the ingredients he needed to make chicken noodle soup. All the grocery stores were closed except for a Jewish deli on Flatbush Avenue. When he got to the deli, the owner was closing and turning out the lights, and he begged her to let him in. He explained that his girlfriend was sick and that he wanted to make her chicken noodle soup. She was so touched, she gave him her recipe for chicken noodle soup and all the ingredients he needed to make it, including what she called her special seasonings. It was delicious.

Osei checks on me every night. On the third day, I tell Osei I'm feeling better.

"Are you sure?"

"Truly, I am so don't worry about me, just focus on winning," I lie.

"But you're my family, and your well-being is much more important to me."

I feel him pouting. "Osei, what are you going to do with me when you find your actual mother?"

"I'll continue to call you my Sese. I'll be home soon, and I'll be your full-time nurse."

Thursday night, the doorbell rings. I turn on the security camera to see Bruce standing there with bags of groceries. I slowly make my way downstairs to let him in.

I don't know whether to be grateful or annoyed.

"What are you doing here?"

"Osei sent me. I'm here to help you feel better, and I'll start by making you my world-renowned chicken noodle soup."

"I'm too sick to argue with you."

"Then don't. Go back to bed. I'll wake you when the soup is ready." He heads to the kitchen as though he belonged there. Bruce wakes me up several hours later with a bowl of his chicken noodle soup. I take a couple of spoonsful, and my insides start to tingle.

"Wow! This is better than I remember."

"I've had twenty years to experiment and make it better."

"You did well, but I don't think I can eat anymore."

I fall asleep. When I wake, it's two in the morning. Bruce is asleep on the sofa. I cover him with a blanket and crawl back into bed. I wake the next morning, and there's a note on the nightstand from Bruce. It reads:

I didn't want to wake you. I'll call you later. Feel better.

Bruce

P.S. I left soup on the stove.

Hours later, Osei rushes into the house, hurrying upstairs and placing his hand on my forehead. "Are you okay? How do you feel?"

"I'm feeling better, but I'm weak."

He gets into the bed beside me. "Osei, get up. I don't want you to get sick. I may still be contagious."

"I doubt it, but I don't care." He turns the TV to ESPN, and I let sleep take me. I get out of bed, trying not to disturb a sleeping Osei. I warm up a bowl of Bruce's chicken noodle soup and call Jack.

"Hello, Jack."

"Sienna, are you feeling better?"

"I'm getting there."

"I hate to do this, but I need you to go to London next week," he says.

"Is there a problem?"

"No. Rhett wants us to present a product line for the new movie he's producing."

"Oh, I see. I'm sure I'll be feeling better by then. I'll have Chloe book the flight and hotel for next Wednesday."

I finish my call and turn to see Osei standing in the doorway.

"What are you cooking? It smells so good."

"Bruce's world-renowned chicken noodle soup."

"Can I have a bowl?"

"Of course, you can."

"When was Bruce here?"

"I think he was here yesterday. I'm really not sure. I need to feel better soon. I have to go to London next week for work."

"I don't have any games next week. Can I come with you?"

"I'd love for you to come along. I'll have my assistant book our flights."

"No need, I'll reserve a plane for us."

"Are you sure?"

"When do you want to leave? I'll make the arrangements."

"Wednesday. We can kill two birds with one stone. I have a plan. Do you think Ms. Hannah would meet us in London?"

"Probably, but what's your plan?"

"Ms. Hannah knows I'm not your mother. I want her to continue to think I'm using you for your money. I'm one hundred percent convinced she wants to have access to you and your bank account, and she's going to do everything in her power to make that come true. If she sees me as a gold-digging imposter, it'll be upsetting enough for her to tell you who your birth parents are. Knowing I have access to your finances, and she doesn't, I need her to think that my greed surpasses hers.

"I'll email her tomorrow to see if she can meet me in London. Can I have another bowl of soup?"

"Sure, and I'll give you some to take home. Let me know when you hear back from Ms. Hannah."

My cell vibrates on the kitchen counter. It's Bruce calling. I nod for Osei to answer it. He pressed the speaker button.

"Hello, who's calling?"

"Is Sese there?" Bruce asks.

"Hold on, please."

He hands me the phone. "Hello, Bruce."

"Was that Osei?"

"Yes. That was the young messiah."

"Are you feeling better?"

"Yes. Thank you for the soup. Both Osei and I are enjoying it immensely."

Osei shouts, "I want the recipe."

Bruce says, "It's a family recipe which has been passed down for generations."

"Okay, Dad. I'm ready to learn. When can we start cooking?"

Bruce laughs. "I'm on my way over."

Ten minutes later, Osei greets Bruce with a hug. "

Osei fills Bruce in on our trip to London, and he says, "Can I come along?"

"Sure, why not? The more, the merrier." I say.

20

So Easy to Love

I wave goodbye to Osei and Bruce. Osei, heading to practice, has offered to drop Bruce off at 30th Street Station. I notice a file folder Bruce left on the table near the front door and call him.

"You miss me already?" he answers.

"Not exactly, you left a file on the table."

"Osei and I are stuck in traffic. I'll be seeing you in three days. Can you bring it with you to the airport?"

"Sure, see you then."

I'm about to hang up the phone when I hear Bruce say, "I can tell you have grown very fond of Sese. Will you continue to want her in your life once you find your birth parents?"

"As far as I'm concerned, Sese will always be a part of my life."

"Good. I don't want her to be hurt. Sese has endured a lot of hurt and disappointment in her lifetime, and the majority of it was because she loved me."

"Why couldn't you love her when she's so easy to love?"

I feel bad for eavesdropping, but I can't bring myself to stop.

"When I first met Sese, she was the extrovert, and I was the introvert. I was happy to have this exceptionally beautiful, outgoing person love me. When we moved to New York, I started to find myself, and I changed. I wanted her to change as well. I wanted to be the leader and not be led by her. She never felt comfortable in the academic world, and I needed someone who could work the room and be political."

"So, you needed someone more of a business partner," Osei mockingly says, "How did that work out for you?"

"Not very well," Bruce says with a chuckle.

"Bruce, I know what I want from Sese. Can I ask you what you want from her? It seems you are more capable than I of hurting her."

"I'm not expecting her to love me. I want her to talk to me and be able to listen to her every word. I've missed her. I found out yesterday that Sese tried to kill herself after I left her, and in doing so, she had a miscarriage. This was the second child she and I lost, which is why she has taken to you. You could be the son she never had. To be perfectly honest with you, if push came to shove, and she had to choose between the two of us, I believe hands down, she would choose you."

Osei says, "I hope it never has to come to that."

I hear Osei exchange warm goodbyes, and the car door closing.

I don't know what to do, should I hang up the phone, or should I say something? Before I can decide, Bruce says, Oh my God, Sese, are you there?"

"Yes, I'm here."

"Did you hear my conversation with Osei?"

"Yes."

"I'm sorry you had to hear that, and also for the intervention you had to endure over the weekend with Rainey."

"How do you know about what happened with Rainey?"

Sensing her irritation, he quickly says, "Jackson told me he overheard the conversation with Gloria and Dee. Clearly, everyone was upset with Rainey. Sese, can I come back to see you?"

"Why?"

"Because I need to see you. I can take an Uber."

"Bruce, it's late."

"Since when has six-thirty been considered late?"

Twenty minutes later, Bruce is ringing the doorbell.

Opening the door, I say, "Bruce, we've already talked about this."

"I know, but I need to apologize for breaking your heart and for not listening to mine. It wasn't worth you trying to take your life. Why didn't you tell me you were pregnant again?"

"Would you have stayed with me if you knew? You hated me so much after I had the abortion. I knew you loved me less afterward, and I couldn't blame you because I loved myself a lot less as well. So, I ask you, would you have stayed with me if you knew I was pregnant?"

"I don't know."

"When I tried to take my life, I didn't know either if we'd be able to love each other ever again."

"Sese, why did you do that? I wouldn't be able to live if you weren't on the planet."

"Please stop. If you couldn't live on the planet without me, why did you leave me?"

"I was angry, hurt, and I wanted a change. I thought if I started over with someone new, I'd be okay."

"Bruce, you wanted to start over. You wanted a change. Can we stop? I don't have the energy for this."

"I want to know if we can start."

"Start what?"

"Can we start by being friends? Can I call you and ask how you are doing? How was your day? I want to be able to call you and not have to worry if you'll answer my call."

"Sure. We can start there."

He turns to leave, offering a quiet "Thank you." I watch as he slowly walks to the waiting Uber, and I can't take my eyes off him.

21

Hot Water with Lemon

As soon as the plane takes off, I go into planning mode. "I'd like to discuss the plan for Ms. Hannah."

"Ready," Osei says.

"Osei, you'll invite her to breakfast, not letting on that I will be there as well. I'll play the role of the gold-digging Mama, and Osei, you'll be the whatever-my-mama-wants son. The goal is to infuriate Ms. Hannah. I'll suggest the two of you meet later without me. She'll try to convince you I'm the mother who abandoned you, and I am not to be trusted. Even if she doesn't reveal who your real parents are, it will be difficult for her to backtrack. We'll get a sense of her agenda."

"What's my role?" Bruce says.

"You're the sixth man off the bench," I answer.

"Look at you, using basketball terminology. We have a plan," Osei proudly says.

"Osei, how much did this flight cost? That bathroom is way more elegant than mine. I'd like to help pay for this," Bruce says.

"That's not necessary."

"Then I'll pay for the hotel rooms."

"I've taken care of the hotel as well."

"By the way, where are we staying?" I ask.

"At the Savoy, in a double adjoining suite overlooking the Thames."

"Boy, are you crazy?"

"No, just rich. Speaking of rich, did you know all three of us have the same car?"

"Bruce, why do you need a car? You can ride the subway," I say.

"I'm pretty sure the New York subway system doesn't have any stops in Philly," he replies.

He and Osei high-five each other.

I can't win with you two. I settle into a cozy spot, wrapped in a cashmere throw, and drift off. A couple of hours later, I wake to Bruce and Osei playing backgammon.

"Who's winning?" I ask.

Pointing at Osei, Bruce says, "He's cheating."

Osei flashes a wide grin, his perfect teeth on full display—nothing about him suggests a life of an orphan.

"Ms. Lewis, would you like something to drink?" the flight attendant asks.

"Yes, hot water with lemon."

"You can have anything, and that's your choice?" Osei laughs.

"It relaxes me. I'll drink later, speaking of which, just wait until you meet Rhett. He'll drink us all under the table."

"Who's Rhett?" Bruce asks.

"My client."

22

The Dungeon

"Rhett, we've arrived. How are you doing?"
"All is well. Where are you staying?"
"At the Savoy."
"Is Jack paying for that?"
"No. My godson is here, and he's paying."
"I'd like to meet him. Do you all have plans for tonight?"
"I'll call you back shortly after I check. I'm looking forward to seeing you."
"The feeling is mutual."
"Are you guys up to hanging out tonight?" I ask, entering the adjoining room.
"Hell yes!" Bruce exclaims.
I called Rhett and he gives me the address of a club.
When we reach the address Rhett gave us, we're directed down two dark, gloomy flights of stairs. At the bottom, a massive padded red door with gold stitching looms. Osei opens it eagerly, and we step into a space swallowed in shadows, lit only by bursts of electric blue, hot pink, and acid green neon.
"Wow, this place is unreal," Osei says.
"Is this a club or a dungeon?" Bruce mutters, eyeing the room.
"We should've brought bodyguards," Osei jokes.
Bruce walks in behind him and says, "Look at that! That's the longest bar I have ever seen. There has to be at least fifteen bartenders."

In the center of the room is a massive stage. Plush velvet booths encircle it, each with a perfect view of the stage. The anticipation that hangs in the air is electric.

Rhett is standing beside one of the booths. We walk over to him. He pulls me in for a hug before I turn, and I introduce him to Osei and Bruce.

"Oh my God, Osei Wharton, I'm a huge fan of yours." He turns to me, saying, "Osei Wharton is your godson?"

Before I can answer, Osei says, "I'm not her godson. I'm her son."

Confused, Rhett glances at me and then at Osei.

"He's joking, it's a long story," I reply.

"What's this place?" Bruce asks.

"Pretty cool, huh? It's a karaoke bar," Rhett says.

"Wow. I always wanted to come to a place like this," Osei says.

"You'll love it," Rhett assures him.

"Let's order some drinks," Bruce says.

Rhett looks at me, grinning. "And do a bit of singing."

"No way! Please tell me you didn't sign me up."

"I did," he says triumphantly.

I give him a sideways glance, narrowing my eyes. "I hate you right now." He knows I don't mean it.

"Sienna, you can sing?" asks Osei.

Rhett grins, arms wide. "You're in for a treat, and Bruce, my man, this will be the last round of drinks you'll have to buy. Once she sings, drinks will start showing up."

"Why would people buy us drinks?" Osei asks.

"To keep her on stage singing," Rhett says as the announcer pipes in. "Please welcome to the stage, Tiffany Terrell."

"Truly, I'm going to kill you," I mutter, half joking, half serious, as I reluctantly make my way to the stage.

Tiffany Terrell was the alias Rhett gave me when I performed at karaoke bars. It's been years since I've sung anywhere but the shower.

Handing me a mic, the announcer says, "The first song by Tiffany will be 'Ain't No Stoppin' Us Now, ' by McFadden & Whitehead."

"This song is dedicated to Osei and Bruce." I sway and move across the stage while the horns and piano play. Trying not to look at them, I force myself to begin as people yell my name. I'm soon lost in the music. I glance at the man-child I have come to love, his face aglow with pride, and tears well in my eyes. After the song, I hand the mic to the announcer and hurry off the stage.

He blocks my way. "Not so fast. They want another song."

I look at Rhett, and he raises his glass. I sigh and take the mic, and I start to sing "The Way" by Jill Scott.

I finish the song to thunderous applause. Again, I hand the mic to the announcer, and he says, "Can't you hear the crowd? You're still up."

I look at Rhett, and he raises his glass again, indicating someone has bought them another round of drinks. As long as they keep getting drinks, I have to keep singing.

"This is the last song for me, and I want to dedicate it to Osei, a beautiful spirit the world gave us and a bright addition to my world." I start to sing "Welcome to My Love" by Rachelle Ferrell.

I finish the song, and Osei runs to me and sweeps me off my feet.

"Sese, you are fantastic." He carries me back to where Bruce and Rhett are sitting.

"Osei, please put me down."

All eyes are no longer on me, but on the player who no doubt will lead the 76ers to victory. Soon, our table is swarmed with people seeking his autograph.

Bruce gives me a high five, and Rhett gives me a gigantic smile. I look at the table, and it's filled with drinks.

Bruce, laughing, says, "I see you've progressed from the shower."

"What is so funny?" Rhett asks.

"It's an inside joke," Bruce says as he looks at me.

"You remember I told you about the love of my life, who left me for another woman? Well, I'd like for you to meet him." I say, pointing to Bruce.

"I see," Rhett says, " So, Bruce, what part are you playing in this telenovela? It seems you've come to your senses."

"I'm the lookout."

Finally, Osei signs a last autograph and asks the crowd to be considerate and not interrupt the show.

"And you, Osei?" Rhett asks.

"I'm their long-lost son."

Rhett chokes on his drink. I pat his back. "Rhett, he's kidding, just breathe."

After gaining his composure, Rhett says, "Sese, when are you going to quit your day job and start singing full-time?"

"Never, and please pass me the scotch."

On our way back to the hotel, Osei is still talking about my performance.

"Sienna, am I welcome in your world?" Osei asks.

"Always," I whisper.

Bruce and I share a warm smile.

23

The Evil Woman Appears

Osei is scheduled to have breakfast at the hotel at 9:00 A.M. tomorrow with Ms. Hannah. Afterward, I'll meet with Rhett to work on the project.

Osei sees Bruce lounging in his sweats and a T-shirt, ordering room service. He raises an eyebrow. "I'm jealous."

I laugh and pull him by the arm. "Come on. You can come back and play video games to your heart's content."

We arrive at the hotel restaurant and see Ms. Hannah seated at a table in the back. She stands as Osei, and I approach the table and outstretches her arms.

"Ms. Hannah, you look fabulous," Osei says, embracing her to make it all seem as normal as possible.

"Thank you, son." She looks at me with a piercing gaze. "What a surprise to see you, Sienna," her jaw tightens and her lips barely move.

"So lovely to see you again, Ms. Hannah." *In this lighting, she looks more her age, and I can tell she'd had a lot of work done to keep her youthful look.*

Osei hands her the menu, and Ms. Hannah only orders coffee.

Osei and I share an order of the Belgian waffles, turkey sausage, and scrambled eggs.

"So, Sienna, what brings you here?" she says.

I'd made a point to wear the diamond ring Osei gave me, and, of course, she notices it right away.

"Just looking out for my son's best interest."

"People can't believe she has a son my age," Osei says, adding fuel to the fire.

Ms. Hannah's smile gets tighter as she stares at the ring, saying, "That's a lovely ring."

"Isn't it? Osei bought it for me."

"How many carats?" Ms. Hannah asks.

"I don't know," I reply.

"It's eight, but next time I'll buy her a ten-carat," he looks at me, mischief written on his face.

"Yes, but I'm keeping this one too, if you don't mind." Waving my hand flamboyantly in the air. "Thank you, son."

"Osei, you can't just throw your money away buying expensive gifts," Ms. Hannah says, visibly annoyed.

"Yeah, I know, but whatever my mom wants, she gets. Ms. Hannah," Osei says in a very beguiling voice, "I'm so grateful to you for helping me to locate Mom. So, thank you so very much."

"You are welcome. I can certainly understand that you want to take care of your mother. Which brings me to why I wanted to meet. It's the least I could do for you, my dear. I'd like you to please give some thought to talking to an investment and sports management firm I'll recommend to you. They're both excellent to work with…"

Before she can finish her sentence, I interrupt her. "I don't think he'll need them. He's hired the firms that I recommended."

Her expression froze, but even in fury, she's sharp.

"Let's not focus on his finances and his bank account, as all is taken care of. You and Osei should spend some time catching up on each other's lives. And I personally wanted to show my gratitude for the care you gave my son." I continued. "Truly, I am so grateful to you." I lather it on.

"I'm only thinking of his future and what's best for him," Ms. Hannah says.

"Your concern is truly appreciated, but a lot has changed. Osei," I ask, "When was the last time you saw her before our trip to Germany?"

"When I went to Germany for her sixtieth birthday," he says, "And the time before that?" I ask.

"When I was twelve."

"Ms. Hannah, I'd like for us to talk about something other than Osei's finances."

"Seems I have offended you. Which wasn't my intent," Ms. Hannah says, eyes glaring with fury.

"Not at all. Perhaps." I turn to Osei, "You and Ms. Hannah should meet again without me. I am sure you have so much to catch up on," I suggest.

"I'd like that," she replies.

"Ms. Hannah, I have something to do now. Are you free for lunch?" Osei asks.

"Yes, of course," she says. "We can meet back here for a late lunch, say at two."

"You could have won an Academy Award for your performance," Osei says, as he heads up to the suite to let Bruce know what happened at breakfast, and I'm off to meet Rhett.

After a very productive meeting. Rhett is curious about Bruce and Osei. So, I give him the Reader's Digest version.

"Wow! Are you serious? Sienna, are you sure you want to take this on?"

"Rhett, I have to help him."

"What are you going to do when he finds his birth parents?"

"I'll cherish this time, and if I'm not able to be a part of his life, I'll continue to love and cherish him from afar."

"And what's going on between you and Bruce?"

"Nothing is going on."

"Do you love him?"

"I want to love him, but I'm afraid to."

"Why the fear?"

"I can't trust that we won't hurt each other again. I don't want to try again."

"You should follow your heart."

"I tried that, and it didn't work," I say, rather harshly.

As I walk into the hotel suite, Bruce says, "I hear you could have won an Academy Award for your performance at breakfast."

"Osei was a great co-star. I hope I wasn't too over the top. My goal was to irritate the heck out of her."

"If pissing her off was your goal, then you succeeded." Osei laughs.

"So, are you ready to meet with her later today?" I ask.

"She seems quite eager! Ms. Hannah has texted me twice."

"Really, what did she say?"

"If we could meet somewhere other than the hotel."

Alarmed, I ask, "Did you agree to that?"

"No, of course not."

"Why would she want to change the location?" I ask.

"I'll find out in thirty minutes."

Bruce, sensing my concern, says, "I don't trust her, so I hired some guys to watch Osei's back. I called your friend Rhett, and he recommended a security company for Osei while we're in London. Like I say, I don't trust her, and I'll be there too, keeping an eye on Osei."

"She wouldn't do anything to harm Osei, would she?"

"Why take any chances?" Bruce says. I'm going to head down before anyone gets there."

Bruce FaceTime's me as he's arriving at the restaurant. There before Osei and Ms. Hannah, cap pulled low, he takes a seat at the bar.
Osei arrives shortly afterward.
"Can you see Osei?" Bruce asks.
"Yes, I'll be able to see everything going on."

Ms. Hannah arrives, waves at Osei, and heads over to his table. I notice two men entered with her, but pause, not approaching the table. After a few minutes, she beckons them over. I can see Osei is baffled, but he stays focused and speaks directly to Ms. Hannah, not glancing in the direction of the two uninvited men. The conversation with Ms. Hannah seems to be light. Osei is laughing, which makes me feel less nervous. One of the men opens his briefcase and hands Osei some documents. After reviewing the documents, his eyes return to Ms. Hannah. She says something, and the look on Osei's face changes immediately. He's fidgeting. I can tell the tenor of the conversation has changed; he is no longer laughing. One man is talking fast and pointing to the document.
Osei is focused on Ms. Hannah, looking her directly in her eyes without smiling, which is making her extremely uncomfortable. Osei looks at the papers and again at Ms. Hannah. He says something to her and begins to stand. As he does, one of the suits grabs him by the arm. The other suit shoves a pen in his face, demanding he sign the papers. Osei's bodyguards emerge, swiftly restraining both men. Ms. Hannah is surprised and annoyed by unwanted attention, is visibly upset, and doesn't

want a scene. Osei says something to the bodyguards, and they leave the table. Ms. Hannah is asking Osei to stay, but it's apparent he's leaving.

As he's walking away, she whispers something to him, and his expression says it all: cold, angry, and ready to fight. Osei and Bruce return to the suite, both visibly flustered.

"I can't believe that woman. Trying to strong-arm me into signing papers allowing the companies the suits represent to manage my financial portfolio and my career."

"Why would you hire a firm in the UK to manage your finances?"

"The firms are located in Washington, DC, and in Manhattan. This was her plan from the beginning."

"I'm sure she has some sort of agreement with those firms. Osei, what did she say when you were leaving?" I ask.

"She told me that I'd regret my decision, and others could be hurt as a result of it."

"That old bat. She threatened you?"

"Sese, she was threatening you. Do you need to meet with Rhett tomorrow?" Bruce asks.

"No. We're done."

"Let's get out of here, Osei. How soon can we leave?"

"We can leave now. I'll make the arrangements."

On our way to the airport, I receive a text message from Ms. Hannah. *You and I both know you are not Osei's mother. If you don't want him to know this, I suggest you have him sign the contract hiring the firms I recommend representing him.*

I showed the text to Osei and Bruce.

"That woman is the devil," Bruce says.

I text back. *I have a number for you, and it's zero. Not because zero means nothing, but because it's important. What makes Osei of interest to you now is the number of zeroes he has in his bank account. Believe me when I say you won't get anywhere near him or his finances.*

"Thank you," Osei says, as he puts his arm around my shoulders.

"For what?" I ask.

"For saving me from Ms. Hannah."

"Stop pretending I saved you. You know darn well you wouldn't have signed those papers."

"Don't worry, Sese. I'll protect you," Osei says.

"You'll need protection once she finds out what you've done," Bruce chimes in.

I look at both of them. "Whatever it is, I'll deal with it later. I'm exhausted."

24

A Penny for Your Thoughts

Awakened by turbulence, I glance at my watch and realize we've been in the air for two hours. Osei and Bruce are both asleep. I look at Osei, and I can't imagine who would abandon such a lovely child. I ask myself if I'll be able to walk away from him when the time comes for me to do so. He refers to himself as a well-raised orphan, and he has never let being an orphan negatively impact his life. How was he able to overcome such hardship?

"A penny for your thoughts?" Osei whispers.

I'm so deep in thought, I didn't realize he was awake.

"This thought is worth a quarter."

He comes over and sits next to me on the sofa.

"What were you thinking about?"

"How to neutralize Ms. Hannah, because you and I both know she won't give up trying to get her hands on your money. Osei, she's serious about hurting someone close to you or threatening you with a scandal to get you to sign those papers."

"You're the only one close to me, and what could she possibly use as a scandal? I'm an open book. There's nothing in my personal life she could use as leverage against me. While you were sleeping, Bruce and I discussed hiring security to watch over you."

"Ms. Hannah doesn't scare me, so hiring security isn't necessary. I won't live in fear, and I'm definitely not going to be a victim of that old bat."

"She may not scare you, but she scares the hell out of me, and I'm going to take every precaution to keep you safe from her," Bruce says.

"I'm sorry, Bruce. We didn't mean to wake you. Do you think meeting her again was a bad idea?"

"No. Now, we know her agenda. We wouldn't have known had you two not met with her a second time."

"In addition to the contract with the firm to manage my affairs, there was another document which would give her a monthly salary," Osei says.

"What? Are you serious?"

"Yes. She wants me to give her fifty thousand dollars a month for three years."

"Is she crazy?" I say.

"Crazy like a fox. She hopes I'd feel indebted to her and her husband. It was framed as a donation in his memory."

"But there were two things for which she hadn't planned. Osei is financially savvy, and you, Sese. She must have felt sure you'd reject Osei, and she would be there to pick up the pieces," Bruce says.

"But how would Ms. Hannah know Osei would be a successful basketball player?"

"I think she figured that out when she came to see you play when you were twelve. Osei, how did you do in that tournament?" Bruce asks.

"My team won, and I was MVP. There were a lot of college scouts, as well as NBA scouts. I explained to my coach who Ms. Hannah was, and he allowed me to meet with her after the game. She took me out to dinner and told me she had found my birth parents and gave me the papers where you guys signed me over to the orphanage."

"What were you like at twelve?" As I look lovingly at him.

"I was very shy, and I didn't talk much. I don't think I spoke more than ten words at dinner."

"Bruce, do you think she started planning this when Osei was twelve?"

"If it wasn't a plan, it definitely was a thought," Bruce says.

"Why is she just now inserting herself into your life? Why didn't she show up sooner?" I ask.

"I'm guessing Ms. Hannah didn't come off as motherly when she met you after the game," Bruce says.

"I was shy. I didn't say much, but I didn't feel anything toward her," Osei replies.

"Sese," Bruce continues. "Ms. Hannah assumed you'd send Osei packing, and she'd swoop in to be the support he needed."

"Looks like I'm not the only one doing the protecting here," I say.

"Speaking of protection," Osei says, glancing at Bruce. "Can we switch seats?"

Bruce raises an eyebrow. "No, I don't want her hitting me by mistake."

Osei nervously turns to me. "Sese, I have something to tell you."

"What is it?" I ask, now impatient.

Osei hesitates. "Just… maybe let me get out of arm's reach first. Well, there are two things I need to tell you, and I think both will make you angry. First, I made you my beneficiary. Secondly, I uploaded the karaoke video to my Facebook, Instagram, Twitter, and YouTube accounts."

I'm speechless, and I look at them both. Bruce throws his hands in the air. "He's your son."

I give him an annoying look. "I've asked you not to do things like this without asking me."

"The beneficiary thing was business, and the video thing was for fun. I'm so proud of you, and I wanted people to know."

I'm trying extremely hard not to show how angry I am. My speech is slow and methodical as I say. "Osei, you know how I feel about my privacy. Here is what I need you to do. First, remove my name from any of your business documents. I generally don't agree to things I don't read. And second, take down the video immediately."

Osei pulls out his iPhone, saying, "Sese, the video has at least a million views and has been shared just as many times. It's useless to take it down now."

"I don't care, take it down."

Hours later, we arrive in Philadelphia. I have nothing to say; Osei knows I'm not happy with him.

25

I Wasn't Lost

My ringtone echoes, breaking the silence. It's Gloria. "Hey. What's up?"

"You are. Jackson and the boys are upset with you. The boys are questioning whether or not you're their godmother."

"What's going on? Did I forget their birthdays, or some other important date?"

"Hold on. I'll let them tell you."

"Auntie Sese, why didn't you tell us you know Osei Wharton? We follow him on Facebook and Instagram, and we saw the video of you singing."

"Sese, I didn't know you graduated from singing in the shower," Jackson shouts over the boys.

I glare at Bruce, and he winks at me. I hand the phone to Osei. "Their names are Justin and Jason. You need to speak with them."

"Hey, J and J. This is Osei. Sienna has told me you are my biggest fans, and I want to thank you both for your support."

Jason says, "Wow! Is this really Osei Wharton?"

"Yes, it's me. Next time you visit Sienna, I'll get you tickets to a game, and we can grab a bite before the game."

"We would love it," Justin squeals.

"We'll make it happen," Osei says, and hands me back the phone.

"You've made their year. Jackson wants to know how you know Osei," Gloria says.

"I'll explain it all to you later."

We drop Bruce off at 30th Street Station.

As we drive away, Osei asks, "Sese, are you still upset with me?"

"Yes, I am."

"Okay, I'll take down the video, but I'm not removing your name as my beneficiary."

"Why not?"

"Because you're the only family I have. Sese, please let me do this."

"Osei, you have to involve me when you do things like this. Don't you understand you and I are on a quest to find someone who did the same thing to me, using my name without my permission?"

He looks at me with his beautiful brown eyes. "I'm sorry, and it won't happen again. Do I have to take down the video? Everyone loves it."

"Osei, my patience is wearing thin. Please take it down."

"Okay. I'll take it down."

"I truly mean it. I'm happy you're a part of my world."

He says, "But..."

"What I was going to say before you cut me off was, I'm not ready to share what we have with the world. Have you given any thought to what's going to happen once you find your birth parents?"

"I have. You'll always be a part of my life, and that will never change."

"Ms. Hannah's reaction to me will pale in comparison to how your birth mother will react."

"She has no right to react to anything. Did you forget she left me?"

"We don't know why she left you."

"That may be the case, but she's had years to find me. I wasn't lost. Who knows? I may be the one to leave her this time."

We arrive at my home; I can barely keep my eyes open. Osei takes my luggage inside. I hug him and we make plans to have lunch in a couple of days.

"Oh, by the way, so you're aware, Bruce and I hired a company to provide around-the-clock security for you."

"You did what? You're kidding me."

"I'm not kidding," he says, backing out of the driveway.

26

Dead Serious

Millie kissing my hand awakens me. "Good morning, big girl. I missed you."

We go downstairs, and I make coffee. I relax in my special chair and begin reading emails. Right on time, Osei makes his morning call.

"Good morning, Sese."

"Good morning, Osei. What's happening in your world?"

"I asked Mark to look into the DC management company, and he and I also discussed wanting to start a foundation."

"When would you have time to run a foundation?" There's silence. "Osei, are you there?"

"Yes, I'm here, and wondering if you would help me get the foundation off the ground. I'll eventually hire someone to be the CEO, but until then, can you help me?"

"I don't think I have the bandwidth."

"Okay, but promise me you'll give it some thought."

"Okay. I'll think about it, but right now, we'll need to concentrate on getting the names of your birth parents from Ms. Hannah. All of this is mentally overwhelming. I need to unpack the events and plan our next steps."

"I have dinner plans for tonight. Are you available for breakfast tomorrow morning?" he asks.

"Osei, it's Sunday, we can do brunch instead."

Ms. Hannah's actions linger between us; we both know that this isn't over.

I can't wait to discuss the recent events in London with Dee. She won't be surprised that Ms. Hannah threatened me and attempted to coerce Osei into signing a contract with her. She answers on the first ring, and I lay it all out.

"I told you the woman is evil. Sese, you won't be able to do this alone. Ms. Hannah is a ruthless human being. Be prepared for her to come after you. Her number one priority will be to remove you from Osei's life."

"My number one priority right now is to protect Osei and expose her for the criminal that she is."

We need to develop a network around you and Osei. Don't you think it's time to involve everyone?"

"Yes, Dee, will you arrange everything? Please let them know this is an emergency."

"I will. And remember, you have us. You are not alone," Dee says.

I need to get some fresh air, so I take Millie for a walk. As we reach the end of the driveway, a man approaches us.

"Ms. Lewis, my name is Rob Ackerman, and I'm the head of WD Security. My company has been assigned as your protection detail."

"My what?"

"Your protection detail," he repeats. O&B Management hired us. If you're leaving, a team will escort you wherever you need to go."

"Will you excuse me?"

I go back inside, and I call Osei.

"Osei, I told you I could take care of myself. I thought we agreed that security was not necessary."

"Bruce insisted," he says.

"Really, hold on," and I added Bruce to the call.

"Bruce, Osei is also on the phone."

I say in a loud but very calm voice, "I need O&B Management to fire WD security now."

Laughing, Bruce says, "Osei, I told you O&B Management wasn't a good name."

"Do you think this is funny? I'm not going to ask you again. Fire the security company." I hang up the phone.

Bruce immediately calls back. "We're not firing the security company."

"Yes, you are." I hang up the phone again. Millie and I take our walk with Mr. Ackerman's team close behind.

I receive a text from Dee. *We're on for 8:30 tonight. I'll send out the Zoom invite.*

I respond with a smiley face emoji. I have a few hours to get my mind right for the call. I have never kept anything of this magnitude from them.

Millie and I finish our walk and head home, the watchdogs in tailored suits trailing after us. The phone rings. It's Bruce. I debate sending him to voicemail, but relent and answer.

"Please don't hang up."

"That depends on what you have to say?"

"I want you to calm down and accept the fact that you'll have around-the-clock protection for the foreseeable future."

"Bruce, you, and Osei can't decide what I need and what I don't need. You are taking this a bit too far."

"You were threatened by someone who has a motive and the means, and we're not giving her any opportunity whatsoever to make good on her threat. I'll do everything in our power to protect you."

"Bruce, I can't have this kind of interference in my professional life."

"They won't enter your office or your client's. However, they will be outside and will follow you to your appointments. I understand you and Osei are meeting tomorrow."

"Yes, we're having brunch."

"Good. He'll discuss the extent of the protection perimeters with you."

"Are you serious?"

"Yes, dead serious."

27

The Network of Love

I spend most of the afternoon thinking about what I'm going to say to the girls. I know they'll be upset because I didn't tell them about Osei sooner. As the time for the call approaches, I'm extremely nervous. I take a few deep breaths, reminding myself to stay focused. My lifelong friendship with these women is riding on this, and I need to be at my best.

At 8:30 pm sharp, I log into the Zoom call, and Dee is already on.

"Hello, Dee."

"Hey, Sese. Are you okay?"

Before I could reply, Taylor, Rainey, and Gloria joined the call.

"Hello, my loves, thank you for joining the call."

Rainey says, "Like we had a choice. You know we can't ignore a request when it's urgent."

"Sese, why the SOS? What is going on?" Gloria asks.

I retell the entire story. Everyone is silent. Their expressions are a mix of concern and frustration.

"I pledged to this young man I'd help him find his birth parents."

"Why?" Gloria asks.

"Because he's a lovely person, and I'm pissed that someone would steal my identity. For the past few months, I've been helping him find his parents."

"So, is Bruce involved?" Rainey asks,

"Rainey, would you please give it a rest?" Gloria says.

"This kid is a famous athlete."

"Oh my God, is it Osei Wharton?" Gloria asks.

"Yes."

"Holy shit! He was the person stalking you at Saks," Taylor says.

"Yes, and now we know why. I'll answer all your questions later. I need to get through this."

"Okay. We won't interrupt you again," Rainey says.

"I realize now I should have discussed this with all of you sooner. But I needed to be certain...to make sure none of you were his mother."

"Are you serious? Are you saying you thought one of us gave birth without telling anyone, and then gave the child up for adoption using your name?" Rainey says.

"That sums it up nicely," Taylor annoyingly says.

"And what makes you think one of us isn't his mother?" Gloria says.

I look into the camera. "You all love me as much as I love you and would never fraudulently use my name in any shape, form, or fashion."

"Well..." Rainey began.

Gloria cut her off, saying, "Sese, how can we help?"

"Do you know of anyone who was pregnant during our senior year or the year after we graduated?"

They all say, "No."

"What if someone in the administration office used your credentials? Didn't you have a job in the bursar's office during your senior year?" Taylor asks.

"Yes, but I only worked there for a week, not even long enough to collect a paycheck."

"Sese, your personal information would be on file there, and there were a lot of people who had access to your information and could have forged your signature," Dee says.

"But why you, Sese? Why would someone use your name, and why add Bruce's name? Gloria asks.

"Ms. Hannah knows I'm not Osei's mother. She's the one who gave him the adoption papers. I suspect that she has the information about his real birth parents. When we met her in London. I portrayed a gold-digging mama to irritate her, and it worked. She became very agitated when I flashed the ring Osei gave me in her face. Later, she sent me a text message saying she knew I was not Osei's mother and that I'd remain unharmed if I had him sign the contract. Ms. Hannah has her own agenda and is going after Osei's money. Therefore, she sees me as a roadblock."

"Please be careful. She's pure evil," Dee says.

"You know her?" Rainey asks.

"She ran the cafeteria when I worked there and was a mean racist."

I try to interrupt Dee before she says anything else.

Sensing my attempt to deflect, she says, "It's okay, Sese, I need to tell my story because they need to know how evil Ms. Hannah is."

Dee tells everyone about being raped and how Ms. Hannah tried to extort her when she became famous. When she finished, we were all crying.

"Sese, what are you going to do?" Taylor asks.

"Everything I can to help Osei find his birth parents."

Gloria shares her screen. "Look at this. This is the video Osei uploaded. I saw something that was amazing," she says.

"What did you see?" Taylor asks.

"Love," Gloria replies. "Look at the way Osei looks at Sese and the way she looks at him."

I watch their faces as the video plays, and I'm embarrassed.

"You're right, Gloria. There's an undeniable bond between them," Rainey says.

"Are you going to be alright once he finds his mother?" Taylor asks. "I can see that you really care about this kid."

"That I do… and yes, I'll be fine."

"Are you sure you're not his mother? He has your eyes," Rainey says.

"Sese, he has your entire face," Dee says.

"There's a slight resemblance," I say.

"Slight resemblance, my foot. He could be your son—or at least your younger brother," Gloria says.

"I deal with kids who have been abandoned every day, and one thing I can tell you, not all of them want to find their birth parents, and a large number may never make the parent–child bond after finding them. There's a chance Osei won't bond with his birth mother," Rainey says.

"Why do you think that could be the case?" I ask.

"I know the answer," Taylor says. "Osei stayed at the orphanage for all those years. He wasn't lost. His mother knew where he was and could have come for him at any time."

"Bingo," Rainey says.

"Don't downplay the threat from Ms. Hannah. She's an extremely dangerous person," Dee says.

"I won't, Osei and Bruce hired a security company to protect me."

"I have a line to all the legal and illegal adoption agencies. I'm sure someone knows if she's active in the adoption arena," Rainey says.

"Taylor, will you talk to some of your sorority sisters? They may know of a girl or girls who were pregnant our senior year or the year after."

Gloria's boys come into the room, hug their mother, wave at us, and in unison say, "Hello Aunties."

"I have to go. The hungry bears are home. Oh my God, you guys smell like bears. Get off me," Gloria exclaims.

We all say goodbye, and I think how blessed I am to have these women as my sisters. I looked at the clock. It's almost 10:00 P.M. Before I fell off to sleep, I remembered how happy Osei was in London. I want him to feel wanted for the rest of his life.

28

Battle on the Trail

Millie is making a racket at the ringing doorbell. I roll over and turn on the camera. The UPS guy is leaving a package at the front door. I fluff my pillow, deciding to stay in bed an hour or so more. Unfortunately, the darn phone rings. "Bruce, hello!"

"Good morning, Sese, the security company called to say you received a package. They want to know if you'd like them to open it," Bruce says.

"No." I hang up the phone and roll over. I'm going to sleep for two more hours. Whatever is in the package will have to wait until I get up.

I pick up the package and place it on the counter. Millie is squirming, so it'll have to wait until I return to open it. I put on her leash, and we head for the trail. I look behind to see a guy following me. I relax knowing he's there to protect me. The trail is where I can reflect and be with nature. The beautiful tulip poplar trees, wild cucumber magnolia, and flowering dogwood trees, their roots intertwining and growing across the trail, are always a quiet wonder. As I walk farther into the woods, I notice the security guy is no longer behind me. I let Millie off her leash, and she starts exploring, sniffing, and running through the woods.

I hear someone calling me, and I turn to see the security guy coming up behind me.

The man looks around nervously, then says, "It's clear you don't follow directions very well."

My heart begins to pound in my chest as I realize he isn't part of my security detail.

"Who are you?" I nervously ask.

"Look, Miss. No one needs to get hurt here. I'm here to warn you that you should do what you've been told."

"What are you talking about? Please leave."

"This is a public area, and I have a right to be here."

"Yes. But you don't have permission to talk to me or block my way."

"Who's going to stop me?"

"I am." And I pull out my expandable baton and whistle for Millie, who comes barreling out of the woods, heading directly for my unwanted visitor. While Millie is distracting him, I take his photo. He turns to me, and I step toward him, swinging the baton. I hit his forearm. Clutching his arm, he winces in pain as the impact reverberates. His eyes locked onto mine, a mixture of shock and anger. Millie has a hold of his leg, and he's hitting at her, but not connecting.

"Get your dog off me, you bitch!" he yells.

Two men on mountain bikes are coming up the trail. I whistle, and Millie releases his leg.

"Lady, do you need help?" the bikers shout.

"Yes, help me," I scream.

My unwanted visitor runs, and I lose sight of him as he disappears into the trees.

"Can you walk with me to the bottom of the trail?"

"Shouldn't we call the police?"

"Please walk me home. I'll make a report when I get there."

When I get home, Osei is standing in the driveway. He looks at the bikers and at Millie's bloody mouth.

He runs over to me. "What happened? Sese are you okay?" he frantically asks.

One of the guys says, "We found her fighting with a man on the trail."

"You were doing what?" Osei says. He grabs me by both of my shoulders.

"Are you hurt anywhere?"

"I'm fine, I'll tell you what happened when we get inside."

"Thank you so very much for helping my mom," Osei says.

One of the guys asks, "Aren't you Osei Wharton?"

"Yes, can I have your contact information? I'd like to send you both a gift to show my appreciation."

Osei calls 911, and afterward, I explain what happened, but before I can finish, he holds up his hand.

"Hold on."

He dials Bruce, "We have a problem, someone threatened and attacked Sese while she was walking on the trail."

"Where the hell was the security detail?"

"That's the million-dollar question," Osei says.

"Sese, are you hurt anywhere?" Bruce asks.

Before I can answer, Osei says, "She's okay, a bit shaken up, but okay."

"Sese, what happened out there?" Bruce says, steady and focused.

"I was walking the trail when a man approached me. At first, I thought he was part of the security detail. He told me I should do what I was told. I'm sure Ms. Hannah sent him."

The doorbell rings, and Osei says, "Bruce, the police are here. We'll call you back later."

"I'm heading to Newark Airport. I'll be there in about an hour," Bruce says.

The police take the report and leave. Osei, call the security company to find out what happened."

Bruce arrives about an hour and a half later in an Uber, and we all convene in the kitchen.

Osei says to Bruce, "The security company was very apologetic. They explained there was coverage overnight, but the morning guy didn't show up," Osei says to Bruce. "Someone was dispatched to his home about twenty minutes ago. The man impersonating the morning guy attacked Sese."

"Bruce, who called you about the package that was delivered this morning?" I ask anxiously.

I start to open the package.

"Don't open it," Bruce shouts!

I gingerly place the package back on the counter, realizing for the first time it could be something dangerous.

Bruce carefully opens it. He empties the contents on the kitchen counter. Inside is a typed note and a photo. *You need to do what you're told.*

I look at the picture, Bruce and I are kissing. I'm topless, wearing only pants. It was taken when we were in college.

Osei looks at both of us and breaks out laughing.

"Gimme that." I grab the photo. "Damn, look at me. I was so fine back then."

Bruce takes a deep breath, running his hands through his hair as his eyes dart from me to the photo. "Am I the only one embarrassed here?" he mutters, his voice laced with discomfort.

"Yes, you are. You know what this means. Ms. Hannah has been conspiring all these years."

Looking closer at the photo, Bruce says, "This photo was taken inside my apartment. There wasn't a window in that little rinky-dink room."

Now, understanding what this means. "Who the hell took this picture?" I ask.

"Why would she bug my apartment?" Bruce says.

We both look at each other, wondering what else she may have, and my mouth drops at the thought.

Osei laughs and says, "I want to know what happened next."

Bruce says, "If you were my son, I'd say that was the night you were conceived."

I'm starting to understand what Bruce and Osei have been saying. I step outside to breathe. A few minutes later, Bruce joins me on the deck with a cup of coffee.

"I need something a little stronger."

He hands me the glass in his other hand.

I take a sip, and my insides tingle—cognac, cinnamon, and cherry liqueur.

"I haven't had a cognac sidecar in years."

"That's because I wasn't around to make it for you. Do you remember what happened between us the night that photo was taken?"

"Yes, we made love for the first time."

"That's what you called it? You bit me several times. I thought I was going to need a tetanus shot," he says.

I give Bruce a worried look. "Do you think Ms. Hannah has more photos?"

"I'll bet my last dollar that she does."

Osei and Millie join us. He too has a cup.

"There better not be any alcohol in your cup," I say.

"Of course not. It's hot chocolate."

"Sese, how were you able to fight that guy off?" Bruce asks.

I reach into my pocket, and I dramatically whip out my expandable baton. Osei, choking on his hot chocolate, says, "Sese, you never cease to amaze me."

"Millie and I know how to defend ourselves. I was trained to protect myself, and Millie was trained to protect me."

The security company calls Osei. "Can I put you on speaker? Sienna and Bruce are here."

"Yes, please do. Hello everyone. This is Rob Ackerman..."

Before he can finish, Bruce angrily says, "What the hell happened today?"

"Two men broke into the home of the guard assigned to the morning shift protecting Ms. Lewis and beat and tied him up. He is unconscious and being transported to the hospital as we speak. Ms. Lewis, can you give us a description of the person who attacked you? I need to confirm if he was one of the people who harmed my employee," Mr. Ackerman asks.

"I took his picture, and I can text it to you."

"In light of what happened today, you may be considering another company. I'd ask you to give us another opportunity."

Osei says, "Why should we?"

Mr. Ackerman replies, "Because this is now personal. One of our team members went to the hospital today."

"Let us discuss it, and we'll get back to you," Osei says.

"Mr. Ackerman, this is Bruce. In the meantime, you'll still need to protect Ms. Lewis."

"Yes, we'll continue until we're told otherwise," Mr. Ackerman says.

While rubbing Millie's belly, Osei remarks, "Millie, our Sese, is a badass, and you're more than just a pretty face."

29

A Day Late and A Dollar Short

"With the attack on Sese earlier, this is getting serious. Osei, have you heard from Ms. Hannah?" Bruce asks.

"I have not."

"Sese, I'm sure Ms. Hannah thinks you are telling Osei not to sign the contracts."

"I agree, and that's why I asked Mark to look into the DC management agency. According to him, it's a legitimate company, but they have a lot of unhappy clients. A large majority of the athletes who hired them lost all of their money," Osei says.

"How does a company like that stay in business?" Bruce asks.

"By continually signing rookie athletes like me and stealing them blind."

Osei, clearly frustrated, says, "I'm done talking about Ms. Hannah," he says firmly and changes the subject.

"Sese, have you given any thought to heading up my foundation?"

"I have not, you asked me yesterday, and from what I understood from the conversation, I was only helping to get it started, not running it."

"Why can't you?"

"Because Osei Wharton, I have a job that I love."

"Sese, I think you should consider it," Bruce says.

"So now both of you are going to gang up on me?"

"No, we're not, but it makes sense," Osei says.

"Where were you two when I needed to be protected? You both are a day late and a dollar short," I angrily say.

"I'm sorry, Sese. I didn't mean to offend or upset you. If you were at the foundation, you wouldn't have to travel. It would be easier for us to protect you."

Waving my hand in frustration, "Don't worry about me. I'm fine."

"I'm..." Bruce hesitates before he finishes his sentence, saying, "Sese, you better not say it."

"Say what?" Osei asks.

"Whenever Bruce would tell me he was sorry, I'd say, and so is the rest of your family, which would piss him off."

Osei says, "You two are weird."

"And you think you're not," I say.

A text comes in for Osei. The grin on his face gets wider and wider with each word he reads.

"Is everything okay?" I ask.

"More than okay, Mark's been in talks with Nike, and they have agreed to our terms."

"Congratulations," Bruce and I say in unison.

"I want to celebrate. Can we go somewhere nice for dinner tonight?"

"Sure," I say, and Bruce nods in agreement.

Osei gets another text, and we go inside to watch ESPN.

"*Breaking news,*" Cari Champion on ESPN's SportsCenter is announcing. "*Osei Wharton of the 76ers signs a multimillion-dollar contract with Nike. Reportedly over $50 million. Expect to see him in all things Nike soon. Congratulations, Osei. Come visit me soon!*"

I look at Osei and look back at the TV and say, "I think we should stay in and order take-out. It will be pure chaos if you were to go out in public tonight—Chinese, Japanese, Italian, seafood, sushi, or soul food."

"Fifty million dollars? Did I hear her correctly?" Bruce is shaking his head.

"It's worth more than that. The media will never have the exact figure."

"I need a drink. Does anyone else want one?" I ask.

Bruce says, "I'll have what you're having."

"I want one of those Scottish Ales you love so much," Osei says.

My phone's blowing up. Gloria, Taylor, Dee, Rainey. All caps: "HOLY SHIT! CONGRATS, OSEI!" Bruce gets the same from Jackson.

We raise our glasses for a toast.

"Congratulations, Osei. You are deserving of this. You'll be an asset to the NBA and Nike, but more importantly to society," Bruce says.

"Thank you, I'd like to be an asset here. Sese, can I help you pay off the mortgage on your home?"

"No need. There's no mortgage on my home."

"What about your place on the Vineyard?"

"No mortgage there either."

"Wow, I want to do something for you."

"It's not necessary. I'm okay."

"Do you think you could go to Oregon with me to the Nike to sign the contract?"

"I'll be in New York for most of next week. When is the signing?"

"Mark and I are flying out next Thursday morning and coming back on Sunday."

"Osei, I can't commit now. I'll let you know. Am I the only person starving?" I ask. "I want sushi."

"Yes, they both say, and we ordered takeout from my favorite sushi restaurant."

"I'll go pick up the food. It'll be faster," Osei says.

"No, I'll go."

Bruce offers to come.

"I'm going alone, I say, "Clear my head. I'm not used to constant company all the time."

Bruce and Osei look at each other.

"You two forget, I've got the Men in Black outside, I'll be okay."

Bruce and Osei are watching TV in the den when I return thirty minutes later. "Dinner is served," I say.

"You know, I am just noticing how incredibly beautiful this room is. The floor-to-ceiling windows with views of the woods and the creek, and that spectacular rock waterfall, are breathtaking," Bruce exclaims.

"Can we eat here?" Osei asks.

I place the food down on the table by the window along with a few bottles of alcohol.

"This is the best sushi I've ever tasted," Bruce says, having already scoffed down two Hamachi yellowtail rolls.

"Isn't it fantastic?" I say, handing him a mixed drink and Osei a bottle of sweet tea.

He takes a sip, "This is delicious. What is it?"

"It's a Sienna special."

Osei takes a sip of Bruce's drink. "Mmmm...I want one of those."

"Osei, you can't manage this. Have you ever been drunk?"

"No, and I don't plan on starting now, but I want one of those." He points to Bruce's glass.

"I don't know, Osei. This drink has quite a punch. What is it?" Bruce takes another generous swig.

"Korean Soju mixed with beer."

"Sese, please give me one. I'm over twenty-one and today is a good day."

"I hope you're not a sad drunk,"

"There are different types of drunks?" Osei asks.

"Yes, there are at least seven different types of drunks. The drunks whom you'll have the most contact with are the happy drunk, the sad drunk, and last but not least, the mean drunk."

"Wow! I never thought of it that way. I have a teammate who becomes very mean when he's drunk, and he tries to bully everybody around."

"Promise me you'll only drink here or at your place. Never in public."

"I promise," Osei says.

I wake Bruce and show him to the guest bedroom. Osei has already gone to the other guest bedroom.

In bed, I toss and turn, aware of the growing feelings I have for Bruce. I'm glad when a text from Dee interrupts my thoughts: Zoom call tomorrow at 2:00 P.M.

I'm available. I text back.

Coffee and frying onions get me out of bed. Downstairs, Bruce and Osei are in the kitchen cooking breakfast.

"Good morning, sleepyhead," Osei says,

"Good morning. What are you all cooking? It smells amazing."

"I'm cooking, Osei is keeping me company," Bruce says, laughing.

He places a roasted vegetable frittata, buttered toast, and chicken and apple sausage in front of me.

"Yum, I'm hungry."

Osei, who is heavily concentrating on his breakfast, is startled when his phone rings, nearly knocking over his hot chocolate.

It's Mr. Ackerman. He places him on speaker. "Hey, Mr. Ackerman, what's up?"

"Hello, Mr. Wharton, I wanted to report that the man who assaulted Ms. Lewis was located and apprehended by the FBI, trying to board a flight at JFK. He's a part of a crime syndicate operating out of Germany, which is currently being investigated by Interpol. I'll continue to update you all as we get more information."

"A crime syndicate? This is more serious than I thought. Thank you. Please keep us posted."

The impact of Mr. Ackerman's words is written all over Osei's face. "Sese, I'm so sorry for involving you and Bruce in all this. I didn't know Ms. Hannah was so dangerous."

"None of us did, but I'm now well aware of how ruthless and dangerous Ms. Hannah can be. I know for a fact she's extorting several people who attended college with us."

"Unbelievable. That woman is truly despicable. We definitely need to increase your security detail," Bruce says.

"Osei, what about your safety? Do you have security?" I ask.

"She would never hurt me."

"Why is that? Because she would never hurt the goose that lays the golden egg? I beg to differ. If she's desperate enough, she might. If she can't have the golden egg, what then will she go after the goose? In her warped mind, she may try to harm you, Osei."

"I'm a celebrity. She wouldn't dare mess with me," Osei says.

"Maybe she wouldn't, but we know nothing about the people she's associated with," I interject, concern coursing through my body.

"Don't worry, I'll be alright."

"Osei, I'm asking you to take this seriously," I insist.

"Okay, I'll beef up my security as well."

Osei looks at his watch. "I have to go. I'm meeting my accountant at my place. Sese, why don't you bring Bruce over? I want him to see how you decorated my place."

Twenty minutes later, Bruce and I arrive at Osei's. We take the private elevator to his condo, and I enter the code.

"You have the code to his place?" Bruce asks.

"Yes, I've had it for quite some time now."

The elevator doors open, and Millie greets us.

"This is the biggest Rottweiler I have ever seen," Bruce says.

"And I'm sure she's the friendliest," I say.

"I have signed her up for defensive and protective training. She needs to have your Millie's skills," Osei chimes in.

Osei excuses himself to finish up with the preparations to meet the accountant. Bruce and I walk into the space. "This place is spectacular, and the city skyline is breathtaking," Bruce says.

Osei joins us when we reach the game room. "All my teammates want to hang out here. They find it to be peaceful and relaxing. Which reminds me, Sese, a couple of them would like you to talk to them about decorating their apartments."

I give him an annoying look. "Osei, why don't you think I have a real job?"

"A thousand apologies."

I go into the kitchen and open the refrigerator. To my delight, there are fruits, vegetables, fish, and an abundance of bottled water.

"Hey Bruce, would you like a full tour of my place?"

"Wow, I want to live here. Sese, what inspired you?" Bruce asks.

"Osei was my inspiration. I wanted to make sure he had a place where he could close the door and relax his mind, body, and spirit."

I point toward the spacious living area. "I wanted to define the open space, so I laid down hand-knotted silk and wool rugs in warm earth tones. The modular seating in the living and den areas gives him room to stretch out. The den has oversized pillows and a cushioned window seat."

The house was designed for comfort and function. A kitchen with a breakfast nook overlooking the view, a game room for his friends, a bonus half-court, and a full entertainment setup with a pool table, poker table, and theater system. We head upstairs, where I added an office with a projection TV, converted a guest room into a gym, and upgraded the master bath with a steam room and soaking tub.

The tour is interrupted by the doorbell. Osei heads downstairs, and Bruce and I join him a few minutes later.

We find him reviewing documents with a well-dressed man, who looks up and greets us with a warm smile.

"This is Mr. Walker," Osei says, "the head accountant at the firm that manages my portfolio."

Mr. Walker extends his hand. "Pleasure to meet you both. I'm glad you're here. So Perfect! Osei needs witnesses for a document he's about to sign."

Without thinking. Bruce and I both sign as witnesses.

Mr. Walker leaves and assures Osei he'll file the necessary paperwork.

"Osei, is it okay if I use your office for the call with the girls in a few minutes?"

"Of course."

"By the way, what were the papers Sese and I signed earlier? I'm not big on signing things I don't read, but just for you," Bruce says.

I echo his sentiment.

"Nothing really. I needed to transfer a piece of property."

"How many properties do you own?" I ask.

"I owned three units in this building. Now I own two."

"Osei, why would you sell a unit? This building is prime real estate. This apartment alone is valued well over a million dollars." I shake my head, still trying to understand. "You handed us the papers to sign when we were distracted. I shouldn't have signed it."

"Well, Sese, I didn't exactly sell it," he says, a sheepish look on his face.

"Did you donate it?" Bruce says.

"Why would he do a thing like that, and to whom would he donate it?" I say annoyed.

"I guess you could say I donated it. I signed it over to you."

Bruce and I both exclaim, "You did what?"

"So, if you decide to evict me, I'll move into the other penthouse apartment," Osei says.

Very sternly, I say, "Please call that man back here right now. We need to destroy that document."

"No, I'm not changing my mind."

"This isn't over." I head upstairs. "It's time for the call with the girls. I can't be late." As I make my way upstairs, I add, "Osei, we'll discuss this later. No matter what you say, this isn't a done deal."

30

The Elephant in the Room

I log onto the computer, and I see the lovely faces of my friends. Dee says, "Hello Lovelies, before we get started, I have news. My beautiful daughter, Marie, is moving to Scotland to live with her boyfriend."

"Dee, are you serious? I thought she loved living in London," Taylor says.

"They're getting married next year, and he's going back to work in the family business. His family owns one of the largest whisky distilleries in Scotland."

"I definitely want some samples," I say with a grin.

"Where in Scotland is she moving?" Rainey asks.

"Somewhere in the Highlands. Colin has a small estate on his parents' property."

"How small?" I ask.

"A hundred acres."

"Holy Cow," Gloria says.

"Dee, tell Marie, I wish her the best, and I'm happy for her," I say.

"Sese, didn't you date a Scottish Highlander a few years ago? Whatever happened to him?" Rainey mockingly says.

He lives in London. I see him on occasion, and he's an American of Scottish descent.

"What is his name again?" Gloria asks.

"Rhett. In fact, I saw him when I was in London with Osei and Bruce."

"Why was Bruce there?" Rainey says.

"Because he and I are both involved with this, and Osei asked him to come along. But let me address the elephant in the room. Bruce and I are both trying to get to the bottom of this, nothing more, nothing less. Neither one of us is interested in being in a relationship."

Bruce walks in and kneels beside me, "Hello, ladies, for the record, Sese is speaking for herself. I have every intention of being in a relationship with her."

Handing me a glass of scotch, he says, "I thought you would need this."

He pats me on the top of my head and walks out.

I'm catatonic. Osei is doubled over in silent laughter.

I'm stuttering; I truly have no words.

"Well, damn, I've never seen Sese at a loss for words. We need to reschedule this call for later today. Sese needs time to compose herself," Gloria says.

"We're rooting for you, Bruce," Taylor says.

"Is everyone available at six tonight?" Dee asks.

"Great, I'll send a Zoom invite," she adds.

They leave the meeting, and I sit staring at the blank computer screen. I'm frustrated beyond belief, baffled by what just happened. I compose myself and I head downstairs. Osei and Bruce are watching golf. Without saying a word to either of them, I pick up my purse and keys and leave.

They arrive at my place ten minutes later.

"Sese, why did you leave without saying goodbye?" Osei asks.

"I'm feeling smothered by you two. What I want doesn't matter because you two have decided what is best for me. News Flash! I have survived for twenty years without either of you."

"We're..."

"Shut up, Osei."

Bruce tries to say something. "Not a single word from you either. Osei, I want you in my life, and you don't have to buy me gifts or give me property. Please trust me when I say I'll be there, regardless. So please, stop."

"Okay, but I'm not taking back the condo."

"Osei, there are many in need of financial assistance. Everyone isn't as fortunate as you. Only a small percentage of the country has your wealth."

"There will be enough to go around. Sese, you always ask about what happens when I find my family. Even if I find out I have siblings, aunts, and uncles, please don't forget you'll always be a part of my family, and I would be honored to be your son. I don't think I'll find anyone else I'd like to acknowledge as my mom."

"One thing is for sure. You are as stubborn as she is," Bruce says.

"And as for you! I have no words to express how angry I am with you," I say to Bruce.

"Sese, you have a right to be angry, but I also have the right to be honest. In fact, I wasn't going to say anything, but when I heard you talking about your Scottish American boyfriend, I was jealous."

"You mean the American guy we met in London. I think he still has a thing for Sese for sure," Osei says.

"Yes, that's him," Bruce says.

"So what? Rhett and I dated five years ago."

Bruce starts to speak, and I raise my finger. "Not another word from you. I think you have said enough. Now it's time for me to speak. Twenty years ago, I prayed every night that you would love me again. I also prayed every night I'd stop loving you. Do you think you have the right to show up twenty years later asking for a do-over? Did it ever occur to you how devastated I was when you left me, for the future we both dreamed about?"

Osei tried to creep out of the room.

"Freeze!" I commanded my focus, never leaving Bruce. "Regardless, I don't hate you. Rhett and I broke up because I was afraid to commit to him, thinking he would leave me, so I left him first. He was someone I should have run to without any hesitation, but my wounded soul refused to believe his love for me was solid and pure. He moved to London, and it took some time before he would allow me access to his life again. I did everything I could to be his friend because I missed him, and I needed him to be a part of my life. Today we are friends, and it will always be that way." Pointing at Bruce, I say, "So, no more declarations of how you feel about me, understand!"

"I understand, and I apologize if I made you uncomfortable."

Osei, wanting to change the mood and escape, says. "Sese, what time should I pick you up on Thursday?"

"What is happening on Thursday?"

"We're flying to Oregon. Did you forget?"

"No, I'm good. I took Friday off. What time is the flight?"

"When we get there," Osei replied.

"Good luck. I'll see you all when you return," Bruce says, stepping back to give me space.

"There's room if you want to come," Osei says.

"I don't want to wear out my welcome. Sese isn't too happy with me right now."

"That is an understatement. Don't you have a job you have to go to?"

"I'm on a six-month sabbatical."

"I hope you don't plan on taking your sabbatical in Philly."

"I'll be in Philly doing research. Don't worry, the majority of the time I'll be in NY."

"I'm not worried," I reply.

"I like it when you two argue. Too bad you can't kiss and make up," Osei says.

In unison, Bruce and I say, "Shut up."

"Okay, I'm leaving."

I point at Bruce and say to Osei, "Please take him with you."

After they leave, I wonder how I became the damsel in distress, or why they both see me as someone needing to be rescued. A few hours later, rested, I logged onto the call with the girls.

Dee starts the call by saying, "Ms. Hannah is extorting two people I know, but they both are afraid to talk to me. I'll continue to try to win them over. On a lighter note, "Sese, Marie wants me to thank you for your well wishes. She says you can expect a case of scotch very soon."

"That is why I love her."

"Can we expect someone to be giving you a drink?" Rainey sarcastically asks.

"So, what if someone happens to place a drink on Sese's desk? That is her business," Taylor says, smiling.

Gloria joins the call a few minutes late and says, "Sese, the boys want Osei's autograph. Can you get it for them?"

"Of course."

Dee continues her story. "The two women I suspect Ms. Hannah extorted have been paying her for years. One is a politician's widow hiding a past pregnancy from her strip club days.

The other is in the city government. Neither will talk to me," Dee says,

"Are you serious? Is this really true?" Taylor asks.

"As serious as a heart attack, and I'm sure there are others I don't know about."

"Well, I found out that she's been involved with illegal adoptions, placing American children with families in England and Germany. These families pay hundreds of thousands of dollars for American children. If you have the money, you can have a child."

"Sese, this is extremely dangerous. Will you be okay?" There is a grave concern in Gloria's voice.

"I have bodyguards."

"Good, I'm glad you have protection," Gloria says, asking us to "hold on." She closes her camera and mutes her microphone. A few minutes later, she is back on camera. "Sorry, Justin has a bump on his butt; he wanted me to look at it."

Totally embarrassed, Justin says, "Mom! Why are you telling everyone my business?"

"On that note, I think we can end here. Can you all be available next Thursday evening?" Dee says.

"Weekends are better for me. I see patients until late during the week," Gloria says.

Dee asks, "How about next Sunday?"

Everyone nods.

"Okay, I'll send out the new invite shortly."

A few minutes later, I received the invite from Dee for next Sunday at 5:00 P.M. I accepted the invite and logged off the computer.

Osei calls, and I tell him what I learned from the girls about Ms. Hannah.

"I truly didn't know her."

"Ms. Hannah is a soulless individual whose moral compass is truly broken."

"She needs to go straight to jail," Osei says.

"Are you still angry with me and Bruce?"

"Yes, I am. Where are you, anyway?"

"I'm taking Bruce to his hotel."

"Sese, I'm sorry," Bruce says.

"You should be, both of you, but what exactly are you sorry for?" I ask.

"For treating you like a damsel in distress and thinking I had to mansplain everything."

"I think he's got it! Thank you," I say, hanging up the phone.

31

Ditto

"Sese, wait," Bruce says, "While we're on the subject."

"What subject?" Osei asks.

"The damsel in distress," Bruce says.

"Are you guys kidding me right now?" I ask.

"Sese, even with bodyguards, I'm worried about you getting hurt."

"I agree," Osei says.

"I have a friend who is extremely high up at the FBI. I'm going to ask his advice on what can be done about Ms. Hannah."

"You know people in the FBI?" Osei asks.

"Yes, a friend from college. He'll definitely help."

"Why would he help us?" Osei asks.

"One, because he had a huge crush on Sese in college, and two, blackmail, illegal adoptions, and racketeering are right up his alley.

"Is there anyone who doesn't like Sese?"

"I know of one person who doesn't like her very much," Bruce says.

"Who would that be?" I ask.

"Well, Ms. Hannah. I think we'll need to hire security for Oregon?" Bruce says with a smirk.

"By all means, I'll reach out to Mr. Ackerman," Osei says.

"Earth to Osei and Bruce—have you lost your minds. What part of I'm not a damsel in distress that you don't get?"

I am bewildered by their behavior of ignoring me.

Bruce, in an assuring tone, says, "I'll reach out to Dave Miller. Sese, do you remember Dave?"

"No, should I?"

"You should. Big Dave from Oakland."

"Any other clue?" I deadpan.

"The guy I got into a huge fight with."

"Oh yeah, but I never knew his last name. I always wanted to ask you why you guys fought."

"Because he was stalking you, and it pissed me off."

"Stalking me, no way, you're making that up."

"No! I'm not. I told him to stop following you around campus. He had a crush on you in the worst way, and he thought I wasn't good enough for you. The day we fought, he came to tell me he was going to pursue you regardless of how I felt about it. So, he and I had a physical discussion."

"A discussion that ended with both of you in the infirmary getting stitches."

Bruce chuckled. "Yes. Well, Dave is now the Deputy Director of the FBI in New York."

"Really," Osei asks.

"Yes, I'm sure he'll help us. We've kept in touch over the years. He's happily married now, so I'm sure he has forgotten all about Sese."

"Good for him," I say.

"I'll ask him to look into Ms. Hannah."

I'd had enough, so I changed the subject. "Osei, I have an important call tomorrow. Can we leave in the afternoon?"

"Sure, how about 2:00 P.M., would that work for everyone?" Osei asks.

"Works for me. Good night, all," Bruce says, and I hear the car door slam.

"Sese, want me to pick you up tomorrow?"

"No need, I'll meet you at the terminal. Love you!"

"I don't think I'll ever get used to you saying that. Good night, Sese and Ditto."

32

A Free Man

I call Bruce immediately. Speaking calmly and trying to keep the anger out of my voice, I say, "Meet me in front of the hotel in ten minutes."

"What's going on? I'm not at the hotel, I'm taking a walk in the park at Rittenhouse Square, I need some fresh air."

"Stay there, I'll see you in ten minutes."

I arrive at the park and spot Bruce sitting pensively on a bench, feeding some pigeons. "A penny for your thoughts," I say.

He jumps up and comes toward me.

"Sese. What's wrong?" he asks.

"We really need to set some boundaries around our interaction. I can't have you and Osei dictating how I live my life."

"How about we discuss this over a drink at the hotel bar?"

I reluctantly agree.

"Wait here, Sese," Bruce says, walking over to the front desk. "Excuse me, miss—can you tell me what floor the restaurant is on?"

A bubbly woman behind the desk glances at me, then smiles sweetly at Bruce.

"Will you be needing another room key?"

"No," he replies.

She leans forward slightly, still eyeing me. "Let me know if you change your mind." Bruce doesn't respond. "Which way to the restaurant?" he asks, curtly.

We take the elevator to the restaurant floor. We're waiting to be seated when Bruce's phone rings. "I'll have to call you back," he says, and abruptly hangs up the phone.

Once we're seated, he orders a scotch for himself and a glass of wine for me.

His phone rings again. He ignores it.

"Shouldn't you answer?" I ask.

He nods and answers, "Didn't I say I'd call you back? What is so important, Charlotte?"

Bruce steps away to take the call while I sit quietly observing the man who still makes my heart flutter. Time has been good to him. His style is now more professorial, which gives him an air of distinction. His sharp features are even more so, and his body is still to die for.

When he returns, I meet his gaze. "Bad news?" I ask.

"As a matter of fact, good news. I am officially divorced. That was my now ex-wife. Congratulating me on being a free man. What she doesn't understand is that I've always been free."

"Isn't she happy?"

"Well, she thinks that she needs to apologize for keeping me from being happy all these years. It wasn't about my happiness. I was there because she and my daughter needed me." Bruce looks at the phone, shakes his head, and murmurs, "I pray she and I both will find happiness."

His phone rings again.

"It's my daughter, I haven't spoken to her in days, I have to take this call."

He doesn't step away this time but speaks at the table. His voice is soft and kind as he speaks with his child. When he finally hangs up, he says, "My daughter is finally done with exams, and she wants to meet for dinner."

Again, his phone rings. "What on earth! Sese, I'm sorry."

"Really, Charlotte, why are you calling again? Shouldn't you be calling Janice? We didn't talk this much when we were married. What's going on with you? Is everything okay?"

"No. I don't miss you, but I do miss being a part of a family. I'm not trying to be harsh. Shouldn't you be calling Janet?"

He pauses, "You're no longer a couple. I'm sorry to hear that."

He knows that I'm following the conversation, and he seems anxious. Growing uneasy, he says, "I have to go."

"I know you heard that my wife left me to be with a woman."

I try to look surprised.

"Is she going to be alright?"

I'm looking at the sadness in his eyes, and I don't have the heart to tell him what I had planned to say to him thirty minutes before, which was, I don't see a path forward for us.

Instead, I say, "I heard that the steaks are exceptionally good here."

33

Signing Bonus

When we arrive at the airport in Oregon there's a fleet of Range Rovers waiting for us.

"Osei, why do we need three SUVs?"

"One is for us, and the other two are for the security detail."

"Tell me why we need security here?"

"Until Ms. Hannah is neutralized, we'll have security for the foreseeable future," Bruce responds.

Mark, Osei's agent, greets us. Osei introduces him to Bruce.

"It's a pleasure to meet you, Bruce, and even more of a pleasure to see you again, Ms. Lewis," he says, "I'm still receiving calls from some men who were at the game wanting to meet you."

Osei looks at Bruce jokingly and says, "I may get a daddy real soon."

Bruce throws an air punch his way.

"Ms. Lewis, you and I can talk later," Mark says.

"No need. I have no interest in meeting anyone."

"Even if one of them is a billionaire who owns half of Connecticut?" Mark says.

"Not even a billionaire who owns half the world." I take his arm as we walk to the Range Rovers. "How far are we from the hotel?"

"You're not staying at a hotel. One of the Nike board members is letting Osei stay at his estate."

Osei recognizes the puzzled look on my face and explains. "Sese, it's easier for the security team if we stay where people have limited access to us."

We arrive at a gray-stone chalet, nestled in a beautiful, wooded area flanked by the most amazing gardens. It's magnificent.

"Wow! This is a beautiful estate," Bruce says.

"Isn't it?" Mark says, "It's seldom used except when board members are in town for the annual meeting."

The SUVs pull up under the portico. A man and two women greet us.

Lucas, the property caretaker, introduces us to the two women—Hilda, who will be our chef, and Grace, who will assist with our needs. The palatial Chalet, straight out of *Architectural Digest*, has vaulted ceilings and wooden beams. Lucas explains the layout: Each first-floor room opens to the patio and a heated infinity pool. As he speaks, light pours through the clerestory windows, which casts soft streaks across the rich wood floors. I walked into the kitchen. I gasped, "Oh my God!"

It is enormous. On the right, a walk-in wine cellar, a sleek kitchen with white pristine cabinets, stainless-steel appliances, and a cozy nook with striped yellow and white cushions completes the breathtaking room.

"Lucas, I have never seen a kitchen this big."

He smiles. "It is extraordinary."

The bedroom I'm shown overlooks the backyard and has a stunning view of the Oregon mountains. The wooded area behind the property, I am told, is Tualatin Nature Park. I change my clothes and head back downstairs. Osei and Bruce are outside, engaged in a putting contest.

"Who's winning?" I ask.

"Osei is the clear winner. He won fifty dollars off of me so far," Bruce says, and hands me the putter.

In the end, I walk away with a lot of Osei's money in my pocket.

We're seated on the patio when Lucas, Hilda, and Grace place trays of food on the table before us: Lobster and steak, grilled vegetables, and potatoes au gratin.

"This all looks delicious," Bruce says.

We enjoy dinner, overlooking the majestic mountains and listening to Miles Davis. There couldn't have been a more perfect setting.

After dinner, stuffed and tired, I ask, "Osei, what time do we have to be at Nike tomorrow?"

"Ten o'clock."

"Okay. I'm calling it a night. I'll see you all in the morning."

Bruce raises his glass, and Osei blows me a kiss.

Tired as I was, sleep was sketchy. At two in the morning, I decide to take a dip in the pool, hoping the exercise will help me sleep. I'm on my third lap when I notice Bruce sitting on the side of the pool. I swim over to him.

"How long have you been sitting here?"

"Only for a few minutes. I can't sleep, and Osei can't either. He's in the gym working out."

I get out, and Bruce hands me a towel.

"Can you get Osei? I'm going to make us all a cup of warm milk. It may help us sleep."

I gather what I needed, and when the milk was ready, I added a dash of cinnamon, and we drank with hope.

"Thanks for the milk," Osei says, gloomier than I've ever seen him.

"You are welcome. You need to be well rested for tomorrow."

Osei, pressing his hands together, says, "Too late for that... it's 3:00 A.M. I've never been this nervous before."

"Why would you be nervous?"

"All this is happening so fast. I keep thinking I don't deserve all that's happening. I've spent my life dreaming of this, but now that it's happening, I feel I'm not deserving of it."

Bruce goes to Osei and hugs him. " It's here. Embrace it. This is a big deal, and it means you are among the elite. You deserve all the good coming your way because you have worked hard all of your life for this moment. Now isn't the time to doubt yourself. It's the time to grab the brass ring you've earned."

Osei starts to cry, and Bruce beckons me over. I take Osei in my arms. "Osei, I might not have been with you from the beginning, but I am here for you from now on. I believe something magical happens when you love someone unconditionally. You and I have decided to let love bestow all the magic on each other. Even if all of this goes away, you'll still have me, and what I have emotionally as well as financially is yours. You'll have to continue to work to be the best player, the best role model, and the best son." I pause for a moment.

"Sese... It's just... " he wipes away tears using the back of his hand. Bruce hands him a tissue.

"Osei, tomorrow is the beginning, not the end. Don't fear what could happen. Own your success. Now close your eyes. On the count of three, open them and be greatful and ready to embrace your fate. One, two, three."

Osei opens his eyes and looks at me and Bruce. He hugs me so hard I can hardly breathe.

"I'm grateful to embrace my fate," he says.

"Boy, let me go. I can't breathe."

"I'll breathe for you, Sese."

"You are so silly." I stay put in his embrace for several more seconds.

We make our way to our bedrooms. Before I enter a deep sleep, I receive a text from Bruce. *Sese, you are truly a blessing.* I fall asleep, thinking about how Bruce and Osei are becoming my blessings.

Our transportation arrives at nine in the morning. We were too nervous to have breakfast, so as we made our way to the waiting cars, Lucas hands us thermal bottles filled with green tea and honey. Mark is in the front seat. He turns to greet us. "How did you all sleep?"

Bruce smiles, "I slept like a baby. I woke up every thirty minutes."

"Osei, my man, you good?" Mark asks.

"Yeah, I'm good."

I take Osei's hand, and we interlock fingers and share a smile.

The Nike campus is mammoth, with more than seventy-five buildings on the property. Mark points out the window. "Osei, look!" Commanding attention at the entrance to the Nike campus are two colossal banners. One with Osei's name in bold, unstoppable letters, the other freezing time as it soars through the air, slam-dunking a basketball. I tap the driver on the shoulder. "Can you stop? I want to take a picture of the banners."

"Mark, is there time for me to stand in front of the banners for a picture?" Osei asks.

"This day is all about you, man." Mark replies.

The driver pulls over. Osei grabs my hand, and he and I stand in front of the banner as Bruce snaps the picture.

Minutes later, we're met by Osei's Nike team. Osei is managing himself with poise and grace as he shakes each person's hand. With pleasantries over, they get down to business. The signing of the contract is relatively short, and everyone except me takes a tour of the campus. I need to answer a few work emails.

Because no one is allowed to walk around the campus unattended, a tour guide was left with me. My work done, I ask the tour guide to take me to the lovely Japanese Gardens I'd recently read about. The area is truly exquisite. I take a seat on one of the stone benches and take in the beauty of the garden. The fountain's gentle flow brings a sense of relaxation and calm. I can feel the peaceful energy surrounding me. I imagine how much the girls would appreciate this peaceful solitude, everyone except Rainey, of course. The guide looks at her phone and says. "Ms. Lewis, we have to leave. Everyone has arrived back at the main building."

We head there, a quick ride walk from the garden. I see Osei. He waves me over.

"Sese, I want you to meet Marni Stiller. She and I will be working closely to develop my product line," Osei says.

"You must be so proud of Osei," she smiles genuinely.

"Yes, and I know you all will create a great product line together."

We head back to the house, with Osei and Bruce talking nonstop about the Nike Campus.

"Sese, do you think I'll have a building named after me on the campus one day?"

"That's completely up to you. Are you ready to be the best of the best?"

"Yes," Osei says.

As we pull up to the house, a man from the security rushes over. "Please just give us a minute. We apprehended an unauthorized person earlier trying to enter the premises."

"Where's that person now?" Bruce angrily says.

"In police custody in Beaverton."

Both Bruce and Osei are visibly upset and call Rob Ackerman.

Rob answers on the first ring. "Hello, Mr. Wharton, I was expecting your call. A man walked onto the property at about ten this morning. The security team noticed him last night and kept him under surveillance. We wanted to make sure he was not someone camping in Tualatin Hills Nature Park. After you all left this morning, he made his way onto the property and was caught trying to unlock one of the patio doors."

"Why didn't you contact us immediately?" Bruce says.

"We didn't notify you earlier because I knew you were at an important meeting."

"Rob, do you know anything about this individual, and who could have hired him?" Osei asks.

"We know who hired him, Ms. Hannah," I say.

"All we know now is that he has a German passport and claims not to speak English. The police there provided him with an interpreter, and now he's refusing to speak at all.

"Thank you, Mr. Ackerman. Is there anything we need to do?" Osei asks.

"No, not at this time," Rob answers.

"Good, we don't want this incident to be associated in any way with Osei," Bruce says.

"Mr. Ackerman. If there are any new developments, please contact us right away," Osei says.

"How would Ms. Hannah know we're here?" I ask.

"It's no secret, Osei's contract made National News. More than likely, we were followed from Philadelphia. I'll reach out to Dave and let him know what happened."

We arrive at the house, and I head to a covered pergola by the swimming pool. Lucas has prepared a light spread, grilled chicken, spinach salad, and seafood pasta salad. Thoughts of Ms. Hannah and her merry band of criminals are gone.

Lucas brings out a gorgeous sheet cake and places it on the table. It reads CONGRATULATIONS, OSEI. EMBRACE YOUR GREATNESS!

Osei says, "Thank you, Lucas."

"You have to thank Ms. Lewis. She asked me to order the cake for you."

Before Osei can say anything, I look at him and say, "You are welcome."

We relax and listen to jazz until the sun sets, then go get cleaned up for dinner.

"For dinner, I've prepared Mr. Wharton's favorites—turkey and beef hot dogs with buns, grilled onions, and turkey chili," Lucas announces.

Bruce cracks up. "This is your favorite food?"

"Yes, why?"

"Sese, are you sure he isn't your son?" Bruce asks.

"I'm one hundred percent certain he's not. Lucas, could you bring out fresh-cut onions for the chili dogs?" I ask.

"Yes, I'll bring out the fried onion rings and the French fries as well."

Osei looks at Bruce and me with a puzzled look.

"Osei, back in the day, this was the only food Sese wanted to eat when we went out on dates."

"I only ordered a hot dog because I knew that was all you could afford."

"Sese," Osei asks out of the blue. "How much money do you earn in a year?"

"Where did that come from. And how does what I earn any of your business? You are entirely out of line."

"Bruce, it seems Sese is uncomfortable discussing her salary. So, how much money did you make last year?"

"Let's just say enough. With my University salary, guest lecturing, investment dividends, and royalties from my books, I made a comfortable living," Bruce says.

"Sese, you know how much I make, and Bruce has an amazingly comfortable life. So, I ask you again, how much do you make?"

"Osei Wharton, if you must know, I made $725,000 last year, and it was an off year."

"I'll give you a yearly salary of 1.6 million to run my foundation."

"I don't know how to run a foundation. Please hire a professional to oversee it."

"Wow," Bruce whistles. "If she doesn't want to do it, I definitely will. I wonder how much Rainey makes, since she runs a foundation."

"I have no idea," I reply.

Bruce takes out his phone and places it on speaker. "Hey Jackson, you're on speaker, Osei and Sese are here. I have a question for you. Do you know what Rainey's salary is for running the nonprofit?"

"Last I heard, it was well over $900,000."

"I should quit being a professor and head up a foundation," Bruce says.

"How is everyone doing?" I ask.

"The boys are fine. We picked up their cars today. I got them both Mini Coopers. Gloria was not happy. I'll be exiled to the guest bedroom for at least a week."

We say our goodbyes and hang up.

"Sese, will you at least give it some thought?" Osei pleadingly asks.

"Yes, but I also want you to give some thought to hiring a professional manager."

I leave Bruce and Osei for some much-needed alone time. Sitting out on the bedroom balcony, I wrap myself in the tranquility of the night, watching the stars sparkle and the moon reflect off the mountains. What a spectacular way to end a fantastic day.

Taylor calls, and I go inside to take her call.

"Hey Taylor, I was thinking about calling you earlier."

"Really, what's on your mind?"

"Do I need a reason to call you?"

"Certainly not. So, why were you thinking of me?"

"I wanted your advice on something."

"Okay, I won't charge you my normal hourly rate," she says jokingly.

"Taylor, if I wanted to, could I retire and live comfortably?"

"Sese, are you having problems at work?"

"No, everything at work is fine. I was offered a position running a nonprofit. I'd like to consider it. If things don't work out, I don't want to worry about money."

"You passed that point a long time ago. You won't be able to spend all your money in two lifetimes. You have nothing to worry about."

"I'll fill you in on the particulars a little later. I want to give it some more thought before I discuss it with you all."

"This must be serious if you are involving us."

"Yes, I'll call you next week. Love you."

"I love you more," Taylor says.

I step back out on the balcony. Osei and Bruce are still sitting by the pool, laughing and enjoying themselves. Their laughter fills me with warmth, like the honey drizzling over a hot, buttered biscuit.

Bruce says, "You better not tell Sese."

"Tell me what?" Startled, they look up at me with awkward smiles.

"I'll see you all later," Osei says and runs inside.

Bruce looks up at me. "Good night." Then he follows Osei inside.

"Both of you stop right now! Osei Wharton, you are in for a world of hurt. What have you done?" I yell.

I have no idea where their bedrooms are, and I don't have the energy to look for them. I'll find out tomorrow what he's done wrong.

Lucas greets me with a warm smile as I enter the kitchen.

"Lucas, where are Bruce's and Osei's bedrooms?"

"Mr. Wharton is on this floor, and Mr. Leblanc is on the second floor. But they left an hour ago."

"Thanks."

I call Osei.

"Hello, Sese, are you still upset with me?"

"No, only because I don't know what you have done. Where are you?"

"I'm at the campus with Mark. There were a few things I needed to do here. Bruce is at the police station in Beaverton."

"Why is he at the police station? I thought we were not going to get involved with the police."

"Mr. Ackerman called. He needed one of us to go to the police station to file a formal report."

"Oh, I see. What time will you be back?"

"Shortly. I'm finishing up here."

"Okay, I'll call Bruce to see how things are going at the police station. Talk to you soon."

I call Bruce. He answers, "Sese, I can't talk to you right now. I'll have to call you back."

"Is there a problem?"

"Everything is fine."

Thirty minutes later, Osei arrives. He knocks on my bedroom door and comes in.

My phone beeps. A text message pops up.

"Can we meet—H. Becker?"

He takes my phone and texts back, *NO*.

Another text comes in.

"I'm calling you now," I answer. It's Ms. Hannah whom I place on speaker.

"Hello, Sienna."

"Hello, Ms. Hannah, what can I do for you?"

"I understand you are in Oregon with Osei."

"Why are you concerning yourself with my whereabouts?"

"My only concern is for Osei to sign with the management and investments firm, which will ensure his future. I'm sure he would listen to you. We both want what is best for him."

"I don't have that type of influence over what Osei does or doesn't do with his finances or the management of his career."

"You and I both know you are not his mother."

"You are the one who made me his mother."

Osei is about to say something, but before he does, I put my finger to my lips and shake my head for him to be quiet.

"Do you know who his mother is?" I ask.

"Yes, of course," she replies.

"Until you tell Osei who she is, I'm his mother." With that, I hang up the phone.

"Sese, why didn't you let me speak to her!"

"For now, this fight has to be between Ms. Hannah and me."

"Why can't I let her know that I know she lied to me?"

"Osei, once she knows you know she lied about me being your mother, the situation could escalate, and she might try to force you to sign those documents."

"Hello! Anybody here?" Bruce yells.

Osei answers him, "We're upstairs, in Sese's room!"

"Wow, this space is incredible," Bruce says, looking around.

"Only the best for Sese," Osei replies.

"The best would be owning this masterpiece," I say.

Osei bursts into laughter, and I can't help but join in.

Bruce grins, "You both are crazy."

Catching his breath, Osei says, "This house, and everything in it, belongs to you."

Stunned, I ask, "What are you talking about?"

"Sese, this place is jointly owned by you and the Osei Wharton Foundation. It'll become our West Coast headquarters. I worked it into my Nike deal. That's what my meeting with Nike was about earlier."

Tears are unabashedly flowing down my cheeks. "Enough is enough. I can't accept this. Please stop, you are making me into what Ms. Hannah says I am, a gold digger!"

"Sese, you certainly don't know the meaning of a gold digger. Have you ever asked me for anything, and do you care for me because of how much money I have?" He pauses. "No, so please stop crying, because if you don't, Bruce is going to hit me."

I take a series of deep breaths to compose myself.

Bruce playfully places Osei in a headlock.

"Osei, I'm not comfortable accepting expensive and outrageous gifts from you. You absolutely have to stop. You promised."

"I know, but think of it not as a gift but a signing bonus. It'll be jointly owned by you and the Foundation, so technically, we're true partners."

"I don't understand. What's a signing bonus?"

"I got this," Bruce says to Osei, "This property is given to you by Osei as an incentive for you to head up the foundation, and this is part of your compensation package."

"I haven't decided what I'm going to do."

"It won't matter what you do. Either way, the property is ours," Osei says.

"I'll give Taylor a call. I need to know the ramifications of accepting these properties."

"What type of ramifications could there be?" Bruce asks.

"I don't know. That's why I'm discussing everything with Taylor."

The next morning, we board the jet back home.

When I get home, I text Taylor to see if she has time to speak with me. She replies, *Yes, call me anytime*. I call her, and I tell her everything about the Foundation and the Oregon property.

She's silent.

"Taylor, are you there?"

"Yes, I'm here. I was putting the property into your portfolio."

"So, what do you think? Should I accept the offer?"

"If you don't, you'd be nuts?"

"These are really high-value properties. The only drawback is the higher tax bracket, but that's irrelevant if the Foundation co-owns the property. As a nonprofit, taxes won't be an issue. We can figure out capital gains if the property is ever sold."

"So," Taylor, done with the subject, asks. "How is it going with Bruce? I understand you two are spending a lot of time together."

"He has been helpful, and Osei likes him a lot."

"Is there a possibility you and Bruce will get back together?"

"The time spent with him has shown me how much I missed him. I'm afraid to care for him again. It took me a long time to collect all the pieces of me, and to be honest, I'm still missing a few."

"If I'm not mistaken, you had a major role in his deciding to leave."

I stay silent; her words sting and bring memories that were tamped down deep in my heart.

"You both shoulder some blame," Taylor says, interrupting the silence.

"I admit I was selfish. I didn't want to give up everything I had worked for to become a mother. I wasn't ready."

"You took something away from him, something he wanted to have his entire life? You were born with parents who loved you. Give him some grace and maybe a little forgiveness. Did you forget that his parents left him in an apartment by himself when he was six, and he was placed in foster care? Thank goodness his grandparents found him after a year, but he still carries the trauma of abandonment. He wanted to prove to himself, to you, and society."

Impatient, I interrupt her this time. "What did he have to prove?"

"That he could be a loving parent, but.... You took that away from him. Sese, are you listening?"

"Yes, I'm listening. How can we forget all that has happened, all the hurt and pain we caused one another?"

"Sese, people make mistakes. You both have to decide to trust and love each other again. Anyway, life is too short for regrets."

"I want to, but I'm afraid I wouldn't be able to survive him leaving me again."

"Well, try to be brave like me."

"What's that supposed to mean?"

"Do you remember Eric?" Taylor asks.

"Yes, and I never understood why you all broke up."

"Believe me, I was devastated. I wanted him more than anything, but he didn't want me."

"Taylor, I'm sure he loved you."

"In our case, love was not enough, but we've decided to give ourselves another chance."

"Are you serious? How did you two reconnect?"

"Believe it or not, we ran into each other at a fundraising event in the city for Rainey's nonprofit. Her husband and Eric are colleagues at Sloan Kettering. Eric is an orthopedic surgeon. Only you and Dee knew about my relationship with Eric. Gloria was completing her residency, so I didn't want to distract her. Rainey, being Rainey, was always too negative and judgmental. So, they never knew about me and Eric."

"I was invited to Rainey's event, but due to a last-minute issue at work, I arrived extremely late. Of course, she was upset, yelling and screaming at me. So, to calm her down, I committed to writing her an excessively big check. 'Forget about the check,' she screamed.'"

"Are you kidding? She never turns down money."

"I know! I was totally shocked, but what she said to me afterward left me numb."

"What did she say?"

"In the most humiliating way possible, she says, 'I've been trying to squash the rumors about you being gay. There's someone I want you to meet. I was trying to keep him occupied until you got here.' She then grabbed me by the arm and drags me over to her husband and Eric. 'I'd like for you to meet Dr. Eric Thompson. You remember you met him on the train when we were on our way to Philly to Sese's party.'"

"I did all I could to keep it together, avoiding Eri's laughing eyes. He was quite happy to play along. After the introduction, Eric leaves and returns with a drink for me."

"You can imagine the look on Rainey's face when he returns with a Martini. Everyone knows it's my favorite drink. I finally told her that he and I went out on a few dates years ago, and I wasn't looking to date him again."

"Oh my God! He was the good-looking guy at 30th Street Station. I knew he looked familiar. Taylor, did Rainey actually believe you were gay?"

"I'm sure she didn't, but that was her way of getting back at me for being late. Sese, I never told anyone, not even you, why

Eric left me. There was a guy at the first firm I worked at who helped me a lot."

"Yes, you were the first of us to get a real job."

"He was one of the only Black men in his role at the company and became my mentor, connecting me with key people in the investment world. I was grateful and wanted to thank him, so I invited him to dinner at my place. During the meal, he drugged my drink. I woke up the next morning naked in bed beside him, with no memory of the night. I looked up to see Eric standing in the doorway, his face etched with disdain. I tried to explain, but he wouldn't listen. He couldn't deal with it, and he walked away."

"How long have you two been back together?"

"Five months now."

"And it took you this long to tell me."

"I wanted to make sure we could work everything out."

"Taylor! I'm so happy for you."

"Thank you, Sese. I plan on telling everyone soon. In the meantime, can you keep this between us?"

"Yes, it's in the vault."

"Where's he now?"

"Taking a nap. He just returned from a conference in LA."

"I love you."

"I love you more," I reply.

34

The Threat is Alive and Well

Osei, Bruce, and I are enjoying cups of hot chocolate when Osei's agent, Mark, calls.

"Hello Mark, what's up?"

"Is Ms. Lewis there by any chance?" Mark asks.

"Yes, she's sitting next to me. You're on speaker."

"Hello Mark," I say.

"I just wanted to share that the Nike folks absolutely love Osei, and they're impressed with you, and glad he has a stable team around him—you and Bruce."

"A stable team?" Osei, surprised, repeats.

"Ms. Lewis, I swear you have everyone in the palm of your hand," Mark says.

Osei winks at Bruce and says, "I agree, and the beauty of Sese is she's oblivious to her charm."

"Thanks, Mark. Please let them know I'm more than proud to be part of Osei's posse. And thank you for sharing this with us."

"All right then. Hey Osei, I'll see you at the photo shoot next week," Mark says.

The following week, Bruce, Osei, and I meet with Mr. Ackerman at his office to review what he calls a "Threat Report." "This is rather alarming," he says, handing me the report.

"Alarming how?" I ask.

"Ms. Hannah has no intention of going away," Osei answers.

"This is a breakdown of threat activities for the past few weeks," Ackerman says. "Miss Lewis, you and Osei were followed and photographed by an unknown person on multiple occasions."

He then opens a folder, which contains photos, with timelines and locations. The make and model of the cars used, and the license plate numbers that turned out to be fake.

"Ms. Lewis, the man following you, we suspect, is a German operative who was staying at the Marriott, under an assumed name. We alerted the police, but by the time they got there, he was gone."

" I see Ms. Hannah has no intention of going away," Osei says, looking alarmed.

"This definitely confirms that she's connected to a crime syndicate. "

"This means that Ms. Hannah is involved in something ominous," Bruce says.

Osei and I look at each other.

"These men are pros," Mr. Ackerman says. "If they get a hint of suspicion, real or imagined, they will disappear. And even if they're caught, they're unlikely to talk. We know that from the man apprehended in Beaverton."

"Sese, and that is why you'll always have security around you. Just think what could happen if you were alone," Bruce says.

"Okay, I will no longer fight having a protection detail."

"Our men are on the highest alert, and I'll call immediately if we suspect that the situation is escalating."

Standing outside Mr. Ackerman's office, Bruce orders an Uber.

"Are you staying in Philly tonight?" Osei asks.

"Yes. I'm at the Westin Downtown?"

"You are welcome to stay with me," Osei says.

"I appreciate the offer, but I need to work and make a few calls."

"What time is your train tomorrow?" I ask.

"It's at 2:45 P.M. I was hoping to have breakfast with you all before I leave."

"I think we can make that happen. You guys can come over to my place," Osei offered.

"Great, I'll see you both tomorrow," Bruce says as he hops into the Uber.

Osei's phone rings; it's Tony, one of his teammates.

"Hello Tony, what's up?"

"A few of us are getting together tonight at Micah's place to hang out and play games. You should stop by. We want to toast you for getting the Nike deal."

"Cool, what time is everything jumping off?"

"Eight thirty."

"Okay, should I bring anything?"

"No, food and drinks are being delivered."

"Catch you later then," Osei says.

Osei walks me to my front door, hugs me and says, "I thank God for the blessing that is you." Walking to his car, he looks back at me and shouts, "I'm so happy I could burst."

"Stop playing around and drive safely."

35

Security Is A Necessary Evil

"Hello, Sese."

"Hello Bruce, I'm checking to see if you made it to the hotel safely."

"I did. But something came up, and as it turns out, I need to take an early train home tomorrow morning. I'm going to have to pass on breakfast tomorrow. I'm only a phone call away, though, so don't hesitate to call if you all need me."

"Don't stay away too long."

There's silence.

"Bruce, are you there?" I ask.

"Wow—I wasn't expecting that. I'll go water my plants and give you a little space. I know it's been a lot. You need room to breathe."

"Good night, Bruce, and safe travels."

Just then, Osei's name flashes across my screen.

"I'm on my way to New Jersey to hang out with some of my teammates."

"Have fun and live it up. Bruce can't join us for breakfast tomorrow."

"Okay, be careful. Call me when you leave there."

"Why. Anything wrong?"

"Not that I know of."

"Okay, I'll see you tomorrow."

"Be careful. Call me when you leave there."

"Sese, I'm not a ten-year-old. It'll be late when I leave New Jersey, and I don't want to wake you. Why don't we talk until I get there?"

"I'd like that."

Osei arrives at Micah's.

"What the hell is going on?" I hear him say, but he isn't speaking to me.

"Osei, is everything alright?"

"I'm fine, just too many unfamiliar faces. The place is swarming with people. Sese, hold on. I need to speak with Tony."

I hear his car window roll down. "Hey, Tony. What's with all the people? I thought it was just us hanging out tonight."

"We weren't expecting this either," Tony says.

"Where's Micah?" Osei asks.

A new voice cuts in. "Hello, superstar."

A man introduces two women, saying they're friends of his girlfriend.

"Micah, I appreciate this, but you know I don't do crowds like this," Osei says.

"Man, relax. I wanted to celebrate with you, so I invited a few friends."

"I'm out. I'm not comfortable here. I'll see you at practice next week, and thanks for the thought, bro," Osei replies.

I hear Micah shout, "Where are you going? Get over yourself. You're a celebrity now!"

"Osei, are you okay?" I ask.

"Sese, I forgot you were still on the phone. I'm okay. So…" he continues. "…you think everything is okay with Bruce? Shall we call him?"

"No! It was an excuse because he thinks I need space. That I might feel smothered."

"Are you?" Osei asks. "By him and by me?"

I pause. "Sometimes. There are moments when the two of you take my breath away, in every sense of the phrase. And then, there are times when I can't breathe. I'll let you both know when I need to come up for air."

"There's a black Range Rover following me. The same car that was parked in front of Micah's place. Sese, I'm going to have to call you back. I need to call Rob. This could be one of Miss Hannah's plants."

"Call me right back."

I frantically answer Osei's call back. "Are you okay?"

"Yes, as I suspected, I was being followed, but it's not by Ms. Hannah but some groupies. The girls from Micah's party."

"Is your security detail there?"

"Yup. Rob's team is taking care of it."

"Once I cross the bridge, instead of taking the expressway, at the last minute, I'll change lanes to the local route. The security team will block them, and they will be forced to merge onto the expressway. The security team is behind me. Very few people know where I live, and I want to keep it that way."

"I have peace of mind knowing that you have a security detail. Let's hang up so you can concentrate. Call me when you get home."

36

Welcome to the World of Motherhood

After hanging up with Osei, I notice a missed text from Dee: *Call me.*

"Hello, Dee."

"So, Sese, are you falling in love all over again?"

"Well, that is a weird question to start a conversation with."

"I take that as a yes," Dee says.

"Bruce left today, and I miss him, but it's a far cry from being in love."

"I wasn't talking about him. I was referring to Osei. I looked at the video again that he posted of you singing to him in London."

"I'm going to kill him. I've asked him a million times to take it down."

"As of ten minutes ago, it has over two million views, and all the comments are positive," Dee says.

My interest is piqued. "What comments?"

"I'll read one to you."

Osei, man, you are blessed to have a mother who isn't afraid to tell you she loves you.

"I'm going to hurt him! But what about you? What's been going on? I know you didn't call me to ask questions about who I love. For the record, I truly do love Osei."

"You know me too well." Then, more seriously, "Sese, are you being careful?"

"I have a security detail that follows me relentlessly. Dee, I need your advice. Please be completely honest."

"This sounds serious," Dee gasps.

I tell her about Osei's offer for me to lead his foundation, outlining the pros and cons.

"Whoa, she says, "I can't believe it..."

"I know! I can't believe it either."

"Sese, what I was going to say before you interrupted me was, I can't believe you haven't agreed to do this. What is there to think about? It's not like you actually need to work a nine-to-five. Is it about money? Would you be making less?"

"No, I'd make considerably more."

"I've told you what I think. Now you have to have the confidence in yourself to take a leap of faith."

"Dee, there's another reason I'm hesitant. What happens when he finds his birth parents? Wouldn't they object to me having such a major role in their son's life, not to mention being involved with his finances?"

"I have to agree with Rainey here. Who's to say he'll bond with them? Osei wasn't lost. His parents knew where he was, but they decided not to reclaim him. What you feel for him is real, and what he feels for you is also real."

"Dee, I don't want to lose the connection I have with him. The love I feel for him is more intense than anything I have ever felt before."

"Welcome to the world of motherhood. I can't wait to meet him."

"Good night, Dee. I'll talk to you soon."

37

Can't You Love Me Again

The next morning, Millie is happy to be running the trail, sniffing everything under the sun. We haven't done this since she and I had to fight off one of Ms. Hannah's thugs. With security detail in tow, I'm feeling free in the company of an abundance of wildlife to keep me company. Today, the birds are singing, the trees sway, deer prance, and Millie and I are content.

With a sigh, I pull my phone from my pocket to answer Osei's call.

"I'm at your place. Where are you?" he asks.

"I'm hiking the trail. I'll be home in about ten minutes."

Osei is waiting in the driveway when we arrive.

"Why didn't you go inside?" I ask.

Millie, excited to see him, runs and jumps on him. The two guys on my security team who were on the trail with me introduced themselves to Osei. He thanks them for looking after me. I go inside and bring back bottles of water for them.

"So, Osei," I loop my arms through his. "What brings you here so early in the morning?"

"I couldn't wait to tell you what Mark told me this morning about the DC firm associated with Ms. Hannah. They denied reaching out to me and had no idea who Ms. Hannah was."

"What?"

"Mark spoke directly to the firm's CEO. The man with Ms. Hannah in London didn't work for the company."

"Ms. Hannah keeps surprising me. She's a true con artist."

"She definitely has a plan and is dead set on accomplishing it," Osei says.

"Well, in the words of Mike Tyson, everybody has a plan until they get punched in the mouth, and it's time for us to punch Ms. Hannah in the mouth."

Laughing, Osei says, "I'm glad you are on my side."

"We need to let Bruce know what Mark found out."

"While I was waiting for you, I called him. He told me to tell you he's having lunch with your college crush tomorrow."

"He's referring to Big Dave. I didn't have a crush on him."

"I can only imagine the number of men following you around on campus. I'm sure Bruce had his hands full trying to keep them away from you."

"As far as I could tell, Bruce and Dave had a serious man-crush thing going on."

"Speak of the devil!" Osei points to his cell phone.

"Hey, Bruce. I'm here with Sese. Placing you on speaker. What's up? Did you make it home safely?"

"I'm still at the hotel. I'm not feeling well."

"Do you have a temperature?" I ask.

"I don't know. One minute I'm hot, and the next minute, I'm cold."

"Sounds like you're coming down with something," I reply.

"I went down to grab a bite before heading out, and I felt fine. I was about to leave when suddenly I began feeling sick. I have an excruciating headache."

"We're on our way to get you. Can you make it to the car, or should I come and get you?" Osei says.

"I can make it down to the car."

"Okay, we'll be there in fifteen minutes."

"Osei, you go pick him up. I'll stay here, get everything ready, and start making his famous chicken noodle soup."

I head downstairs to the guest room to change the linens and place fresh towels in the guest bathroom. I turn on the humidifier and add eucalyptus to help him breathe easier. Comfortable. Then, I return to the kitchen to check if I have all the ingredients for Bruce's famous chicken noodle soup. According to Bruce, the chicken should be baked, not boiled. So, I place it in the oven and begin preparing the vegetables, herbs, and spices.

Osei arrives, and indeed, Bruce isn't doing well at all.

Concerned, I say, "Bruce, I think we should take you to the hospital."

"I'll be fine. I just need to rest."

Osei helps him to the guest bedroom and makes sure he's settled in. Two hours later, Osei and I take the chicken noodle soup to him. He's sound asleep. We quietly leave the room, not to wake him.

Upstairs in the den, I turn on Netflix.

"What are you watching?" Osei asks.

"A Korean drama."

He looks perplexed. "Why are you looking at a Korean drama?"

"Why not? This is my guilty pleasure. K-dramas highlight culture, family, love, and respect, promoting heartwarming stories with rich, well-developed characters. The cinematography is spectacular, and I can relate to it all—it refreshes me. And then the men… oh Lord!"

"So, what are we watching tonight?"

I select the drama I'm currently watching and scroll back to episode one.

"You were on episode twelve. I can watch that episode. You don't have to start over."

"Believe me, starting over is a treat."

We finished the first episode, and Osei says, "Sese, that was very entertaining. They seem to be masters of cliff hangers!"

"Wait." I lowered the volume on the TV. "Osei, did you hear something?"

We hear Bruce calling out, "Osei, Sese, are you there?"

"Yes, we're coming," I say.

We open the door, and he's lying in bed with his eyes closed.

"I heard my phone ringing, but I can't find it," he says.

"Here it is," Osei says, and hands Bruce his phone.

"It was Dave Miller. Sienna, can you call him back for me?"

"You must be really sick if you are asking me to speak with Dave Miller."

"I'm scheduled to have lunch with him tomorrow to discuss Ms. Hannah. You and Osei can talk to him and bring him up to speed on what is happening."

He groans softly as he moves to get more comfortable. "Sese, that's all you need to discuss with him and nothing else."

"I didn't have much to say to him twenty years ago, and if it wasn't for Ms. Hannah, I'd have even less to discuss with him now."

"Bruce, get some rest. We'll call Mr. Miller," Osei says.

We call Dave from Bruce's phone, and he answers right away, "Hey, Bruce."

"Hello, Dave, this is Sienna. Bruce isn't feeling well. He asked me to call you."

"Hey, Sienna. It's good to hear your voice. When do you think he'll be better?"

"Can't you speak to me?"

"No. This is a serious issue. It cannot be discussed over the phone."

"Dave, you are scaring me. I need to know what you know?'

Osei gestures for me to let it go.

"Okay, I'll have Bruce call you," I relent.

I check on Bruce before I go to bed. I softly knock on the door. In a very weak voice, he says, "Come in."

I open the door; he's sitting on the side of the bed. "You should be lying down."

"I'm going to go back to the hotel. I don't want to bother you."

"It's no bother."

"What did Big Dave say?"

"He'll only talk to you."

"Talking about talking. Sese, I was hoping we could talk."

"Talk about what?"

"About us."

"Since when has there been an us?"

"Since always."

With a sad look on his face. He continues, "Sese, can't you love me again?"

Feeling nervous, I say, "Can't I just like you a lot? I'm not ready to love you. I'll be back with a cup of tea." I quickly escape the room.

I set the tea tray on the nightstand and smile. "Good night, Bruce."

"Good night, Sese, I'll meet you in my dreams."

"Sweet dreams." I turn to leave. My heart is tugging in the opposite direction. I keep walking. Not wanting to think about what Bruce said earlier, I turn on the Korean drama I had started.

38

Not Your Virgin Mary

Early morning, I sit with Bruce as he calls Big Dave. He beckons me to be quiet.

"I now have a personal reason for finding Ms. Hannah," Dave says.

"Why? What is going on?"

"It seems Ms. Hannah has been victimizing my wife."

"Oh my God, was she being blackmailed?"

"Apparently. For almost twelve years. I'll fill you in later."

"Dave, did she have a baby?"

"I'll fill you in on the details when we meet."

Bruce ends the call, and he and I look at each other in disbelief.

In shock, before I could move my hand from my mouth, Rainey calls.

"Sese, have you been watching the news?" Rainey asks.

"No. Why?"

"Ms. Hannah made national news; she's allegedly tied to an illegal adoption ring. A London family unknowingly adopted a kidnapped child from New York. While visiting, they saw a news report, recognized Ms. Hannah, and alerted authorities. Several arrests have been made, and she's now wanted for questioning."

"If she's in the US, I'm sure she has gone underground," I say, not entirely shocked.

"Dave Miller was on the news earlier, making a statement to the press about the illegal adoption ring. Sese, are you any closer to finding Osei's birth mother?" Rainey asks in a serious and steady tone.

"No, but I have a hunch, which I haven't shared with him yet."

"Is it anything you care to share with me?"

"No, not yet."

For once, Rainey does not press me for more information. Instead, she says, "Sese, it's okay to love Bruce."

I look over at Bruce, who has a smile on his face.

"Is it okay just to like him?" I ask.

He frowns.

"Liking him is okay, too."

"I see Dave Miller has made it his mission to capture Ms. Hannah."

After hanging up with Rainey, I call Osei.

"Are you available tomorrow?"

"I have a practice this morning, but I'll be done in the afternoon."

"Okay, I'll see you after practice," I say, not wanting to disturb his focus.

When Osei arrives, I let him know that Ms. Hannah is wanted for questioning.

"Does Bruce know? How is he doing today?" he asks, heading downstairs.

"Yes, we've got to be extra careful now. If Ms. Hannah's anonymity is gone, she could be trying to escalate her plan before going into hiding. We're both in danger."

"I know, and I think she probably still has minions doing her dirty work," Osei says.

"Osei, do you still have contacts at Wharton? People who were there when Mr. Albert was alive?"

"Yes, why?"

"Can you find out what Mr. Albert's health status was before he died?"

"Do you think she killed him?"

"She's capable of doing anything, and killing someone would not be out of the realm of possibility for Ms. Hannah."

"I'll see what I can find out." Osei taps on the door. No answer. "Let me go check on Bruce."

Bruce is out cold, so we go back upstairs. Osei leaves, and I watch a K-drama until I fall asleep.

I wake to the sound of Millie running around in the kitchen, which is unusual for her unless someone is downstairs. I grab my robe and head downstairs. Bruce is playing with Millie and drinking coffee.

"Good morning." Bruce looks up as I enter.

"Morning," I say. I touch his forehead, and then mine. "Your fever is gone."

"I'm feeling much better, thanks for taking care of me. Ms. Millie wants to have some coffee."

"Ms. Millie is adorable, but she doesn't want coffee. She wants food. Isn't that right, girl?"

"I should have known. She doesn't look like she has ever missed a meal."

"Are you calling my dog fat?"

"No, but she's extremely healthy. Would you like breakfast?"

"I'm good with the coffee for now."

While we're enjoying our coffee, I tell Bruce about my conversation with Osei while he was sleeping.

"What's our plan now?"

"With Dave hot on Ms. Hannah's heels, I think we should leave it up to the experts."

"The net is tightening around Ms. Hannah and her minions," he says.

"I hope so, but I don't think for one second this will weaken her resolve to get her hands on Osei's money. I'm happy to know that Dave Miller is giving this his full attention."

"I'm not surprised," Bruce says.

"Really, why not?"

"You do know who Dave married, don't you?"

"No, who did he marry?"

"Mary Thomas."

"Are you Serious? As in, I'm not your Virgin Mary from Chicago?"

"Yes."

"But Mary was no pushover!"

"Still isn't. She works for the Manhattan DA's office as the Chief Assistant District Attorney. She oversees an office of nearly five hundred lawyers and a support staff of six hundred or more. She's the real deal, and a prime target for the likes of Ms. Hannah. I wonder what Ms. Hannah has on her?" Bruce says.

"Bruce, she wasn't a Saint, but none of us were. How dare she use youthful mistakes to threaten people? What gives her the right? I despise her more every day."

"I agree."

The TV flashed breaking news. And there looming large was Dave Miller.

Bruce calls Dave, "Yes, dinner, I'll see you tomorrow night."

"Where are you all meeting for dinner?" I ask.

"At my place. I'll be back in a couple of days," Bruce says.

The next evening, I ring Bruce's doorbell. He opens the door, shocked to see me.

"Why are you here? Did you miss me?" he asks.

"No, I want to join your conversation with Dave. I need to know from him what Ms. Hannah is capable of."

The doorbell rings again, and Bruce opens it, surprised to see Dave with his wife, Mary.

He thought they were meeting alone. Bruce has seen Mary on TV countless times, but it's been years since he last saw her in person. She still looks stunning, with the same youthful appearance as Sese. Now he knows why Dave married I'm Not Your Virgin Mary from Chicago. Both Dave and Mary are startled to see Sese. To break the tension, Sese hugs Mary and says, "Wow, you are still drop-dead gorgeous."

Smiling, Mary says, "That is the pot calling the kettle black."

Everyone erupts in laughter.

Bruce pours a dram of scotch for Dave and himself, and hands Mary and me a glass of red wine. We all relax on the deck while Bruce grills the steaks.

"Wow, look at the Manhattan skyline, absolutely stunning," Dave says.

"The steaks are ready. I have also prepared potatoes au gratin and a salad," Bruce says.

"Man, I didn't know you could cook!" Dave chuckles.

"I learned to cook when Sese and I lived in Brooklyn. In fact, we learned to cook together."

"Sienna, I heard you live in Philly now," Mary says.

"Yes, Philly is my home."

"I admired you when we were in school. You were so glamorous."

Suddenly, Mary starts to cry. "I wanted to be like you. To be liked and to be popular. Back then, I thought the way to attain popularity was to have boyfriends. I wanted the other girls to envy me. But they didn't envy me. Instead, they pitied and gossiped about me behind my back."

Dave hugs her. "It's alright, honey, those days are over. You don't have to talk about school anymore. And look what you got!" He beamed.

"I need to say this. I've never told Dave this before, but with this case, I have to come clean. Maybe if I had, Osei wouldn't be in this mess with Ms. Hannah. While I was in school, I had two abortions. Ms. Hannah arranged everything, the doctor, transport, and even had me recover at the orphanage in a wing for girls like me."

Mary pauses. "She's been extorting me for the last ten years. I've paid her over half a million dollars. Even when I didn't have it, I took out loans. I stole from our joint account." She looks at Bruce. "After Dave told me about Ms. Hannah and what's happening with Sese and the basketball player, I realized I wasn't alone."

Mary takes my hand. "If anyone can take her down, it's you. That's why I finally told Dave, after all these years."

"You can imagine how shocked I was. I was upset with Mary for not telling me, but that shock soon turned into anger. I was determined to hunt down this Ms. Hannah and kill her with my bare hands. Man, do you know what we could have done with five hundred thousand dollars? I get mad all over again, just thinking about it," Dave says.

"Mary, when was the last time you spoke to Ms. Hannah?" Bruce asks.

"You never speak to her unless the money isn't deposited into her account."

"How often did you deposit money into the account?" I ask.

"Every three months. If your payments were late, she would send you emails, and if you didn't respond, she would call you."

"When she called, what did she say exactly?" I asked.

"She'd ask how things were going and, depending on her mood, either say something civil like, *'If you need more time, let me know,'* or threaten to expose everything. Then she'd read an email detailing the abortions—addressed to my boss, the District Attorney—and say, *'Isn't he your boss?'* She loved saying that phrase, always chuckling afterward. I always wanted to snap, *'No one even uses that antiquated term anymore, you archaic bitch.'*"

Dave takes a sip of his drink and says, "Ms. Hannah is under investigation for her role in an illegal adoption syndicate and for extorting at least ten people. After seeing her in the news, they all came forward and filed complaints with the FBI. She's gone into hiding, and we believe she may have fled to Canada. We're coordinating with Canadian authorities now."

"Dave, if she's found in Europe, will you be able to bring her back to face charges here?" Bruce asks.

"We're working in conjunction with several European agencies. In the meantime, if you all hear from her, let me know."

"Sese is waiting with bated breath. She's from the school of I wish a mother would," Bruce says, laughing.

"Oh, Ms. Hannah better watch her back. I've no patience for her nonsense."

Mary says, "I know if anybody can bring Ms. Hannah to her knees, it will be you, Sese."

39

Follow the Money

I decide to stay over at Bruce's. We stand on his balcony, admiring the Manhattan skyline, enjoying a glass of wine. I am unable to stop thinking about that brute of a woman, Ms. Hannah.

"Bruce, I've been giving some thought as to who Osei's birth parents could be. The way Ms. Hannah operates, she would definitely use Osei's parents in her plan to get his money."

"I can think of two reasons why she isn't. One, she doesn't know who his parents are, or two, they're both dead," Bruce answers.

"Even so, I still don't understand why she chose me as his mother and went out of her way to convince Osei I was."

"I bet she was banking on you sending him away."

"Why would she assume I'd do that? She doesn't know me. I still can't wrap my mind around all this. Why me?"

"She got us both stumped. I wish I knew."

"A trust was established in Osei's name when he was a baby. Maybe there are clues there."

"A trust for a baby without a name? How's that even possible?"

"Osei thinks he chose his name, but what if that's just what he was told?"

"It's a deliberate name. Osei is an African name, which means 'noble' or 'honorable.' A child wouldn't know that," Bruce says.

"Osei says there's a million dollars in the trust."

"We should look into the trust. We may not be able to find Ms. Hannah, but we can follow the money. First, we need to identify the trust administrator."

"Osei can give us that information. I'll ask him when I get back to Philly."

With no classes, Bruce decides to ride back with me to Philly. Being with him is starting to feel so familiar that I invite him to stay at my place instead of a hotel. I also invite Osei over for dinner to learn more about his trust fund. Of course, all Osei wants to talk about is me heading up his foundation.

"If you headed up the foundation, you would work for yourself."

"That's where you are wrong. I'd work for you and be very cognizant of the Osei Wharton brand and image." I groan. "Oh, I couldn't manage that type of pressure."

"Sese, you would do an excellent job. You have a remarkable personality, a million-dollar smile, and, not to mention, your unwavering commitment to do what is right."

"Osei Wharton, flattery will get you nowhere."

Bruce yells to us, "Would the basketball star and the woman with a million-dollar smile like dinner?"

"Hell yeah!" Osei says.

Bruce is outside on the deck, grilling chicken, and he has made a delicious spinach salad. For dessert, there are also double chocolate brownies.

"Where did the brownies come from?" I ask.

"Osei bought them."

"Wow, they look delicious."

"Sese, I can't believe how relaxed I feel out here. Just a few minutes ago, I saw a deer wandering through the trees. Look—do you see that?" he exclaims, pointing. "A fox chasing a groundhog! It really feels like I'm in the middle of nature."

"Bruce, you have to hike the trail with me and Sese. It's so peaceful and relaxing."

I glance at Osei, switching gears. "We had dinner with Dave Miller last night. He has a vendetta against Ms. Hannah. His wife was also a victim of Ms. Hannah. We couldn't have a better ally."

"Speaking of Ms. Hannah, I made a call to the orphanage today," Osei says.

"Good, before you tell us about that, we have a few questions about your trust fund," Bruce says to Osei.

"Why?"

"If we follow the money, it could lead us to your birth parents or, at the least, to the person who set it up," Bruce replies.

"I don't know very much. The director of the orphanage handled the trust. Sese, remember I told you about the argument he had with Ms. Hannah. I don't know any more than that."

"Okay, go on. Why did you call the orphanage?"

"Sese wanted me to see if I could find out the status of Mr. Albert's health before he died."

"Sese, do you think he didn't die from natural causes?" Bruce asks.

"We're talking about Ms. Hannah. She's capable of anything, and getting rid of a husband would be child's play for her."

"The director told me that he was doing fine, but then all of a sudden. No one saw him for several weeks before his death. So, it's difficult for anyone to provide an account of his health leading up to his death," Osei says.

Furious, I say, "Wow, Ms. Hannah should watch her back, because I'm going to be a step behind her with a brick in my hand. She has messed with the wrong people, and I'm going to do all I can to make sure she doesn't harm anyone else."

On Wednesday morning, I give Bruce a ride to the train station. We made meaningless small talk, but we both know something is changing. There are times when I want to slap him, and there are times when I want to hug him. When he gets out of the car, he hesitates and leans back inside the window. "I did something twenty years ago that I've regretted every day since. I'm not going to make that mistake again. So, take all the time you need to figure things out. But know this, I'm not going anywhere. I'm here no matter what. Take care of yourself. I'll call you when I get home."

Before I can respond, he walks away. I watch him until he disappears into the train station.

If ever there was heavenly intervention, Taylor's call was it. "Hello." I can hear her speaking, but my thoughts are on Bruce, and the feeling of being alone consumes me as I watch him walk away.

"Sese, are you there?"

"Yes, who is this?"

"It's Taylor. Are you drunk this early in the morning? What is going on?"

"I was distracted. What's up?"

"Now, I have to repeat myself."

"Yes, you do."

"Sese, you better be glad that I'm not there, I'd..."

Before she can finish the sentence, "If you were here, I wouldn't be distracted."

"Stop being a smartass."

"I miss you, Taylor."

"You know how to manage me when you say, 'I miss you' or 'I love you,' I concede. Anyway, I ran the numbers, and you can retire now if you want to. In fact, you'll come out financially ahead if you manage the foundation versus working in your current situation."

"Are you sure?"

"Yup, my question to you is, when are you going to resign?"

"Taylor, I'm afraid. What if I'm not good at running the foundation?"

"If Rainey can run a successful Foundation, I know you can. Do you remember when we were in school, we all took turns tutoring her? In some cases, we took her exams for her. She would have never graduated if it weren't for us helping her."

"You know, I have never equated a college degree with intelligence. I can honestly say Rainey is smarter than all of us combined. She may not be book smart, but there's nothing like having common sense, which she has a PhD in."

"You have to decide within the month, right?"

"Yes."

"Well, you have a week left to decide."

"I know, and I'm no closer to deciding. Taylor, what would you do?"

"If I had the opportunity you have, I wouldn't hesitate. I absolutely love what I do, but if I could impact a child's life, I'd do it in a heartbeat. But I don't write policies or save lives—I manage money for the ultra-wealthy and make them richer."

"Taylor, do I have what it takes to truly impact a child's life and make a difference?"

"Sienna, you have never failed at anything. Why would you start now? Out of everybody I know, your heart is the biggest."

"Thank you, Taylor. How is Eric doing?"

"He's doing fine. In fact, we're doing very well. I'll fill you in on the details later. I have to run."

As I'm about to leave, I notice Bruce by the car. I roll down the window and, channeling Nancy Wilson, ask, "Did you miss your train or were you caught in the rain?"

He grins, "I won't bother to explain. My train is running thirty-five minutes late due to track issues. I saw you sitting here and thought something was wrong."

"There's no problem. I was just talking with Taylor."

"Do you have time for a cup of coffee?"

"No, I need to get going. Call me when you get home." I drive off. As I look in the rear-view mirror, I see Bruce turning to go back into the train station. Suddenly, I want to turn the car around and have a cup of coffee with him. The thought of having a warm cup of coffee with him feels very soothing. I merge onto the expressway, saying out loud, "Sienna Lewis, you are a coward. Stop running away from him. Be brave and..."

Before I can finish the sentence, the Apple CarPlay announces an incoming call, and I connect to Osei.

"Hello, my prince. It's such a nice day. I've decided to go to the driving range to hit a bucket of golf balls," I say in a cheerful voice.

"May I join you?"

"Of course. I'll text you the address."

Osei arrives fifteen minutes later. As he walks toward me, people start snapping photos.

He is gracious and signs a few autographs. One man is insisting on having a photo. He grins and says, "How about a selfie with everyone instead?" That's all it takes. They all rush over.

After the selfies, he finally gets to hit a few balls.

"Boy, I didn't know you could hit the ball a mile," I say, impressed.

"You are not bad yourself. In fact, you are incredibly good."

Afterwards, we relax, enjoying a cold bottle of water. "Sese, I called the orphanage and spoke to Dr. Simms, one of the directors who worked at Wharton when I was there. You may be on to something about Ms. Hannah killing Mr. Albert. He corroborated the same story the old director told me, that until the day he died, he was good and had no issues with his health. Ms. Hannah told him that Mr. Albert had the flu, and he would be out for a few days. A week later, she called back to say he had died."

"He died of a heart attack, right?"

"Yes, and it was quite unexpected, according to Dr. Simms. Ms. Hannah told everyone that his brother and father both died from heart attacks at an early age. Sese, when I went to visit Ms. Hannah for her birthday a few years ago, I met Mr. Albert's father there."

"What about his brother? Did you meet him?"

"Mr. Albert doesn't have a brother—he has a sister."

"I'm even more convinced that she killed him."

"Maybe Bruce can ask Dave if an autopsy can be done twenty-plus years after death to determine if someone was murdered. I'll text him to ask Dave that question," Osei says.

Minutes after sending the text to Bruce, his phone rings.

"Hey Bruce, Sese and I are at the driving range. We'll call you from the car."

"Okay," Bruce replies

We call Bruce and share with him what Dr. Simms told Osei.

Bruce says, "I'm pulling into Newark Amtrak station. I'll ask Dave about the timeframe for an autopsy."

We say our goodbyes.

On my way home, Osei calls, "What's up? Didn't I just leave you?"

"Yes, you did. I want to invite you and Millie over for dinner."

"What time?"

Six-thirty. I'm going to prepare my signature dish for you."

"I'd like Sushi."

"How did you know I was ordering out?"

"Knowing you and the ego you have, if you could cook, it would definitely be something you would constantly brag about."

"You know me all too well."

After showering and changing, I head to Osei's with Millie.

I have a missed text from Gloria. I don't bother replying. I call her instead.

She answers.

"Sese, I have bad news. Jackson's Dad died today."

"I'm so sorry. Is there anything I can do?"

"No, we'll be in Philly tomorrow morning. We're leaving for the airport shortly."

"If you haven't made hotel reservations, you all can stay with me. I have plenty of room."

"Thank you. We'll take you up on your offer."

"Is there anything special in the food department I should have the housekeeper buy for the boys?"

"No. They will eat anything and everything."

"Okay. What time will you all arrive?"

"We land at 7:45 A.M."

"I'll see you all in the morning. Give Jackson a hug for me."

"Will do. We'll see you in the morning, and thank you," Gloria says.

"Do you think we could fit in a girl's night? We all want to be there for you and Jackson during this time."

"Yes, but I'll leave it to you to plan."

I call Dee and tell her about Jackson's dad's passing and ask her to get in touch with everyone and let them know.

"We should plan a girl's night," Dee says.

"Yes, you read my mind. We'll need one after the drama that's about to happen."

"Why, what have you heard?"

"Nothing, but there can be a boatload of drama when someone wealthy dies. Family members fight over money. Greed is a beast."

"I hope that's not the case. Bye, Sese."

"Bye, Mama Dee."

Millie and I arrive at Osei's building, and we take the elevator to his apartment. As soon as he opens the door, the dogs excitedly greet each other. I was barely able to make it inside from all their romping.

"I can't believe how well they get along," Osei says.

"That's because they were raised right. Did you order sushi?"

"Not just any sushi."

"Oh no, you didn't."

"Oh yes, I did. This sushi is from your favorite restaurant in New Jersey."

"I also bought some Sake, Soju, and wine. Which would you prefer?"

"No drinks for me tonight. I have to be up early to pick up Gloria and her family from the airport. You spoke to her boys on the phone. Well, her father-in-law died. Can I borrow your Range Rover tomorrow?"

"Sese, I can drive you if you want me to."

"Really, in that case, pass me the Sake, please."

We relaxed on the deck, looking at the skyline of Center City. I break the silence. "Does the other apartment have a skyline view?"

"I forgot." Osei hits his head with his palm. "You haven't seen the other apartment. Would you like to see it now?"

"Yes, of course."

We take the elevator to the twelfth floor. Unlike the apartment on the seventh floor, this place is all white, with dark wood floors—no exposed brick walls.

"Wow, Osei, this place is extremely elegant."

"I thought you would like it."

"Like it, I love it."

"This is exquisite," I say, pointing to the floor.

"I think it's Black Oak. What I love is that it's all on one floor."

"The apartment has four en-suite bedrooms, a guest powder room, and a fully equipped exercise room."

"Which place did you buy first?"

"I bought them both at the same time. Actually, this is the apartment you own. If you had read the papers before you signed them, you would have noticed the different floor number and the difference in square footage. This place is much larger than the space downstairs."

"That's what I get for trusting you! So you're right, it's my fault for not having read the documents."

"If the shoe fits."

"I won't make that mistake again." Ignoring him further, I go over to the floor-to-ceiling windows. Osei presses a switch on the wall, and four of the windows open, folding back like an accordion. They open onto a huge deck with a magnificent view of the city.

"Oh my God, Osei, why did you decide to live in the other apartment and not this one?"

"This place is too girly."

The patio is fully furnished with gorgeous furniture and a huge electric grill.

"The girls are coming to town in a few days. Can I borrow this place for an evening?"

"What part of this is your apartment you don't understand?" Osei says, handing me the keys.

I start to tear up.

"Sese, please don't cry."

"Osei, I don't know what to say."

"You don't have to say anything. Sese, do you know how much I appreciate you and how much I love you? Do you know this is the first time I'm telling someone I love them? I've never said that to any of the girls I have dated."

"Why not?"

I used to believe love was a privilege for the truly cherished, that I didn't deserve it. No one ever loved me enough to keep me safe. But you do, every day. Yours is the kind of love I dreamed a mother's love would be. Please let me show mine the way I can."

I take his hand. "This love is mutual. You have also given me something that I thought I'd never have: a child to love unconditionally. Thank you, Osei Wharton."

40

Hindsight is Twenty-Twenty.

Osei and I leave the apartment. When we get back to his place, the dogs are asleep.

"Millie loves the dog bed you bought. She doesn't want to crawl in next to me."

"My Millie loves hers too, but still battles for mine every night. Good night, my prince."

I kiss Osei on the cheek and head home.

I wake filled with excitement at the thought of seeing Gloria and Jackson.

Osei calls as I'm making coffee and hot chocolate for us.

"Hello, Osei."

"Good morning, Sese. I'm ten minutes away."

"Okay, I'll be out front waiting."

I walk outside, greet the security detail, handing them coffee and bagels. I pass Osei a thermos filled with hot chocolate.

"Oh my God. Thank you. I wanted some hot chocolate."

"You are welcome."

"Rob tells me you take coffee and bagels to the security team every morning, and they all love you."

"Well, I have an ulterior motive."

Osei gives me a puzzled look.

"I'm being nice, but I also want to see their faces. So, when I'm out and about, I don't mistake them for the bad guys."

"That's very smart."

The expressway is a parking lot.

I text Gloria to see if they have landed and to let her know we're stuck in traffic.. She texts me back. *At the gate.*

I text back. *Meet me outside the American Airlines Terminal B baggage claim.*

"Sese, you mentioned having a girls' night. I'd like to plan something for the men. Xbox sent me some new video games to review before they hit the market. I think the boys, and everyone, would enjoy playing them."

"Speaking of the boys, be prepared. Gloria's boys are going to lose their minds when they see you."

When we finally arrive at Terminal B baggage claim, I spot Gloria and her men.

Osei says, "Wow, Sese, do you know any ugly people? Everybody you know looks like they stepped out of the pages of *Vogue* and *GQ*."

Gloria is looking absolutely beautiful. You wouldn't have known she had flown all night. She has her hair pulled back in a high ponytail, wearing a long T-shirt under a knotted Balenciaga sweater, Oscar de la Renta pencil leg pants, and a pair of Valentino Rockstud flats.

"Is she a model?" Osei asks.

"No, she's a plastic surgeon who will never need any work done."

Jackson and the boys look extremely healthy and athletic as Osei pulls up beside them.

I roll down my window and say, "Going my way?"

The boys and Jackson laugh, and Gloria says, "Did you get a new car?"

"No, this belongs to Osei."

He leans over me and waves at everyone. The boys drop their luggage, open the back door, jump in, and mob Osei.

Jackson smiles. "Thank You."

"I thought a little distraction was needed," I say.

"Thank you, Auntie Sese!" Gloria says.

Jackson loads the luggage into the cargo space. He rides in the front with Osei. I get in the back with Gloria and the boys.

Gloria takes my hand. "Thank you, the boys are having a hard time with this. They loved their Popa."

We drop Jackson off at his dad's place in Chestnut Hill. We watch in silence as he walks to the front door with grief and loss written all over him.

Osei, sensing the mood change, immediately says, "Gloria, can the boys go with me to the arena. I need to get a workout in?"

The boys, in unison, "Please, Mama, please?"

In a mocking tone, Justin says, "I'm sure you and Auntie Sese have a lot of *girly* grown-up stuff to talk about."

"I need to check with your dad first. He may have plans for you all."

"Jackson." She gets him on the phone. "Osei has invited the boys to work out with him. Do you have plans for them later? Okay, call me when you are ready to be picked up."

"Your dad is okay with you hanging out with Osei, but you need to eat first."

"I'll make sure they get something to eat," Osei says.

When we arrive home, the boys and Osei bring the luggage inside and leave.

"Gloria, wine, scotch, or coffee?" I ask.

"I drank a pot of coffee on the plane. Now I need Tig."

Tignanello is her favorite wine.

"It has been a rough couple of days."

"I hope there's no drama."

"No, Jackson and his dad sorted everything out while he was alive. All the Philadelphia property will go to the boys, which will be placed in a trust managed by Jackson."

"What about your father-in-law's wife?"

"He left her a boatload of money, and she has nothing to complain about."

"Is she disappointed about losing the Ocean Park house on the Vineyard?" I ask.

"No, with the money she inherited, she's buying a place up island in Makonikey overlooking Vineyard Sound. "Poppa Jake made sure everyone was happy."

"Perfect. We all want to support you. The girls are coming down for a girls' night. When is the funeral?"

"There won't be a funeral. Poppa Jake wanted to be cremated, and that's happening tomorrow morning. The only ones present will be Jackson, the Minister, and me. Poppa Jake wanted the boys to remember him as a living entity, and not a body in a casket. He loved his grandsons, and this gesture proves it even more."

"When are you all planning to leave?" I ask.

"We're here until next weekend."

"Good, I planned the girls' night for Saturday. Osei wants to have a boys' night at his place, so everyone is bringing their spouses and significant others."

"What about Taylor? I don't want her to feel left out."

"She'll be fine. I won't have anyone here either. Taylor and I have always been each other's significant other." I pretend not to know about Eric.

"You have Bruce."

"I beg to differ."

"So, he won't be here?"

"I'm not inviting him."

"So, you are going to use Osei to invite him."

"I'm not using anyone. Osei can invite whomever he wants to. I'm sure Bruce will come because his best friend, your husband, is in town."

Changing the subject, I say, "I need to bring you up to speed on all that's happening with me. I've decided to resign and head up Osei's foundation."

"You are going to resign? When did you decide to do that?"

"I made up my mind to do so about five seconds before I told you. You're the first to know. Can you keep it to yourself for a few days? I haven't told Osei yet."

"Of course, it's in the vault."

"Also, Ms. Hannah's on the run. She is tied to a busted illegal adoption ring. The CIA, FBI, and Interpol are all after her."

Gloria's phone rings. "Hey, honey," she says.

She looks at me and whispers, "He's ready to be picked up. Are you okay to drive?"

I look at my glass and realize I haven't taken a sip. "I'm good," I say.

"We're on our way. Anyone there I need to see?"

He must have said no. Gloria grabs my wine and drinks it.

"I didn't want to waste it."

"You are such a Tig wino."

We drive to Jackson's father's house. Jackson comes out and says to Gloria, "My uncle wants to see you."

"Jackson, I just drank two glasses of wine."

"I guess it's five o'clock somewhere," he says.

Glancing at me, he adds, "You are such a bad influence on my wife. I'm going to stop you two from hanging out."

"Jackson, I can't help it if your wife is a wino."

Jackson opens the car door for Gloria, and they go inside.

I text Dee and ask her to call me.

My phone rings. It's Dee. "You're quick."

"We'll be there Saturday morning on the ten forty-five train. Can you arrange transportation, or should we take a rideshare?"

"For how many people?"

"Six, us and our men."

"I'll come and get you all."

"Is Bruce coming?"

"I didn't invite him."

"Sese, why didn't you?"

"No particular reason, I just haven't gotten around to extending an invite. I'm sure that Osei will invite him."

"Sese, stop being a coward, and invite him."

"Okay, I'll call him."

"How are Gloria and Jackson doing?"

"Jackson and Gloria are doing fine. In fact, the lovebirds are marvelous. They're getting in the car as we speak. Say hello."

Jackson excitedly says, "Hey, Dee, can you make Bourbon Glazed Ribs for me?"

"Of course," Dee says.

"Jackson, would you drive?" I ask.

"Sure, I'll never turn down the opportunity to drive a Porsche."

"Sese, there's a car following us. It was parked down the block from my dad's house when we left. Should I be concerned?" he asks.

I look out the back window. "No, that's my security detail."

"Wow, Bruce told me about the issues you all were having with Ms. Hannah, and with her being on the run, is she still a threat?" Jackson asks.

"You never know with her. I suspect that she isn't going anywhere until she has access to Osei's life, and especially his finances."

"Even if you weren't in the picture, what makes her think Osei would give her access to his money?" Gloria asks.

"Ms. Hannah thinks highly of herself and her ability to lie her way into any situation. Especially when there are millions of dollars involved."

Jackson pulls into my driveway and says, "Excuse us for an hour. I need my wife to bring me back to life, having spent the day dealing with the business of the dead."

"Be my guest. Millie and I will go check on Osei and the boys."

It's time for me to be a big girl. On my drive to Osei's, I call Bruce.

He answers, saying, "Hello, Sese, what's up?"

"I'm calling to let you know we're planning a gathering here in Philly supporting Gloria and Jackson. You are invited to join the festivities."

"Osei called me this morning and mentioned it. I told him I'd think about it."

"Why didn't you accept his invitation?" I ask.

"Because I wanted the invite to come from you."

"Well, you have been invited. Where are you?"

"I'm on my way to Philly. I should be there in two hours."

"You were coming whether I invited you or not."

"Yes, but I feel a lot better now that I have an official invite from you. Are you out and about?

"Yes, I'm on my way to Osei's to hang out with him and the boys. Jackson and Gloria are at my place, having some alone time."

"Some things never change."

"And some things do," I say.

I arrive at Osei's place, and the boys are so excited to be there.

Jason says, "Auntie, Osei told us you decorated his apartment. We love it."

Justin chimes in, "I want to live in a place like this when I grow up."

"Okay, are you guys hungry?" I ask.

"Osei ordered pizza," Jason says.

Justin excitedly says, "Auntie, Osei says we could spend the night with him. Can you ask our parents for us?"

"Sure, I'll call them."

I look at Osei, and he nods in agreement, saying, "I want them to play the new video games. Their feedback would be invaluable."

"Osei, you guys can't play video games all night!"

"We won't. I've invited a couple of teammates. We're going to watch movies and play some ball."

"I can't believe Osei has a half-court in his apartment," Jason says.

"Your godsons have some skills. They were showing off today and got the attention of the coaches," Osei says.

The twins are very tall for their age. Jackson is six feet five, and Gloria is six feet, so they're bound to be tall.

"We have skills. Did you hear that, Auntie?" Justin says proudly. "Jason is a better scorer, but I'm better at defending."

"I'm sponsoring a summer camp. Could you both come and work out with me and my teammates?"

Jason says, "We would love to, but we have to discuss it with our parents because…"

Before he can finish his sentence, Justin chimes in, saying, "because our mom plans a lot of activities for us during the summer."

"Ok, discuss it with them and I'll keep two slots open for you guys until I hear otherwise."

The front desk calls, the pizzas have arrived.

On my way to the lobby to pick them up, I called Gloria, who drowsily says, "Hello."

"Earth to Gloria."

"Hey, Sese, there's nothing on this planet that can take me to another universe like my husband and a bottle of Tig."

"Too much information," I say, laughing.

"Osei has invited the boys to spend the night at his place. Are you okay with them staying?"

"I'm okay with it. Jackson is in the shower. I'll call you back once I talk to him."

I take the pizzas and salads upstairs. While they all eat, I step outside to relax on the balcony, letting the Philadelphia skyline impress me. I look at my watch, 6:30 P.M., which means it's 11:30 P.M. in London.

I call Rhett. "I was just thinking about you," he says.

"You were? Good thoughts, I hope."

"Always, what's shaking in your world?"

"I wanted to let you know I'm resigning on Monday. Osei has asked me to head up his foundation."

"I can't believe it has taken you this long."

"Why would you say that?"

"Because you need to be doing something that will feed your spirit, something where you can make a difference. This is a perfect fit for you."

"You think so? I'm warming up to the idea."

"I know a few companies that may want to donate to the foundation."

"That would be fantastic. I'll call you next week, and we can discuss it further."

"Until then."

Osei joins me on the patio. "Where are the boys?"

"In a pizza coma watching TV in the den."

"Are you absolutely okay with them spending the night?"

"Of course I am. I'm enjoying their company."

Gloria calls me back, "Jackson is okay with the boys spending the night. We'll bring their pajamas and a change of clothes for tomorrow."

"I'll be there shortly to pick you all up," I say.

"No worries, Bruce called Jackson, and he's a few minutes away. He'll bring us."

Twenty minutes later, Gloria, Bruce, and Jackson arrive. The boys meet them at the elevator, saying, "Mom, look at this place! Auntie Sese designed it. Isn't it fantastic?"

Jackson looks around in awe, "Sese, I'm impressed."

With a bit of pride, I say, "I'm the interior designer extraordinaire."

"Damn girl, I must agree with the boys. This place is fantastic," Jackson says.

"I see why you guys want to spend the night here," Gloria says.

Osei invites Bruce and Jackson to his place on Saturday for a boys' night.

Justin and Jason both ask at the same time, "Can we come?"

Osei says, "Of course! It wouldn't be any fun if you all weren't here."

Jackson pulls Osei aside. "Thanks for spending time with my boys. This has been a positive distraction for them. Their grandfather was a huge fan of yours. He would've loved to meet you and was thrilled when you got drafted by the Sixers."

"I'm flattered. I know what it feels like when someone you love dies."

Jackson says, "I'm sorry. I didn't mean to bring to mind any bad memories. I know how devastating it can be to mourn a loved one. Did you know your parents?"

"No, I convinced myself my parents must have died, that's why I'm in an orphanage, and I mourned them every day of my life until I met Sese."

"Justin and Jason, it's time to get in bed," Gloria says.

"Okay, Mom." The boys say good night and make their way upstairs.

Osei yells to them, "Hey, guys, the towels are in the hall closet." He turns to Jackson. "I'll drop them off tomorrow morning."

Gloria and I drive back together.

"Are you going to make Bruce stay in a hotel?" Gloria asks.

"I'm not making Bruce do anything. I think we'll both be embarrassed if I invite him to stay with me. He should walk in with his luggage, no invitation needed."

We pull into the driveway. Moments later, Bruce parks next to us, and he pops his trunk and pulls out a suitcase.

"Who wants a drink?" Gloria asks, her wink screaming. *You're going to need one.*

"I'm hungry, Sese, what do you have to eat?" Jackson asks.

"We can order out. There's a Thai Restaurant that's still open, and they deliver."

"Shrimp Pad Thai for me," Jackson says.

Jackson, feeling nostalgic, says, "I never thought in a million years the four of us would ever break bread together again."

"I agree with Jackson, I'm feeling very nostalgic myself," Bruce says all of a sudden. He and Jackson get up and hug one another, and start fake crying.

"You two are silly," Gloria says.

We leave them confessing their love for one another to go inside to make coffee. I turn to see Gloria staring at me.

"Gloria, why are you staring at me?"

"You guys still look good together."

"I'm sure you all enjoyed getting together with Bruce and his ex-wife. Gloria, why aren't you answering me, and what's with the look?"

"I have never met her, and she has never set foot in my house."

I look at her, dumbfounded. "Why not?"

"Bruce never brought her around. When he visited us in LA, or met us here in Philly, he was always alone, and I got the sense he was not happily married."

I put the coffee tray together, and Gloria and I rejoined the guys on the deck. I turn on the outside speakers, and we listen to Miles Davis's album, *Ascenseur pour l'echafaud*.

We sit in silence, grooving to the music.

"This definitely feels like old times," Gloria says.

"You wait until Saturday. It will feel like the good old times."

"What is happening on Saturday?" Bruce asks.

"The girls will be all together. Let the good times roll," Jackson sarcastically says.

Gloria and I high-five each other.

Jackson says to Bruce, "I guess you'll be leaving on Friday."

"No, we'll be playing poker at Osei's on Saturday night while the girls pamper themselves."

As Gloria and I left the patio, we hear Jackson say to Bruce.

"A blind man can see you still love her."

"I never stopped loving her," Bruce answers.

I tug Gloria's arm; she wants to eavesdrop, but I refuse and pull her away.

The patio door opens, and Gloria steps out. "You guys have had enough alone time," she says with a smile. "Jackson, come to bed. I can't sleep without you."

"You can't sleep either, want some company?" Bruce says.

"No, I need the stars."

He looks up. "All I see are trees, not a star in sight."

"You have to sit at the back of the patio."

He grabs two chairs, and we face south. The night's silent beauty is outshone by the silence between us, which seems like an eternity. I sense that he wants to take my hand, but I also sense he knows I wouldn't want him to. Finally, I break the silence.

"I have decided to accept Osei's offer and head up the foundation."

"Congratulations, I know this will be the right move for you and Osei. Are you excited?"

"Yes, I'm excited, but I'm also extremely nervous. I haven't told Osei yet, but I plan on doing so this weekend."

"I'll support you in every way I can."

I take his hand and thank him. "I want to surround Osei with people he can trust and create a village for him, something he hasn't had before."

Bruce's hand is wrapped around mine. I tug gently, trying to break free. Reluctantly, he releases his grip.

"What were you and Jackson talking about for so long?" I ask.

"We were reminiscing."

"Would you care to elaborate?"

"We were talking mostly about you and me and how I saw your career as a way for you to grow and leave behind."

"No! I wanted us to grow together, but instead we started to grow apart. I knew that you loved me, but I didn't feel that you were in love with me any longer."

"Sese, how could you say that? I never stopped being in love with you."

"Well, Mr. Leblanc, you stopped showing it."

"I've had years to think about what I did wrong, and I don't plan on making those mistakes again."

His words fade into twinkling stars and the beauty of the night.

"Good night, Bruce. I'd like to say we can continue the discussion about our past and future later. If I saw a path forward for us, which I don't."

I see him searching for words, not lost in the night, but lost in our hearts.

A sharp thrill cuts through the silence.

It's Osei. "What's up? Breakfast is at 9:00 A.M. I'm making chicken and waffles. I'll see you in the morning." Bruce says.

"I'm going to bed."

"Good night, Sese. I'm going to stay out here a little longer."

Bruce watches me as I leave and smiles; it's clear he has definitely missed me.

41

Punched in the Face

Morning comes too soon. When I make my way to the kitchen, Gloria, Jackson, and Bruce are having coffee.

"Good morning, beautiful!" Gloria beams at me.

"Good morning, gorgeous," I say back.

"So I guess Bruce and I aren't beautiful or gorgeous," Jackson says.

"No, you are just pretty," I tease.

"Pretty average," Gloria adds, handing me a cup of coffee. We high-five.

"What smells amazing?" I ask.

"There's chicken in the oven, and I'm taking waffle orders, regular or stuffed," Bruce says.

"Stuffed with what?"

"Walnuts and fruit. Blueberries, peaches, or strawberries."

"That sounds incredible. Peaches and walnuts for me."

"Coming right up," he says.

The front door opens, and Osei and the boys come barreling in.

"It smells so good in here. I'm hungry," Justin says.

We sit down for a wonderful breakfast. After that, Gloria and Jackson get ready to leave for the crematory.

"Wait for us. We're going with you," Jason says.

"Your Poppa is being cremated, and I don't think you should come," Jackson says.

Justin says, "We know, and we want to be there to celebrate Poppa's transition as a family."

"Plus, Poppa talked to us about what he wanted when he died, and we told him we would be there to help pick out his urn," Jason says.

Jackson takes his sons in his arms and, tearing up, says, "Thank you."

"Don't cry, daddy," Justin says. "Everything will be alright."

Osei hands Jackson the keys to his Range Rover.

As Osei and Bruce argue over the last piece of chicken, Osei casually mentions a call he got from Ms. Hannah.

"Ms. Hannah called me. She wants to meet in two days when she's in Philly."

"That woman is relentless. The FBI's after her, and she still has the nerve to reach out. How is she so sure you won't turn her in?" I ask.

"I know. She's unbelievable. I told her that, and she asked me to trust her, just once more. I'm hoping she'll finally tell me who my parents are."

Bruce leans forward. "Osei, I get it. But you realize her being in Philly is because of you." We need a plan."

"She wants me to come alone," Osei says, his voice tight.

"I'm sure she does. And you and I both know that's not happening. Where does she want to meet?"

"She'll text me the location today."

"Bruce, please call Dave and let him know Ms. Hannah is planning to come to Philly."

"I'll call him now. He is very interested in Ms. Hannah's whereabouts."

Bruce finishes his call with Dave and says, "He wants us to contact him as soon as we hear from Ms. Hannah. In the meantime, he is going to alert the local police as well as the FBI."

"Osei, call Rob and have him increase security," Bruce says. Looking dejected, Osei dials Rob Ackerman.

I listen keenly and pour myself another cup of coffee. I know I need to think like Ms. Hannah.

"I don't trust that woman one iota. Can you check with Rob to see if he has a man and a woman on his team who could pass for us?"

Osei and Bruce give me a puzzled look.

"We may need a decoy. Ms. Hannah has always been a step ahead. She knows I won't let her meet with her alone. So, she'll find a way to separate us. I'll bet my last dollar that she won't show up at whatever location she texts you. She'll come when you least expect it. Using the element of surprise to catch everyone off guard. The only place she can have access to you without anyone around is your apartment. Call your management office and ask if any major deliveries or repairs are scheduled."

Osei calls his management office and puts the phone on speaker. "Hello Matt, is there anything happening at the condo in the coming days I should be aware of?"

"Hello, Mr. Wharton, I was just getting ready to call you. We received a call. A new tenant is moving into the unit next to yours tonight."

"When did the new owner notify the management office?"

"About twenty minutes ago, and we're not thrilled about it."

"Thanks, Matt, keep me posted."

"I'm calling Dave. He can look into the owner of the unit," Bruce says.

"Osei, I know this may not be a good time, but I want to let you know I'm accepting your offer to head up the foundation."

Rushing over to me, Osei hugs and says, "Thank you, Sese."

I kiss him on his forehead. "You are very welcome."

"I hate to interrupt this love fest, but the owner of the unit lives in Manhattan. According to Dave, he has not rented or sold the unit to anyone," Bruce says.

"Oh my God, Sese, you are correct," Osei exclaims.

"Bruce, does Dave have a plan?" I ask.

"Yes, he and his team will land in forty-five minutes."

Osei's phone rings, "Hello, Rob."

"Hello, Mr. Wharton, my men reported you were followed when you left your home this morning, and the car is parked down the block from Ms. Lewis's home now."

"Hello, Rob, it's Sese." I grab the phone. "Can your men see who's in the car?"

"There are two men in the front, but we don't have a visual on the people or persons in the back seat. The windows are heavily tinted."

"Thanks, Rob," Osei says, and hangs up.

"What do we do now?" Osei asks.

We'll keep them occupied until Dave sets everything up at your place." Bruce says.

Osei calls the management office to inform them that Dave and his team will be on-site and need access to his apartment and the vacant unit next door. He assures them the FBI will have the necessary paperwork and will explain the situation.

Gloria and her men arrive, and the boys head straight to the den to play video games. We bring Gloria and Jackson up to speed on the latest developments with Ms. Hannah.

"Is there anything we can do?" Gloria asks.

"Yes. We're going shopping," I say.

"How's that helping?" Jackson asks.

"We need a distraction while the FBI is setting everything up at Osei's place, and nothing will irritate Ms. Hannah more than seeing Sese spend Osei's money," Bruce says.

"I'll wait here while you and Gloria shop," Osei says.

"No, you won't. You are coming with us. I'm not letting you out of my sight. Besides, her minions are following you."

Bruce calls Rob. "Osei and Sese are going to Saks. We need you to have a team in place before they arrive. They should be there in thirty minutes."

"I'm dispatching a team now, and I'll inform security at Saks that Osei will be there with his security detail," Rob says.

"Sese, I swear there's never a dull moment with you," Gloria says.

"I know. Now let's go spend some money."

"Only beautiful and gorgeous people get to go shopping," Jackson adds.

"Which one am I?" Osei asks. "Beautiful or gorgeous?"

"You are both my darlings, so get ready to spend some money!" I say.

Osei opens the driver's door to get in, but I nudge him aside and hop behind the wheel. "I'm driving, because I'm the only one who has taken defensive driving training."

"Sese's taken multiple defensive driving classes," Gloria says. Osei gives her a baffled look. "What? Why?"

"Don't ask, Gloria replies. "It's an exhaustingly long story."

"Osei, let's just say, I'm a well-trained operative."

"I definitely want to hear this story," Osei says.

"Osei, at one point in her life, Sese dated an African Prince?" Gloria adds.

His eyes widen. "Are you serious? I didn't even know there were still monarchies in Africa."

Gloria laughs, "Oh, Osei, you have a lot to learn about Sese."

"It seems like it," he says, shaking his head.

As I maneuver through traffic, I glance at him in the rearview mirror. "I have lived an exciting life, and I'll tell you about it someday."

"You must tell me about the African Prince, where you met and how," he says.

"I was working in DC, and I met him at a nightclub called Kilimanjaro, in Adams Morgan."

"No way," Osei says, "Are you kidding me?"

"Trust me, Osei, she isn't kidding," Gloria says.

"We're here," I say, easing the car into a parking space. "This story will have to wait for another time. And just so you know, personal villains are parked two rows behind us."

When we enter the store, I head to the perfume counter, and Gloria heads to the shoe department. Osei is still at the entrance of the store, signing autographs for some of his young fans. I notice one of the guys from the car that tailed us lurking around Osei.

I walk over and grab Osei's arm. "There are a couple of perfumes I want your opinion on," I say. "This is my excuse to put some distance between you and Ms. Hannah's henchman," I whisper.

"I know. I saw him when he came into the store. I also saw Rob standing close by. I wasn't worried."

We spent three hours in Saks, spending a small fortune. Bruce calls to update us that Dave and his team have set up surveillance at the condo.

We drop Gloria and the shopping bags off at home.

Osei and I drive to his place.

I look at him. "I pray the nightmare that is Ms. Hannah is over tonight. Are you nervous?" I ask.

"Only for you. I'm not interested in hearing what Ms. Hannah has to say."

Osei and agree that we'll play good cop, bad cop. I'm the bad cop.

Dave calls to give us the lay of the land. "Cameras and listening devices have been installed in Osei's apartment, and men are in position in his apartment as well as the apartment next door. Bruce is the security officer with two members of his team. Rob, head of your security detail, is on site with his men as well."

I park, and Osei and I take the elevator to his place. Once we get inside, Bruce calls. "Sese, the moving van and Ms. Hannah have arrived."

"Where's Dave?" I impatiently ask.

Before he could answer, Dave opened the bathroom door, and I nearly fainted.

"God, Dave, you nearly gave me a heart attack."

"We're here. No need for either of you to be afraid. If at any point you feel threatened, use the word *aquarium* in a sentence, and we'll come out."

"How many people are here with you?" Osei asks.

"Besides me, there are four other agents. I can arrest her as soon as she walks into the apartment, but I know you and Osei have questions you need answers to," Dave replies.

Dave answers his ringing phone, listening intently. "Three guys carrying boxes. Professionals, huh? Alright… It's go time."

I look at Dave, "What type of professionals?"

"The kind who carry weapons, not boxes," he says.

We hear movement next door. A few minutes later, the doorbell rings. Osei opens the door.

"Hello, Ms. Hannah," he says, greeting her with the customary cheek kiss.

"I wasn't expecting you," Osei says. "I thought we were meeting later."

"Hello, my dear," she replies. "Slight change in plans."

I walk into the foyer from the kitchen. "Ms. Hannah, why didn't you text Osei to let him know you were coming?" I ask, indignantly.

Ms. Hannah looks at me, "Hello, Sienna. What are you doing here?"

"Visiting my son, what else?"

"I was in the neighborhood, and I'm sure Osei doesn't mind me stopping by."

"No, I don't mind at all," Osei says. "And who are you?" Osei extends his hand to the man standing next to Mrs. Hannah. The man barely touches Osei's hand and, in a thick German accent, says, "Nice to meet you. I'm Hans Muller."

"Ms. Hannah, why would you show up unannounced at Osei's home?" I ask again.

"I'm leaving the country, and I need to discuss a very important matter with him."

"What do we need to discuss?" Osei asks.

"Osei, I want us to have a private conversation."

"I don't know about Mr. Muller, but I'm not going anywhere," I say.

I take a seat at the kitchen counter, and Mr. Muller sits across from me. Ms. Hannah looks around. "Osei, this is a nice apartment."

"Thanks to Sese. She decorated it for me. So, what do you need to discuss with me?"

"I'm leaving the country tomorrow, heading back to Germany. I've been away from home much too long. I wanted to see if you reconsidered signing with the sports agency and the investment company I recommend. I only want the best for you, dear, she looks scornfully at me."

"Ms. Hannah, Osei isn't changing his management company. Since I'm his mother, you can talk to me about anything to do with his career and his investment portfolio."

She says in a sharp tone, "Sienna, I'm not talking to you."

"Well, you are basically talking to yourself because I'm his mother, and anything to do with Osei you'll have to speak to me."

She gives a commanding look at Mr. Muller, who says, "Ms. Lewis, could I have a glass of water?" As I move toward the refrigerator, I notice the front door is open. I hand him the water, and I walk to the closet near the front door. I take off my jacket, hang it in the closet, and take the opportunity to close the front door. I sit back down, and I look to see Ms. Hannah whispering to Osei. He looks over to me and says indignantly, "If Sese isn't my mother, then who is? What are you talking about?"

"What the hell are you saying to him?" I demand.

"I did some investigating, and you are not his mother."

"Why did you tell me she was?" Osei angrily says.

"I never told you that. I only gave you the adoption papers. As you know, documents can be altered."

Followed closely by Mr. Muller, I sit next to Osei.

"Ms. Hannah, why are you saying this? Sese is my mother."

"Sienna isn't your mother. She's only hanging around you to get her hands on your money."

"You haven't answered Osei's earlier question. Who is his mother if it's not me? We took a DNA test. I'm his mother. Mrs. Hannah, I'll give you this, you've got nerve. Do you think we live under a rock? We've seen the news. We could call the police right now. Aren't you a fugitive? I've had enough. If you want to catch that plane tomorrow, it's time for both of you to leave."

Mr. Muller comes over to where we're sitting, saying, "Ms. Lewis, I think you should refrain from speaking. I wouldn't want this conversation to get ugly. Mr. Wharton, all you need to do is sign a few papers, and we'll leave."

"I'm not signing anything. Ms. Hannah and I have had this conversation, and nothing has changed."

"Osei, I'm afraid you no longer have a say in the matter."

"Are you threatening me?"

"Of course not, I'm helping you to make a very wise decision," she says, dripping with sarcasm.

"So, before you leave the country, you're going to rob me?"

"Osei, don't look at it like that. Think of it as payment for the years my husband took care of you."

"Mr. Albert died when I was young. I barely remember him, and you left soon after. What I do remember is Mr. Albert took care of all the children, not just me."

With tight lips, she sighs. "What I remember is that man was an absolute bore. You know what his problem was?" Answering her own questions, she continues. "He cared too much for people who had no value, who couldn't contribute to his life or wealth."

"I remember him being kind and loving," Osei says.

"That man was content living a nondescript life, caring for nondescript people."

"Is that why you killed him?" I ask.

"Dead men tell no tales," Mr. Muller says as he moves to stand behind me. I see the concern on Osei's face.

Ms. Hannah, feeling amazingly comfortable, says, "We're not leaving here tonight until you sign the papers."

In a hostile tone, Mr. Muller says, "If you don't sign them, something bad is going to happen to Ms. Lewis while you watch it."

"I remember the last gift Mr. Albert gave me, Osei says quietly. An aquarium. And if I remember correctly, you poured the fish and everything down the toilet."

He fixes his gaze on Ms. Hannah, unblinking.

On cue, Dave and his men come out of hiding with their weapons drawn.

Mr. Muller tries to get away and is thrown to the floor by two men and handcuffed.

Ms. Hannah lunges at Osei. I grab the Tom Dixon aluminum vase from the coffee table and hit her in the face with it. Blood pours from her nose, and I hit her again. Before I could hit her a third time, Osei grabbed my hand.

"Let go of me. How dare she come into your home and threaten you!" I yell.

He lets go of my arm, and I hit her again. Dave runs over, picks me up, and carries me away. I scream at him, "Dave, put me down!"

"Sese, calm down. She won't be able to harm either of you."

There's a commotion at the front door, and one of Dave's men steps in. Five men in the hallway, two of them in handcuffs. Bruce stands behind them, looking triumphant. Dave's team escorts Ms. Hannah and her accomplices.

"Thank you, Sese, " Dave says. I'll keep you updated. We need to get them back to New York quickly."

Bruce turns to Dave. "I owe you."

Dave shakes his head. "No, I owe you and Sese."

"You'll regret this," Ms. Hannah is shouting as they cart her away.

After Dave leaves, Osei pulls me into a hug. "I'm relieved, the chapter that is Ms. Hannah is officially closed. Sese, I think you broke her nose."

"I didn't hit her that hard."

Bruce grins. "Yeah, you did. I have it on video."

"No way, show me." Osei eagerly says.

Bruce takes out his phone and plays the clip.

"Damn, Sese," Osei says as he watches. "I definitely broke her nose."

"She's lucky that's all I broke." I reach for my glass of water, but my hand is shaking so badly I almost drop it.

Bruce takes the glass, "Sese, are you okay?'

Months of bottled-up hatred and fear finally rise to the surface. I collapse on the sofa as the weight of everything crashes down. I begin to cry, deep sobs come hard, uncontrollable.

"Sese, are you okay? What's wrong?" Osei rushes to my side, panic in his voice.

"You see, Osei," I manage between breaths, I'm not as brave as you all think I am."

"She's crying because this is over, and you are safe," Bruce says gently.

"I'm crying," I correct him, wiping my face, "because I couldn't break Ms. Hannah's legs. She caused so much hardship and pain to so many people."

Minutes later, I pull myself together and hug Osei. "I'm so glad this is all over."

"Me too," he says.

"What do you say we pick up something for dinner and celebrate?"

"Oh, yes, I'm famished," he replies. "All this drama can make a man hungry."

"Boy, when are you not hungry?" Bruce asks.

I call Gloria.

"Is it over?" she asks.

"Yes. Everyone is safe, and Osei is starving. We're grabbing Mexican Food, and we'll see you shortly."

"Don't bother, Dee is here, and she's cooking up a storm."

I scream, "Oh my God, I'm on my way!"

"Is something wrong?" Bruce asks. "What happened?"

"Dee is here."

Bruce grabs his cat. "Wait for me."

"Who is Dee?" Osei asks.

"One of your four godmothers," I reply. "We don't need to pick up dinner."

"I'll drive you." Bruce gathers up my purse.

"No, thank you. I just need a moment."

Driving home, I'm a wreck and need to collect my thoughts. I didn't want to admit how worried I was for both Osei and myself. I could see the perverted look in Mr. Muller's eyes. He wanted to hurt someone, and the hurt was directed toward me and Osei. I was afraid for our lives. I shiver and take a deep breath. I want to leave Ms. Hannah behind me and enjoy my friends. I say a prayer of gratitude and step on the gas. Osei and Bruce, following close behind, did the same.

When I get home, Taylor, Dee, Gloria, and Rainey all greet me.

"I don't believe this. How did you all know I needed you here?"

"Gloria called us and told us what was happening. We thought you might need some support," Taylor says. I'm overcome and start to cry.

Dee hugs me. "Thank you for doing something about that wretched woman." She pats my back in comfort. "There are a lot of people who will be able to move on with their lives."

"Hello, everyone. You all must be my godmothers," Osei says as he and Bruce walk in. "I'm Osei Wharton."

Rushing over to give him a hug, Rainey says, "Yes, we are, and I'm sure I'm going to be your favorite."

"You must be my Aunt Rainey. I have heard a lot about you," Osei says.

I give Osei a look, and he immediately changes the subject, knowing he does not need to elaborate on what he has heard about Aunt Rainey.

"Where are Justin and Jason?" he asks.

Hearing Osei's voice, the twins come running up the stairs and give him an overly complicated handshake.

Osei says, "What smells so good? I'm starving."

"Let's go find out," I grab Osei's hand and head to the kitchen.

"Hey Bruce, you're looking as handsome as ever," Taylor says.

"Yes, I have to agree with Taylor," Dee chimes in.

"Give me a break," Rainey and I both say in unison.

Still focused on his stomach, Ose says, "I'm serious, what smells so good?"

"Well, we're having Jackson's favorite bourbon ribs. Sese's lobster mac and cheese, bourbon-glazed salmon, spicy corn muffins, and Rainey's favorite, string beans sauteed in a garlic sauce."

"When did you have time to cook all this food?" Osei says.

"I brought most of it with me already cooked. For dessert, I made Taylor's and Gloria's favorite, chocolate crepe cake."

"Too bad your men aren't here. When are they joining us?" I ask.

"Our menfolk will be here tomorrow."

The boys help their mother set the table, and we all sit down to an amazing meal. Finally, at peace, knowing Ms. Hannah was out of our lives for good.

"Jackson, would you bless the meal?" I ask.

"Sese, instead of me saying a prayer, I'd like for everyone sitting here to say what they're grateful for today, and every day. I'll start," he takes Gloria's hand. "Losing my father has been extremely hard for me. He was the first person I ever loved. I'm grateful to have been raised by a wonderful man, and grateful these three people allow me to share their lives with them." Gloria leans over and kisses him on the cheek.

Dee says, "My turn. I'm grateful for being a mother to a very headstrong young woman, but I'm so grateful to my girls for always being there for me."

Rainey stands up and looks around the table. "Please turn all recording devices off." She continues. "I'm so incredibly grateful for you all. You've accepted me for twenty-five years, and you've all loved, and will continue to love who I am, and all who I'm not. I'm grateful for all of you. I'm also grateful we're all healthy," she says. "You may turn your devices back on."

Jackson turns to his boys.

"Dad, do we have to?" Jason says.

"Yes."

"I'm grateful for my family, and I'm grateful for my Poppa. May he rest in peace."

Justin looks at his dad. "I second what Jason just said, but I want to add I'm grateful that Osei is our cousin."

Osei, seated next to Jason, gives him a high five. Osei stands up. "I'm grateful to Sese for taking me in, for protecting me, and introducing me to my new family. I have never experienced a gathering like this, and I'm happy and feel blessed to be here."

Gloria clears her throat. "I'm grateful for my family, which goes without saying. But I'm so grateful for my sisters. Through it all, I have had my girls."

Bruce stands, and we can see that he's nervous when he says, "I'm grateful I'm able to be with you all again. I have missed you all, and like Osei, I'm happy and blessed to be here."

Fighting away tears, I say, "I'm grateful to you all. I draw strength from every one of you. I'm blessed to have Osei in my life. Thank you for welcoming him. He's a lovely addition to our family."

Taylor is the last to stand. "I have cherished all of you, and I know you've cherished me too. Not a day goes by that I don't thank God for each and every one of you."

Caught up in the moment, we all raise our glasses and the room is soon filled with love and joy. Dessert is fantastic. The boys say, "Auntie Dee made this cake for our birthday last year."

"Osei, when is your birthday?" Dee asks.

"December 30th."

"You can expect a cake for your birthday this year."

"Thank you," Osei says.

Osei and the boys are the first to leave the dinner table. They have plans to visit one of Osei's teammates. Bruce and Jackson retire to the deck to smoke cigars. We make our way down to the den.

"I'm just going to say what everyone is thinking," Rainey says.

Unsure of what is coming, we exchange glances and look at her with raised eyebrows, and brace for classic Rainey.

"I don't know when it could have happened, but Sese, you can tell us. Osei is your son. I was watching the two of you during dinner, and you both have the same mannerisms and expressions, not to mention looks. It was very disconcerting."

I throw a paper cup at her. "I didn't give birth to him, but he's my son. Isn't he handsome?"

"Yes," Dee replies with a grin. "He's drop-dead gorgeous. I think he and Marie would make a good couple."

"Nobody in their right mind would marry Marie," Rainey quips.

Dee throws another cup at Rainey.

"Come with me, I want to take you to where we're having our girls' night party." I take them to the empty apartment. Once inside, they're speechless.

"He gave this to you?" Gloria asks.

"Not exactly, it belongs to the foundation."

"Damn, Sese, this is a chef's kitchen," Dee says, admiring the high-end appliances.

Everyone scatters, exploring every inch of the place. Gloria and Taylor rave about the bathrooms with their multiple shower heads, a steam room, and separate toilets for men and women. Rainey smiles as she steps into the bedroom. She and I are both bedroom people. "If I owned this place, I'd sleep in a different room every night," she says.

We eventually gather on the deck, glasses of adult beverage in hand, taking in the fabulous view of the city skyline.

"We'll stay here tomorrow for our girls' night," I say. "We can drink, cook, and be merry. Which reminds me, we need to go shopping for a few things: candles, a couple of nice rugs, and plenty of pillows. I have air mattresses for us to sleep on. Are you all okay with that?"

Dee says, "Hell yeah. Let's do this."

"Okay, let's do it."

"What will the menfolk be doing?" Rainey asks.

"Trust me, they won't be bored." I take them to Osei's apartment.

Gloria, who'd seen it before, says. "Isn't this place gorgeous? Our very own Sese decorated the entire apartment."

"Shut the front door. Are you kidding me?" Taylor says.

"The men will totally be in heaven here," Dee chimes in.

"Osei has a poker and games night planned. Food will be catered by one of the stadium restaurants. We'll have to pick up the alcohol when we go shopping. Osei has water, soda, and sports drinks covered."

Rainey says, "My husband will never want to leave."

"This is going to be so much fun!" Taylor says.

"Is it okay if my husband sleeps with me on the air mattress?" Gloria asks playfully.

We all give her the classic you've got to be kidding me look, grab our bags, and head on our shopping expedition.

"Seriously, can't you sleep without him for one night?" Rainey asks.

Gloria gives Rainey the middle finger.

"You are addicted to the middle finger," Rainey sarcastically says.

"You got that right, and I make no excuses," Gloria replies.

"You go, girl, own it," Dee says.

On the way back to my house after shopping, I call Osei.

"Hey Sese, what's up?"

"Where are you all?" I ask.

"We're on our way back to your place. I have to place the food order for tomorrow night. How many people should I order for?"

"There will be eight, including you. I think you should order enough for twelve."

He says, "Okay, will do. We'll see you all soon."

"Should there be a car following us?" Rainey says.

"Yes. It's the security team. Until we know what's what, we're keeping them in place. I feel safer with them around."

"I have an idea. Why don't we order sushi for tomorrow instead of cooking?" I say.

"In that case, I'll make breakfast for everyone on Sunday," Dee chimes in.

42

The Calm After the Storm

"What time should I pick up the guys from the train station in the morning?" I ask.

They're traveling together and will arrive on the nine 9:45 am train," Rainey says.

Taylor volunteers to go with me to pick them up.

"I'm looking forward to seeing Eric again," I say.

"Who is Eric?" Gloria asks.

"He's a colleague of Kelvin's. I introduced them, but I don't know why Taylor invited him," Rainey says.

"Because we're dating," Taylor replies.

"Since when, and why?" Rainey asks."

"For a while now. Since your party and because we can," Taylor replies flatly, shutting down any further questions from Rainey.

Back at my place, I find Bruce and Osei on the deck, deep in conversation. I join them and hand each a cup of hot chocolate.

"What's with the serious faces?" I ask.

"Dave called," Bruce says, "Ms. Hannah was found hanging in her cell."

"Oh my God! Is she dead?"

"No, she's in a coma," Osei says.

"Where did she get the stuff to hang herself with?" I ask.

"That's the question everyone is asking," Bruce replies.

"Do you think someone tried to kill her?" Osei asks with concern.

"She was in federal custody. How could that be?" I ask.

"Dave and his team are doing an investigation. It could have been done by someone in the FBI, or someone in the local law enforcement," Bruce answers.

"What about the men who were arrested with her?"

"They're not talking, especially after what happened to Ms. Hannah," Bruce says.

"Is this the end, or the beginning, of something worse? Should we be worried?" I anxiously ask.

"Dave thinks that Ms. Hannah knew a lot about the organization behind the illegal adoptions and child trafficking. So, she was silenced. You and Osei are both safe. Dave will keep us updated on her condition and any other pertinent information."

"I'll feel better if Sese's security detail stays intact for now," Osei says.

"I totally agree," Bruce replies.

Jackson opens the patio door. "Dee is warming up leftovers. Are you guys hungry?"

Osei pushes Bruce and me aside and rushes inside. Dinner tonight is less formal. Some of us are standing at the kitchen island, while others sit at the dining room table.

"Sese, how were you able to control your temper when Ms. Hannah threatened Osei?" Gloria asks.

"There were moments when I was afraid, and plenty when I was angry. But I knew I had to stay calm to protect Osei and not put us at risk."

"I was calm because she was calm," Osei says. If I had seen fear in her eyes, then I'd have panicked."

"I still can't believe Sese actually hit Ms. Hannah," Bruce adds.

"Sese, you hit her?" Dee asks.

"Yes, she did, and I have the video to prove it," Bruce says, grinning.

Everyone rushes over. When the clip plays, they see me land a hit squarely on Ms. Hannah's nose and the entire room erupts into a collective "Damn," followed by uncontrollable laughter that echoes through the house.

"Will you all stop? You're embarrassing me," I plead.

Dee hugs me, "You'll forever be my hero. That woman took advantage of so many young women and made us hate ourselves."

The girls and I head upstairs to my bedroom, where we all pile onto the bed in a tangle of laughter and whispers, like teenagers at a slumber party.

Taylor and I are the first to wake up. We get dressed and head out to pick up the men from the train station.

"Traffic is crazy, and you are driving too slow. We'll never get there," Taylor complains.

"Taylor, will you stop complaining about every little thing?"

"I'm so excited to see him, but I'm also very nervous."

"Why would you be nervous?"

"I want you all to accept him because I love him."

"We'll welcome him with open arms."

The men are exiting the station when we arrive. "Did those men just step out of the pages of *GQ*?" I ask.

Kelvin, Rainey's husband, leads the way. He's tall with a long stride.

Taylor says, "That man is way too handsome for Rainey. She should thank God every night."

Next to him is Arjun with café brown and shoulder-length hair framing a face even more magnetic in person than on TV.

"He looks incredible," I say.

"When you hear him speak, you'll want to fall right into his arms." Taylor grins.

The last of the trio, graceful and a chiseled, makes me pause. "OMG, Taylor. That man is drop-dead gorgeous. I don't remember Eric being so good-looking."

Taylor glances at me and nods. "I know. He's gorgeous."

Heavenly aromas greet us at the door. "Dee's doing her thing," Arjun says proudly. He walks up behind her and wraps his arms around her waist. Dee tilts her head and smiles. "Hello, honey. I'm making your favorite breakfast."

Rainey hands Kelvin a mimosa, and he smiles. "I missed you."

"I missed you more," Rainey responds with a kiss.

Osei and the boys arrive, also following the delicious aroma to the kitchen.

"Wow, what smells so good?" Osei asks.

I introduce him to the guys, and their jaws drop. They didn't know about him.

"Osei, how do you know Sese?" Kelvin asks.

"She's my mom."

All the guys look at Bruce, and he says, "It's a long story."

Justin and Jason pile a lot of food on their plates. Gloria says, "Please save some food for the rest of us."

While we're all enjoying breakfast, I lay out the plan for the weekend. The men are excited; their evening will include good food, poker, dominoes, and basketball. We, however, are looking forward to sushi, wine, and simply being together. It's been months since we all gathered, and we all need this time to relax and recharge.

43

Voulez-vous coucher avec moi ce soir?

I make sure the men are all settled in and the food has been delivered. We all step onto the balcony of Osei's apartment just in time to see the brilliant hues of the setting sun erupt in a blaze of color.

We bid our menfolk goodnight and head upstairs.

To create a relaxing spa atmosphere, I layer the floors with rich red Persian rugs and scattered oversized pillows throughout the space. Large crystal vases, each holding a softly glowing scented candle, are placed in every corner. Chiffon-beaded curtains drape the windows, casting delicate patterns of light across the room. When the girls first walk in, they screamed with delight. Even Rainey, usually critical, has kind words to share.

"This is the reaction I was hoping for. I want to transport us to a peaceful and calm place."

Sitting next to Dee, I take a sip of the most glorious wine and let out a sigh.

Dee places a hand on my arm and says softly, "Sese, let it go. You've been through hell these past ten months."

"You're right. It has felt like a lifetime. I'm glad the Ms. Hannah chapter is closed. Now Osei and I have one mission to accomplish: finding his parents."

"Why even bother?" Dee asks.

"Because I promised him and I intend to keep that promise."

"Osei is happy. Don't you think you should just forget about finding his birth mother?" Gloria says.

"Sese, let me answer that question. Sese has to find his birth mother because he needs closure, and so does she. Osei may be happy now, but deep down, there will always be the uncertainty of whether or not he has parents or siblings. For him, it will be like the boogie man lurking in the closet, waiting for some unexpected soul to open the door," Rainey says.

Dee takes my hand. "Sese, thank you for neutralizing Ms. Hannah. She was always lurking, waiting to come after me again. I had to put so much on hold, never knowing when she'd strike," Dee says.

"It's over now. Your life is your own. You never let her control you," I reply.

"In some ways, I did," Dee says. "Every sponsor I landed, I worried about my past ruining it, not just for me, but for the forty people who count on me. So let's toast to Sese. Ladies, raise your glasses. To our brave and committed Sese, we love you."

"We certainly do," say Taylor, Dee, and Rainey, their voices full of love and deep respect.

"Thank you. I love you all, too."

"Well, I've got news," Dee says, a mischievous glint in her eye. "There's something that I've been holding back, and now I can finally share it with all of you."

"I'm sure we don't want or need to know about it." Rainey counters.

"I want to know," Taylor says.

"Me too," I enthusiastically add.

Dee reaches into her pocket and pulls out a ring, The luminous saphire is framed by sparkling tiny diamonds, and says, "Six months ago, Arjun and I got married, and Marie was our witness."

We all look at her in amazement and shock.

"I don't know whether to be happy or mad. You got married without us. It's going to take me a while to forgive you," Rainey says.

Gloria takes out her phone and calls Jackson, saying, "Sweetie, can you guys come up here? We all need to talk."

"Yes, something is wrong, and you all will find out what it is when you get here."

Within minutes, the front door opens, and all the men come rushing in, including the boys.

Gloria points at Dee and says, "Dee has something to tell us."

Arjun rushes over to Dee, "Are you okay?"

"I'm fine, in fact, we are both fine. I want to make a toast to all of you, and especially to my husband Arjun, whom I love with all my heart and soul. I love this man with every fiber of my body, and now I can share and celebrate our love with all of you."

Bruce and Jackson are pouring champagne for everyone. The boys and Osei grab bottles of water.

Arjun says, "I want to thank you all for loving my wife, and I hope you can spare a bit of it for me as well."

"You have it," Gloria says.

"Since we were not present at the ceremony, you all need to reenact the first kiss as husband and wife," Eric teasingly says.

Arjun grabs Dee, and the two of them kiss passionately.

Justin scans the room with curiosity and asks, "Aunt Sese, what is the vibe here?" As he gestures toward the décor. "Bordello, or opium den?"

We all look around and laugh until we're wiping tears. Justin, still serious, says, "I'm trying to figure this out."

"My money is on the bordello," Bruce says, spinning me into his arms. With a wicked grin, he adds, "Voulez-vous coucher avec moi ce soir?"

Justin's eyes go wide. "What does that mean?"

Bruce leans in and whispers, "Would you like to sleep with me tonight?" Then, louder, to the room: "Do you take cash or credit?"

Again, the room fills with laughter. We settle down, and everyone takes a seat on the pillows or on the floor. After about thirty minutes, Rainey says, "Okay, time for you all to leave. This is our time together. We may or may not see you later."

The men reluctantly leave.

Gloria yells out to Jackson, "Honey, I'll see you later."

Taylor hits her on the shoulder.

"Can't you sleep alone for just one night?"

"I didn't get married so I could sleep alone," Gloria says.

"Let's get this party started. We need some Michael Jackson," I yell.

Taylor raises her hands and says, "Before we do, I have a confession as well. Eric and I have been living together for two months, and we plan on getting married."

"I can't with you two," Rainey says, pointing a finger at both Dee and Taylor. "We all live within a two-mile radius, and neither of you could share this news with me?"

Dee and Taylor walk over to Rainey, and they hug her.

"Okay, it's my turn to come clean," I say.

Rainey says, "Don't tell me you and Bruce are together, because I understand his wife is no longer a lesbian and wants him back."

"Good to know, but that isn't my news. I've decided to quit my job and head up Osei's foundation. In fact, you all are standing in my new office."

"Good for you," Dee says.

"I'm glad you are finally using your talents for good," Rainey jokes.

"Rainey, you make it seem as if I've been using my talents for evil."

"Sese, please ignore her. She means well." Taylor looks at Rainey with a scorching look.

"When will you resign?" Dee asks.

"On Monday, I'm excited, but I'm also very scared."

"Sese, I know you'll do an amazing job," Rainey says.

The rest of the night we drink, dance, and sing our favorite songs. Dee and Rainey fall asleep on the floor.

"We should wake them up," Gloria says.

"They look so comfortable. Let's just leave them be," I say, reaching for a blanket to cover them.

Gloria hands me her phone, and I read the text from Jackson: *Girl's night is over, we're coming up.* Minutes later, Jackson, Eric, Kelvin, and Arjun walk in. Kelvin sees Rainey on the floor.

"Where's she sleeping?" he asks.

"Rainey's sleeping in the first bedroom on the right, and Dee's in the second," I say to Arjun.

"Jackson, where's Bruce?" Gloria asks.

"He's downstairs, playing dominoes with Osei and the boys."

"Taylor, you and Eric can have the master suite."

"We'll see you all in the morning," Gloria says with a grin, taking Jackson's hand as they head down the hallway.

"Sese, you and I can sleep in the master suite, and Eric can sleep out here," Taylor says.

"It's okay. I can crash at Osei's."

I take the elevator to the seventh floor. Osei, Bruce, and the boys are in the game room playing dominoes.

"I take it girls' night turned into a couple's night," Osei says.

"Yes, and there's no room at the inn for me. I'll see you all in the morning. I'm going home."

"Sese, it's late, you can't leave now," Bruce says.

"I live less than ten minutes away, and I have a security detail. I'll text you all when I arrive."

"Sese, why are you leaving? You can stay here," Osei pleads.

"I know I can stay here, but I feel better going home." Before anyone can respond, I leave.

Bruce follows me to the elevator and steps in front of the buttons. "If you are leaving, I'm going with you," he says, eyes locked on mine. "I want to go with you."

I give him a look of quiet resignation.

"I plan on crashing in the guest bedroom," he adds.

44

Golden Milk

At home, I say goodnight to Bruce in the foyer and head upstairs with Millie. Two hours later, still wide awake, I go downstairs for some water. A soft, warm glow spills from the kitchen. To my surprise, Bruce is standing at the stove, gently stirring a small pot.

"Couldn't sleep either?" I ask.

He glances over his shoulder. "I knew you wouldn't be able to sleep."

"What makes you say that?"

"You weren't sleepy when you left Osei's. You used to fall asleep before midnight, so I figured it would take you some time to unwind."

"A lot has changed in twenty years, especially my sleeping habits."

He hands me a cup of whatever he's been stirring. I take a sip and pause.

"What's this? It makes me tingle inside."

"Golden milk," he says.

I take another sip. "This is so soothing. You have to give me the recipe."

"I thought it would be something you would like. I pinned the recipe to the fridge with the Martha's Vineyard magnet."

I walk over to the fridge and read the ingredients: milk, turmeric, honey, cinnamon, and ginger. I take a seat across from Bruce. "Thank you, I'm sure this will help me sleep."

"How are you really doing? You have gone through a lot."

"I'm fine," I say.

"Sese, you are far from fine. Over the last eight months, you have gained a son, and a very evil enemy, not to mention me reentering your life."

"You think I'm allowing you to reenter my life?"

"Okay, okay, me trying to reenter your life, and the icing on the cake, quitting your job to become CEO of Osei's foundation. How are you even okay with all this?"

"Maybe I'm not fine, but I'm trying to be."

"Sese, I'm here if you need to talk or a shoulder to cry on. I'm willing to do what you need."

"Why?"

"Because I want to be a part of your mornings, and especially your nights. I want to listen to all you want to say and let your body tell me all you are afraid of."

"It's that easy for you?"

"What do you mean?" Bruce asks, as he avoids my eyes.

"To pick up where we left off? To act like nothing happened?"

"Sese, it has taken me twenty years to get here, and it wasn't easy. I hated you for doing what you did, but I never stopped loving you. It took me all this time to understand it was okay for me to hate you, but it was also okay for me to love you. We never talked about it. You said what you had to say, and then I left. I'm not saying we need to talk about it now. But honestly, not a day has gone by in twenty years that I haven't wished for those moments back."

"What would you have done differently?" I ask, as my mind drifts back to that night.

"Everything," he says, voice at a whisper. "We would have argued, because we needed to, but I wouldn't have stormed out. I'd have made coffee, we'd have talked all night, and fallen asleep in each other's arms. Sese, I was jealous of anything that took you away from me. I blamed your job and your ambition to succeed for taking away our child, never myself, for distancing myself, and trying to punish you. I'm sorry for hurting you," he pauses. "For hurting us."

Tears are rolling down his face. I wipe them away.

"Bruce, I'm sorry too, but I'm too tired to talk about it now. Can we agree to discuss what happened twenty years ago in twenty years? Whether we do it together or separately, we have to move on."

"Moving on separately isn't an option," he says.

As I leave the kitchen, I glance over my shoulder. "By the way, do you have pajamas here?" I ask.

"Yes, my luggage is downstairs."

"When you get changed, if you want to, you can hang out with me and Millie upstairs."

"I'll see you all in fifteen minutes," he eagerly says.

I get into bed feeling awkward beyond belief.

Bruce slides into the bed next to me, "Good night, Sese, and thank you."

"For what?"

"For liking me a lot," he whispers.

I fall asleep with Bruce gently patting my back, the rhythm easing me into rest.

I awaken to Bruce's ringtone. He reaches over me to turn it off.

"I'm sorry."

"What time is it? I ask.

"6:00 A.M."

"Six o'clock, are you serious?"

"I wanted to make you breakfast before we left for Osei's."

I give him an annoying look.

"Don't look at me like that," he says with a grin. "I'll see you in the kitchen."

I make my way to the kitchen guided by a divine aroma.

"No way, you still have that robe," Bruce says, in disbelief.

"Why wouldn't I still have it?" I ask.

Sese, that robe's twenty years old. I bought it for you with my first paycheck. I remember falling in love with the Asian dragon and lotus design on the back."

"I have other robes, but none compares to this one."

"It warms my heart to know you still enjoy wearing it."

"Sese, did our conversation last night upset you?"

"No, but I understand your ex-wife no longer wants to be an ex-wife."

He chokes on his coffee. "Where did you hear that?"

"Take a wild guess."

"Radio Rainey," he says jokingly.

"Bingo."

"Yes, she has been making overtures to that effect, but we're over."

"How can you be so sure?"

"I know exactly where I want and need to be, and that's by your side. Do you know how much I've prayed for a night like last night, where I could hold you?"

I look at him and think to myself, *Not as much as I have because, when I close my eyes at night, I fall asleep picturing his face.*

As we head to Osei's, my mind drifts to a possibility I never expected: how easy it might be to slip back into something with Bruce. The idea is barely formed when the car's Bluetooth chimes. Osei Wharton flashes on the dashboard.

Bruce taps the steering wheel button. "Hey, Osei. You're on speaker."

"Good morning, Sese, the caterers are here. Should they set up here or upstairs?"

"Your place is fine. We're only minutes away. We'll see you soon. I'll text everyone to let them know that breakfast is at your place."

When we arrive at Osei's, he and the boys are drinking virgin Bloody Marys.

Justin holds up his glass and says, "Auntie Sese, this is out of this world good. Have you ever had one?"

"Yes. I'll have one of those, minus the virgin," I say to the bartender.

"Same here," Bruce says.

Everyone strolls in looking relaxed and well-rested.

Gloria looks at her sons.

"What are you all drinking?"

"A Bloody Mary," Jason says.

Justin corrects him. "A virgin Bloody Mary, and this is good. It's like drinking V8 on steroids. Mom, can you make these for us at home?"

"No, but your dad makes the best Bloody Mary. I'm sure he wouldn't mind," Gloria says.

With mimosas and Bloody Marys in hand, everyone heads to the buffet.

"Osei, how is the new shoe for Nike coming along?" Jackson asks.

"I'm heading to the campus next Thursday to give my input on the latest designs."

Osei looks at the boys. "Would you two be interested in evaluating the shoe for me?"

Both Justin and Jason scream, "Yes!"

"Osei, you are totally spoiling them," Jackson says.

"That's what family does," he says, looking at the boys. "Am I right, cuz?"

"Absolutely," Justin says.

Bruce excuses himself to take a phone call. When he returns, he has a very strange look on his face.

"Bruce, is everything okay?" I ask.

"Well, that will depend on your perspective. Ms. Hannah died this morning," he says.

"Did she really kill herself?" Gloria asks.

"That evil woman is too vain and ornery to kill herself under any circumstances," Dee replies.

"Dee, I think you're right. She didn't kill herself. She was murdered. Ms. Hannah's friends didn't trust her to keep quiet. Dave is investigating how she was killed. Only FBI agents and the police were allowed in the area where she was being held. It's a mystery. And get this! He told me that the autopsy performed on Ms. Hannah's husband proves he was murdered," Bruce says.

"I knew it. She killed him!" I exclaim.

May God rest her soul." Rainey sighs. "Since we only have a few hours to be together, the last thing I want to do is waste another minute talking about Ms. Hannah."

"Gloria, when are you heading home?" Dee asks.

"Wednesday evening. The reading of the will is tomorrow, and Jackson is meeting with lawyers on Tuesday. Jackson's dad left mostly everything to the boys, but guess what? He left the Vineyard property to me."

We all squeal with excitement.

"Wow, I can walk to the Inkwell now," Rainey says.

"Perfect. Now you can charm donors and work the beach, just try not to get us kicked out," Taylor quips.

"My dad loved my family more than he did me," Jackson says.

"You should be ashamed of yourself," Gloria says. "Your trust is the biggest of all."

"What did I do wrong? Am I the only one on welfare?" Bruce says.

Osei raises his glass for a toast, saying, "What matters most is family. To family!"

"What time is our train?" Eric asks.

"6:45 P.M.," Dee responds.

"Good, we can have drinks made with a bit more of a kick," Eric says.

"Better yet, we can skip the train and let someone else drive us back to Manhattan. I can rent a luxury party bus, which will pick us up at Sese's at nine o'clock tonight," Arjun says.

"Hey, bartender, I guess you can keep the drinks coming," Kelvin says.

Later, everyone, including Bruce, leaves on the party bus. Osei heads to New Jersey to hang out with some of his teammates. Jackson and the boys leave to watch a baseball game on TV, and Gloria and I enjoy a soothing cup of coffee on the deck.

"Sese, where did Bruce spend the night?"

"Here. With me. But nothing happened."

"Whether anything happened or not, you all are heading in the right direction."

"Only time will tell," I say.

We watch the stars and drink our coffee in silence. Jackson opens the patio door. "Osei's called, he's ten minutes away."

45

New Heart

Osei arrives and joins us on the deck, while Gloria goes inside to help Jackson with the boys.

"Sese, I want to thank you for allowing me to be a part of this family you've created."

"You are welcome. Let's talk for a minute while they're getting ready. We need to discuss the next steps. Now that Ms. Hannah is out of the picture, we need to resume the search for your birth mother."

"What if I don't want to?"

"This isn't about want, it's about need. You have to close this chapter, or you won't be able to start new ones. For your sake and mine. Do I have to remind you about regret?"

"No, regret is the most painful thing in life," he sheepishly says.

"Then there's only one thing left to do. We finish what we started."

"Okay, we can resume the search. Are you nervous?"

"Nervous about what?"

"Your big day tomorrow."

"I'm resigning. I'm not nervous. I don't know what I'm feeling, but it isn't nerves. Now that it's happening, I just want it to be over."

Osei hugs me goodnight and leaves with the boys. Jackson and Gloria head downstairs. I want to call Rhett. It's 11:30 pm here. Depending on how you see it, it's either late-night or early-morning in London. I choose early morning and hope he does too.

"Good morning."

"Hello, Rhett, I was hoping you were awake."

"I'm starting my workout. What's up?"

"I want you to know I'm resigning."

"Good. I'm very happy for you."

"Are you really?"

"Sese, I told you earlier, this is a good move for you. Also, I may have a sponsor for Osei."

"Seriously?"

"Yes. I had a meeting with the CEO of a PR firm, and they have a high-end European luxury auto manufacturer looking for an athlete to be the face of the brand in North America. Do you think it would be okay to bring up Osei's name?"

"I'll get back to you after I talk to Osei."

"Good luck, and don't let Jack talk you out of leaving."

"I won't. I've made a promise to Osei that I can't break. Rhett, thank you."

"For what?"

"For always supporting me."

I hear a female voice in the background, "Rhett, who are you talking to?"

"I'm talking to Sese," he replies.

The voice responds, "Does she know what time it is in London?"

"Yes, she knows, and apologizes for waking you."

I lower my voice and say, "Why didn't you tell me you had company?"

"I found someone I want you to meet. I really like her. Actually, I'm completely smitten."

"This is splendid news. I can't wait to meet her."

46

Save Those Happy Tears for Me

Early Monday morning, I arrive to pack and clean out my desk. Chloe walks in, notices the empty spaces where photos and plaques used to be, and her eyes instantly well up.

Trying my best to assure her, I say, "Chloe, don't cry, I have plans for you. I need time to set everything up at the foundation. In two months, I can bring you on board."

"Why can't I leave with you now?" she asks.

"I'm here for at least another month, so technically, it will only be a month."

"You promise," she says, wiping her face. "Jack is looking for you."

"Thank you, I need to see him too."

I knock softly on Jack's door.

"Come in," he says.

"Good morning, Jack."

"Morning, Sienna. I need you to work your magic once again. There's an issue."

Before he can finish his sentence, I choke back tears and say, "I thought this would be easy, but now that I'm seeing you, I'm having a hard time."

"What's wrong? Please don't tell me you're leaving."

"Yes, I have an opportunity I absolutely can't say no to."

"Are you going to one of our competitors? I'll match what they're offering."

"I'm not going to a competitor. In fact, I'm leaving the industry and creating a foundation for my son."

He looks puzzled and says, "Your son?"

"Let me clarify, my adopted son."

"Your adopted son? When did this happen?"

"About eight months ago," I say. "His name is Osei Wharton." It hits me. This is the first time I'm saying it out loud.

He stares in disbelief. "Osei Wharton is your son? My boys and I absolutely love him, and they will love you forever if you get his autograph."

"Of course, Jack, I want to make sure there's a smooth transition of accounts. I'm giving a month's notice unless you want me to leave sooner?"

We're interrupted by a knock on the door.

Chloe steps in and says, "Sienna, you have visitors."

"Really, I don't have any appointments this morning."

"It's Osei Wharton and another man. I took them to your office."

Jack jumps up from his chair and bolts down the hall. Chloe and I follow him to my office, where Osei and Bruce are standing, waiting.

Osei hands me a large bouquet. I make the introductions. Jack is like a kid on Christmas morning; he can't contain his excitement. I suspect he forgot about my resignation; my departure is now old news. Osei signs autographs for Jack and others in the office.

Bruce, shaking Jack's hand, says, "I hope you don't mind. Osei and I ordered a coffee and an ice cream truck for the office as a farewell gift from Sese."

We all go make our way to the parking lot. A large banner is draped across the front of the trucks. It reads GOOD LUCK, SIENNA. I start to cry, and Osei hugs me.

"We weren't going to let you go through this by yourself. You have spent too many years on your own, and from now on, we'll always be by your side. Sienna, I'm sure your co-workers have never seen you cry. So don't let them see you cry today. Save those happy tears for me and Osei. You are not allowed to share them with anyone else," Bruce says.

Jack and I step away while everyone else stays with Osei, enjoying the coffee and ice cream. We pick up our conversation, agreeing on a month's notice, so we can reassure clients that the level of service they're used to won't change after I leave.

"It will be hard to replace you," Jack says.

"You can never replace me," I tease. "But if you need to brainstorm, I'm a phone call away. And my new office is directly across the street,"

"Don't forget about us." He takes my hands and gives them a warm squeeze.

"I'm not gone yet," I say. "Save the mushy stuff for later."

Chloe helps me take several small boxes filled with photos and awards to my car. "You'll be here tomorrow, right?" she asks.

"Sure, I'm here for a month."

I get in my car, and I take a deep breath and slowly let it out. All in all, today was a good day.

Gloria and Jackson are at my place when I get home.

"How did the reading of the will go?" I ask.

"There were no surprises," Jackson answers.

Gloria hands me a glass of wine, and I raise it. "Here's a toast to no surprises!"

Osei and Bruce arrive a few minutes later.

"I can't believe you all started drinking without me," Bruce says.

"We just started, so there's no need for you to scold us," Gloria says while pouring a glass for him.

"Let's order out, I'm starving." I grab the menu. "Pizza, Italian, Chinese, or Thai?"

After dinner, Bruce and Jackson step outside to smoke cigars in memory of Jackson's father, who loved a good cigar.

The boys leave with Osei to work out at his place.

Gloria sips on her wine. "It has been a long time since I have seen this Sese."

"Really? And exactly what Sese are you seeing now?"

"A happy Sese."

"I've been happy before."

"Maybe, but not in the last few years. You've lived a life of contentment, not happiness. You never even showed any desire to achieve true happiness. You pushed away anyone who showed interest, settling for situationships because they were easier. Still, something always felt missing. Not anymore."

"So what do you think was missing? Pray tell?"

"Sese, you were missing, you were in denial about wanting a family."

"You are wrong. You all are my family."

"You are right about that, and we'll always be your family, but Osei has captured your heart in a way only a child can."

With measured words, I say, "Gloria, all these years I've pretended not to feel anything. It was how I coped with the emptiness."

"I know." She raises her glass. "A toast to Sese and her son."

Bruce and Jackson walk in just as we're toasting.

"We have a couple of alcoholics on our hands," Bruce jokes to Jackson.

"When we left, you were toasting. What are you all celebrating now?" Jackson asks.

"I'm making a toast to Sese and Osei," Gloria announces.

"I'll drink to that," Jackson says.

The next day. Bruce leaves to meet a colleague downtown. Osei and I take Gloria and her men to the airport. I hate seeing her leave. It has been nice having her around.

Pulling away from the Terminal, Osei says, "Sese, will you be able to go with me to Oregon to meet with the Nike design team? I need to review the designs for the new shoe."

"I hadn't planned on going. I didn't think I was needed, but... Osei, I have an idea. Do you want to hear it?"

"Sure."

"I thought we should set up a meeting with everyone who will be involved with the foundation. Since a majority of the potential board members are on the West Coast, why not have the meeting at the house in Oregon over the course of a week?"

"I like the idea, a brainstorming session," he replies.

"Yes, I was thinking we could do this in two months or so. I want to give everyone time to schedule it on their calendars."

"I'll send you the contact info of the people whom I'd like to be on the board."

"Great!"

"Sese, would you have an issue with Bruce being on the board?"

"No, of course not. Working in academia all these years, his knowledge would be invaluable."

"Do you want to ask him, or should I do so?" Osei asks.

"We both should."

"I agree."

"I'm thinking of asking Rhett. Why do you think? He has strong global contacts and might have an opportunity for you. Want to hear it?" I fill him conversation about the high-end

European luxury car brand that he wants him to be the face of their brand in the US, as well as the company's CEO's interest in helping to fund the foundation."

"I'm willing to speak to them. I'll ask Mark to set up a meeting."

47

Who Could She Be?

Once I'm home, I call Taylor. I have to talk to her immediately because the suspicion gnawing at me about who could be Osei's birth mother might be is growing stronger.

She picks up on the second ring. "Please hold on," she says quickly, her voice low and sharp, giving rapid instructions to her assistant.

"Hey, lovely, how are you doing?" Taylor asks.

"Why are you working so late?"

"I need to save up money for my wedding."

"Are you serious?"

"Just kidding about why I am working late. Last-minute project that has to be done, but as serious as a heart attack about getting married," she amusingly says.

"Congratulations, Taylor, I'm so happy for you. Have you set a date?"

"Not yet, maybe in the spring. But enough about me. How are you holding up? You've been through so much lately, an intense emotional rollercoaster."

"I'm fine, but I need your help. Looks like I'm about to buy another ticket for the emotional rollercoaster."

"Talk to me. What do you need?"

"I've restarted the search for Osei's birth mother." I hear her groan.

"Sese, I know you have your reasons, but can't you and Osei just move on?"

"Which is precisely why we need to start the search for his birth mother...because both he and I need to move on."

"I can't win with you! Okay, what do you need from me?"

"I need to find out everything you can about Vanessa Henry. If my memory serves me correctly, you and she were both finance majors."

"We were, but we weren't friends. But why did you think of her?"

"Because people on campus always mixed us up. And with how much Osei looks like me... she and I could've been sisters, right?"

"Yeah, but I doubt she could be Osei's mother. Her father was the president of the university, and she kept to herself. There were also rumors that she struggles with mental issues, which isolated her even more. But you might be right. For whatever reason, she really didn't like you."

"How could she not like me? She didn't know me at all."

"Don't quote me, but I think it was because of Bruce. She knew Bruce liked you, and she had a thing for Bruce. In fact, did you know Bruce went out on a few dates with her?"

"When?"

"Before he met you."

I don't say anything for a few seconds, my mind racing as I try to find the right words. Do I dare say this out loud? The silence hangs heavy between us.

"Sese, are you there?"

I take a deep breath and exhale slowly before speaking, my voice barely above a whisper.

"I'm here... and I do think Vanessa may be Osei's mother."

"What makes you think so?"

"Taylor, there was talk about her being pregnant."

"Yes, I remember, she was supposedly dating a naval officer."

"Is there any way you could find out if she had a baby?"

"I think there are a couple of people in my sorority who may know. I can reach out to them."

"Is it true she committed suicide?"

"I don't know. College rumors aren't always reliable. I heard she committed suicide, died in a car crash, or was killed by her boyfriend. No one seemed to know the truth."

"What happened to the boyfriend?"

"No one knows for sure, but if they were Osei's parents, then he truly is an orphan."

"What about her boyfriend? Maybe his parents are still alive?"

"You should also ask Bruce."

"Why?"

"Didn't you know Vanessa's boyfriend and Bruce were friends?"

"No, I didn't. I'll reach out to him. One more thing, can you also look into who set up the trust fund for Osei?"

"Sure, I'll see what I can do."

"Thank you, I promise to buy you an expensive wedding gift."

"Please don't. We don't need anything."

"Good night, Taylor."

The house feels so empty without Gloria and her men. I make myself a cup of tea and enjoy it sitting on the deck. My phone rings, and it's Rhett.

"Hello, Rhett, Osei is interested in knowing more about the auto endorsement."

"Good, because they're interested in talking to him."

"Perfect, he and his agent will be reaching out to you."

"I look forward to hearing from them," Rhett replies.

Afterward, I call Bruce.

"I was just about to call you," he says,

"You were?"

"Yes."

"To say what?" I ask.

"To say I missed you and want to see you."

I let my silence speak for me.

"I apologize for making you uncomfortable."

"No apologies necessary. I was calling because we need to talk."

"I'm a few minutes away from your place. I'll be there soon."

He hangs up, leaving me staring at my phone in disbelief.

My frustration builds. Does he really think he can just show up at my home? Yet the moment he walks up the driveway, my anger disappears. *Trust Sese. Trust.*

Millie and I greet him at the door. I hand him a scotch on the rocks. He takes a slow sip, eyes on mine.

"This must be a serious talk."

"I want to talk to you about Vanessa Henry."

"That's a name I haven't heard in twenty-plus years. Why do you want to talk about her?"

"I understand that you dated her after you dated Rainey."

"Whoa, I never dated Rainey. We went out a few times."

"Seriously?"

"Yes, seriously. I was never intimate with Rainey. I don't think we even kissed."

"Why not?"

"Because her mouth was never closed long enough for me to kiss her, she talked nonstop, and if you haven't noticed, she's been that way for these past twenty years. As for Vanessa, yes, we kissed, but we were never intimate."

"Do you remember anything about her death?"

"The rumor mill says suicide, but I know for a fact she died in a car accident."

"How do you know for a fact?"

"She was in the car with a friend of mine. They hit an underpass on the highway, and both of them died."

"Who was that?"

"It was Phillip Douglass."

"I don't think I knew him."

"He was in the navy, and he and Vanessa were on their way to get married when they died."

"Oh, my God. Was she pregnant?"

"No, she had given birth a few months before she died."

"I wonder where the child is now?"

A light went on in Bruce's eyes. "You don't...mean..."

"I do."

Bruce exhales. "I can see it now. Why didn't I think of this sooner? I heard President Henry sent the baby to live with a relative in New York."

"But why wouldn't he keep the baby?"

"President Henry was a widower and a busy man. Running the university and serving on several Fortune 500 boards kept him away constantly. I'm sure he thought about the baby's welfare and knew he wasn't equipped to raise a child."

"What about Phillip's family? Why didn't they take the baby?"

"Phillip was an orphan. He grew up in foster care in Detroit. Do you really think they may be Osei's parents?"

"I don't know, but it's worth looking into."

"From what I understand, Vanessa gave birth to a girl, so while it seems plausible, it may not be the case."

"Are you one hundred percent sure? Did you see the baby? Who told you it was a girl?" I rapid-fire questions.

"Sese, I can only answer one question at a time. No, I'm not one hundred percent sure, and no, I did not see the baby. It was rumored she had a girl."

"So, the baby could have been a boy for all we know. Bruce, do you want to know what I think?"

"I'm sure you are going to tell me."

"What if President Henry lied and didn't send the baby to New York after all, but to Wharton instead? And to cover it, he told everyone he had a granddaughter. Can you imagine the scandal if people found out he placed his own grandchild in an orphanage? Wasn't he a board member at Wharton?"

"Yes. I saw him whenever I worked the fundraising galas there."

"Do you think he was the one who started the trust for Osei? Osei was only six when President Henry died. Did he ever visit him? How could he just leave him there? What kind of person does that?"

"I honestly don't know, Sese. You need to slow down. You're spiraling. There's no way that he would have left his only living relative at an orphanage."

"I remember you saying we should follow the money. If we dig deeper into who really funded Osei's Trust, we might start connecting the dots. Until I have something solid, we can't bring Osei into this. I just can't."

"I agree."

"I asked Taylor earlier to look into the origins of the trust."

"She's a financial bloodhound, and if anyone can follow the money, it will be her," Bruce says.

"What happened between you and Vanessa?"

"You happened to Vanessa. After I saw you, you were all I could think about."

Probing, I ask, "When was the first time you saw me?"

"You were playing ping-pong with the tennis player from Brazil. What was his name again?"

"Roger De Souza."

"Yes, you were playing ping-pong with him at the Student Union."

"That was the beginning of my first year. I didn't meet you until the beginning of my second year."

"I had to do some research before I could approach you."

"Research? What type of research?" I inquire.

"I had to make sure you weren't seriously seeing anyone. That you were a good person, and that you were comfortable being you. I knew your parents were wealthy, so I wanted to make sure you weren't a spoiled brat."

"What do you mean, comfortable being me?"

"Someone who isn't easily led around by others, someone grounded and comfortable in the skin your parents gave you."

"Here I was thinking it was love at first sight," I quip.

"Sese, it was for me. Haven't I always told you I loved you more than you loved me? I was in love with you for at least seven months before we accidentally bumped into one another during homecoming weekend, your sophomore year."

"Couldn't you have introduced yourself without spilling a pitcher of beer on me and ruining my favorite sweater?"

"Every time I tried to approach you, some other guy was already talking to you. By the way, did your sweater really cost five hundred dollars?"

"It costs more. My mom bought it for me while she was in Paris. Why did it take you six months to pay me?"

"I dragged out the payments so I could see you."

"Your plan was successful. You grew on me."

"Sese, when did you fall in love with me?"

"Honestly, I knew I liked you when you spilled the beer on my new cashmere sweater, but I fell in love with you the first time you took me out to dinner. I drank too much wine, ended up wasted, and you held my hair every time I threw up. I'll never forget how you carried me back to campus, on your back. That's when I knew I'd love you with all my heart and soul, sober or not."

"You serenaded me all the way back to campus."

"I don't remember that. What did I sing?"

"Somewhere Over the Rainbow."

"Which version, Judy Garland's, or Patti LaBelle's?"

"The drunkard's version. Thank you for loving me back then. I hope you'll do so again."

Before I can respond, Osei walks right in.

"What are you doing here? I thought you would be at practice," I ask.

"Practice, we're talking about practice," Bruce says, laughing.

"In the words of Allen Iverson, you can't be talking about practice," Osei adds.

He turns to me and says, "Sese, don't you remember what Iverson famously said about practice?"

I give him a blank stare, and he quickly adds, "Never mind. Did you tell Bruce about the foundation summit you are planning at the house in Oregon?"

"No, I didn't have the chance."

"Then what were you two talking about?" Osei asks.

"I'm trying to convince her to fall in love with me again," Bruce says.

"Man, you are not afraid to put your feelings out there, and you don't care who knows how you feel about Sese," Osei says.

"I spent so many years not being able to express my feelings. I intend to make up for lost time. Sese, I'm sorry if I'm making you uncomfortable again," Bruce says.

"You can't prove that by me," I say, irritated.

Changing the subject, Bruce says, "I want to hear more about the summit you are planning."

"I'm still flushing out the details and...."

Osei interrupts, saying, "Bruce, Sese, and I would like for you to be our first board member."

Bruce exchanges a glance with Osei before turning to me. "I'd be honored."

"Great! Now that you are a board member, you can help me prepare the agenda for the summit," I add, laughing.

"For sure. I'm at your beck and call," Bruce says.

"That statement just made me cringe," Osei says.

"Oh my God, this is what makes you cringe. Not all the nonsense he said earlier about loving me? Osei Wharton, you are a very weird person."

48

Poppa Henry

"Speaking of boards, Osei, have you considered being on the board at Wharton?" Bruce asks.

"I think it will be enough if the foundation has a relationship with the orphanage," Osei says, fidgeting, clearly irritated.

"What is it you are not telling us?" I ask.

"There's nothing I'm not telling you. I don't want to be on the Wharton board."

I fix him with my "I don't believe you" look.

"Okay, when did you become a mind reader?"

A strange look comes over his face. "I don't know what any of this means, but recently I've been having dreams about a man I called Poppa Henry. It feels mostly like a dream, but it feels real, too. This Poppa Henry would play with me at the orphanage and often took me to the playground and to go fishing. Once, I even caught a fish. When he came around, we played board games, and he bought me my first basketball. Then one day he told me that he was sick, and he wasn't going to be able to come and see me anymore. I actually remember crying, for some reason, when I was six, but honestly, I don't know why. I truly didn't remember much from back there, but this memory or dream has been making me sad."

.

I look at Bruce, not believing my ears.

"I don't want to think about Wharton. It brings back memories I don't understand."

"Perhaps you blocked them out because it was a painful memory," I say softly.

"I had happy memories, too. Anyway, Sese, if it's a real memory, he was so nice to me? If it's a dream, it makes me sad."

I take Osei's hand. "Osei, we think Poppa Henry was actually President Henry and your grandfather."

"What? Is there really someone called Poppa Henry? What are you talking about?"

"Yes, Osei... there was."

Tears welled up in his eyes.

"Poppa Henry was the father of a woman named Vanessa Henry. Her boyfriend was Phillip Douglass. I believe they may be your parents, but I'm not one hundred percent sure. There were rumors that Vanessa and Phillip had a baby girl."

Osei seems frozen, struggling to process what he just heard. After a long pause, he draws a sharp breath.

"I need to make a call," he says, pulling out his phone.

"Hello, Mr. Thomas. This is Osei Wharton. I need you to investigate three individuals who lived in Virginia." He gives the names, then hangs up.

Sliding the phone back into his pocket, he says, "We'll know soon enough if this is my family."

"Who is Mr. Thomas?" I ask delicately.

"The private investigator who found you."

"Sese, I think you should send Mr. Thomas a thank-you gift," Bruce says quietly.

I look at Bruce and I acknowledge his statement with a smile.

"Sese what are you thinking?" Osei says.

"Why me? I keep asking myself this question. Who decided to give you to me and make me your mother? If Ms. Hannah knew about your parents and grandfather, why did she forge our names on your birth certificate?"

"What if she had nothing to do with it?" Bruce says. "What if Vanessa, on her own, decided to give her baby up for adoption and used our names?"

"It's a plausible explanation, but until we have all the facts, I think we should table this conversation for now," I say.

Bruce heads home, and Osei and I head out for a hike. Looking over my shoulder at the three men trailing us, remembering the attack ordered by Mrs. Hannah.

"Osei, Ms. Hannah is gone. I don't need a security detail."

"As long as I'm famous, you'll have one. Once people know we're connected, you become a target for someone to get to me."

I take his arm. "You've got quite the imagination."

"Maybe, but Fan is short for fanatical for a reason."

Jokingly, I ask, "How much would you pay for my safe return?"

"Every dime I have, but I'm sure Bruce would do a Mission Impossible rescue before I had to."

"Sese, it's okay."

I glance at him. "Okay, to do what?"

"To love Bruce."

"We've got a lot of healing to do. But I'm glad you like him."

Back home, we relax on the deck with tall glasses of iced tea.

"If Poppa Henry was my grandfather, why did he leave me at Wharton?"

"I can't answer that question. Osei, do you have a sense of how long President Henry visited you?"

"My memories are all jumbled together, and I don't have a sense of time. There were birthday gifts and Christmas gifts from him, but the gifts stopped coming after Mr. Albert died. Why couldn't he love me?"

I start to answer, but I see tears rolling down his face. I cradle his face in my hands and wipe them away. "Osei, you were loved. Maybe they couldn't tell you, but you were."

He rests his head on my shoulder, and we sit in silence. I look down and I realize he's fallen asleep. Carefully, I ease his head off my shoulder, get a blanket, and tuck it around him. I sit down next to him, and soon drift off, too.

When I wake up, Osei is standing at the edge of the deck. I walk over to him. "A penny for your thoughts?"

"This thought is worth a quarter."

"I remember who named me Osei, it was Poppa Henry."

"What was your name before he and others started calling you Osei?"

"I don't remember. I've always been Osei."

"With your memories coming back, are you going to be okay? Do you want to spend the night?"

"I can't. I'm leaving for Oregon tomorrow. Did you forget?"

"I did. But are you okay to travel?"

"I am. I'll be okay. I'll wait until I hear from the private detective before jumping to any conclusions."

I take my car keys from the counter.

"Where are you going?" he asks.

"I'm going to follow you home and pick up Millie. She can stay with us while you are gone."

"I've made plans for her."

"Okay." He walks toward the door, and I follow him.

"You are determined to follow me home."

"Yes, for an intelligent person, you are not very bright. You should know by now, when it comes to your well-being, I'll not waiver, and I won't take no for an answer. Even if I must protect you from yourself."

We arrive at Osei's apartment.

"Osei, would you like a cup of hot chocolate?" I ask.

"Yes, I'm going to shower. I'll be back shortly."

I call Bruce because I know he's worried about Osei. And to tell him about my conversation with Osei.

"Bruce, I'm worried about him," I say quietly.

"Sese, I didn't think much of your theory because I couldn't wrap my mind around either scenario. The parents giving Osei up for adoption, or President Henry leaving him at Wharton knowing he was his grandson. If what Osei remembers is the truth, then the truth lies somewhere in those two scenarios."

"Osei is pretending he's fine, but I can tell he's not. He leaves for Nike tomorrow to review his shoe design. I can't go. I have a meeting with Jack tomorrow morning, and Mark is on vacation. Are you available to go with him?"

"Yes, I'll pack and head to Philly. He's growing on me, too. I know he is going to be fine. After all, he has you, Sese. If what Osei remembers is the truth, then we are on our way to solving this mystery," Bruce says.

Osei comes downstairs, and I hand him a mug of hot chocolate.

"Who were you talking to earlier?"

"Bruce," I say.

Before I can say anything else, Osei says, "Do you think he could go to Oregon with me tomorrow?"

"He's packing his bags, and he'll be here later tonight."

He gives me a hug. "Thank you."

"You are welcome. Osei, I can stay here tonight."

"Sese, I'm really okay."

I kiss him on the cheek. "I'll see you on Sunday."

Hugging me, he says, "Sese, I'm glad you are my mom."

"I love you too, and don't you forget it."

"Oh, by the way, where's Bruce spending tonight?"

"He has the code to your door. He'll be staying with you and Millie."

"I'm sure he won't be happy with that scenario."

"Good night, Osei. Call me before you leave tomorrow."

49

Worth the Wait

That night, I dream of being back in college. I'm talking with Vanessa.

"I know you think I don't like you," she's saying. "It's not that I don't like you. I just hate that Bruce does."

"I'm not going to apologize for that."

"There's no need to," she says. "Just promise me you'll take care of him."

"I can't promise you that I'll take care of Bruce."

She takes my hand. "I'm not asking you to take care of Bruce."

I lie still, replaying the dream in my head, struggling to make sense of it. Was it really just a dream?

The sudden ring of my phone jolts me. It's 1:00 A.M. Bruce is calling. I fumble to answer it. Why was he calling so late? Worried that Osei might have had a meltdown.

"Is Osei okay?" I ask, heart pounding.

"He's fine," Bruce says. He told me to stay at your place tonight."

"I'm going to hurt him. Where are you now?"

"In your driveway."

"I'll be down shortly."

I unlock the door and step aside to let him in.

"Sorry for waking you up."

"You should be. You know where the guest room is. I'm going back to bed. I need my beauty rest."

He catches my arm. "Mind if I sleep upstairs with you?"

"Sure, as long as you know we're just sleeping, and nothing else."

"I understand," he says, following me upstairs. I slip into bed as he heads to the bathroom to change. When he returns, I shift closer, melting into him as we settle into a warm embrace.

"Do you remember how many nights we slept together before you and I made love for the first time?" He asks.

"Yes, it was two months."

He kisses me on my shoulder and says, "It was worth the wait." I smile back at him. "Go to sleep."

I awake to the smell of coffee and an empty bed.

On my phone, a message from the council member: *Good morning, Sienna. I'm not feeling well and need to reschedule our meeting for Monday.*

I reply: *No problem, feel better. I'll see you on Monday.*

In the kitchen, Bruce is talking on his cell phone. He hands me a cup of coffee, and I go outside to enjoy it on the deck.

"Is everything okay?" I ask when he joins me.

"Not really. That was Charlotte. She wants to get back together. Sese, I have no intention of reconciling with my ex-wife. She knows that, and I want to make sure you know it as well."

"The thought never crossed my mind."

"Good. I was worried you thought otherwise."

"If I thought otherwise, you wouldn't be in my bed."

"While we're on the subject, will I have to wait three months?"

"Only time will tell my friend."

"I can wait." He pulls me close.

I pull away from him.

"Are you uncomfortable in my arms?"

"In your arms is where I want to be," I say, smiling.

"Then, where are you going?"

"To pack. My schedule cleared, so I'm coming to Oregon with you. I need to pack."

"Osei will be very happy."

"Don't say anything to him. I want to see the look on his face when I board the plane."

"It will be priceless," he says. "He really needs you now."

While I'm packing, I call Osei.

"Good morning Sese."

"Hey, handsome. What's happening? Are you excited about seeing the new shoe designs?"

"Yes, this will be it. No more changes."

"Are you nervous?"

"No, should I be?"

"If I were in your shoes, no pun intended, I'd be incredibly nervous. Bruce will be there to help you if you need advice."

"I know, but I wish you were coming with us."

"You both will be fine. Hugs and kisses. Call me when you all land."

"Tell Bruce I need to stop by the stadium, and I'll be a few minutes late."

Bruce and I head to the airport. Osei running late actually works in my favor. I board before he arrives, grab a blanket, and slip to the back of the plane.

"He's coming up the steps," Bruce announces.

I cover my head and Osei boards without noticing me. He embraces Bruce, but his energy is off.

"Are you okay? Was there an issue at the stadium?"

"No, I left my travel bag in my locker. I needed it for this trip."

"Why the long face?"

"I wish Sese could have come with us."

I tiptoe behind him, put my arms around his waist, and say, "Hello, my prince."

He turns around, and I can see joy return to his eyes.

"Sese, you're here. Thank you for coming."

"I guess now…" Bruce says. "…All is right in the world."

"Yeah. It is."

Osei hugs me like he'll never let go.

Once airborne, Bruce and Osei look over the shoe designs. I cover up and listen to a book on Audible.

I wake up to Bruce and Osei laughing.

"What is so funny?" I ask.

"We find it hilarious that you talk in your sleep," Osei says.

"I do not."

"Yes, you do," they both say.

"What did I say that was so funny?"

"You were asking someone to love you," Bruce says, with raised eyebrows.

I frown. "Apart from this not being true, why would it be funny?"

"It was humorous because you are in the presence of two people who love you more than you'll ever know," Bruce says.

Dismissing his statement, I walk to the galley. "I need a drink. Do you guys want anything?"

At Portland International Airport, I'm happy to see only one Range Rover waiting for us. Osei drops me off at the house, and he and Bruce head to the Nike campus.

"Welcome back, Ms. Lewis," Lucas says, opening the door.

"Hello, Lucas, I'm happy to see you."

"I'm putting your bags in the master suite on the third floor."

I give him a puzzled look. "I'll stay in the same bedroom as before—I love the view."

He smiles, "Ms. Lewis, this is your home, not a hotel."

He's right. This is my home. I head to the kitchen to get a glass of water and check my emails. Lucas shares the dinner menu with me. Grilled shrimp tacos with avocado salsa, Spanish rice, and a Mexican chopped salad.

"Let me guess, Osei called you."

"Yes, when he was leaving his appointment. Ms. Lewis, you know your son very well."

"Sese, where are you?" Osei yells as he and Bruce enter the house.

"In the kitchen," I yell back.

Lucas hands them both a glass of water.

"Do you have something a little stronger?" Bruce asks.

"How about a margarita?"

"Perfect, just what I need," Bruce says.

We eat dinner outside, lounging by the pool.

"Osei, how did the design review meeting go?" I ask.

"It went very well. I'll be in New York soon to start filming the commercials for the launch."

"How exciting. Your commercial's being directed by the one and only Spike Lee! He did Jordan's commercials back in the day. Imagine if he actually resurrected Mars Blackmon. Now that would be hilarious," Bruce says, clearly thrilled.

I raise my glass for a toast to his success, but before I can say anything, Osei says, "Sese?"

Bruce smiles, trying to hold back the laughter. "Just wait for it."

I look at both of them, confused. "Wait for what? Osei, what have you done now?"

Osei grins, "I'm not saying. It's a little surprise."

"A little surprise, with you, nothing is little."

Bruce chuckles, "He made the design team put the word Sese on his shoe."

"I asked them nicely, and when they told me no, I told them the matter was not up for debate."

"Why on earth would you do that?"

"Because you inspire me. Even before I met you, I'd think about you before each game I played in. I imagined you being in the stands, cheering me on."

"Have you given any thought as to how you'll explain my nickname on your shoe?"

"To me, it means courage and self-esteem."

"Sese, don't even try. This debate lasted for hours," Bruce says. "Are you upset?"

"Are you happy with your decision?" I ask.

"I'm over the moon," he excitedly says.

"Then so am I."

After dinner, I head upstairs and fall asleep almost instantly. I wake to the soft rustle of sheets and find Bruce sleeping next to me. I gently touch his face, and he opens his eyes.

Taking my face, he kisses my forehead and nose, and then our lips touch. His kiss is magical and makes my head spin. I don't want him to stop. The slow, melodic rhythm of our lips, touching, pulling, remembering. My body responds instinctively, willingly. I pause, gently stroke his face, grounding us both.

"What I want to do with you won't happen tonight."

"Why?" His desire is unmistakable.

"Bruce, I have decided to give us a real chance. I want to be in my bed, alone with you, when this happens, and I don't want to rush. I want it to be never-ending, no meetings, no alarm clocks, and most of all, no Osei. I promise you it will be worth the wait."

"In that case, I need to go take a cold shower."

"I'm sorry."

"You have nothing to be sorry for. I'll be back in a few minutes."

I don't remember him coming back to bed. I slept soundly through the night.

Bruce and Osei are in the kitchen, eating and watching ESPN, when I head down for breakfast. Lucas hands me a cup of coffee.

"Thank you, Lucas, may I have an egg white omelet with onions, avocado, and tomatoes?"

"Of course. Coming right up."

"Good morning, handsome." I kiss Osei on the cheek.

He smiles, looks at me, and then at Bruce. "How was your night?" he asks.

"I can only speak for myself, but I slept very well," I say, not looking at Bruce.

"And yours, Bruce?"

"Just great," he says dryly, biting into his toast.

Bruce and Osei leave for the Nike campus to finalize some paperwork. Lucas and I go to the pergola to discuss menu ideas for the upcoming foundation summit.

"I can give you a list of local caterers to choose from," Lucas says.

"I already have a caterer, and it would be great if you would assist her."

"Is she local?" he asks.

"No, Dee Patterson and her team will be flying in from New York."

"You know Dee Patterson?" he exclaimed.

"Yes, she's one of my best friends, and one of Osei's godmothers."

"I'm a huge fan of hers. I watch her show every Sunday."

"I'll be sure to tell her."

"I would be more than honored to assist her." Lucas beamed, leaving to go prepare dinner. Maybe I spoke too soon. I haven't formally asked Dee to cater the summit, and it would be horrible if she isn't available. I immediately call her.

"Dee, were your ears burning? I was just talking about you?"

"Talking to someone, or just yourself again?"

"Ha, ha, ha. I'm in Oregon with Osei, and I was talking with the estate manager. Turns out he's a big fan of yours."

"Send me his contact information and I'll send him a signed cookbook."

"I'm hoping you will give it to him personally."

"If he wants tickets to a live show, I'll make it happen."

"Of course, you can, but I was hoping you would come to Beaverton, Oregon, in October."

"And why would I be coming to Beaverton, Oregon?"

"You make it seem like Beaverton is two blocks south of hell."

"Convince me otherwise."

I explained the details of the summit to her, covering the agenda and what we hoped to accomplish.

"October is two months from now. What are the dates?"

"Dee, I can plan the dates according to your schedule."

"Okay, I'll check with my crew and get back to you. In the meantime, I'll need you to send me pictures of the kitchen, storage, and of any appliances, such as freezers and/or refrigerators, not located in the main kitchen."

Lucas emails me photos of everything Dee requested, along with a blueprint of the main and prep kitchens. He also sends an *Architectural Digest* article featuring the property, which I forward to Dee.

Relieved, I change into my swimsuit and head to the pool. I am on my third lap when I see Bruce and Osei standing at the edge of the pool. I swim over to them.

"You should join me. The water is outstanding."

"I can't, I need to make a few calls. I'll catch up with you two later," Bruce says.

Osei kicks off his shoes, and he dangles his feet in the water.

"What's up, why the long face?"

"I was forced to remove your name from my shoe."

"You can always write my name on your shoe."

"I know, but I wanted you to know how much you inspire me."

I pull on his toes. "We inspire each other. Having my nickname on your shoe isn't a big deal."

I say, eyeing his feet in the water.

"Your feet are huge! What size are those?"

"Sixteen."

"Seriously?" You could fit all fifty states and still have room for my full name."

He laughs so hard he nearly falls in, and his laugh is so infectious it makes me double over.

"Osei, stop! You're killing me."

"Can you two keep it down?" Bruce calls from the balcony. "What is so funny?"

Osei and I look at each other and burst out laughing all over again.

At the end of another perfect day, I slip into bed next to Bruce.

"You've got the magic touch," he says. "Osei was upset after we left the campus, but you helped him to put it all in perspective."

I give him a puzzled look. "Perspective?"

"He now understands that having your name on his shoe isn't important. What matters is having you in his life. It's all about perspective."

"Hmm, perspective, I like that. Good night, Bruce."

"Good night, Sese."

I can't sleep, so I slip out of bed and go downstairs for a warm cup of milk. Only to find Osei sitting at the counter watching TV.

I hug him from behind. "Osei, is the TV in your room broken?"

"No, just sleep."

"Same here. I'm going to make myself a cup of golden milk. Want some?"

"Sure, what is golden milk?"

"Bruce makes it when I can't sleep."

I hand him a cup. He takes a sip. "This is toe-tapping good."

"What's on your mind that's keeping you from sleeping?"

He mumbles. "Nothing in particular. I haven't heard from Mr. Thomas. It's making me anxious."

"I'm sure you'll hear something soon."

He pauses. "While we're on the topic of nothing in particular. What's going on with you and Bruce?"

I shoot him a look.

"Don't give me that look. I'm curious."

"Honestly? I'm not sure. Are you familiar with the meaning of the French word *dépaysement*?"

"No."

"It means feeling out of place, like you don't have a home. But when I'm with you and Bruce, it feels like home. We're trying to work through some things."

I read the look on his face. It says everything.

"Osei, don't worry. If Bruce and I ever hurt each other, we'll walk away. We'll either be together or we won't."

"I'm hoping you will be."

"Thank you, Osei Wharton."

I pull him close, resting his head on my shoulder. I grow heavy.

I nudge him. "Don't you dare go to sleep. I can't carry you upstairs."

"My suite's down here next to the gym."

I hug him goodnight and head upstairs.

I slip back into bed next to Bruce. He pulls me close. "Sese, I'm never going to hurt you, and I'm not walking away again." He kisses me deeply, then rests my head on his chest.

"Good night, Bruce."

As I drift off to sleep, it hits me. He overheard my conversation with Osei. My last thought before sleep, we need to have a conversation about eavesdropping.

The next morning on the plane, Bruce and Osei are looking at the final shoe design, exchanging thoughts. I watch them and smile, thinking, *Dépaysement no more. They are my home. My refuge."*

50

Someone Stole My Steering Wheel

Thanks to the time difference, we land in Philly in the early afternoon. The familiar skyline warms my heart. I love this city.

Osei needs to stop by the arena.

As we pull up, we see crowds gathered out front, and traffic is bumper to bumper.

Osei rolls down his window. "Hey, Tyler, what is going on?"

Tyler, the parking manager, grins. "They're here to buy your jersey!"

"My jersey has been out of stock for months. Why all the fuss?"

Bruce pulls out his phone and Googles Osei's name.

"Not anymore. According to this article, your jersey is back in stock, and it's the top-selling jersey in the NBA. Congratulations."

"We need to get out of here. I'll come back later."

"We're going to have a hard time getting out of here," Bruce says.

Osei's phone rings, "Hey Mark," he says.

"Congratulations, Osei, your Jersey went on sale today, and it sold out in a matter of hours."

"Thanks, man, I'm at the stadium now, and it's crazy here."

"Let's switch seats," Bruce says, noticing Osei fidgeting. "Are you okay?"

"I don't think I'll ever get used to everything that's happening. On and off the court. I don't deserve it."

"You deserve it. Your talents are undeniable. I'm just glad you are humble and staying grounded," Bruce replies.

"Thank you for saying so. I'm trying to come to terms with all the fame and accolades."

They're too tall to just climb over, so Tyler stops traffic. Osei pulls his hat low, they quickly switch spots, and he reclines his seat. Looking back at me, he says, "I'm glad I have you to help me navigate the good and the bad times."

Bruce looks through the rear-view mirror and carefully pulls out while Tyler holds the oncoming traffic at bay.

"So, Bruce," Osei says with a sly grin. "I know you love her, and I know she loves you. What can I do to move things along?"

Bruce looks at me through the rearview mirror, smirking. "Help?"

"Yes, help," Osei echoes, grinning at me.

I glare at him. He's acting like a mischievous twelve-year-old! "You're on your own," I say to Bruce.

Bruce turns serious. "Osei, Sese, and I are exploring possibilities. You can help by respecting the natural course we need to take. What I need is for her to openly love me. When she is ready. Sese loving me is a gift. But neither of us can force it. We can't rush or interfere with the rhythm, and neither can you. Do you understand? You must not do anything to disrupt the rhythm."

Poor Osei has no idea what Bruce is talking about.

"What is the best route to get out of here?" Bruce asks.

Osei amusingly replies, "You must decide. I wouldn't want to suggest anything which might interfere with your rhythm."

Bruce looks at him and they both burst out in laughter.

"Okay, smart-ass, how about we stop somewhere and get a drink?" Bruce suggests.

"I promised Sese I'd only drink alcohol at her house or my house, never in public. Right, Sese?"

"Yes, you promised. Bruce, you can drop me off at home, and you and Osei can drink to your heart's delight at his place."

"Osei, we'll have a drink at your place and call it a night," Bruce says.

Tomorrow is my last day at work, and I need to settle myself. Mike Tyson's quote comes to mind, *Everybody has a plan until you get punched in the mouth.* I hope and pray this works out, and I'm not walking around with a permanent black eye.

I feel a sense of relief when my cell phone rings.

"Oh my God, Sese the photos of the kitchen, are to die for. I showed them to my producer, and he lost his mind. He wants to film an episode of the show there before the start of the summit. Is it possible? Please say yes?" Dee pleads.

"Of course, it is. I'll connect your producer with Lucas, and they can work out the details. Does this mean you'll oversee the food preparation for the summit?"

"Yes," Dee excitedly says.

"Have your manager send me a contract to sign."

"No way, Sese. You are doing me a favor by letting me film my show there."

"Okay, but you must bring Arjun."

"I wouldn't dream of leaving him behind. In fact, I've already started to work on the menu. Here are my suggestions: a light breakfast with several food stations, a build-your-own yogurt station, a smoothie station, a breakfast meat station with both vegetarian, beef, and pork options, a waffle station with all the toppings, and last but not least, a muffin tin omelet with prosciutto, feta, and spinach station. Nothing that would put folk in a food coma."

Dee continues, "There would be a beverage station with water, tea, sodas, and coffee, which would be available from morning until the end of the meeting. We continue the light theme for lunch. A turkey spinach salad with Oregon Bigleaf Maple syrup, a salmon Caesar salad, an almond strawberry salad, tomato clubs, basil chicken sandwiches, and grilled shrimp tacos."

"Can we have two sandwich options?" I ask.

"Sure, we can eliminate one of the salads and go with a grilled steak sandwich instead."

"I like the salad choices. I think we should eliminate the tomato club."

"Okay."

We move on to desserts.

"Oh, by the way, include Godiva hot chocolate on the beverage cart. It's Osei's favorite. Let's have drinks and desserts at the close of each session. Make the desserts decadent."

"How about a chocolate crepe cake, strawberry cheesecake, an ice cream station, individual fried apple pies, and banana meringue pudding cups?"

"Dee, I have to go. Osei is on the other line. Let me know if you need anything else."

"Hello, my prince. I thought you'd be in a drunken stupor by now. Are you having a hard time sleeping?" I ask.

"No, I plan on being up for a while. I have a set play in my head, and I want to write it down to share with Coach. It will take me a while to put it all together."

"Excuse my ignorance, but what is a set play?"

"A set play is a designed and choreographed sequence of movements to get open shots and score points."

"Sounds like fun. Speaking of which, did you and Bruce have fun tonight?"

"Sese, hold on, I have another call coming in."

He comes back on the line, he says, "That was someone from your security team. There's a car parked in your driveway."

"Why did they call you and not me?"

Laughing hysterically, he says, "It's Bruce."

"Osei Wharton, what is going on? Why is he just sitting outside in his car?"

"That's a question you should ask him. I'll stay on the line."

I walk outside to find Bruce sitting in the passenger seat. I tap on the window, and he bolts upright. It takes him a few seconds to get his bearings.

"Bruce, are you alright?"

"Osei, seriously. Why did you let him drive?"

"Sese, I didn't. He had a driver to take him to the Four Seasons. He must have told the driver to bring him there instead."

"Sese, what are you doing here?" Bruce asks.

"Bruce, that's what I was going to ask you."

Bruce, in his inebriated drunk logic, says, "Sese, I was trying to drive to the hotel, but someone stole the steering wheel. Do you have an extra steering wheel?"

"He's drunk," Osei says, laughing uncontrollably.

"I know, Captain Obvious." I can barely keep a straight face myself.

"Bruce, you are sitting in the passenger seat. The steering wheel is on the other side of the car."

"Are you sure?" he asks.

"Can you walk inside? I ask.

He looks around and says, "I'm already inside."

"Yes, you are inside your car, come in the house with me."

Bruce looks at me, saying, "Okay."

"Osei, I'll call you back when we get inside."

"I'm on my way over. I have to see this," he replies.

Osei arrives in time to help me take Bruce inside.

"I told you, Sese and I have a natural rhythm," Bruce says to Osei.

"Yes, honey, we have a natural rhythm."

He points to Osei. "I told you." And he falls back onto the pillow.

Osei, not believing his eyes, says, "He's out like a light."

I hit Osei on his shoulder. "You are to blame for this. How much did he drink?"

"A half bottle of scotch." Wanting to change the subject, he asks, "How is everything going with the planning for the summit?"

"So far, so good. I'd like to extend a board membership to everyone we invite. What are your thoughts on that?"

"I totally agree."

Hugging me, he says, "I'll call you tomorrow."

I debate whether I should check on Bruce, but decide not to. Instead, I go upstairs and get into bed.

The sound of the phone ringing wakes me up I look at the clock, and it's 6:30 AM.

"Hello, it's me. I'm sorry for being a nuisance last night," Bruce says.

"It's okay, you were very entertaining, but not a nuisance."

I sit up in bed, noticing how distant he sounds. "Are you downstairs?"

"No, I didn't want to wake you. I'm heading home. I've got meetings today I can't reschedule."

"When will you return?"

"Tomorrow, I haven't forgotten that we have a meeting to discuss the foundation."

"I'll see you tomorrow. Drive safely," I reply.

51

Second Chance

It's my last day at work. These thirty days have flown by. I stand at the window, excitement rising in my chest, the air filled with a sense of possibility.

There's a knock on the door.

"Come in."

"Good Morning, Sese. Are you sure about this?" Jack asks.

"I'm sure. Jack, it has been a pleasure being a part of your team. We didn't always agree on everything, but our respect for one another was genuine."

"You are going to make me cry," Jack says.

Tears begin to roll down my face. He comes over and hugs me and says, "I heard what Bruce said to you the day you resigned. He told you your tears were reserved for those you love. Sienna Lewis, if you keep this up, you're going to make me think you love me."

"This is for you," he says, and hands me an envelope.

I open it and find a check for one hundred and fifty thousand dollars. "What is this for?" I ask. "Your bonus, but if you decide to stay, I'm willing to double it."

"No, I can't stay, but I'm willing to consult from time to time, if you need me to."

"Sese, are you serious?" Jack excitedly says.

"I'm willing, but if I feel like you are taking advantage of me. I'll stop."

He extends his hand. "We have a deal."

Chloe knocks on the door and says, "Excuse me, Rhett is on hold for you."

Jack leaves, saying, "Give Rhett my best."

"Rhett. How are you doing?"

"I'm doing very well. How about you?"

"I'm good. Has Osei been in touch with you?"

"He most certainly has. I just received an email from him asking me if I'd consider being on the board of his Foundation. I wanted to talk to you before I accepted."

"Rhett, you'd be invaluable. Why doubt yourself?"

"Are you sure?"

"Rhett, I'm absolutely sure. Mark your calendar for the first summit at the end of October. Do you think you can attend?"

"I'll check and get back to you. Congratulations on the next chapter."

"Hugs and kisses, I hope to see you soon."

Jack stops by and says, "The legal department is preparing the contract for you to become a consultant. You should have it early next week. Sese, you can't change your mind."

"I won't, I promise."

The phone, relentless as ever, rings once more!

"Congratulations, how do you feel?" Taylor asks. "I feel like I'm floating on a cloud, and I'm looking down at a shiny new toy."

"Good, do you think you could come down from the clouds and meet me in New York next Friday?"

"Sure, what is going on?" I ask.

"Eric and I are getting married, and I want you there."

"Wait, what! Did you say getting married on Friday, as in this Friday? Oh my God, Taylor, I'm so happy for you. What can I do to help?"

"Yup, there's nothing to do. I've made all the plans. I just want you beside me. We're not making a production of it. Dinner at Nobu after the ceremony. Rainey and Dee can't make the ceremony, but they'll join us for dinner. I don't expect Gloria and Jackson to come all the way out here for a City Hall wedding. Since you are in between jobs, I thought you could stand next to me."

"Taylor, I'd be honored."

This cannot be. Taylor can't get married without all of us being there! I immediately dial Gloria.

"Gloria, have you spoken with Taylor?"

"Yes, I cried tears of joy when she told me about her wedding. I want to surprise her! Jackson and I are flying into Philly on Thursday night. Can we stay with you?"

"Of course you can. We can all drive to New York on Friday morning."

I turned off the lights in my office for the last time. Instead of going home, I go to the foundation's office. Walking into the foyer of my new office still takes my breath away.

The electronic lock beeps, and I turn to see Osei walk in.

"Don't you have practice?"

"Yes, but I saw you driving into the garage and I wanted to say hello."

"I'm glad you did because I need a hug." I walk over, but he looks away. "Osei, are you alright?"

"Yes."

"If you are alright, then why can't you look at me?"

"Sese, I want you to be happy."

"Osei, I'm happy."

"Did I pressure you to head up the foundation?"

"Osei Wharton, I thought you knew me. If you did, you'd know I don't do anything I don't want to. So put your mind at ease. I'm doing this because I want to. Have you had a change of heart?"

"Absolutely not! I want you to head the foundation. I just want to make sure you want to."

"I'm all in. A handshake will seal the deal."

"A handshake and a hug will seal the deal," he says, pulling me into a bear hug.

"Good. Now get going… leave. You're going to be late for practice. Oh, by the way, Gloria and Jackson are flying in on Thursday. Can I use your SUV to pick them up?"

"Sure, I'll see you later." He leans in and gives me a peck on the cheek. "Thank You."

I watch him leave. A few minutes later, I leave the office, feeling good about my decision and imagining what lies ahead. My phone vibrates in my purse, and I'm instantly annoyed.

Today is one of those days I wish cell phones had never been invented. It's Bruce calling.

"Hey, Sese, can I stay at your place tonight?"

"Sure, what time will you arrive?"

"About 6:30 P.M., I'll pick up Chinese food and a bottle of wine."

"Mr. LeBlanc, are you trying to seduce me?"

Laughing, he says, "Not tonight, but hot and heavy seduction is in our future."

I take a deep breath. The visual I'm having is too graphic for me to manage.

During Dinner, I feel off balance, avoiding his eyes because there's too much I need to say. One look, and I'll lose my nerve. I drain my wine for courage.

"Slow down, cowboy!" he says, "What's going on? You haven't looked at me all night. Should I leave?

"No!" I say a little too fast.

"I have something to say, and I can't if you're not here."

"Sese, I'm listening. Take all night if you need. I'm not going anywhere."

"Do you know what I have learned over the past twenty years?" I ask.

"No, what?"

"There's no perfect way to love. There are seven billion people on the planet, so there are seven billion ways to love someone. I thought our love would last a lifetime and beyond."

"Sese, I'm sorry."

I place my hand on his lips. "Bruce, please don't interrupt me. If you do, I won't be able to say what I need to say. I thought we were committed to one another, and nothing or no one could break our bond. Do you know what I realized?"

He silently shakes his head.

"I took you and your love for granted. I knew you'd never leave me, so I acted like having a baby was no big deal because that was the story I needed to believe. I was so insensitive to your feelings. When you left, everything fell apart. I couldn't face life without you. Nothing mattered anymore..." My voice trails. "It was so unbearable. Two months after you left, I filled the bathtub with water, drank a bottle of wine, and took sleeping pills. I cut my wrists. I just needed to turn off my feelings for you."

Eyes shining with tears, he whispers, "Sese... why didn't you tell me?"

"After surviving, I couldn't tell you that I tried to kill myself, and because of that, I lost our second baby. I didn't want or need your pity. After years of extensive counseling and self-reflection, I could move forward with my life without you. Rhett was my healing balm. I couldn't love him in the way he needed to be loved, and I hurt him so badly he ran away to London. Bruce, if I had a time machine, do you know what moment I'd relive?"

Again, he just shakes his head.

"The moment I found out I was pregnant. I'd have picked up a cheesecake from Juniors and brought a box of expensive chocolates and a bouquet, opened a bottle of champagne for you, sparkling water for me, and celebrated us expecting our baby."

Tears lingered on Bruce's eyelashes, threatening to fall.

"When I first met Osei, I did everything I could to care for him. Then one day he told me, 'Sienna, I'm still going to love you.' When I asked him why, he said, 'Because I decided to.' I accused you earlier of not believing in us, when it was me who didn't believe in us. Forgive me, Bruce."

"I didn't know. I'd have been by your side. Why didn't you tell me?"

"I couldn't because you were getting married. I didn't want to interfere with your future and your happiness."

"Do you know how much I regret getting married?"

"Yes, I saw the pain on your face."

"Wait… What. You were at my wedding?"

"Yes, I slipped into the back of the church. The atmosphere was more like a funeral. When I saw you standing at the altar, I knew a part of you had died. I cried at that moment, knowing we would never be together. I wasn't strong enough to grab your hand and run away from the church, and from the pain we were both in."

Kissing the tears away from his eyes, I say, "We'll be alright. From now on, we'll love each other for an eternity. Because like Osei said, I've decided to."

As usual, Osei opens the patio door at the most inopportune moment. He stops at the sight of Bruce and me, both wiping away tears.

"Are you all okay?" he asks.

"Better than alright," Bruce says.

Osei looks at me, eyes dark with worry, as if bracing for a storm.

"Truly, I'm fine. Are you hungry, Osei?" I ask.

"Of course, I'm always hungry."

"There's Chinese food in the kitchen. I'll bring it out to you."

"Is she drunk?" I hear Osei whisper to Bruce.

"A bit, but I'm in heaven. Sese and I are going to be a couple again, and I thank the alcohol for allowing her to open up."

"Going to be a couple?" Osei's voice rose an octave.

"Yes. We'll be doing the things couples do." Bruce winks at him.

"Sese," Osei calls. "I need you to use protection when you all do the couple's thing."

"Boy, what are you talking about? Stop being silly."

Osei leaves to rest for an early practice tomorrow.

While Bruce is cleaning the kitchen, I make a call to Taylor to confirm the plans for her wedding.

She answers, "Sese, I'm so freaking happy. I can't sleep, eat, or breathe."

"Taylor, I'd highly recommend you do at least two of those things, or else you'll end up in the morgue rather than at the courthouse."

"Who is going to be Eric's best man?"

"It's Bruce, you didn't know? Eric's best friend is in the military, stationed in Germany, and he can't make it."

"Bruce has been terribly busy lately. It probably slipped his mind. Is there a specific color or style of dress I should wear?"

"Yes, white." A beat passes before she says. "I'm not serious, but I trust your taste and style, wear whatever you feel like wearing."

"Okay, Taylor, please eat and by all means, breathe. I'll see you soon."

Bruce finishes cleaning the kitchen and calls up to me, asking, "Sese, are you busy? Can I come up?"

"Sure, come on up."

He stops at the top of the stairs. "I'm going to crash at Osei's tonight. I'll see you in the morning."

"Bruce, you are welcome to stay here tonight."

"I need to think about what you told me. It makes me sick to think you tried to take your life because of me."

"I tried to kill myself because of me, not because of you. The hopelessness I was feeling was a result of not trusting myself to live without you."

"Every day, over five hundred thousand couples end their relationships. They survived. They moved on," he says.

"Bruce, are you saying we should continue to move on?"

"Sese, that's not what I'm saying or want. I just need to think. I'll see you tomorrow morning."

Osei calls. "Bruce asks if he could crash over here. Is everything okay between you two?"

"We're fine. He needs to think about a few things."

"Think about what?"

"Mind your business. There's nothing to worry about. We're okay."

"I thought it may have something to do with the couple's thing."

"Good night, and take care of Bruce."

"Roger that. Good night, I love you, Sese."

"I love you more."

"Bruce is at the door," Osei says.

"Okay, ask him to call me before he goes to bed."

Bruce calls and, in a sorrowful voice, says, "Sese, why didn't you tell me about the second baby?"

"I didn't know about the second baby until it was too late. There was no need to complicate your life or mind any further."

"Sese, I'm so very sorry I wasn't there to kiss away the tears."

"No, you were not, but you are here now. Bruce, there's nothing between us now but space and time. We have to let the past go and fill the space we have now with wonderful memories. Tonight, I took the first step to rid myself of the pain and the guilt. I don't blame you for anything that happened because blame is like a sore. It never heals."

"I'm taking two giant steps. I'll see you shortly," he says.

Osei calls again, saying, "Sese, what is going on? Why is Bruce playing musical houses?"

"Mind your business, Osei Wharton, be here tomorrow morning for breakfast."

52

Jupiter

I open the door for Bruce. He lifts me into his arms, and I wrap my legs around his waist, resting my head on his shoulder as he carries me upstairs. We lie facing one another. I kiss his nose and whisper, "I want us to do the couple's thing."

"Sese, do you know how many times I've dreamed of this? You and me doing the couple's thing?"

As I unbutton his shirt, I murmur, "The mind can fantasize, but the body never forgets."

I kiss his chest and take his nipple in my mouth. Moaning, he says, "Sese, you'll have to slow down." He lifts my face, kisses me, and rolls on top of me. His taste is unforgettable.

I pull away from him. "Is it my heart or your heart I hear pounding?"

"Both," he says. "But don't worry, it will synchronize soon."

He kisses me again, slow and deliberate. Our eyes meet. "Sese, are you as nervous as I am?"

"Yes," I say softly. "But don't worry, we still have the magic."

He kisses, moving lower, and when his lips reach my breast, my nipples harden. I moan and move slowly underneath him. "Where are you taking me tonight?" I whisper in his ear.

"We're going to Jupiter," he murmurs, his hands guiding my hips, pulling me softly toward him.

"I haven't been to Jupiter in years," I say with a breathless smile. "I've missed it."

I gently push him down, opening myself for him, wrapping my legs around him as our bodies fall into rhythm. His voice breaks as he whispers my name.

"Sese, can we go to Jupiter next time? I think we're only going to make it to Mars."

We both tremble and shake in ecstasy. Afterwards, he looks at me, eyes glistening.

"I'm never going to let you go again."

I gently wipe his tears. "Promise? Because I can't go twenty seconds without you?"

I start to rise from the bed.

"Where are you going?" he asks softly.

"I'm going to get some water. Would you like a glass?"

"You are so beautiful. Your body hasn't changed."

"You don't have to flatter me. It all belongs to you."

He wakes me in the middle of the night.

"How about we orbit around Earth?"

I push my bottom into his, and as we orbit Earth, I see stars and the moon, again and again. When I wake up, I look at us, and I can't tell where his body ends, and mine begins. Bruce pulls me closer. "What time is it?" he asks.

I look at the clock. "It's 5:30 A.M. We have two more hours before we have to get out of bed."

"Good, I need to recharge my battery."

I turn to him and ask, "How are we going to navigate this?"

"Sese, I know how your logical mind works. We'll be okay."

Before drifting off to sleep, I find myself smiling as I remember the first time we started galaxy travelling. It was the first time he and I made love.

We'd snuck onto the roof of my dorm to watch a meteor shower. The sky was lit by the brilliance of the meteors falling from the sky. We both made wishes.

"What did you wish for?" I asked.

"I wished for a trip to Jupiter."

"If you want to go to Jupiter, I think I can make your wish come true," I replied.

He grabs my hand, and we walk to his apartment. He undresses me, saying, "I want you to take me to Jupiter tonight."

"Be careful what you ask for," I said. "I am a galaxy traveler."

I wake to the smell of Bruce in my bed and the smell of coffee in the kitchen.

It's okay to love Bruce LeBlanc again and again.

Bruce is making breakfast. He kisses me, saying, "Good morning."

"Good morning," I say, as I gently kiss his bottom lip.

"Go get cleaned up. Your son is on his way here."

"I need coffee."

He hands me a cup, pats me on the derriere, and I head back upstairs.

After the night Bruce and I had, I should be exhausted, but I feel alive and energized. Osei is standing in the kitchen when I return. I grab him from behind. "Good morning, handsome, are you hungry?"

"Why do you always ask him that? You should know by now he's always hungry," Bruce says.

Right on cue, Osei says, "Sese, can you pass me the French toast?"

After breakfast, we discuss the foundation, agreeing on a ten-member board. Osei will invite representatives from Nike, his management company, law firm, accountant, and his best friend, Mason, the financial sector, and educational sectors, as well as Rhett, and the CEO of the European auto manufacturer.

Osei is in talks to become the American spokesperson. I suggest forming an advisory council; Bruce and Osei like the idea, so we decide to table it until the summit. We spend a few more hours refining the agenda, but there's still work to do.

It's time to go to the airport to pick up Gloria and Jackson.

Osei hands me the keys to his Range Rover.

"Can you drive?" I ask, handing the keys to Bruce.

"Sure. But when we get back, the three of us need to have a meeting."

Osei and I exchanged confused looks.

"Isn't that what we just had?" Osei asks.

"That was for the foundation. This one's a family meeting," Bruce says.

"About what?" I ask.

"Sese, we'll talk later," he replies.

Osei laughs. "Bruce, my man, this is going to be a long ride to the airport."

As Bruce pulls out of the driveway, he says, "Sese, don't be upset, everything is okay."

I study him. "Are you okay?"

He smiles. "I'm more than okay."

"Good, that's all that matters."

We're silent and listening to WDAS's Quiet Storm, as Bruce weaves in and out of traffic. The silky, soulful voice of Tony Brown comes through the speakers: "*I'm Tony Brown, and up next is the prince of sophisticated soul, Will Downing.*"

Will Downing starts singing the lyrics to "Sorry, I."

Bruce turns off the radio.

"Why did you turn it off? I like that song."

"That has to be one of the saddest songs on the planet."

"What would you like to hear?"

He lifts my hand to his lips, pressing a gentle kiss before softly repeating the lyrics from Luther Vandross, "Forever, for always, for love."

We arrive at the airport and immediately spot Gloria and Jackson.

Jackson places their luggage in the cargo space, and I move to the back seat with Gloria.

Jackson says to Bruce, "I wasn't expecting you to be here."

"Sese and I are back together," Bruce says.

Embarrassed, I smack him on his shoulder.

"It's about time," Gloria says.

53

Prayers for a Lost Soul

My cell rings. It's Rainey. "Gloria, does Rainey know you're coming to the reception tomorrow?" I ask.

"No, I want to surprise everyone."

I press the speaker button. "Hey Rainey, what's happening?"

"Is Bruce with you?" Rainey asks.

Bruce raises an eyebrow and mouths, "No."

"No Rainey. Why do you ask?"

"His ex-wife tried to kill herself and was found in her apartment this morning unresponsive."

"How do you know?"

"She's at Lenox Hill. You know Kelvin is on staff there."

"Rainey, I'm in the car. I'll call you when I get home."

The car falls silent, the only sound is the hum of the engine. When we arrive, Bruce pulls out his cellphone. "I need to call my daughter."

We leave him behind to make the call.

Osei greets us. "I spoke to the boys last night," he tells Jackson.

"Gloria and I are grateful you've taken an interest," Jackson replies.

"What's up with Bruce? Why is he still in the car?" Osei asks.

I explain briefly and head upstairs to pack.

"Osei, can you keep Millie for me?"

"Of course. Anything else?"

"No, that's all for now."

Bruce comes inside and says, "I spoke to my daughter. She confirmed what Rainey told us. Charlotte is in the ICU, and the prognosis isn't good. She's preparing herself for the worst. I need to leave for New York immediately."

"We're going with you," I say.

"Thank you, I need you by my side," he says.

Osei hugs Bruce and says, "I'll send up a prayer for her recovery. I'll see you tomorrow."

"Bruce, I'll drive. You might need to make a few calls," Jackson says.

Gloria and I get into the back seat, and we immediately start to text one another.

> Gloria: *Do you think this will have an effect on your relationship?*
>
> Me: *No, Bruce will do what he needs to do because of his daughter.*
>
> Gloria: *These things have a way of sucking you back in. By the way, where are we staying tonight?*

I look at her and hunch my shoulders.

"I'm booking rooms for us at the W Hotel. Is that okay?" I ask.

Bruce looks over his shoulder and says, "You all are staying at my place."

Jackson glances at me in the rear-view mirror with a smirk. "Thanks, Bruce. We'll take you up on your offer."

We arrive at Bruce's apartment, and when we enter, our eyes widen. The magnificent view of the Manhattan skyline stretches out through the floor-to-ceiling windows in the living and dining rooms. It's a breathtaking sight. The lights of the city's iconic buildings are twinkling like stars in the night.

"Man, this is an incredible view," Jackson says.

"How long have you lived here?" I ask.

"I bought the place ten years ago. I started living here full-time after my separation from Charlotte."

He takes my hand and guides me down the hallway, opens the door to his bedroom, and pulls me to him.

"Will you be okay?" I ask.

"I'm fine. I need to go be with my daughter. This isn't the first time this has happened, but this is the worst it has ever been. I'll be back as soon as I can."

I look up at him, pull his face to mine, and give him a long, tender kiss.

"Take care of what you need to do. I'll be here when you get back."

After Bruce leaves, Gloria, Jackson, and I huddle in the kitchen. I find the whisky and pour us a glass.

"This is a hard time for Bruce, but he'll be okay because he has you," Jackson says.

"Bruce told me this isn't the first time his ex-wife tried to kill herself."

"Oh my God, what a tormented soul," Gloria sadly says.

Jackson angrily says, "Yes, a tormented soul whose life mission has been to torment others."

Surprised by his harsh words, Gloria asks, "What are you talking about?"

"This is her third attempt. The second attempt was five years ago when Bruce filed for a divorce. He withdrew the divorce papers because he felt it was not the time to leave his daughter alone with her mother," Jackson says.

"Didn't his ex-wife file for divorce because she had fallen in love with a woman?" Gloria asks.

"Yes, that train soon crashed and burned," Jackson replies.

I look at Jackson with a sense of shame because talking about Bruce's relationship with his ex-wife was a violation of his privacy.

"Enough about Bruce and his ex-wife. Jackson, you are his best friend, and I'm sure he has told you things he would never tell me or anyone else about his marriage. So, let's respect his privacy and leave this here."

"I'm not respecting anything. Tell me, please," Gloria pleads.

"Gloria, enough already. I'm serious," I say.

"Okay, I'll let it go." She winks at Jackson, saying, "We'll talk later."

"I agree with Sese. I'm not telling you anything."

Osei calls, "Hey, Sese, I'm checking to make sure you all arrived safely."

"Yes, we made it."

"How is Bruce doing?" he asks.

"He's keeping it together. Osei, Bruce, is calling me now. I'll see you tomorrow in Manhattan."

"I'll be there."

"Bruce? Are you okay? What happened?" My voice is tight with worry.

There's a pause, just long enough for my heart to sink.

"The ride into Manhattan is forty-five minutes," he says quietly. "It gives me time to think."

"Is it Charlotte?" I ask.

"I need to hear your voice," he admits. "I wasn't sure if I should call. I don't want to drag you into this chaos."

"You're not dragging me into anything," I say gently. "I'm already in it. With you. Whatever this is, we face it together."

"Did I tell you how I met Charlotte?"

"No," I reply.

"I met her at a fundraiser held at the Studio Museum in Harlem, and we were married a year later. Charlotte's controlling nature and bipolar disorder made her a difficult person to love. I tried my best to help and to love her. Sese, Charlotte won't survive this. She drank a deadly dose of antifreeze, and her organs are all failing. She has only a few hours left."

"I'm so sorry, Bruce."

"How am I going to prepare my daughter for the inevitable?"

"Your love for her will help you to find a way."

"My daughter has survived her mother's madness. She may not be able to survive this. I'm arriving at the hospital. I'll see you later."

54

The Boathouse

It's two o'clock in the morning when Bruce walks in. I'm on the sofa drinking a cup of tea. He walks over to me, and we hold onto each other with all our might.

"I was so worried. How is your daughter?"

"She's doing better than I expected. No matter what, she'll be okay."

"Can I have a cup of tea?"

"Of course."

"Have you been sitting here long?"

"Not really. Lovely apartment, but the walls are paper-thin. Jackson and Gloria have visited Mars a few times tonight."

He grins. "I'm surprised they only have two children. We'll have to show them we've got interplanetary skills too."

"Yes, we will."

As we orbit Jupiter again, I wonder how I've lived without him, without his touch.

Bruce left early in the morning to see his daughter and meet with the doctors. He'll meet us later at the courthouse for Taylor's wedding.

Jackson jokingly says, "I didn't want to burn down the kitchen. There won't be any elaborate stuffed waffles, just toast and coffee."

After breakfast, we leave for the courthouse.

I'm meeting Bruce on the corner of Worth Street near the City Clerk's office. I can't help but smile. Of course, Taylor is getting married for sixty dollars. Thirty-five for the license and twenty-five for the ceremony. A woman worth millions, and she's still the queen of bargain weddings.

My eyes scan the crowd for Bruce, and I see him walking toward me, moving effortlessly through the sea of people. My heart skips a beat. I can't believe how handsome he looks. The crowd seems to move in slow motion as he approaches.

"Wow, Sese, you look beautiful," he says.

"Thank you, you don't look too bad yourself."

I glance up, and Taylor and Eric are standing at the top of the stairs.

"Oh my God, Taylor! You are absolutely stunning!" I yell up to her.

Tall and lean with the correct amount of bumps, both top and bottom. The crepe sheath wedding dress flatters her figure with a high halter neck and splits at the hem in an off-center split. A sheer illusion back is concealed by a trail of pearl buttons. In her hands is a simple bouquet of Calla lilies and baby's breath.

Tears well up in her eyes. "Taylor, please don't cry. Those happy tears will ruin your makeup."

The ceremony is brief, a courtroom wedding with just the four of us, a photographer, and the judge.

But as we walk outside into the sunlight, a burst of cheers fills the air. Our friends are gathered around, clapping and shouting with joy.

Taylor, touched by the overwhelming support, can no longer hold back the tears. "Gloria, I told you not to come. Why are you here?"

"If I had to take a plane, an automobile, and a train. I was not missing your wedding," Gloria replies.

Taylor and Eric look in disbelief at the party bus with *Just Married* on the back, and their names spelled out in white roses.

We board the bus and receive a flute of Champagne.

"What is going on? Why aren't we at Nobu?" Taylor asks.

"Because this is your wedding day, and your reception is being held at the Central Park Boathouse!" I exclaim. This time, Taylor burst into a full-blown meltdown.

Taking her hand, Dee smiles. Taylor says, "I've never been this happy before. But I hope you got my money back from Nobu."

"This is the cheap Taylor we know and love."

At the entrance of Central Park on Sixty-Second Street, three elegant horse-drawn carriages awaited, their brass gleaming and velvet seats inviting. As we climb in, the rhythmic sound of hooves echoes through the trees, carrying us along the water's edge toward Seventy-Second Street. The ride felt timeless as the iconic Loeb Boathouse came into view, glowing softly at the lake, ready to usher in an unforgettable evening. A crowd of about fifty people gathers to celebrate their glorious day. The Boathouse veranda is reserved for Taylor and Eric.

We dance, drink, and toast the happy couple. Dinner is beyond scrumptious, and when we are tipsy enough, our forever group serenades Taylor with Patti LaBelle's "You Are My Friend, I never knew it till then. My friend, my friend." The tears are flowing as freely as the champagne.

Taylor and Eric thank us for making their special day even more memorable, and a waiting limo whisks them away.

Bruce heads to the hospital. Osei drives Gloria, Jackson, and me back to Bruce's place in New Jersey.

As soon as we arrive, Gloria and Jackson disappear into the bedroom.

"Osei, if you hear any noise, it's just Gloria and Jackson hittin' it."

"You're kidding."

"Nope. Dead serious."

"In that case, we'd better turn on the TV," he says.

55

Heloise and Abelard

Hours later, I look up to see Bruce standing over us, smiling gently.

"Come on, let's get you both to bed."

Osei rubs his eyes. "Wow! I must've dozed off."

"How's your daughter?" I ask.

"Not good at all. The decision to resuscitate, if needed, will be made by her. I found out that she and her boyfriend have been living together for the past three months. I've known him since they were in preschool together. He'll be there to support her through all of this."

"Did her mother know about this?" I ask.

"I don't know. Life with her mother hasn't been easy for my daughter. They're complete opposites. She's caring, loving, and compassionate. Her mother thought that was a weakness and would belittle her for it. Charlotte picked fights over anything. My daughter is all about keeping the peace. If I was happy about work or the Yankees, it set her off. I'm sorry my daughter had to witness the worst parts of our relationship. What kept me sane, Sese, were the letters I wrote to you. Ones I never sent."

"Letters? Why didn't you send them to me?"

"Maybe I was scared of what you'd think, or maybe I wasn't ready to confront my feelings and admit I made a mistake. I wrote them every time I missed you or needed to tell you something. Writing to you was my way of preserving our love and the memory of it. They went missing, and I thought Charlotte had destroyed them. Tonight, I found out that Adia had them. She had hidden them away and told me that reading them restored her faith in love."

Bruce looks away from me, his voice softening. "She gave them back to me tonight. I cried because my daughter knows all the things I couldn't say to you, and she knows that I didn't love her mother. I thank God that she turned out to be such a beautiful young lady, because the household she was raised in was so dysfunctional."

He pulls out a leather box from his bag.

I open the box, stunned. "Bruce, how many letters are there?"

"I don't know, hundreds. Sese, I missed you so much, and writing to you was my way of staying connected to you."

"So, the first letter you wrote is on the bottom?"

"Yes."

I flip through the letters. "Then I want to read them in the order you wrote them," I say, moved beyond words.

Bruce's phone rings, and he puts it on speaker. "Hello, darling." His face tightens with worry as he listens to his daughter.

"Daddy, please come to the hospital. Mommy isn't doing well. I need you." Adia's voice trembles through the phone.

"I'm on my way," he says, his tone steady, but his eyes reflecting deep concern.

I walk him to the elevator, and I plant a soft kiss on his cheek, "I'll be praying for you all."

He gives me a grateful smile before stepping into the elevator. The doors close. I return to the apartment to find Gloria pouring herself a glass of water. She looks up. "Where have you been?" she asks, her tone curious but gentle.

"I walked Bruce to the elevator. He's on his way to the hospital."

"This has to be so very hard on his daughter," Gloria says.

"Sese," she repeats, more firmly. "Sese."

I look at her.

"Are you okay?" she asks.

"Yes, I was thinking about Bruce's daughter. For a moment, I could feel her pain. It was like an out-of-body experience."

Gloria's concern changes to amusement. "You are certifiably crazy."

"Gloria, I need you to do something for me."

I hand her the first letter from Bruce, my fingers trembling. "Can you read this? I don't think I can."

She reads in silence. As she reaches the end, tears begin to stream down her face.

"Gloria, what is wrong? Are you okay?"

She wipes her face and folds the letter. "This is so Heloise and Abelard," she says, her voice thick with emotion. "I need a drink."

Feeling a mixture of anticipation, fear, and curiosity, wondering what words made her so emotional. "A drink of what?" I ask.

"Something strong…over eighty proof. If I'm going to read this letter to you, we're both going to need it."

"Who are Heloise and Abelard?" I ask.

"Sese, I told you! I need a drink first."

She returns with a bottle of Aged Bourbon. Pouring me a glass, she says, "The story of Heloise and Abelard is one of the most romantic and tragic stories in history. They were separated by circumstances beyond their control, but their love never faded. Over twenty years, they exchanged heartfelt letters. Even now, people travel from around the world to visit their graves to leave love letters."

She begins to read the letter out loud.

"My Darling Sese, I'm married, and I can't wrap my mind around the fact that it isn't you. I'm asking myself, how did I get here without you? Will I ever be able to forgive myself for abandoning our love? I can't tell you how many times I've longed to see you. I'll never stop loving you. I have made a promise to myself that I'll never love anyone else. Charlotte is a good woman, but I don't love her. She knows this, and I'll do my best to be a good husband to her. Will I ever be able to stop loving you? I've started a journey, and I ask myself every day if I can walk this road without you. I'll write to you for the rest of my life. If I can only communicate my feelings for you in this way, I will, because you are the owner of my heart and my soul until death takes me away. Love BL."

She puts the letter down.

"Gloria, I now know the pain I felt on his wedding day was mutual."

I take a sip of the bourbon, and it stings, but not as much as Bruce's letter stings my heart.

"Oh my God, how miserable have they both been all these years? He loving someone else. She knowing it and is making their lives miserable because of it," Gloria says.

Gloria lifts the letters. Astonished, she says, "Damn, there have to be over a hundred letters here. Geez Louise, it will take you forever to read all these."

I look at the stack of letters, "If it takes a lifetime, I'm determined to read every letter."

"I'm happy you and Bruce found a way back to each other. You looked so good together today. Even Rainey commented on how you both were beaming."

"It's as if a part of me has been missing all these years, and now, at last, I've found it."

The phone rings, it's Bruce, his voice heavy with pain.

"Sese, the doctors say Charlotte has only a few hours. She's in and out, but ten minutes ago, she asked to see you."

"Me? Why?"

"I don't know. But I need you here too. Will you come?"

"Will my being there upset your daughter?"

"No. She's okay with it."

Sensing the gravity, I say, "I'll be there as soon as possible."

Gloria's eyes widen. "You're going to the hospital?"

"Yes, Charlotte asks to see me."

"No way! That woman is crazy. This is her way of getting back at you."

"I haven't done anything to her," I exclaimed.

"The man she loves, loves you." Her voice rises with every word. "You don't need to hear nothing she has to say."

"Neither one of us can control how he feels. Why would she blame me?"

She grabs my shoulders, her voice trembling and loud. "You are not going. I won't let you!" she screams.

Osei and Jackson rush in, alarmed.

Osei says, "Sese, are you okay? What's going on?"

Before I can answer, Gloria says, "She has lost her mind."

"Gloria, calm down. Tell us what is going on?" Jackson says.

"Bruce's ex-wife, with hours to live, wants Sese to come to the hospital," she screams.

Both Jackson and Osei turn to look at me.

"I'm going, I have to go."

"I think I understand, but you are not going alone. I'm coming with you." Osei says.

"Jackson and I are coming too," Gloria adds.

We leave Gloria and Jackson in a coffee shop near the hospital. I call Bruce to let him know that Osei and I are in the lobby. We enter the room, and Bruce's daughter is standing next to her mom's bed. I'm struck by her beauty. She's strikingly tall, with skin the color of honey, high cheekbones, and dimpled cheeks. She has Bruce's eyes, and they're red and swollen from crying.

"Thank you for coming. My name is Adia," she says.

"I'm Sienna." I beckon for Osei to join us. "This is my son Osei Wharton."

This young woman is calm and poised, creating a sense of calm in this very overwhelming moment. Her steady presence eases my nerves.

In a very weak voice, Charlotte says, "Adia."

Osei and Bruce both stand at the foot of the bed. Adia and I stand on the opposite side of her mother's bed.

Charlotte says to Adia, "I'm sorry, baby, I'm tired."

The tears stream down Adia's beautiful face. Charlotte looks at me and reaches for my hand. I take her hand, and I'm shocked at how cold it is.

"Thank you for coming. This is hard for me to do, but I want to ask you a favor," Charlotte says.

I grip her hand tightly, "Whatever you want, I'll do my best to do it for you."

"I want you to take care of my daughter. My child and my husband suffered because I didn't know how to love them."

"Mommy, what are you saying?"

"Baby, you are nineteen years old, and soon to be without me. It may take time, but you'll need someone like her in your life. Your father has loved this woman all his life, and he wouldn't have if she weren't deserving of his love. Sienna, my daughter, will need someone to help her become an even more beautiful woman. Promise me that you'll take care of her."

I look over at Adia, and she looks away. "If she'll have me, I'll take care of her."

"Thank you," she murmurs, her voice fading away. "I'm tired." She closes her eyes slowly, as if surrendering the weight of everything she's carried.

I go over to Adia, and I take her hand.

She slides her hand out of mine and says, "I appreciate what you are doing, but I need time to think about this," Adia says, with a weak smile.

"I understand, and I'm here if you need me." I hug her, and I grab Osei's hand, and we leave the room.

I text Bruce: *We will wait for you at the coffee shop across the street from the hospital.*

As we wait for the elevator, Osei says, "Unbelievable! She gave you her daughter and her husband on her deathbed. Unbelievable."

"I wasn't expecting that," I say, slightly taken aback.

We meet Gloria and Jackson, and I take a deep breath before recounting my conversation with Charlotte.

"That was creepy," Osei says.

Jackson, listening intently, leans in. "I swear to God that woman is a witch."

We all stare at him.

"All that drama? Bruce raised Adia her whole life. He doesn't need her permission to proceed with his life, and neither does Adia. Charlotte was diagnosed with schizophrenia early on and rejected Adia," Jackson exclaims.

Just then, I get a text from Bruce: *Charlotte has died, and I'm taking Adia home. Can you wait for me?*

Me: *Yes. We'll be here.*

"Is she gone?" Jackson asks.

"Yes, Bruce wants us to wait here. He'll be here soon."

Osei shakes his head, "Wow! I have a mother, stepfather, stepsister, cousins, aunts, and uncles. This is definitely next-level stuff."

"Be careful what you ask for," I say.

Bruce walks in, silent but heavy with emotion. He nods. We all rise and head out together.

It's five in the morning when we all walk into Bruce's place, totally exhausted.

"Are you really okay?" I ask.

"Yes. Charlotte was herself until the very end. What she did was all for her benefit. She didn't want a memorial service and will be cremated later today. Her ashes are to be scattered. Charlotte donated all her clothes and jewelry and burned every photo of her, Adia, and us as a family. Adia won't have anything of hers. Did she expect her child to live as if her mother never existed? Adia left a part of herself at the hospital. My poor baby was told by her mother on her deathbed that she never loved her. How can I help my child, Sese? How can I help her?"

"You'll continue to love her, and if she allows me, I'll love her too. Our village will embrace her the same way they have embraced Osei."

We fall asleep in each other's arms. At last, a moment of peace.

I wake to a sharp knock on the door and Osei entering.

"Good morning, Sese. Bruce wants to know what time you want to leave to go back to Philly?"

"What time is it?"

"It's 10:30 am and Bruce is making breakfast, not to alarm you, but Adia is here, and you're in her daddy's bed."

I throw a pillow at him as he quickly closes the door.

I walk into the kitchen, and Adia comes over and wraps me in a tight hug. "I'm so sorry for what happened at the hospital last night."

"How are you doing?" I ask.

"I'm still trying to process everything. May I have a word with you in private?" she asks.

"Sure," I reply nervously.

We go into Bruce's bedroom and close the door. She sees the leather box on the dresser and walks over and touches it gently.

"I see Dad gave you the letters, still touching the lid. The letters in this box made me believe in love. I found them when I was sixteen. I apologized to my Dad for reading them, but I'm not sorry that I did. These letters restored my faith in love, teaching me how to express it. He wrote these letters to you, the person he always loved, and I wanted to meet you and let you know that it's okay for you to love him."

My heart pounds as the gravity of her words sinks in.

"Adia, your father, and I are working through things. There's a lot of healing ahead for all of us."

She takes my hand. "I know, but we'll always have love."

Adia and Osei quickly bond over basketball. Her knowledge of the game pulls him into a full-on sports talk. She's now immersed in the world of Osei Wharton.

I smile to myself. *Osei Wharton, the human antidepressant.*

Over breakfast, Bruce announces, "I have news."

"What now?" I groan. "We can't take much more."

"I have accepted a position at the University of Pennsylvania. We've been in talks for over a year, and we came to an agreement last week. Sese, this is what I wanted to discuss with you and Osei yesterday. Adia, I don't have to take it if you need me in New York."

"Daddy, you have to accept it! I'm moving to Philly to start at Penn next semester. Asa is transferring to Drexel."

"When were you going to tell me?"

"Once we had settled in," she says sheepishly.

Osei gives her a high five. "Way to go, Lil sis."

"I'll look for a space big enough for all of us," Bruce says.

"No way," Adia replies. "We're not living with you. Besides, I think you and Sese should live together."

"The thought did cross my mind," I say.

Bruce grins, "Did it now?"

"Yes."

"What will you do with your place?"

"Daddy. This is New York. I can rent out my space for at least $10,000 a month."

"Wow, is your apartment on billionaires' row?" Osei asks.

"My grandfather left me a three-bedroom prewar apartment on the Upper West Side," Adia explains.

"You both are moving to Philly. I'm so excited," Osei says. "Now, when can I give Asa the once-over?"

"Never. I'm not going to allow you to intimidate him."

"Who said anything about allowing me? Call him now. I want to meet him."

Adia's phone rings, Osei grabs it and answers, "Hello Asa? This is Osei, Adia's brother. We need to talk."

Adia chases him around the kitchen island, trying to get her phone back.

Adia kisses her dad. "See you next week, Daddy."

She and Osei head out to meet Asa.

"Osei, the human antidepressant," I say.

"Sienna Lewis, you're mine."

"Yes, I am. And don't you forget it. We've got two hours before anyone gets back. I want to at least leave Earth's orbit."

56

Pizza Night

One wedding and a funeral within days leave us emotionally drained. Osei drives us back to Philly and drops everyone at my place.

"It's Saturday, we should order a pizza," I suggest.

"Pizza night used to be our thing, pizza and beer in bed every Saturday night," Bruce says.

"Eating pizza in bed with my wife. I'm in heaven," Jackson adds.

"And don't forget a cold beer," Bruce chimes in.

Jackson gives Bruce a high five. "You are a mind reader. Definitely the icing on the cake."

We sit out on the deck, drinking soju and enjoying the stars while we wait for the pizzas to arrive.

"This is a good drink," Bruce says.

"I take it you don't know about Sese's obsession with Korean dramas?" Gloria asks.

"Korean what?" he says.

Laughing, Gloria says, "You are in for a treat."

I kiss Bruce on the forehead, "I'll explain my love of Korean Dramas later."

The pizzas arrive, and Jackson and Gloria disappear. I grab a couple of beers and a bottle of soju, and Bruce and I follow suit.

"Sese, tell me about your fascination with Korean dramas."

"Well, one night I was looking for something mindless to watch on Netflix, and I saw a trailer for a Korean drama. To be honest, the male lead reminded me of you. So, I started watching, and it was anything but mindless. I got pulled in by the stories of revenge and romance, and I fell in love with the music."

"I'd like to watch your favorite drama."

"Okay, don't blame me if you get hooked."

After watching one episode, Bruce says, "That was very entertaining."

My cell rings, and it's Taylor, "I apologize for calling so late, but I want to thank you for all you did to make my wedding a very special day."

"Taylor, you deserved to have a momentous day."

"I couldn't imagine a better wedding day. Please give Bruce my condolences. We heard about his ex-wife's passing."

"Thank you, Taylor," Bruce says.

"What are you doing?" I ask.

"Enjoying pizza night. I always wanted to have a pizza night. Now that I have Eric, pizza night will become a part of our lives," Taylor says.

"Thanks for the concept, guys. It's perfect, my wife, beer, pizza, and our bed, where magic happens," Eric calls out in the background.

"You're welcome," Bruce chimes in.

"Bruce and I are doing the same thing, having pizza in bed."

"Aren't Gloria and Jackson at your place?" Taylor asks.

"Yes, and they're also enjoying pizza in bed."

I'll call you back," Taylor says.

Taylor FaceTime me, and when I answer, I see four couples lounging in bed with pizzas.

Bruce raises his glass. "I want to make a toast. Here's to it, and to it again, and may we get to do it again." Everyone raises their glasses.

Jackson grins. "Pizza night's over. Time for the good part."
He and Gloria quickly disconnect.

"I think I'll follow Jackson's lead," Arjun says.

Bruce, Eric, and Kelvin all chime in, "Same here."

Bruce and I enjoy the calorie-burning part of pizza night.

57

Memories

Osei has taken to coming over for breakfast every day since Bruce has been staying at my place. Now he even brings Millie 2.0.

"What's for breakfast?" he asks.

"Bacon, omelets, and sourdough French toast. What would you like in your omelet?" Bruce asks.

"Everything," Osei says, grabbing a slice of bacon. "I got a call from Mark. He got his summit invitation, and he's thrilled."

"I'm glad," Chloe emailed them yesterday."

"I like your idea of having an advisory council. Mason is honored to be considered for the board, but he's working on his doctorate and wouldn't be able to commit to the time needed to be a full-time board member."

"Remind me again, who Mason is?" Bruce asks.

"Mason is my best friend, and the only other person I let beat me at chess."

"I hope you are not implying the other person is me."

Osei takes a bite of his omelet. "If the shoe fits," he says.

I cut in. "Can we get back to discussing the advisory council?"

"Osei, anyone else we should consider for the advisory council?"

"Maybe aunts and uncles."

Gloria walks in. "What about your aunts and uncles?"

"Gloria, would you and Jackson consider joining the foundation's advisory council?"

"I'm swamped, but Jackson might be up for it."

Jackson overhears. "Up for what?"

"Sitting on the advisory council," I say.

"Absolutely, I'd be honored."

"The summit will be the last week in October in Beaverton. Gloria, maybe you and the boys can join us for a long weekend," I suggest.

"They'd love that," she smiles.

After breakfast, Osei and I drive Gloria and her men to the airport for their flight back to LA.

Osei's car phone rings. He taps the screen and puts it on speaker.

"Hello, Mr. Thomas. I was wondering if you were still in business," he says.

"Good morning, Osei. I apologize for taking so long to get back to you."

"No worries, did you find anything?" Osei says.

"Well, Osei, this case is complicated. I found Oliver Henry. He was the president of a Black university in Virginia and died of pancreatic cancer. His sister passed shortly after. The woman you're looking for was his daughter. They were a prominent family, and something about this feels like a cover-up. The reports say a man was driving. I met with a retired officer who was at the scene and insists it was a woman behind the wheel. He helped me track down the attorney who handled the case. I'm trying to schedule a call with him tomorrow, and I'll update you after I speak with him."

"Okay, Mr. Thomas. We'll wait to hear from you. Goodbye."

"I'd feel better if I knew for sure his illness was the reason he left me at Wharton."

I nod my head in agreement. "Yes. The million-dollar question."

Seeing Osei drifting into a sad and dark place. I hurry up and change the subject. Curious about Adia's boyfriend and thinking they'd make great friends for Osei, I ask Osei, "What did you think of Asa?"

Osei smiles. I like him. He reminds me a lot of Mason. He's tall, thin, and looks like that guy from Star Trek."

"Who, William Shatner?"

"No, the other Captain Kirk."

"What other guy?" I ask. Googling Captain Kirk.

A photo of Chris Pine pops up.

"Yeah, that's the one. Asa looks a lot like him."

"Wow, he's definitely good-looking, and you are rigth."

"Sese, how are you dealing with all this?"

"Honestly, I'm not sure. Ten months ago, I was living my life without you or Bruce, and I was happy. My concerns were all centered on me. Now, I'm a mother to you, a potential stepmother to Adia, a girlfriend and partner to Bruce, and not to mention, I quit my job. At times, it all feels overwhelming. Having you now brings about a different type of stress, and I find myself worrying about you every minute of the day."

"Sese, I worry about you too. Is this love?"

"Yes, my love, unconditional love."

"Speaking of worry, the summit is at the top of the list. Osei, we need to make time to iron out some kinks."

"I have a conference call today with Mark, Rhett, and the European auto manufacturer. In fact, if all goes well, I'll be the spokesperson for an electric vehicle."

"Will you have to get rid of your other cars?"

"No, I can still drive and own other vehicles."

"Good. Would you like to go hit a few balls at the driving range? You need to practice before playing golf at Pumpkin Ridge."

"Not particularly," he says.

I place my hand on his forehead. "You are always game for hitting golf balls. Are you okay?"

"I'm okay. Can we watch a movie instead? Maybe one of those Korean dramas you rave about?"

"Sounds good. I'll ditch Bruce and watch a movie at your place. I've got the perfect one with the right mix of action and romance."

I call Bruce.

"Hello, love," he answers.

"Where are you?" I asked.

"I'm out walking Millie, and the neighbors are giving me strange looks. I'm sure if I weren't walking Millie, they would have called the police."

"They'll get used to seeing you. Will you be alright by yourself tonight? Osei and I are going to watch a movie together."

"We're ordering sushi. We can drop dinner off for you if you like," Osei chimes in.

"I'll be fine. I'm going to put a steak on the grill."

"Okay, I'll see you later."

"Are you and Bruce really going to live together?"

"Where did that question come from? Are you okay with Bruce and me living together?"

"Yes, he loves you, and you clearly love him."

"Do you remember when I explained the meaning of the French word, *dépaysement*?"

"Yes, I remember."

"I no longer feel adrift. I have found my home. Enough about me and Bruce. I want to watch a movie."

Osei and I take seats in his screening room. I glance at him and say, "Osei, can we watch the movie in your bedroom?"

"Yes, I wanted to suggest it," he says.

We settle into his extra-large bed, the comfort and the space making everything feel cozy.

"Sese, I'd love to watch one of your Korean dramas, but can we talk instead?"

"Sure. About what?"

"I'm having more memories of Poppa Henry, and they are so vivid."

"What do you remember?"

"I started playing basketball and baseball because of him. He always came to my games and would take me for ice cream afterwards. His favorite was buttered pecan. I sprained my ankle running to first base, and he took me to the hospital. I stayed with him until I was better. We slept in his big bed. It was the biggest bed I had ever seen. I was his Noble Prince, and he was my Superman. He took me fishing and told me he was going on a long trip and didn't know when he'd see me again. I cried all the way back to Wharton. He made me promise to never forget him. It's starting to make sense."

With tears flowing down his face, "Sese, I forgot him. How could I forget him?"

"You were young. Do you remember what he looked like?"

"I Googled his name, and when I saw his picture, I felt a sense of longing, because I did remember him."

"Osei, he loved you very much, and he made sure you were well taken care of."

He starts to cry. I stroke his back as he lies across my lap.

"I resemble him. I remember he was always taller than the people around him. He looked like a giant to me."

"Yes, you do resemble him."

"I looked for a picture of his daughter," he says, then corrects himself. "My mother, but I couldn't find one. I hate Ms. Hannah even more for not telling me. Why did he leave me at Wharton? Why couldn't he love me?"

I start to answer, but I see tears rolling down his face. I take his face in my hands, and I wipe away the tears. "Osei, you were loved. They may not have been able to tell you, but you were loved."

The phone startles us both. I search around the bed and find it under my pillow. It's Bruce calling.

"Hello Sese, is everything alright? When are you coming home?"

"OMG," I say, glancing at my watch. "I didn't realize it was this late."

Osei attempts to get out of bed, but I stop him.

"Relax, Bruce will pick me up."

"I kiss his cheek. Good night, my prince."

"Good night, Sese."

58

When a Plan Comes Together

Bruce picks me up in the garage.

"I missed you," he says.

I lean over and kiss him. "I missed you, too."

I fill him in on Osei's conversation with the private detective and his memories of President Henry.

"Your theory could be correct."

"My theory is one hundred percent correct. What I want to know is who inserted me into Osei's life, and why? I haven't heard from Taylor about Osei's trust."

"I'm sure she has been busy with work," Bruce says.

"I'm sure that's what happened. I'll give her a call."

I shower and then join Bruce, who has settled in bed watching a golf tournament.

"Is Osei okay?" he asks.

"He needs a bit of attention. I'll keep a close watch to make sure he doesn't retreat into himself."

"He has you, and a village that loves and cherishes him."

"With the season starting soon, his focus should be on playing exceptional basketball. This must be resolved by then. Otherwise, it will consume him. When I met him, he never doubted I was his mother, even when it was proven I wasn't. He didn't leave. He held on even tighter."

"Sese, Osei will be okay. And so will you."

I lie on his chest, and Bruce's beating heart lulls me off to sleep.

I wake to the sound of Bruce and Osei in the kitchen and head downstairs to join them.

"Good morning," Bruce says, and plants a kiss on my forehead.

My phone pinged. A text from Dee: *I emailed you the menu for the summit. Take a look at it. Let me know if you want to make any changes. I put my producer in touch with Lucas. They hit it off, and all the arrangements have been made for the filming of my show.*

I pull up the menu on my laptop and share it with Bruce and Osei.

"Yummy, this sounds delicious," Osei says.

I see Bruce staring at me. "I like that look," he says.

Osei looks confused and asks, "What look?"

"The look Sese exhibits when a plan comes together. The look of success."

"Yes, it's coming together. Everyone has accepted their invitation to the summit."

"I think we should have a toast. Here's to…"

Before he can finish, Osei asks, "Isn't it too early to be drinking?"

"Exactly." I pour orange juice and champagne into mine and Bruce's glasses.

"Now it's a breakfast drink. Cheers to new beginnings!"

Bruce chuckles, hands Osei a glass of sparkling water, and we clink our glasses together.

"It's never too early for a celebration."

Osei heads to practice, and Bruce and I leave for the office to work on the agenda for the summit.

"Wow, this place is absolutely beautiful. It has a warm and elegant feel," Bruce says as he walks into the office.

"Ah, so this is your first time seeing it, huh?"

"Yes, and it's beautiful, Sese. I'm serious. I get the same feeling of comfort here that I do when I walk into Osei's apartment or your home."

"You are being kind," I say, correcting him. "Our home."

"This isn't something that can be accidentally achieved. You are a Zen Master, flowing your good chi and energy in everything you touch."

"As long as you and Osei are happy, that's all that matters to me."

I make coffee, and we settle in to work on the agenda. Our work is interrupted by Bruce's cell phone.

"It's Adia," he says to me. "Hello, sweetheart. How are you doing?"

"I'm good, we're in Philly. We just finished looking at apartments, and I was wondering if we could see you?"

Bruce looks at me, and I mouth, "Yes."

"Should I come get you?"

"No, Daddy, we'll come to you. We rented a car," Adia replies.

"We're at the office. I'll text you the address."

"We'll see you shortly."

Fifteen minutes later, Bruce opens the door and welcomes Adia and Asa. Adia glances around and says, "This place is unreal. Daddy, is this your office?"

"No, it's Sese's office."

Adia comes over and hugs me, "Sese, I want you to meet Asa."

He extends his hand. "Is it okay if I give you a hug?" he asks.

"Of course," I say.

Osei calls, "Sese, I'm on my way home and I ordered pizzas for lunch," he says.

"Adia and Asa will be joining us."

"Great. I'll see you soon."

Osei opens the door. Adia pauses as she enters Osei's apartment, "Whoa! Your place is a terrific place, too. Did you decorate it?"

"No, Sese decorated both places," Osei says.

"When we find a place, can you help us put it together?" Asa asks.

"I'd love to help! How did apartment hunting go today? Did you see anything that caught your eye?" Bruce asks.

"No," they say in unison.

"Apartments here are cheaper, but they lack the oomph. There's nothing special about them," Asa says.

"You both are spoiled living in Manhattan," Bruce says.

"Osei, this place has the Tribeca loft feel. We'd love to find a place like this, but smaller," Adia says.

Asa looks at his watch and says, "Adia, we need to check into the hotel."

"Hotel? Adia, why would you stay at a hotel when I have a room here? My feelings are hurt," Osei says.

Laughing, Adia says, "The last thing I want to do is hurt your feelings." She turns to Asa. "Are you okay with us staying here?"

"I'll go get our bags."

"Why don't you all come to dinner at my place? We can throw a few steaks and salmon on the grill and relax on the deck."

Bruce and I leave Adia, Asa, and Osei playing video games.

"Adia and Asa would be good company for him," I say.

"They seem to get along well," Bruce says. "We've got time before they arrive. Care to join me for a nap?"

"Yes, I could use a nap."

We set the alarm for an hour and fell asleep entwined in each other's arms.

59

A New Chapter Begins

The ringtone of a phone startles us awake, "Bruce, your phone is ringing."

"That's your ringtone," he says.

I detangle from him, roll over, and feel around on the nightstand for my phone.

It's Dee. Trying to shake off the grogginess, I answer, my voice barely audible. "Hello."

"Are you asleep?" Dee asks.

"Yes, I was taking a nap."

"Sorry. But I'm too excited to keep this to myself. We just finished taping our first episode at your place, and we're having a blast. The producers are even thinking about replicating your kitchen in our New York studio. Arjun is in heaven, hiking in the woods and finding all sorts of edible plants. Yesterday, he featured lobster mushrooms on his show. This place is stunning! And Sese, Lucas is fantastic. I want to hire him. He's introduced us to amazing organic and sustainable farms, and the vegetables are beyond delicious. My team loves the house and the property so much that they don't want to leave. Thank you again for letting us film here."

"Aren't organic and sustainable farms the same?"

"No, sleepy head, they're completely different."

"Hmm… Okay. I'm glad everyone is having a good time. I guess Beaverton isn't south of hell after all."

"You got that right. So, what did you think of the menu?"

"I thought it was perfect, and so did Bruce and Osei. Thank you."

"You're welcome. Goodbye, I'll see you soon."

I roll back over to Bruce, I rub his stomach, I blow into his ear. "How much time do we have before the kids arrive?"

He looks at the bedside clock. "We have thirty-five minutes."

"How about a quick trip to Mars?"

"I want more than thirty-five minutes," he smiles.

I can't believe how good it feels to be in his arms.

"Do you know what I missed about you the most?" I ask.

"No, what?"

"Your smell. You smell like warm vanilla beans."

"Sese, you can't be serious?"

"I'm profoundly serious. After you left, I slept with your dirty clothes for a week."

"I longed for your smell too," Bruce says.

"You did? What do I smell like?"

"Sienna Lewis, you smell like heaven."

I punch him on his shoulder. "Bruce LeBlanc, you are such a liar."

"If I can smell like warm vanilla beans, why can't you smell like heaven?"

"Because heaven isn't a smell."

He rolls on top of me, saying, "I don't just want to smell heaven. I want to feel it too."

We shower and get ready for the kids to come over. I make a pasta salad, and I stuff poblano peppers with crab meat. Bruce gets the grill ready for salmon and steaks.

I hear Osei come in the front door. Millie picks up her stuffed piggy and greets everyone, and Asa immediately gets down on his knees to play with her.

"I've never seen a dog like this before," Asa says.

"She's a Bouvier," Osei answers.

"She looks like a small bear," Asa replies.

Bruce goes over to Adia and kisses her on the cheek, "Hey, baby."

"Make yourselves at home," I say.

I'm watching the evening unfold, amazed at how much fun Adia and Asa are having. They show no uneasiness around Osei or me, and it feels as if we've been connected for a lifetime.

After dinner, we settle into the living room, quietly enjoying each other's company. I catch the joy on his face, the shimmer in his eyes. Trying not to get teary myself, I mouth, "Man up."

He chuckles, wipes his face, and mutters, "Too Late."

Bruce takes Adia's hand. "Are you okay?"

"Yes, I don't ever remember you being happy, she says, looking at me. I'm glad you have Sese, and I'm over the moon that I have Asa."

"Sese, your home is beautiful. It's so peaceful here," Asa says.

"Feel free to visit anytime," I reply.

"Adia, you'll be okay. You've got a big brother who'll always be there," Osei says.

"Thanks, Osei. I need time to heal, but it's good to know you're there if I need you."

"Did your dad invite you to the summit? We could really use your help," Osei adds.

"No, but do you need me?"

"Yes," I say. "Definitely."

"Can Asa come too?" Adia asks.

"I should probably stay here and look for an apartment," Asa replies.

"No way," Osei insists. "This is a family affair. You can stay with me until you find a place."

"Okay then, just send me the dates and I'll book our flights," Asa says.

"No need," Osei grins. "We're flying private."

"Have you reserved a plane?" I ask.

"No need."

"Why not?"

"Because I bought one, and we can leave whenever we like."

"Really, you bought a plane? Since when?" Bruce asks.

"Since last week," Osei replies.

Excited, Bruce asks, "Which plane did you buy?

"I bought the Dassault Falcon 2000LX."

Bruce immediately pulls out his phone and googles the aircraft. Placing his phone in my face, he says, "Are you freaking kidding me?"

"Osei, why on earth would you buy a plane?" I ask.

"Because he can," Adia quips.

Osei gives her a high five and says, "Sese, don't worry. It isn't that expensive. It's pre-owned."

"Osei, why would you buy a used plane? Is it safe? People usually sell cars, boats, and planes when there's a major repair bill looming. They unload it rather than pay for expensive repairs. Who was the previous owner? Did you thoroughly check out the maintenance records?"

"Several well-qualified companies have inspected it from top to bottom."

"Sese, he didn't buy the plane from a neighborhood shade tree mechanic." Bruce chimes in.

"This is an investment, and it will eventually pay for itself. You can drill, I mean, talk to my accountant at the summit. He was the one who suggested I buy it," Osei says.

"Sese, you'll love this aircraft. Please calm down," Bruce says.

I shoot him a look that says, "Be quiet."

"Daddy, I think you and Sese need to hug it out," Adia chimes in.

"Agreed," I say, wrapping my arms around him and resting my head on his shoulders.

Bruce chuckles, "Sese, I can't breathe."

"Man up, because I'm not letting you go."

Osei, getting a kick out of my antics, but led by his stomach, says, "What's for dessert?"

I look at Bruce, his eyes are laughing. I mouth to him, "Man up."

"Man up," Bruce chuckles, "Please, I baked up a batch of brownies while you and Sese had your movie night."

"Osei, you're in for a treat. My daddy makes the best brownies."

"I'll be the judge of that," Osei says, biting into one. His eyes widen.

"Oh, these are dangerous." He grabs the plate and bolts. "Mine now!"

"Osei, come back here. You can't have all the brownies," Adia yells.

"Okay, I'll have what is left over after you guys get what you want."

"Osei Lewis-Wharton, no, you won't," I say.

Osei stops mid-bite, saying, "Lewis-Wharton, it has a certain ring to it."

We spent the rest of the night as a family, enjoying each other's company. I look over at Bruce, and he looks at me. I see his eyes are glassy and moist. I mouth to him, "Man up."

The kids leave, and we go upstairs to bed. As we lie in each other's arms, I say, "This feels so right. You, me, and the kids. I promise you I'll do all I can to preserve what we have. Will you promise me the same?"

"I promise you with all my heart and soul."

My phone vibrates on the nightstand. It's Rainey.

"Hey, Sese, I heard Bruce is moving to Philadelphia."

"Yes, I heard the same thing," I reply.

"You better not let him stay in a hotel or rent an apartment."

"Why shouldn't I? He's a grown man and can fend for himself."

"Sese, this is a chance for you and him to get back together."

Bruce smiles and pulls me close, kissing me gently. I try not to moan.

"Are you okay?" Rainey asks.

Bruce answers for me. "Hey Rainey, she's fine. I'm just assuring your friend here that I'll take care of her body and soul for the rest of my life."

Laughing, Rainey says, "I'm going to hang up. Sounds like you're about to get very busy."

I'll call you tomorrow, I say, barely above a whisper.

60

Now We Know

I sat up in bed at 3:30 A.M., awakened by a strange dream. Bruce is still asleep. I reach for the water pitcher on my nightstand and pour a glass of water. I take a few sips, trying to understand the meaning of the dream that continues to haunt me.

I'm on a dark road when headlights appear, racing toward me. I run. There's a deafening crash. The car flips over. A bloodied woman and a man are trapped inside. The woman was pointing frantically to the back seat. A baby lies on the floor. I yanked the door, but it won't budge. I reach through the open window, grab the baby, and carry it to the other side of the road. As I turn back, I wake up. Breathless. An unsettling fear clings to me.

"Are you having the same dream again?" Bruce asks.

"Yes, I didn't mean to wake you."

"Come here, I'll rock you back to sleep."

I smile, lay my head on his chest, and he gently rocks me back and forth.

When I wake at 6:30 A.M., Bruce is in the shower. I knock on the shower door.

"Good morning, sunshine," he says.

"Are you going to be long?" I ask.

"I just stepped in, but I'll be quick."

"Can I join you?"

"Be my guest."

While I'm in the shower, Taylor's call go to voicemail. She leaves a message: *Sese, call me as soon as you get this message. It's important.*

Bruce and I rush out the door, with coffee cups in hand, already running late. He has a breakfast meeting with his new colleagues at the university, and today is Chloe's first day at the foundation. I've ordered breakfast, scheduled to arrive in ten minutes! I text Taylor to let her know I got her message and soon, then I send a quick note to Adia asking her to join us for breakfast.

I make it to the office just as Chloe and the breakfast delivery person arrive. As we step inside, morning sunlight floods the space, and the city skyline glows gold through the floor-to-ceiling windows.

Chloe excitedly says, "This is our office?"

"Do you like it?"

"I love it!"

Adia arrives, and I introduce her to Chloe. Minutes later, Osei and Asa walk in.

"Osei, are you a Beagle? Does your nose instinctively know when there's food?" I ask.

"Adia told us that she was having breakfast with you, and I was hoping there would be leftovers."

"There's more than enough."

Adia introduces Asa to Chloe, "This is my husband, Asa."

Adia says, "Sese, we haven't told Daddy, we plan on telling him today."

"Do you think that he'll be upset?" Asa asks.

"No, of course not."

Asa lets out a big sigh of relief.

"I told you everything would be okay," Osei says.

I leave the kids to their breakfast and head to my office. I look at my cell phone and see several missed calls from Taylor. Just as I start dialing her number, my phone rings; it's Taylor.

"Sese, where have you been? Can you talk?"

"I'm in my office. I was just calling you back."

"Where are Osei and Bruce?"

"Bruce is at a meeting, and Osei's here, having breakfast."

"You won't believe what I found. President Henry is Osei's benefactor, and my firm set up the trust."

"You're kidding."

"That isn't the half of it. The firm also manages the estate of President Henry. The estate is massive, and the sole beneficiary is his grandson. The child's name is Osei Henry. It states in the documents that Henry may no longer be his surname. He also instructed the firm to find him. No one here has ever looked. So, everything is just sitting there."

"And it all belongs to Osei," I vehemently say.

"Calm down, Sese, he won't have an issue claiming it. President Henry was very smart and made provisions that ensured Osei would inherit his estate. He stored his DNA, along with his daughter's DNA, at a very reputable DNA testing company. My firm has no affiliation whatsoever. President Henry left a safety deposit box with papers that outline Osei's family history, as well as jewelry that belonged to the Henry family members. Osei has to fill out paperwork to claim the estate. I'm emailing the documents to you, and I'll need them back ASAP."

"Taylor, I need to tell him right away."

"I agree. Besides money, there's significant real estate in Manhattan and Virginia. I'll send the list and the documents he needs to sign."

I go back into the kitchen, where Osei is drinking hot chocolate and joking with Adia. He's back to himself, and I am grateful.

"Osei, we need to finish some last-minute foundation details."

"I'm bringing my hot chocolate."

"No, you are not. I have an all-white office, and you are not about to ruin it with your hot chocolate."

Mocking me, he gingerly places the cup of hot chocolate on the counter.

"Have you heard from Mr. Thomas?"

"I intend to call him when I get home. He left a voicemail earlier."

"Can you call him now?"

"What's up?"

"I'll tell you why after we speak with him."

Looking concerned, Osei calls Mr. Thomas. "Hello, Mr. Wharton, thank you for calling me back. I was able to dig deeper into the car accident. As I suspected, the original police paperwork is bogus. As I told you earlier, the woman involved in the accident came from a very wealthy family, and people were paid off to cover up the facts, including the press. The male was not driving, as it states in the police report. The female was driving, and it seems she deliberately crashed the car into a bridge underpass. A suicide note was found in the console of the car, which was given to her father and was never admitted as evidence. I got this information from a retired police officer who was working at the police station at the time of the accident."

"I'm guessing he wasn't one of the ones paid off," I say.

"No, he wasn't. There was a lot of whispering and gossip, from what he remembered. It's believed the woman was devastated when the man refused to marry her. Some say she decided to give the baby up for adoption and end it all. All this was covered up by her father. The woman's father was a very influential person."

"Mr. Thomas, I'm Sienna Lewis, Osei's adoptive mother. Do you know what happened to the baby?"

"Yes, the child, a boy, was left at the Wharton Orphanage. I also understand it took the grandfather three to four years before he found the child. He spent a small fortune looking for the kid."

"Good to know," Osei says.

"I was trying to meet with the attorney who handled Mr. Henry's legal affairs, but unfortunately, he passed away a few years ago."

"Thank you, Mr. Thomas. Please keep me posted on any new developments."

He looks at me, eyes glassy. "Sese, how did you know she killed herself?"

"I didn't know for sure. I had my suspicions. Your grandfather believed you would find out who you were one day. He placed both his and your mother's DNA at the testing center." I tell him everything Taylor shared with me.

Head bowed, Osei exhales. "This is a lot to process."

"We have to go to New York. You'll need to take a DNA test."

"When the summit is behind us, I want to go to Virginia to visit the graves of my family. Will you go with me?"

"You don't have to ask. The very firm Taylor works for has sat on your inheritance for years." I handed him the paperwork Taylor sent.

We call Taylor to confirm we received the documents and to tell her about the conversation with the private detective.

"Osei, I'm one hundred percent convinced you are President Henry's grandson, and you are Vanessa and Phillip's son. This firm has been sitting on your inheritance for years. They were instructed by your grandfather to find you and to make sure you received your inheritance. They did absolutely nothing to try to locate you. I can recommend a law firm to file the documents for you."

"Auntie Taylor, I have a law firm in New York on retainer that oversees my affairs. Are you familiar with DGA Kipper?"

"Holy shit! They're one of the largest law firms in New York City."

"They oversee all my legal affairs, and the CEO has agreed to be on the foundation board. Sese and I'll reach out to him and fill him in on what's going on."

"This is a lot to unpack, Osei. Are you okay?" I ask.

"I'm more than okay. I have you. I also have the village you surrounded me with. I'm good."

There's a knock at the door. "Come in."

Adia and Asa walk in. "Osei, we're leaving. We have a couple of apartments to look at today," Adia says.

Osei hops up. "Do you need me to go with you?"

"No, we'll be okay." Adia smiles, "Look at you, acting like a big brother."

Laughing, Osei says, "I'm your brother. I don't need to act."

Walking into the office, Bruce asks. "What's so funny?"

In perfect unison, Osei and Adia point accusingly at each other.

"Bruce, do you have a moment?" Asa clears his throat. "I'd like to speak with you."

"Sure." They walk out to the balcony.

Adia anxiously tells me and Osei that Asa is going to ask her father for her hand in marriage.

"Bruce knows that you love each other and support each other, and he'll acknowledge your love," Osei says to Adia.

"Bruce adores Asa. If he didn't, believe me, you'd know it," I say honestly.

We rush over to the window to spy. Osei partially closes the blinds, and we listen intently to the conversation.

Asa starts the conversation by saying, "Mr. LeBlanc, first, I want to tell you how much I love Adia, and I want to share my life with her so we're married. Secondly, I want to apologize for not asking for your permission. If I have to get down on my knees and beg for forgiveness. I will."

"Asa, I know that Adia will always have your love and support. I wanted to walk her down the aisle, but seeing how happy she is with you gives me peace. My daughter loves you more than you'll ever know. You have my permission, and thank you for being by her side all these years. I'll always be your biggest supporter."

Bruce and Asa embrace, then turn to see us peeping through the blinds. Osei, standing next to Adia with his hands on her shoulders, says, "See? Everything is good. I told you it would be."

Tears are streaming down Adia's face. I take her hand and squeeze it. Shortly after, Adia and Asa leave to search for an apartment. Bruce comes over and kisses me on the forehead. "How is the morning going?"

Before I can answer him, Osei says, "I can answer that."

"Wait, what did I miss?" Bruce says eyes wide with curiosity.

"On second thought, I'll let Sese fill you in. I'm still trying to process it all."

I proceed to tell Bruce about the conversation we had with the private detective.

"Wow, Sese, you were right. How did you know?"

"It was your idea to follow the money. Osei's trust fund led me in that direction. Taylor called me this morning after following the money, and you won't believe what she found out."

Osei and I turn to Bruce. He raises an eyebrow.

"Well? What did she find?"

"President Henry left his estate to Osei."

Bruce leans forward. "You have my attention."

"Taylor says the estate is worth well over forty million dollars," Osei blurts out.

"You've got to be joking. That's unbelievable," Bruce says.

"No, we're not. The investment company can keep profiting on the account if it isn't claimed."

"What investment company manages the estate?" Bruce asks.

"The trust was started at the investment company where Auntie Taylor works," Osei says.

"Unbelievable. As if the heavens are directing things down here!"

"We were about to call Osei's attorney to have him file the necessary paperwork."

"If I'm not mistaken, your grandfather owned an apartment in the Dakota," Bruce says, his voice thick with emotion. "I remember hearing about the alumni fundraisers he held there being elegant and attended by the most powerful donors in the city and throughout the country. But what people don't realize is what it took for him to get into the Dakota. That building wasn't just expensive. It was a fortress of privilege, guarded by a board that rarely, if ever, approved a Black resident." He shakes his head slowly. "Your grandfather had everything. Degrees, prestige, influence, but none of that changed the color of his skin. I'm sure he didn't just move in. He had to fight quietly and strategically to get in. Not to mention having to have an ally. Someone on the inside who believed in him. Without that, I doubt they would've let him through those doors."

Sese's voice is tender, full of awe. "He must've carried so much. To break through a barrier like that. Just to live with dignity. Osei, now I understand where your fire comes from. It's your legacy. It's in your blood."

Osei's eyebrows raise, "Wait, what?" he says, shaking his head, trying to process it. Then his eyes widened. "Wait, the Dakota? Isn't that where John Lennon was killed?"

"There are also several pieces of property in Virginia and DC," I add.

"If this basketball thing doesn't work out, you'll have a little something you can fall back on," Bruce quips.

"Bruce, do you think Ms. Hannah knew about Osei's inheritance?"

"I'm sure of it," he answers. "Ms. Hannah's relentless attempts to insert herself into Osei's life finally make sense."

Osei dials the number to his attorney and presses the speaker button. A woman answers, "DGA Kipper, how can I help you?"

"This is Osei Wharton. May I speak with William Sidwell?"

"Please hold, I'll see if he's available."

A few moments pass, and then Mr. Sidwell comes on the line. "Osei, how are you?"

"I'm well, Bill. And you?"

"Doing great and looking forward to the summit. The foundation will be able to impact the lives of vulnerable and marginalized children."

"Thank you, Bill. With your help, I know we'll be able to do remarkable things. Don't forget to bring your sticks. I have reserved some time for us to play at Pumpkin Ridge."

"I'm looking forward to you taking my money."

"When was the last time I beat you at golf?" Osei says.

"Never," Bill proudly exclaims.

"I'm calling because there's an important matter that needs your attention. For full disclosure, I have my adopted mom and a family friend here with me, Sienna Lewis, and Bruce LeBlanc."

"Ms. Lewis, Osei has told me a lot about you, and I'm looking forward to meeting you.

Hello, Mr. LeBlanc. So, Osei, how can I help you?"

"Bill, as you know, while in the orphanage, there was a trust set up for me, and I recently found out the identity of my benefactor. The trust was established from the estate of Oscar Henry, my grandfather. I'm the heir to a large estate estimated to be worth millions."

"What company is managing the estate?" Bill asks.

"Melvin, Wells, and Franklin," Osei replies.

"Mr. Sidwell, apparently Ose's grandfather, stored his and his daughter's DNA for testing. Can we have it done without anyone at Melvin, Wells, and Franklin?" I ask.

"That can certainly be done, " Bill says. "Osei, you'll have something to fall back on if basketball doesn't work out."

Osei shoots Bruce an annoyed look that says, "Why does everyone keep saying, if basketball doesn't work out?"

"I'll file the paperwork with them and email it to you when it's ready," Bill says. "Send it along."

"It's on its way," Osei says.

"Earth to Sese," Bruce says, waving a hand in front of my face.

"Sese, what's wrong?" Osei's concern cuts through her thoughts.

"We need to proceed with caution. I'm sure your grandfather told them where you were. Why didn't anyone look for you, and now that you are famous, everyone knows your story. There aren't too many people on the planet named Osei who grew up in an orphanage in Virginia. The person managing your grandfather's estate at Melvin, Wells, and Franklin could very well be trying to steal your inheritance, and we aren't about to trust them. Osei, we need to call Mr. Sidwell back."

"Why?" Bruce asks.

I shoot him a look that says, "Don't question me right now". Osei redials and gets Bill back on the line.

"Mr. Sidwell, can you hold off contacting MWF? Osei and I will be in New York tomorrow. We need to get the DNA testing done prior to us reaching out to MWF."

"That's not a bad idea."

"The person at MWF managing the Henry Estate doesn't give two cents about the DNA facility. As far as they are concerned, Osei, unless you have a revelation from the heavens, why would you ever suspect you are Oscar Henry's grandson?"

"I'll never get used to how your mind works," Osei says.

Bruce smirks, "Few can challenge the cunning mind of Sienna Lewis."

"Mr. LeBlanc, why can't I just be a deductive thinker? Am I the only one who finds this situation strange?"

Osei nods, "I agree with Sese. I wasn't lost, and I'm sure there are forty million reasons someone at MWF didn't look for me."

There's foundation work to be done, so I kick Bruce and Osei out of my office. They head to the patio with glasses of lemonade. Chloe and I get busy. First up: securing accommodations and arranging transportation for the twenty-six guests staying at the Allison Inn & Spa. Tee times at Pumpkin Ridge Golf Club need confirming, and I've already emailed Lucas's guests' house guest list for their location. Now, it's time to finalize the agenda with Osei. I step onto the patio.

"Osei, Chloe, and I are done with the pre-preparations. All that's left is to finalize the agenda?"

"We were discussing your theory on the investment firm being duplicitous," Osei says.

"When you and Osei met with Ms. Hannah in London, she wanted him to sign with the sports management company, and also with an investment firm to manage his portfolio. We had Mark look into the sports management company, but did we ever ask him to check into the investment company?"

"Osei, do you still have the business cards Ms. Hannah gave you?" Bruce asks.

"Yes. I'll go downstairs and get them."

Osei returns with the two business cards. He hands me the one for the investment company. The name on the card says Charles McCarthy, Senior Investment and Financial Advisor, Melvin, Wells, and Franklin. I hand it to Bruce.

"Well, I'll be damned," Bruce says.

"The plan all along was to steal the estate from me," Osei says, his voice tight with disbelief. "They never meant for me to have it."

"According to Mike Tyson, everybody has a plan until you punch them in the mouth," I say.

"I agree. I'm betting they don't have anyone at the DNA lab," Bruce says.

"Exactly," I reply. "That's why we need to act fast and precisely."

"Bruce, you might want to call Dave because Ms. Hannah's killer could be someone connected with MWF."

I text Taylor: *Call me, it's urgent!*

Chloe comes out on the balcony, "Sese, Taylor is on the line for you."

We rush inside to take Taylor's call. I place her on speaker.

"Sese, I got your text, "What's up?"

"Taylor, call me from your cell, and from a place where you'll have complete privacy."

"You're scaring me, Sese. What's going on?

"I don't mean to, but we all could be in danger, especially Osei."

"I'll call you in fifteen minutes from home."

Taylor calls us back in precisely fifteen minutes, "What the hell is going on? Why all the cloaks and daggers?"

"Taylor, do you know a Charles McCarthy who works at your company?"

"Yes, he works with Alex Greenberg, who manages President Henry's estate."

"Do they know you are acquainted with Osei in any way?"

"No," she says.

"We need to keep it that way. Charles McCarthy was one of the men in London with Ms. Hannah. Can Charles and Alex find out you accessed President Henry's file?"

"No, my clearance is higher than theirs. Sese, are you telling me Alex and Chuck were working with Ms. Hannah?"

"Yes, we're certain that they were. We have a photo of Charles McCarthy taken by the security detail we hired in London. I'm texting it to you."

Osei hands me the phone, I scroll through my photos, find the picture, and send it to Taylor.

She gasps, "Oh my God, this *is* Chuck."

"Taylor, do you think they could be working with anyone else?" I ask.

"Alex reports to someone who is semi-retired, constantly traveling, and golfing. I doubt he has a clue what's going on."

"Okay, we'll be in New York tomorrow morning for Osei's DNA test. It will be expedited, and we'll have confirmation in a few hours. We've scheduled a meeting with Osei's attorney on Friday, at which time he'll file the paperwork for Osei to take possession of the estate. Would you be able to take over the management of the estate?"

"Yes. Osei would have to request it. I'll email his attorney the documents."

"Taylor, the only people who know about this are the four of us and Osei's attorney."

"It's in the vault. I won't mention it to anyone."

We say our goodbyes.

"I'll let Rob know to beef up the security detail on you two, and we'll need two of his men to drive you and Osei to New York tomorrow," Bruce says.

Osei's attorney emails us the paperwork we'll need to present to The Life Sciences Inc., the DNA company. Because of Osei's fame and notoriety, he also emailed a nondisclosure statement to be signed by the staff prior to our visit. As Chloe heads out for the day, I let her know that I'll be in NYC tomorrow and that she can call or email if she needs anything.

As we wrap up our day, Osei says, "Bruce, I have a former teammate who is looking to sublet a one-bedroom, two-bath unit on the fifth floor in this building. I'm thinking Adia and Asa might be interested in it."

"That's great news. We can see how their apartment search went today. If it didn't go well, you can tell them about the unit on the fifth floor."

"Okay," Osei replies.

I key in the code to lock the office door.

Bruce, peering over my shoulder with a curious look in his eyes, says, "That's a very long code."

"It's easy for me to remember."

"You would be in trouble if someone were chasing you," Osei says.

"I bet you twenty-five dollars I know what the code is," Bruce says to Osei.

"I bet you fifty dollars you don't," Osei says.

Bruce looks at Osei, and he smiles, "Why not make it interesting? Why not bet two hundred dollars?"

"You're on. I'll give you three tries to get it right," Osei says.

The first set of numbers Bruce keys in is incorrect. The keypad flashes red.

"One down, two to go."

He tries again, this time the bell chimes, and the light on the lock turns green. "*Voilà!*"

"How did you figure out the code?" Osei says, looking at him incredulously.

"I knew it had to be your birthday, mine, and Sese's. The problem was to figure out the sequence. You're more important to her than I am." He grins, "Sese always puts everyone else first."

"My silly men, I'm changing the code tomorrow, and you won't be able to crack it."

In the elevator, Bruce texts Adia to see what they're doing for dinner.

She responds, "We're on our way back to Osei's. We ordered Thai food. Come join us?"

The smell of the food makes us hungry. Bruce immediately takes the closest empty chair. "Adia, pass me the shrimp Pad Thai, please."

"How did the apartment hunting go today?" Bruce asks, stuffing food in his mouth. "Delicious," he points to the plate.

"Everything we saw today was more than affordable, but nothing we liked."

"You two are spoiled, having lived in your grandfather's apartment."

"Daddy, I'd be happy just to find a place we like. I know nothing can compare to where we live now."

"Osei knows of a place in this building, which might work for you," Bruce says.

"I can show it to you now if you want to see it."

"Yes, we would love to see it," Asa replies.

Bruce and I stay behind and call Dave.

"Hello, Bruce," Dave answers on the first ring. "Have I got news for you! A considerable sum of money was deposited into the accounts of family members of a prison guard assigned to Ms. Hannah's cell block. This Charles McCarthy guy had a very confrontational meeting with Ms. Hannah the day before she was found unconscious in her cell. A warrant is being issued for the prison guard and Mr. McCarthy. We were able to access some of the accounts McCarthy and his boss managed, and from what our forensic accountant told us, they have been taking money from the trust funds and the estates of their deceased clients for years. We have frozen the accounts, and we'll be ceasing all the client portfolios under their responsibility. This will also include President Henry's portfolio. I'm waiting on warrants, but I plan on arresting Charles McCarthy, Alex Greenberg, and the corrections officer tomorrow."

"Thank you, Dave. Keep us posted," I say.

"Sese, I should be thanking you. You were instrumental in putting the pieces of the puzzle together. Call me if you ever need a job."

Adia returns, and she's unable to contain her excitement. "Daddy, we're going to sublet the apartment of Osei's teammate. Would you like to see it?"

"Of course," he says. "I need to make a call, but I'll be up shortly."

I called Taylor. "Sese, I'm still in the office. I'll give you a call when I get home."

I head upstairs to join everyone. The place is as spectacular as the others, just smaller.

"The lease is for two years, and best of all, it comes fully furnished. We won't need to move any furniture, only our clothes. Daddy, isn't this exciting?"

"Yes," Bruce says.

"Asa, you and Adia can sign the lease tomorrow, and you're welcome to stay in the apartment tonight if you'd like," Osei says.

Osei walks Bruce and me to the garage. "S&O Management Company? You couldn't come up with a better name?" I ask, raising an eyebrow.

"It stands for Sienna and Osei."

"I know, and I think O&S Management Company would have been a better choice."

"What are you two talking about?" Bruce asks.

"We didn't tell you earlier, the apartment Adia and Asa will be living in belongs to the foundation," Osei says.

"Really? Then I'm truly grateful to S&O Management."

"You are welcome," I say.

We get home and take Mille out for a walk. The night breeze is crisp and cool, signifying that Fall is coming.

"I can't remember the last time I was this happy," Bruce says.

I take his hand. "I can."

"When were you this happy?" he asks.

"The first time you passionately kissed me."

"I passionately kissed you all the time."

"I'm referring to the first time we kissed while lying in bed together."

"You stopped by my apartment to thank me for carrying you back to the dorm."

"Yes, I bought you flowers and a card."

"Do you remember what happened that night?" I ask.

"Of course." The card read: *To Bruce, thank you for being a gentleman and carrying me home, but mostly for not taking advantage of me. However, in the future, you have my permission to do so. Love Sienna.*

"After I read the card, I picked you up and took you to my bedroom, and the rest is history. In fact, I was the one who was taken advantage of."

"If I remember correctly, I held you hostage and made you spend the entire weekend in bed with me."

Laughing, he says, "You didn't have to twist my arm."

"Bruce, the way you kissed me told me you wanted me as much as I wanted you, and that made me incredibly happy."

"Our diet that weekend consisted of pizza, coffee, and Krispy Kreme donuts. When you get back from New York, we'll have a weekend of pizza and Krispy Kreme donuts."

"We'll have a weekend to ourselves, but there will be no pizza or Krispy Kreme donuts," I exclaimed.

After our walk, I call Taylor and fill her in on our conversation with Dave, letting her know that warrants will be issued, and documents seized because her colleagues are stealing from their clients.

"Sese, are you serious? They're stealing from the firm and clients?"

"Yes. They will be going to jail. Are Alex and Charles at work today?"

"Today is Alex's birthday, and there is an office party in celebration."

"I can guarantee you the mood in the office tomorrow won't be a celebratory one."

"I've been monitoring President Henry's account. There hasn't been any activity since last week. I've also blocked the account where no money can be taken out, or trades done on the account without the CEO's approval."

"Won't they become suspicious?"

"It doesn't matter. They can't touch the money or the real estate. They've left for today, and more than likely, they will be continuing the birthday celebration with expensive alcohol and women."

The next morning, we meet our security team in the parking garage of Osei's apartment. Osei drives his Range Rover, and I sit in the front with him. James and Tony are in the back seat. An Escalade carrying two other guys follows close behind. We arrive at Life Science Inc., the DNA lab, located on the Upper West Side. Osei looks anxious.

"Osei, are you okay?"

"I'm okay."

Osei and I walk in. The lobby is decorated with sleek leather furniture, lush plants, and Persian rugs on black marble floors.

Osei whispers, "This definitely isn't your Maury DNA Lab."

We meet the receptionist.

"I'm Pedro. Have a seat. Doctor Lee is expecting you."

A few minutes later, Doctor Lee appears and leads us through a maze of hallways. We finally arrive in a large space divided by curtains. A nurse approaches and asks Osei to follow her.

"How long will it take before we have results?" I nervously ask.

Looking at his watch, Dr. Lee says, "We'll have the results in three to four hours."

"Is there a restaurant near here where we can get breakfast?"

"We have a private area, and breakfast can be delivered. I'll have someone bring you a few menus for you to take a look at," Dr. Lee says, as he closes the door.

I call Tony, inviting him and the team to come inside. He declines, preferring to stay outside. I look over the menus and place an order, because whatever I choose will be fine with Osei. Twenty minutes later, Doctor Lee walks in with Osei.

He's struggling, and I see tears forming in his eyes. "What's wrong?" I take his hand.

"I'm feeling nauseous," he replies.

His hands are clammy, and he's trembling. Breakfast comes. Osei only sips on his orange juice. He never turns down food, no matter the circumstances, so I know he is really nervous.

"Sese, I'm so afraid this could amount to nothing, but I'm also afraid that it might. I have all these emotions. One second, I want to cry, then the next second, I want to jump up and down and scream with joy."

"Osei, don't be afraid. Whatever happens, there are two things you know for sure. One, you were deeply loved by your grandfather. Second, I deeply and unconditionally love you with all my body and soul forever and a day, regardless."

I text Bruce. *We have arrived, and the testing is being done. We are waiting for the results.*

I move to the sofa. Osei joins me, curling up next to me with his head resting in my lap. I stroke his back and shoulders until he falls asleep. *Regardless of his age and size, he's still a child who has navigated through the trials and tribulations of his life alone.*

Two hours later, Doctor Lee enters the room. He invites Osei and me to a conference room down the hall. We sit at a table across from him.

"Osei, we have the results, and it's a 99.9 percent match that Vanessa Henry is your mother, and Oscar Henry is your grandfather. I have sent the results to your attorney. Your grandfather knew that one day you would come here. When he met with me and my team, he was very precise as to how I was to manage this day." He hands Osei a large manila envelope, which Osei hands to me.

"Sese, can you open this for me?" Osei asks.

The envelope shows clear signs of aging. It had a button with a string fastened around it and sealed with tape, which had turned yellow with age. It clearly hadn't been opened in decades.

Doctor Lee says, "I'll give you both some privacy."

Inside, a handwritten letter and several pictures. I hand Osei the pictures, and I begin to read the letter.

"Sese, why are you crying?"

I touch my face, surprised by the wetness of my tears. I hadn't realized I was crying.

"Are you okay?"

"Yes, I'm okay. I'm just worried about you."

My Dearest Grandson,

At last, I've found you again. First, I want to tell you that you were deeply and sincerely loved. It took me several years to find you, and by then my health was in decline. There was no one I could entrust you to. For better or worse, I made the decision for you to remain at Wharton. Dr. Becker was a great man, and he assured me you would be well taken care of; I trusted him and his wife to do so.

Your real name is Oscar James Henry. You couldn't say Oscar. The closest you could get to Oscar was Osei. So, everyone started to call you Osei. It's important you know your heritage. The firm overseeing my estate has another envelope for you, which will furnish you with detailed information on your heritage and who you are. Melvin, Wells & Franklin, and my good friend Edward Annenberg, manage my estate.

I call Taylor to inform her that President Henry is indeed Osei's grandfather.

"Sese, I can't talk now. All hell is breaking loose here. Every federal alphabet you can imagine is here."

"Wait, Taylor. Answer me this. Is Edward Annenberg still working at the firm?"

"No, he passed away, and the account was handed over to someone who is semi-retired. For all intents and purposes, Alex manages it now. What are the DNA results?" she asks.

"Osei is indeed President Henry's grandson. Osei's attorney will send over the paperwork needed for the estate."

I hang up. Osei is looking at the photos. There are four photos, one of a young Osei and President Henry, fly-fishing. Osei is seated on his grandfather's shoulders, as President Henry stands in the river, the water is midway up his thighs. A picture of Vanessa and Phillip seated at a table, holding hands, and smiling at one another from ear to ear, and the last photo was a picture of Osei standing beside a black car. He looks to be three years old. On the back of the back of photo, written in bold black ink: I FOUND MY BOY.

I look at Osei. He's smiling. "I'm okay, seriously, I'm really okay," he says.

We thank Doctor Lee and his staff, and we head back to Philadelphia.

Osei and I climb into the back of the SUV. He's too emotionally drained to drive. No sooner had his head hit the seat than he's out like a light. I called Mr. Sidwell and sent him a snapshot of the DNA results. "Mr. Sidwell, do you need anything else from Osei to proceed?"

"No, Sienna, I will file the papers and get everything in motion for the estate to be handed over to him."

Taylor calls with news. Charles and Alex, along with four other associates, were arrested, and Osei's estate is secure: she'll be managing everything until further notice. I hang up the phone, and I stare at Osei.

"Sese, why are you staring at me?"

"Oh, I thought you were asleep? I was looking for Oscar, but I didn't see an Oscar. I'm glad you are Osei."

"Me too."

"When I'm upset with you, I'll be using your birth name," I say mockingly, "Oscar James Henry, have you lost your mind?"

"Please don't," he says, resting his head on my shoulder.

"Well, you better not make me upset."

It's late evening when we arrive in Philadelphia, and I have the sense Osei doesn't want to be alone.

"Do you want to spend the night at my place?" I ask.

He jumps at the opportunity. "Yes, I would love that."

"We can grill salmon and steak, and have a garden salad, something light."

"Hey, Bruce," Osei says, putting him on speaker.

"How are you doing, man?" Bruce asks.

"I have my moments, but overall, I'm fine," Osei replies.

"I'm calling to let you know I'm firing up the grill," Bruce says.

"Good, we'll be there soon, and I'm going to invite Adia and Asa to come over," I say.

"The more, the merrier." Bruce chimes in.

Bruce brings in the steaks as Osei and Adia are arguing over who is the greatest boxer of all time, Mike Tyson or Muhammad Ali. We can't help but laugh at their playful banter.

Bruce comes over to kiss me. I turn away. I'm still not comfortable being affectionate in front of Adia just yet.

"Sese, I'm okay with you kissing my dad."

"As long as it's not X-rated," Osei quips, prompting everyone to laugh.

Over dinner, we filled them in on what happened today at the DNA lab and the arrest at the investment firm.

"You don't look like an Oscar," Adia says.

"I dare you to call me Oscar."

"Don't worry, you'll always be Osei to me."

Asa shakes his head. "Adia, that's your takeaway from all of this? I'm still reeling at the forty million dollars, not to mention an apartment in the Dakota."

"Adia, you haven't told Asa that you're wealthy?"

Grinning, Adia says, "He knows. His family runs one of the top gene therapy companies. We work to make a difference, not to increase the zeros in our bank accounts."

After dinner, Osei leaves with Adia and Asa. Bruce and I sit under the night sky, enjoying a glass of wine and filled with the warmth of the evening.

"My heart aches for Osei's parents. They never got to know their wonderful child," I say.

Bruce nods. "Is he going to be okay?"

"He probably shouldn't be alone. Should I at least go check on him?"

"It couldn't hurt," Bruce replies.

I pull into the garage, and I see Osei still in his car, motionless, his eyes closed. Lost in thought, or maybe trying not to feel anything at all. My heart tightens at the sight.

I tap on the car window and smile. "A penny for your thoughts."

With tears rolling down his face, he says, "Why am I such a wreck? I should be happy."

"Come on, I'll make you a cup of hot chocolate and we'll talk about happiness, the book, the sequel, and the prequel."

"Sese, how did you know I needed someone to talk to? Bruce isn't upset, is he?"

"He's fine. He knows you come first, just as I know Adia comes first in his life."

I hand Osei his hot chocolate. "When was the last time you were happy?"

"This morning, before I found out about Poppa Henry and my birth parents."

"When do you think you'll be happy again?

"I was happy the moment I heard your voice in the parking garage."

"Osei, you and I didn't discuss what happened today. What in your life has changed? Other than the fact that the people who gave me life are no longer alive."

"It hasn't," Osei replies.

"You know if your grandfather hadn't become ill, he would have taken care of you, and you should also know if your mother didn't have issues, she would have loved and cared for you. Now you know these two things, how has your life changed?"

"My life hasn't changed, but my heart has."

I place his hand on his heart. "You can hold them there and still be happy. But if you continue to feel sorry for yourself. There won't be any room for them."

"Sese, I don't feel sorry for myself."

"What are you feeling?"

"I'm feeling the pain of not knowing them, of not being able to love them."

"Osei, we'll find out everything we can about them. They would want you to move on. Happiness, the prequel, now you know who your parents are. Happiness, the book is happening right now. Happiness, the sequel, will keep unfolding. Nothing you learned today should make you sad. I'm crashing in your guest bedroom. For better or for worse, we have each other."

"I'll give you something to sleep in."

"Not necessary," I say, opening my coat to reveal my flannel pajamas, "I came prepared."

I text Bruce, *Osei is okay.*

He texts back, *Sweet dreams, I'll see you in the morning.*

61

Soundproof

I can't sleep. The upcoming summit and Osei's learning that he has no living relatives weigh heavily on me. Hearing Osei and Millie snoring peacefully, I tiptoe downstairs and call Gloria.

"Sese, how are you? The boys gave me your message. I apologize for not calling you back. I had three surgeries today."

"I'm fine." I settle into a chair and begin recounting today's events. From Osei's inheritance, the DNA match, and the arrest at Taylor's firm.

"How's Osei doing now that he knows?" she asks.

"He's conflicted, and I'm doing my best to help him cope. Once all this is in the rearview mirror, I'm going to suggest counseling."

"That's a good idea."

"I'm looking forward to seeing everyone at the summit. The boys and Jackson can't contain their excitement about going to the Nike campus. How's Bruce?"

"He's decided to sublet his place in North Jersey, and we're going to live together."

"So, tell me. How are you coming with the letters? I can't imagine the pain both of you have been going through reading them."

"There are times when I laugh until I cry, and others when I just cry. Bruce was miserable, but the good memories of us are what kept him going. All these years, I envisioned something altogether different. I hated him for being married. I hated him for being happy, and most of all, I hated him for being a father.

We have this ritual, after reading a letter, we sit facing each other in a bubble bath, and we talk about anything that comes to mind. Sometimes we talk about the letter I just read, and other times, I tell him what I was doing on the day he wrote the letter."

"I guess misery loves company," Gloria mournfully says.

"Not exactly. I tell him about the times I spent with you all. He gets a kick out of those stories. I told him about Rhett and how I was happy until I wasn't."

"So, what happens after the bubble baths?" Gloria teases.

"None of your business. How's Jackson?" I ask, changing the subject.

"Annoyed, he had to pay to soundproof our bedroom."

"Why on earth would you have him soundproof your bedroom?"

"I had nothing to do with it. The boys were complaining that we kept them up at night doing adult activities. They refused to say the word sex."

I burst out laughing.

"Sese, please stop laughing."

"Gloria, my side hurts. I can't take this. This is the funniest thing I've heard in a long time. Thank you, I needed that release. Good night."

I pour myself a glass of water and quietly head back upstairs, trying not to wake Osei.

"What was so funny?" he asks.

"I didn't mean to wake you."

I tell him about my conversation with Gloria and why Jackson had to soundproof their bedroom. He's crying, and choking at the same time. I hand him the glass of water.

"Here, you need this more than I do."

62

Baby Daddy

I head downstairs. I text Chloe. *I'll be late. Call me if you need anything.*

Then I call Bruce.

"Good morning, sunshine," he says.

"Good morning. Can you bring me something to wear to the office?"

"Anything in particular?"

"No."

"Sure, I'll see you in thirty minutes."

The breakfast I'm making fills the house with a delicious aroma of crispy bacon, fluffy pancakes, and fresh coffee.

"Wow, it smells good in here," Osei says as he joins me in the kitchen.

The doorbell rings. Bruce and I greet each other with a kiss.

"I'm sorry about last night, I didn't mean to take Sese away from you," Osei says.

"Nothing would have kept Sese from checking on you last night. Are you okay?"

"I'm better now. Bruce, you knew my father. Am I at all like him? Do I resemble him?"

"To be honest, you don't resemble him, but you have the look of him. You have his height, his mannerisms, and you definitely have his sense of humor. He loved playing basketball and was competitive at everything. Come to think of it, he was also very generous. Being a few years older than me and an established officer in the Navy, he would often treat me to dinner. There were times, unsolicited, mind you, he would give me a couple of dollars. Your sense of generosity comes from him. I was the one who introduced your parents to each other, so you could say I'm partly responsible for your existence."

"Really, I owe you one," he says playfully.

"Did he love Vanessa?"

"I think he did. Vanessa was a difficult person to love. She lived mostly within herself. You know, she and I dated for a few months," Bruce says.

"So technically, you could have been my daddy. What happened between you two?"

"Sienna happened. If I hadn't met Sienna, maybe who knows?"

"Sese, if it hadn't been for you, Bruce could have been my daddy."

"If it hadn't been for me, Bruce would have been a lot of babies' daddy."

Smiling at them, I say, "I'm late for work. I can't believe we're leaving for Oregon tomorrow."

"Yes, in my used jet," Osei sarcastically says.

I glare at him from over my shoulder, "You'd better stop playing with me. It had better not look used, and you better email me the Carfax report."

When I get to the office, Chloe and I review the summit itinerary for what seems like the hundredth time.

"How many times will we go over this? We've crossed every 'T' and dotted every 'I,' so please relax," Chloe says, annoyance speckling her voice.

I can tell she's had it with me, so when she leaves for lunch, I quickly call Dee.

"Sese, everything will be fine. Please relax."

"This has to be perfect."

"It's natural to feel nervous, but the summit will be just another thing you'll conquer."

Bruce and I have lunch at La Giorno: mussels marinara, seared sea scallops, and spinach in a Beurre Blanc sauce.

"How did you know?"

"Know what?" I ask.

"That Vanessa and Phillip were Osei's birth parents."

"I had my suspicions, but it became crystal clear when Osei told me about his memories of President Henry. What I still haven't figured out is why me? Who decided to place Osei in my care?"

Bruce takes a bite of the seared scallops. "That's the missing piece of the puzzle. Ms. Hannah was high on the list, but how she resented you, she couldn't have done it."

"After the summit, Osei and I are going to visit his family's burial grounds. Can you come with us?"

"Of course."

Changing the subject, I ask, "Are you excited to start your new position at the university?"

"Yes, and I'm looking forward to the semester starting and..." He's interrupted by my phone vibrating on the table.

"Hey, Taylor."

"I need to speak with you and Osei. Can you make time tonight?"

"Sure, what is this about?"

"His grandfather's estate is much larger than what we originally thought. I'll give you a call at eight thirty tonight to update you both."

I look at Bruce in disbelief and say, "This is unreal."

"If this kid never bounces another basketball, he's set for life, and his children are set. This is true generational wealth," Bruce says.

Back at the office, I text Osei to let him know we have a call with Taylor tonight.

"I'm off. I'll be back before the call with Taylor," Bruce says.

I'm sitting by the fireplace when Osei arrives.

"How was your day?" I ask.

"I had an incredible day."

"What made it so incredible?"

"I didn't feel alone, and you're asking me about my day? Made this an even more incredible day. After practice, I took a nap. I've never been relaxed enough to sleep during the day. I feel at ease, knowing who I am. This journey would never have happened without you by my side."

"Osei, I'm happy to walk with you wherever the road takes you."

"I'm curious what Aunt Taylor has to say."

Walking into the living room, Bruce says, "That makes two of us."

The phone rings at exactly eight thirty.

"Hello, gorgeous," I say.

"Right back at you. Are Osei and Bruce with you?"

"Yes, I'm going to place you on speaker."

"Hey, Auntie Taylor."

"Marvelous, the gang is all here. At the present time, the estate is worth sixty-five million dollars, and we are still assessing everything. Osei, we'll need you to come in as soon as possible to sign the necessary paperwork to turn the estate over to you."

Bruce lets out a low whistle. Osei, seemingly missing Taylor's point, says, "We can come after the summit?"

"Sure, that will be fine," Taylor replies.

"Holy cow, this is ridiculous. Taylor, I'd be curious to know what the original amount of the estate was," Bruce says.

"Good question," Osei says in agreement.

"Well, from what we can tell, the estate's original value was twenty-five million. Before running the university, your grandfather was a partner at a prominent New York law firm. Some early property purchases added to the estate's value. And get this, your grandmother was the only daughter of a wealthy New York family with real estate holdings in Harlem and Manhattan. That has also contributed to its value. Osei Henry, you're a descendant of Black New York aristocracy," Taylor says proudly.

"Thank you, Auntie Taylor. This is a lot to digest. We'll see you soon."

"One thing we know for sure is even though those guys were crooks, they were savvy investors," I say.

"I'm in a betting mood, Bruce says with a grin at Osei. "How about a game of chess? Ready to get schooled?"

Osei raises an eyebrow and smirks, "Oh, I'm ready. But just so you know, I'm about to turn you into a pawn in my master plan."

I leave them trash-talking. I'm sitting in bed reading when Osei comes and plops down beside me and says, "I'm leaving. I'll be here at ten in the morning."

"We'll be ready."

A few minutes later, Bruce gets into the bed beside me, snuggles close, and kisses my neck.

"Next week we'll be surrounded by family and friends with little time to ourselves. So, I propose we have our private time tonight."

I give him a confused look. "Are you suggesting we cram a week's worth of private time into one night?"

"Yes, if you don't mind."

I gave him a playful look as I unbuttoned his shirt, kissing his neck.

"I thought I'd get some resistance," he says.

I stop and glance around the room. "From whom? Is there somebody else here I don't know about?"

I gently push him onto the pillow. "Mr. LeBlanc, be careful what you ask for."

The alarm clock rings. Bruce rolls over with a smirk. "I can't believe you kept me up all night."

I grab my robe, and I head to the kitchen. "I need coffee. Do you want a cup?"

"We have another ten minutes. I need you."

"Ten minutes will turn into twenty, and the kids will be here before we know it."

He throws back the sheets.

"Mr. LeBlanc, you need a cold shower."

"I can't believe you're going to leave me like this!" he yells after me.

I return with the coffee and settle in next to him.

"What's with the look? We have been up all night making love. Aren't you happy? I gave you what you asked for."

"I'm over the moon, but I think about all the time we were apart, and I get angry."

I take a sip of my coffee. "Yum, this is the best coffee ever."

"Are you changing the subject?"

"Yes, because neither one of us can change what happened in the past. So, we must guard our love and make sure nothing, or no one, will be able to come between us. From now on, our time together will be filled with loving one another."

"Yes, you know, it's the little things that matter. Like this moment, simple, but perfect."

We touch our cups together, "Yes, simple, but perfect. Now get up and take your shower."

He jumps out of bed and grabs me. "We're going to take a shower together."

"Hey, family, I'm here. Asa and Adia are waiting in the car."

"We're in the kitchen," Bruce says.

I hand him a travel mug of hot chocolate. I pick up my toiletry bag, and Bruce carries both our briefcases. We join Adia in the back seat.

"Good morning," Bruce and I say in unison.

"Where's your luggage?" Adia asks.

"We already have clothes at the house. This keeps everything really simple," Osei responds.

We arrive at Philadelphia Atlantic Aviation, and Chloe is waiting inside. After checking in, we head out to Osei's new plane, a Dassault Falcon 2000LX. Bruce and Asa are the first to board, but they stop in their tracks. I bump into Bruce, and Chloe—who is right behind me—collides into me. Annoyed, I give Bruce a push. "Will you move?"

"Sese, you won't believe this," he excitedly says.

As he and Asa move down the aisle. The plane in all its splendor comes into view.

"Wow, Osei, I'm impressed. I feel like I've walked into the lobby of a five-star hotel and there's more than enough room for everyone," I exclaim.

Chloe and Adia sit across from each other, while Bruce, Osei, and Asa sit at a table so they can play chess and dominoes. I settle in on the couch, too tired after staying up all night, and hand Chloe and Adia cashmere throws.

"It gets cold on the plane, so you'll need these."

I'll inspect the plane later.

An hour into the flight, I get up to look around. I examine the bathroom and the galley. I open the refrigerator, and there's soda, water, and juice. There are also sandwiches, salads, guacamole, and several types of sliced cheese. The cabinets were filled with cookies, crackers, potato chips, and Twizzlers.

"Hey, Mr. Wharton, I'll take care of the galley on the way back. Look at all this junk food you bought."

Adia joins me in the galley and points her finger at Osei. "Mr. Wharton, did you think you were feeding a bunch of toddlers?"

Osei enters the galley and opens up the warming drawers. One with roasted chicken, steaks, and salmon, the other with rice and steamed vegetables.

"Wow, this is fantastic. You did good, Mr. Wharton. I think I'm going to like your used plane," I say.

I blow a kiss to Bruce and snuggle under the throws.

I wake up to Osei playing chess with Asa. I look around and see Bruce asleep at the other end of the couch.

The captain announces, "Please prepare for landing in forty-five minutes."

When we land, two SUVs are waiting. The kids take one to the house, while Bruce and I head to the Airport to pick up Rhett and the president of the European auto company Osei just signed with. Rhett is accompanied by a woman and introduces Maxwell Wagner, the European executive, and his fiancée, Song Min-Ah. I'm so happy for them that I nearly jump into the back seat to hug her.

"Congratulations to you both," Bruce says.

"Are you sure we're not in the Swiss Alps?" Maxwell asks as we pull up to the house. "This place is beautiful."

"It does feel like we've been transported to some idyllic spot in Switzerland, doesn't it? I'm glad you like it because it's where you'll be staying."

Osei greets us, and I introduce him to everyone. He grips Maxwell's hand in a firm handshake and gives Rhett and Min-Ah a big hug. "Min-Ah," he says. "I want to warn you, Sese is a Korean drama fanatic."

"So am I," Min-Ah exclaims.

We lock arms and begin talking about our favorite Korean dramas.

In the kitchen, Dee and Arjun are cooking and talking with Jackson.

"What are you doing here?" I say to Jackson, grabbing him in a bear hug.

"I came a day early because I want to spend some time with my best friend."

Once everyone settles, I look around and realize I can escape for a few minutes by myself. Osei and Maxwell are talking about sports and cars. Rhett and Min-Ah are mesmerized by seeing Dee and Arjun. Their cooking shows are syndicated in London. Bruce and Jackson are getting ready to go swimming. *Tomorrow will be where the rubber meets the road, so tonight, I'm going to relax and enjoy myself.*

I take a cat nap, dress, and join Rhett, Min-Ah, Dee, and Arjun in the kitchen. Dee hands me a glass of wine, whispering in my ear, "Sex with Bruce agrees with you. You are glowing!"

"Mind your business," I whisper back.

"Arjun, "What are you cooking?" I ask.

"Some dishes for Osei, butter chicken and fish curry, and Dee is making lobster mac and cheese, herb-crusted beef brisket, and a boatload of veggies."

"Dee, I thought we were having drinks and appetizers tonight."

"We are, but Osei says he's starving, so Arjun and I are cooking for him."

"Honestly, Dee, when isn't he starving?"

Dinner is served poolside. The delicate white twinkling lights hang in the trees, and floating candles drift aimlessly across the pool. The atmosphere is enchanting, as if we're floating among the stars. Osei, Rhett, Bruce, Jackson, and Maxwell dine at the same table, while the rest of us sit at adjacent tables.

After dinner, Osei challenges Asa to a game of dominoes. Arjun, Jackson, and Bruce follow Osei and Asa into the game room.

With Jackson yelling, "I'm playing the winner."

Fighting jet lag, Rhett, Min-Ah, and the European executive retire for the evening.

"Thank you for letting me film my show here. We had a sensational time, which translates into a sensational show, which translates into high ratings. I can't believe Vanessa Henry was Osei's mother, and President Henry his grandfather. Who would have thunk it?" Dee says, brows furrowed. "This is unbelievable."

"Dee, why are you staring at me like that?"

"Until now, I didn't realize how much you and Vanessa Henry resembled each other, and that's why Osei looks like he could be your son. Sese, how did he end up at your front door?"

"That's the million-dollar question I'm determined to find an answer to. After the summit, Osei and I'll be in New York. Apparently, President Henry left him sealed letters in a safe in the Dakota apartment. Maybe the answer is there."

Dee chokes on her drink. "He left Osei, an apartment in the Dakota."

"Yes, can you believe it?"

"You can't make this stuff up," Dee says.

We look up as Arjun brings us chai latte. He sets the tray on the table.

"I didn't want you drinking wine all night. Enjoy the tea." He winks at Dee. "I'll see *you* later."

"Aren't you going to join us?" Dee asks.

"I'm going back to the game room. The domino matches are too exciting to leave. Jackson and Bruce are playing now, and the trash-talking is better than the game." He waves back and disappears inside.

"Sese, I really meant what I said earlier. You look truly happy."

"I'm over the moon happy. Osei and Bruce are filling a void I never dared to admit existed. I feared that loneliness would consume me, but I have released that fear. "

"Bruce is moving to Philly to teach at the University of Penn."

"Good, you can see each other often."

"Yes, every day and every night. He's going to move in with me."

"Oh my God, let me tell Rainey, I know something she doesn't."

As Dee and I are heading inside, we're hijacked by Osei. He drags us into the game room to see the domino showdown between Bruce and Jackson.

Bruce says to Jackson, "You are done for now. My lucky charm just walked in."

Needless to say, Bruce's lucky charm didn't work. He lost very badly to Jackson.

An hour later, I kissed Bruce on the cheek, "Your lucky charm is tired and going to bed."

Adia says, "Me too." She grabs my arm, and we leave, arms linked together. I walk Adia to the adjoining suite she and Asa are sharing with Osei.

"Sese, can you come in for a few minutes? I need to tell you something."

"Sure."

She nervously turns to me, whispering, "Thank you."

"For what?"

"For allowing my dad to be himself. I have never seen him this happy. I witnessed the light in his eyes slowly fade. Do you know how many years he has had an apartment in New Jersey?"

"Yes, he told me. Ten years."

"Mom found out about it because she hired a private detective to follow him, because she thought he was having an affair. He took photos of my dad doing everyday stuff, shopping for groceries, reading in the park, and riding his bike along the river. There was one photo of him standing on the balcony, crying. When my mom saw the picture, she showed it to me and said, 'I'm happy to know he's miserable too.' I was ten years old at the time. I went to my room and cried and prayed that one day they both would be happy. Thank you for allowing Dad to love and be happy."

"You're welcome." We hug and say goodnight, and I head to my suite.

I'm just about to get into bed when a knock sounds at my door. Before I can answer, Osei walks in and drops onto the bed.

"Just came to say good night and to get plenty of rest tonight. Bruce is making golden milk for everyone, and he wants to know if you would like one."

"No, I'm so tired. Tell Bruce I don't need golden milk. I need him."

"You are scandalous," Osei says.

"Only on occasion."

A short time later, Bruce gets into bed beside me, saying, "I heard you need me."

I rest my head on his chest. "Yes, I need you." Our breathing synchronizes, and we fall asleep.

63

Here's to Family

I awake to Bruce kissing my forehead.

"Good morning," he says, and hands me a cup of coffee.

I glance at the clock: 5:00 am "Why did you make coffee this early?" I ask, still groggy.

"I didn't make it. Adia did. She and Chloe are heading to the Allison Inn to check in the early arrivals."

I head downstairs to catch them before they leave. Chloe and Adia are having breakfast.

"You didn't have to get up," Adia says.

"I know everything is handled, but I couldn't let you leave without seeing you first."

"The welcome bags arrived yesterday at the hotel, and the reception area has been set up by the hotel staff," Chloe says.

"Auntie Dee worked with the food service staff, and everything is set," Adia says.

"What would I do without you?" I say. "This calls for a group hug."

The girls leave with a sense of pride at a job well done.

Osei joins me in the kitchen.

"Good morning, Sese."

"Good morning, how did you sleep?" I ask.

"Not well, I'm not used to having people around me. It reminds me of the orphanage."

"Osei, I can find other accommodations for them."

"That's not necessary. Besides, it will only be for a few more days." He sips his hot chocolate. "I'll get used to it."

"But Adia and Asa stayed at your place in Philly."

"Yes, but we were on different floors. I'll be okay."

"Osei, are you sure?" I ask.

"I'm sure," he winks and kisses the top of my head.

"What time is the New York crew arriving?" Bruce asks.

"All by noon. Gloria and the boys will be here a little after that. Dee and Arjun are already at the hotel, overseeing breakfast for the early guests arriving now."

"Do I have time to get a workout in?" Osei asks.

"You'll have plenty of time. Everyone arrives later for cocktails."

"Great, I'll ask Asa to join me."

"I'm meeting with Lucas to review a few details, then going for a hike," I say, heading to get dressed.

"I'll make sure the security team accompanies you," Bruce says.

"Why? We no longer have Ms. Hannah and her merry thieves lurking around every corner."

Bruce sighs. "You really want me to answer that? Sese, no matter where you go, from now on, you'll have security. Osei and I decided. End of discussion. Enjoy your hike."

"Wow, Lucas, this place is more than a pool house, it's a full-blown apartment!" I say, clearly impressed.

"Yes, it was used by the previous owner's teenage grandson."

I call Osei. "Can you come to the pool house?"

"Yeah, what up?"

"Come now, and you will see."

Five minutes later, Osei walks in. I wave my hand excitedly around. "This place would be perfect for Mason and Zoe. Wouldn't you love having him here with you?"

"Yes," he says and immediately calls Mason.

"Hey Mase, where are you? Well, turn around, you guys are staying here with me. I'm texting you the address now."

I wrapped up the meeting with Lucas. The security team joins me on a hike in Tualatin Hills Park. When I return, Bruce and Jackson are swimming. Dee and Arjun are working with Lucas's team to set up the food stations. I wave, and Dee blows me a kiss. Wanting to rest before everyone arrives, I take a shower and slip into bed. A couple of hours later, I wake to find Osei asleep at the foot of the bed. I move closer and whisper in his ear, "Osei, my son, are you alright?"

His eyes open slowly, shimmering with unshed tears. I rub his back, concern filling my voice.

"Osei, what's wrong?"

"I was fine until you called me son. I can't ever remember anyone using that word for me."

"Well, you better get used to it, because you are mine," I say, smiling as I gently rub his shoulder.

He hesitates, then looks at me with quiet determination.

"Should we make it official?"

"Official, how?" I ask, staring at him.

"I want you to adopt me." He meets my gaze.

Now it's my turn to tear up. "Are you serious? You want me to adopt you?"

"Yes, but I have to keep my last name."

"I'm okay with that. There are plenty of people already with the last name Lewis."

I hear voices downstairs and leap out of bed. Lucas is greeting Taylor and Rainey. I run to them, shouting, "You're here!"

"And happy to see you! But Sese, this place is absolutely fabulous," Rainey says, looking around.

Taylor nods, "For once, I agree with Rainey. This place is magnificent."

"Where are your men?" I ask.

"They saw Bruce, Jackson, and Arjun at the pool, and decided to join them," Taylor replies.

"Hey, Aunties! Welcome to Sese Land," Osei says.

"Hey, everybody." Taylor waves. Where is Dee?"

"In the kitchen, doing her thing. Follow your noses and you'll find her," Osei says,

Dee, lost in her music, is cooking, her shoulders swaying slightly. Taylor moves in quietly and wraps her arms around Dee's waist.

Startled, Dee turns around. Her face softens when she sees Taylor. "Woman, are you trying to give me a heart attack?"

"I missed you," Taylor says with the most tender tone.

"Correction." Dee laughs. "You missed my cooking."

"There is that, but no, I missed you."

"We all know your favorite is Sese, and we still love you," Dee says.

"I'm not her favorite," Taylor mutters.

"I have a new favorite," I smile slyly.

"I heard you and Bruce will be cohabiting soon," Rainey quips.

"I wasn't referring to Bruce, I was referring to Osei."

"Is it true Vanessa Henry was his mother? And that she killed herself, and Phillip too?" Rainey asks.

"Rainey." Dee sighs. "This is why you are nobody's favorite."

Rainey glances around. "What, did I say something wrong?"

Taylor shakes her head. "You have perpetual foot-and-mouth disease. Always saying the wrong thing at the worst time."

Rainey shrugs. "Did I say something that isn't true? I'm sure Osei knows by now."

"Yes, Auntie Rainey, I know who my birth parents are and what happened to them. Did you know my parents?" Osei asks.

"I didn't know your father, and I only met your mother once. From what I remember of her, she and Sese could pass for sisters. Isn't that right, Bruce?" Rainey mockingly says.

Bruce walks in, looks around the room, and says, "Isn't what right?"

"Auntie Rainey was just saying how much Sese resembles my mother. I know you dated my mother, and you also dated Auntie Rainey. Ultimately deciding that Sese was the woman for you," Osei replies. "You got me, and here I was thinking you were going to choose me as your godmother. I guess that ship has sailed," Rainey says.

Osei hugs Rainey, "I was going to ask all of you to be my godmothers, because I know it would be impossible for Sese to decide on just one of you."

"It wouldn't be hard at all," I say.

Everyone turns and points to Taylor. "We have a unanimous decision. Taylor is your godmother."

"Gloria isn't here to vote," Bruce chimes in.

"It doesn't matter," Dee says.

Osei shrugs. "That was easy, Auntie Dee. I'm hungry."

Rhett walks into the kitchen and, in his sexy, posh British accent, he says. "I'm hungry too."

Rainey says, "Rhett, you are as handsome as ever."

"Thank you, Rainey." He winked. "But for the record, I'm here with my future wife."

"Don't worry, I'm not looking for my next husband," she says proudly.

Soon, Gloria arrives with the boys, looking as glamorous as ever. Shortly after Mason and his girlfriend, Zoe, arrive. Osei introduces me to his best friend.

"I'm happy to finally meet you. Thank you for being by Osei's side when I wasn't able to."

Wiping away fake tears, Osei says, "Please stop, you are going to make me cry."

The house is now bustling with activity, and there's an infectious energy as everyone moves with a purpose.

64

Here is to Family

Osei takes my arm, and we walk to the podium at the center of the yard.

He steps up to the microphone.

"I want to thank you all for coming and pledging your support in helping to better the lives of the children this foundation will serve. I started this foundation to provide underserved children with a safe space, a place where they can improve their lives, remove or pave over some of the bumps and potholes on the roads they must travel, to navigate their path to success. I want to help them discover their dreams and give them the tools to pursue them.

As many of you know, I grew up in an orphanage. But I had a group of people supporting me every step of the way—from the beginning until now. Now, I want to give that same support not to just one child, but to hundreds.

Today, I especially want to thank Sienna and Bruce. Sienna has agreed to become the Director of the Osei Wharton Foundation, and Bruce will serve as a board member. For all of you who don't know, Sienna is my mother, and I'm proud to be her son. To be a part of her family means I have aunts, uncles, cousins, a sister, and a brother-in-law."

Jackson raises his glass. "Here's to family."

Everyone toasts. "To family."

With tears beginning to stream down his face, Osei pauses to compose himself. "I asked Sienna today if she would officially adopt me, and she said she would, but only if I kept my surname.

Why? Because she says, there are a lot of people walking around on the planet with the surname of Lewis, but there's only one Osei Wharton. Ladies and gentlemen, I give you my mom, Sienna Lewis."

I beam with pride at his commitment to improving the lives of underprivileged youth. After Osei finishes his speech, my pride is even more.

He hands me the microphone.

"Thank you all for coming and being a part of something special and good. Thank you in advance for all the positive contributions you'll make to the children we'll nurture. I took on this challenge because there are children in this country who face difficult challenges every day. Wondering whether they will have food, if they can go to school, and most importantly, where they will live. I want these children not to worry about those things anymore. I want them to dream of a future they can achieve and not associate hard work with hardships. I want them to know we are here for them and always." I take Osei's hand and we stepped from behind the mic and bowed graciously. "Thank you all. I know we'll do great things together." Osei and I step down from the podium to greet family and board members of the Osei Wharton Foundation.

The next several days are stressful, but incredibly successful. We create a mission statement, and I'm officially voted in as the executive director. We define the roles of the main board members and the advisory council members. Osei establishes the Oscar Henry Scholarship to assist high school seniors with college tuition. With the foundation matters wrapped, we spend our time in the kitchen, talking and eating Dee's amazing meals. The guys play golf, smoke cigars, and drink plenty of whisky. At night, we gather around the fire pit, singing and entertaining Osei with stories about his parents, mostly about his father. A few times, I notice tears welling in his eyes. Bruce was close to Phillip, so he tells the most stories. Osei was all ears when Bruce recounted the night he and Phil fought six drunk and unruly patrons at a bar. Reliving the chaos, "Those guys had no idea what hit them," he says, grinning. "Phil and I cleared the place in five minutes." Osei hung on every word, joy radiating on his face.

We all agree to come back to Oregon for the Thanksgiving Holiday. The boys can barely contain their excitement at the thought of flying back to LA in Osei's plane.

After take-off, everyone settles in. Jackson and Osei are playing dominoes. Bruce and Asa are deep in a chess match. The boys watch while bickering over a video game.

Gloria and I snuggle under a throw.

"I haven't seen this in a very long time," she says.

"Seen what?" I ask.

"The happiness in your eyes. When you are happy, your eyes are bright, and they smile."

"Eyes don't smile."

"I beg to differ, they do, and it seems yours can't stop."

"I must admit, I'm very happy."

I catch Bruce's eye, he winks at me, and my heart skips a beat.

We land in LA and say goodbye to Gloria and her family. Six hours later, we land in Philly.

I stare at the ceiling, willing myself to fall asleep, when my phone beeps. I glance at the clock; it's three thirty in the morning. A text from Osei lights up the screen: *Sese, I can't sleep. Call me if you are awake.* I gingerly slip out of bed and head to the bathroom. I dial his number.

He picks up on the first ring. "Hey, Sese, you can't sleep either?"

"No, I answer softly. What's going on?"

"Being in New York, signing the papers to turn everything over to me, and inspecting the apartment is making me nervous. Auntie Taylor told me there's a safe in the apartment, and according to my grandfather's papers, only I know the combination. I don't have an inkling of what it could be."

"I'm sure there's a clue in the papers President Henry left you. Don't worry."

65

Thank you, Brad Pitt.

Two days later, the three of us, along with two members of our security detail, drive to New York to review President Henry's assets. When we arrive, Taylor and her team are waiting for us in the main conference room. Bruce and I walk in to see six people, including Taylor, sitting around the most beautiful conference table I have ever seen. Osei walks in after signing autographs and says, "This conference table is gorgeous. Where did you get it?"

A young man sitting next to Taylor replies, "It was designed and built by Brad Pitt's furniture company."

"No way, I want one," Osei says.

I pat him on the back and say, "We'll have a smaller version made for you."

I look at Taylor and smile. Because this table has taken all the anxiety Osei was having about this meeting. *Thank you, Brad Pitt.*

Taylor introduces us to the new team that will be managing Osei's portfolio.

"Why do I need this many people?" Osei asks.

"Bear with us. You'll understand in about five minutes," Taylor replies.

A projection screen descends from the ceiling, and Taylor starts her explanation. Three slides in, we all understand why Osei needs a team of six.

Taylor says, "To sum it up, all the firm's holdings on behalf of your grandfather's estate include assets of stocks, bonds, commodities, and real estate. They require different skill sets. That's why you need all of us here."

"Are you serious?" Osei and I both exclaim.

A young woman, a few years older than Osei, says, "As of now, your assets total sixty million, two hundred and fifty thousand dollars. With your shares in a successful Napa Valley Winery and other investments we'll review, you'll also generate steady annual income."

"I imagine you have an accountant, and we'd like to propose working closely together to manage your tax implications," Taylor says.

"Sure?" Osei says.

"Are you kidding me, a winery?" Bruce chimes in.

"Regardless of their morals, the guys who managed this account made some very good and sound investments," Taylor says.

I fervently say. "Yes, I'm sure, after all, they, along with Ms. Hannah, wanted to take everything away from him."

It takes Taylor and her team a couple of hours to lay out everything. Taylor hands Osei the keys to the Dakota apartment, along with an envelope with his birth name written on the front, Oscar Henry.

66

You Are My Everything, And My Everything Is For You

Rather than having the security team drive, we chose to walk the three miles to the Dakota to clear our minds. Osei gives the security team the address of the Dakota. They're hesitant to let us leave unprotected, but Osei assures them that we'll be fine.

"I'll wear my sunglasses and baseball cap. No one will recognize me."

"Osei, you can't disguise your height," Bruce says, laughing.

"They'll all stare, but they won't know it's me. This is good enough."

It's lunchtime in Manhattan. The city's rhythm beats, creating a sea of people. People stare at Osei, but no one approaches him. Thirty minutes later, we arrive at One West Seventy-Second Street, home of the Dakota. The door attendant greets us and gives us directions to the office. Passing through the metal gates and arches, we enter a breathtaking courtyard. We knock on a door with a brass plate engraved Phoebe Silverstein. The property manager introduces herself and asks us to take a seat.

Timidly, he asks for a description of the apartment.

"Certainly, Mr. Wharton, the four-thousand-square-foot, a true palace in New York City, has six bedrooms, a recently renovated kitchen and bathrooms, a media room, high ceilings with floor-to-ceiling windows in the living room, and is one of the building's premier units."

"Phoebe, who has been maintaining the apartment?" I ask.

"Until recently, Melvin, Wells, and Franklin. They often used it for visiting clients, as well as temporary housing for new employees of the firm."

We step into the elevator, and a few minutes later, we exit and walk to the apartment. Osei hands me the keys.

"Sese, my hands are trembling. I'm too nervous to open the door."

I open the door, and we step into a foyer with a large, ornate, round wooden table adorned with a large vase of fresh flowers. There's a card, and I read the card out loud. *This is the start and the end of your journey. With Love, your godmother, Taylor.*

The foyer splits in two directions. Bruce turns to Osei, pointing left then right, and asks, "Which way shall we go?"

Osei points to the left.

"I'm trying not to scream, but this place is freaking fantastic," I say.

The library is the first room we enter. Osei takes a seat and hands me the envelope. Sese, "Can you open it? I'm afraid to."

Inside the envelope, there's a letter addressed to Osei. I slowly start to read the letter.

My Dear Grandson,

Welcome home. I'm sorry I wasn't able to see you grow into the fine warrior I know you would become. First, I want you to know I loved you with all my heart and soul. Though it took me several years to find you. Your mom left you at Wharton when you were six months old, and though I was a board member there, I had no idea you were there. I hired private detectives after private detectives to look for you, but no one could find you.

Unfortunately for both you and me, my daughter, your mother, who suffered from a mental disease, was incapable of raising you. It was difficult for me to reach her, and the Lord knows I tried. I looked everywhere for you, and in the end, it was you who found me.

I was finishing up a board meeting at Wharton, and as I was walking down a hall, you were sitting on the floor crying because you couldn't find your ball. I picked you up, and the moment I looked into your eyes, I knew you were my grandchild. You have your mother's eyes. Albert, bless his soul, allowed me to look at your adoption papers. I knew the people listed as your parents were not your parents.

Bruce looks at me. "I'll be damned."
I continue to read:

I did a DNA test, and it confirmed what I already knew. You were my grandson. Oscar, or should I say, Osei. I hope you might remember how hard I tried to teach you how to pronounce Oscar, but you couldn't do it. So, everyone called you Osei.

Shortly after I found you, I was diagnosed with cancer and given only months to live. So, I made plans for you to be taken care of by Albert and his wife, Hannah. If everything has gone as planned, you are twenty-one, and Albert and Hanna have turned over my estate to you. If you are at the Dakota, you'll find a safe in the library hidden inside the wood-paneled wall behind the desk. The combination is the name you gave the fish you and I caught when we went fishing for the first time. I'm counting on you to remember. If you don't remember, there's a Plan B. Please see the back of this letter.

I turned over the letter, and on the back was the name and telephone number of a safecracking company.

Osei, finding this hilarious, was laughing and crying at the same time. Regaining his composure, he says, "I remember that day. I had never seen a fish before, and I thought it was a funny-looking bunny rabbit. I called it a funny rabbit."

Bruce opened the wood paneling to reveal a six-foot-high safe. A pen and notepad sat on the desk, which I handed to Osei. He wrote "funny rabbit," checked his cell phone, and matched the letters to numbers: 38, 66, 9, 7, 22, 24, 88. Bruce entered the code, then nodded to Osei, who turned the handle. The safe opened with a low whine.

Inside, a folder containing photos and a copy of the Henry family tree. In a large red velvet box, there are diamond rings, diamond earrings, pearl earrings, and a wealth of gold jewelry with a note: THIS JEWELRY BELONGED TO YOUR MOTHER, YOUR GRANDMOTHER, AND MY SISTER. And there's a letter stating where he is buried, along with Vanessa and Phillip.

Another envelope contains photos of Vanessa and Phillip: Phillip in his navy uniform, of him on the ship's brig, playing volleyball, a smiling photo of him and Vanessa holding hands, and finally, a picture of them holding an infant who must be Osei.

I stopped reading. Osei is doubled over in tears. "Hey," I hug him tight. We can do the rest later."

"No, please, Sese. Go on."

There was a letter explaining Phillips' history.

President Henry writes,

Your father, Phillip, was an orphan. He was adopted several times but always managed to escape and return to the orphanage. He was a world-class sprinter in high school and college. He was also a decorated naval officer and a fine man. When you have a spare moment, look into his military history. You'll be impressed and proud.

"I guess I got my speed from him?" Osei says.

There's a picture of Vanessa sunning on a beach on Martha's Vineyard. Osei opens the jewelry and takes out his grandfather's wedding band and places it on his finger, which surprisingly fits him perfectly. We leave the library and walk a few more feet to the bedrooms. The master bedroom has a floor-to-ceiling fireplace and opens onto a balcony, which has a spectacular view of Central Park. The other bedrooms and bathrooms are equally magnificent.

Down the hallway in the opposite direction of the library is a large living room with Persian rugs atop magnificent wooden floors. There's an expansive kitchen with a breakfast nook and a media room. Henry's collection of art is beyond impressive: Andrew Turner, Romare Bearden, Lois Mailou Jones, and Jacob Lawrence. Original and signed photos by Gordon Parks and James van der Zee?

"This place feels like a curated museum but also alive and vibrant," Bruce says.

I look at Osei. "Is it just me, or does it seem like someone lived here until recently?"

He nods in agreement.

I text Taylor: *Give me a call.*

"Osei, I know this is a lot to take in. Are you okay?"

"I am. I really am, and now I know why Ms. Hannah was so insistent. She knew about it all along. I will bet my last dollar that she killed Mr. Albert for my inheritance."

"I agree, and then she found her allies in the people conspiring to take it all away from you."

"If you hadn't gotten involved, they would have taken it all from me. Thank you for taking this journey with me."

"It's not done yet. We have one more place to visit."

He looks out the window at the magnificent view of Central Park. "I know we have to go to Virginia," he murmurs.

"Osei, we've come this far, and I'm not stopping now. I still need an answer."

"We already found it," he replies.

"There's still one question left to answer."

He has a puzzled look on his face. "What question is that?"

"I need to know why me and why you were given to me?"

My phone rings, startling us both.

"Taylor, has someone been living in the apartment?" I ask.

"Yes. Apparently, Charles McCarthy's girlfriend was living there. She moved out the day he was arrested. Has Osei given any thought to what he's going to do with the apartment?"

"He's going to keep it. This is his true home." I look over at Osei, and silent tears are rolling down his cheeks.

"I have a true home," he keeps repeating.

"Taylor, I'll call you back. I need to go."

I take Osei's hand, and we sit down. Cupping his face, I wipe away the tears.

"Osei, when we began this journey, we had no idea how it would end, but we committed to see it through. I prayed you'd find your parents and siblings and reunite. It didn't work out that way, and you know the worst part?"

He shakes his head.

"Well, Osei Wharton, the worst part is that you are stuck with me as your mother. I'm so blessed because you knocked on my door."

"I'm blessed, too, and happy you love me. From the way my mom looked at me in that photo, I think she loved me too," Osei says.

"There isn't a doubt in my mind." I cradle him to my breast. "I love you, Osei Wharton."

"Well, that makes two of us. I'm happy she loves me, too," Bruce says.

Looking at my beautiful men. "How could I not? You are both my everything, and my everything is for you."

We decide to spend the night in the apartment and invite the girls and their men over for dinner. When they arrive, they are stunned by the apartment and the breathtaking view of Central Park.

"Damn! We forgot to bring wine," Rainey says.

"There should be a wine cellar in the kitchen," Taylor replies.

"Where we didn't see one," Bruce says.

Curious, we all start searching until Bruce throws open a pair of floor-to-ceiling.

"Eureka!" he exclaims.

Behind them is a magnificent wine cellar, mahogany shelves lined with bottles, soft golden lighting, and a marble tasting table that looks like it came straight out of a château.

Arjun walks over to one of the shelves, admiring a bottle, whistles, and hands Osei a bottle of Château Lafite Rothschild Pauillac.

"Grab a few more. We'll celebrate," Osei says.

Arjun pours. Osei raises his glass. "To family, friends, and to Poppa Henry."

"Damn, this is the best glass of wine I've ever had," Bruce says.

"What we're sipping on is worth nearly five G's a bottle," Arjun says with a grin, lifting his glass as if to toast the extravagance.

"Seriously?" Taylor nearly chokes.

Rainey smirks. "Good, but not that good."

Leave it to Rainey to put things in her own unique perspective.

Taylor, Rainey, Dee, and I take our drinks to the living room overlooking Central Park, while Osei and the guys retire to the media room to watch a sporting event.

Rainey asks, "Sese, when did you start to suspect Vanessa and Phillip were Osei's parents?"

Before I can answer, Taylor's phone rings; it's Gloria. She puts her on speaker.

"Hey, Gloria."

"Where is everyone? I'm in town attending a conference here in New York, and I wanted to surprise you all. Please don't tell me you're all in Philly with Sese."

"They're with me, but we're not in Philly. We're at One West Seventy-Second, apartment eight. See you soon," I add with a touch of urgency.

Twenty minutes later, the doorbell rings. I open it, and Gloria says, "What the hell is going on? Whose apartment is this?"

"Hey, Auntie Gloria, where are Jackson and the boys?" Osei asks.

"They're home." Turning her attention back to us, "Can someone tell me what is going on?"

Osei takes Gloria's luggage, "Auntie, I'll leave it to Sese to explain everything to you."

Rainey hands her a glass of wine, saying, "I think you need this."

We all watch in shock as Gloria drinks the entire glass. Afterwards, she says, "Damn, I want another glass."

Laughing, Rainey pours her another glass while I bring her up to speed.

"I'm glad President Henry made sure Osei was taken care of," Gloria says. Then, rising to her, she adds, "Now, who's giving me a tour?"

Gloria takes out her phone and FaceTimes with Jackson. "Jackson, you won't believe where I am."

We all say, "Hey Jackson."

"I'm in the Dakota, touring the apartment President Henry left Osei."

"Taylor, do you know which pieces were President Henry's? Everything looks new. Do you know what happened to his things?"

'No, but I know all the artwork and the Persian rugs were his. I'll make some calls to find out more."

It's getting late, so I suggest everyone stay over. We all head to the media room to gather our bedfellows.

"Sese, you need to check on your son," Bruce says.

Osei is slumped in a chair in the back of the room. "Son, what's on your mind?"

"I wish I could just disappear for a while," he replies.

"Where would you go if I allowed you to disappear?"

"I'd fly to North Carolina, pick up Mason, and go fishing somewhere in the Caribbean."

"Not a bad idea. However, I'm not going to let you disappear to wallow in your sorrow. The one thing we do know is that you were loved. Your grandfather went to tremendous lengths to preserve all this for you."

"I don't want any of it. I want him here beside me."

"Osei, I won't allow you to hide from your reality, and I definitely won't allow you to have your own pity party. Do you understand me, Osei Wharton?"

"Yes, can I have some hot chocolate?" he asks, clearly deflecting.

We find Bruce in the kitchen. He hands Osei a cup of hot chocolate with marshmallows and me a cup of golden milk.

"Wow! How did you know I needed this?" Osei exclaims.

Osei gently places the photos of his family on the kitchen counter and looks over at Bruce.

"Will you go through these with me again?" he asks quietly.

"Of course," Bruce replies, pulling up a stool beside him.

We stay up all night with Osei, looking at his photos and talking about his parents.

At six in the morning, Arjun and Dee join us and start to prepare breakfast.

I open the refrigerator. "Where did all this food come from?" I ask.

"I ordered everything last night. It was delivered while you and Osei were in the media room."

After breakfast, everyone leaves, including Bruce. Osei and I sit in the living room and gaze out at Central Park, bustling with joggers, families, and people enjoying their day.

"It feels good to know my mom and grandfather sat in this room. I'm starting to feel their presence."

Osei, "Do you need to be alone? I can go for a walk."

"No, I want you here. You are the only family I have. Sese, I don't have practice until next week. Can we go to Virginia to visit my family's graves?"

"Yes, of course," I reply, my tone firm and reassuring.

"Do you think Bruce would join us?"

"I'm sure he'll join us."

"I'd also like Adia and Asa to come along as well," he says, his voice soft, as if unsure whether it's too much to ask, but hopeful all the same.

67

Slaw Dog

A few days later, we leave Philadelphia, heading to Virginia. The mood on the plane is heavy and somber. It feels as if we were heading to a funeral, each of us carrying unspoken words weighing heavily on our hearts. Everyone was lost in their own thoughts, trying to brace for what lay ahead.

The flight time is less than two hours. On the ground, we're greeted by two gentlemen from the security company. The security detail is in the first SUV, and we're all in the second. Osei is seated up front next to Bruce. I'm seated in the back seat behind Bruce with Adia and Asa. I gaze out the window and yell, "Stop."

Bruce slams on the brakes, jerking us all forward, "Sese, what is going on?" he asks.

I take his head gently and turn it to the left.

"I can't believe this place is still standing," he says.

"What is going on? Are you trying to kill us?" Adia says, annoyed.

Bruce pulls off the road into the parking lot of Murray's Hot Dog Stand.

"This is where I took Sese on our first date."

"And many more cheap dates after that," I sheepishly add.

"This place is the epitome of a hole in the wall," Adia says.

Asa cautiously looks around, while Osei points to the menu stapled to the side of the building, saying, "Are you sure this place has been certified by the health department?" he asks.

"You can't go inside. You order your food at the window and wait at the picnic tables until your number is called," I explain.

"All the more reason we shouldn't eat here," Adia says.

We all walk over to view the menu.

"Adia, if you don't, you'll miss out on the best hot dog in the country," Bruce says.

"I'm game, I'm hungry," Osei says.

"Tell us something we don't already know," Adia says mockingly.

Osei playfully punches her in the arm.

The menu reads: HOT DOGS: PLAIN KETCHUP AND MUSTARD $1.75; MURRAY'S FAMOUS MUSTARD; CHILI, SLAW, AND ONIONS $2.05; MURRAY'S DOG WITH CHEESE SAUCE $2.95; AND SHREDDED CHEESE $2.50.

I stick my head into the window and I nearly faint. "Mr. Murray, it's Sese. How are you doing?"

"My world. Girl, it's really you," he says, adjusting his glasses. "How have you been, and why are you in town?"

Before I can answer, he asks, "Where's that cheapskate boyfriend of yours?"

"Right here," I say, pointing to Bruce.

Bruce steps in front of me and shakes Mr. Murray's hand.

Adia orders a slaw dog, topped with lots of creamy coleslaw. She takes a hefty bite, with coleslaw oozing out of the corners of her mouth, "This is delicious. Coleslaw on a hot dog, who knew?"

As we laugh and talk, the weight of this trip fades away.

We introduce Mr. Murray to everyone, and he immediately recognizes Osei.

"You're Oscar's, boy, you don't remember me, but your grandfather used to bring you here," he says.

We all look at him in amazement; his words leave us speechless.

"Mr. Murray, how did you know President Henry was his grandfather?" I ask.

"I knew because Oscar told me. You were the apple of his eye," Mr. Murray says to Osei. "Like your grandfather, you would sit and devour chili hot dogs with onions, your favorite. I heard he passed away from cancer. I'll always be grateful to your grandfather for loaning me money when my business was struggling. When I tried to pay him back, he wouldn't take it. He was a good man."

"We're here to pay our respect to him," Bruce says.

"You'll need the key; you can't get into the cemetery without it," Mr. Murray adamantly says.

We all looked puzzled, waiting for him to explain further.

"The Chaplain at the University Church will have to let you in."

Bruce and I thank and hug Mr. Murray, and we load back into the SUV.

"Osei, now we know why hot dogs with grilled onions and chili are your favorite food," Bruce says.

68

Forgiveness Is Not An Occasional Act;
It Is a Permanent Attitude

Fifteen minutes later, we arrive at the University chapel.
"Osei, this is where Auntie Gloria and Jackson had their wedding. Adia, your dad, was Jackson's best man, and I was Gloria's maid of honor."

Inside the chapel, sunlight streams brightly through the stained-glass windows, casting red, blue, and green reflections on the marble floor and the mahogany pews.

A young man is standing in the back of the chapel, notices us, and approaches with a welcoming smile. He introduces himself as Mr. Willie Gray, the associate pastor.

"How can I help?" he asks.

"We're here to visit the burial site of President Henry and his family," Osei says.

"Please follow me," he replies, and leads us to the pastor's office. We are greeted by Reverend Elbert James. Extending his hand to Osei, saying, "I'm a big fan of yours. I have followed your career since high school."

"Thank you," Osei responds.

Reverend James looks around, bewildered. "Why are you all here?"

"I'm here to visit my grandfather's grave, and I was told I need to get the key from you," Osei says.

The pastor looked more confused. "Who is your grandfather?"

"President Oscar Henry."

Everyone notices the startled look on the pastor's face.

"Is there a problem?" I ask.

"President Henry was your grandfather?"

"Yes," Osei replies.

"I have been the pastor here for five years, and my predecessor gave me plenty of advice on how to be a good pastor. He also informed me to be prepared for the day when a young man would come asking for President Henry's grave. If that day ever came, I was to give him an envelope."

Anticipation showing on his face, Osei asks, "Did my grandfather leave something here for me?"

"No. The envelope I am talking about was left by Vanessa Henry, the President's daughter." He opens a drawer and pulls out a metal box using the key hanging on a chain around his neck to open it. He hands Osei the envelope inside the box. The front of the envelope reads: TO MY SON.

Osei takes the envelope, his hand trembling as if it weighs a ton. The room grows quiet from the cloud settling over us. Seeing the pain on Osei's face, Bruce places his hand on Osei's shoulder, "We're here with you, everything will be okay."

"Sese, will you read it?"

"No, Osei. I think you need to read this yourself, and alone."

"Pastor James, can we have the key to the gate surrounding his family's last resting place?" I ask.

"Of course." He again reaches into the drawer and hands Osei the key and directions to where the graves are located.

As we make our way to the cemetery, Osei hands me the envelope.

"Sese, can you hold on to this for me?"

In the back of the cemetery, there's a large iron gate. Osei opens the gate, and there are several headstones with photos on them. We stand in silence as we look at the headstones with photos of President Henry, Vanessa, and Phillip. There's an epitaph written on President Henry's headstone. It reads: FORGIVENESS IS NOT AN OCCASIONAL ACT; IT IS A PERMANENT ATTITUDE–MARTIN LUTHER KING JR.

We stand in solemn silence until Aida gasps, eyes wide with disbelief. "Sese, you and Vanessa could have been sisters."

Asa leans forward for a closer look. "Not just sisters, you could have been twins. It's eerie how much you resemble her."

Osei kneels in front of his grandfather's grave and clasps his hands together, and prays. Bruce and I kneel beside him, and Adia and Asa place their hands on his shoulders. After a few minutes, he stands, and we all walk away.

Once inside the car, I hand Osei back the envelope.

"Can you keep it for a while? I'm not ready to read it."

I place the envelope back into my bag. As we're driving through the gates of the University, Osei glances back at the cemetery with eyes that are distant and clouded with emotion.

"Osei, trust me, everything is going to be alright," I say.

"I know, is anybody else hungry?" His eyes fill with life again.

"I am," Asa replies.

"Can we stop and get hot dogs?" Osei asks.

"Absolutely," Bruce answers.

"My God, you two are human garbage disposals. Still, I think I could eat another slaw dog," Adia murmurs, gently touching Osei's shoulder.

69

The Moment You Fall In Love

The Dakota has become our second home, and we spend as much time there as possible. Osei, Adia, and Asa are in the media room watching a movie. Bruce and I slip in and sit in the back of the room after the movie begins. The room is dark as the glow of the credits at the end flickers softly on the walls. While watching the credits, Adia turns to Osei and asks, "How do you feel about Sese?"

The kids, unaware of our presence, remained glued to the screen. I grab his hand to leave, but he stays still.

"Why do you ask?"

"You behave as if she's your real mother."

Osei, his eyes fixed on the dark screen, says, "As far as I'm concerned, she's my mother. Before I met her, I refused to love anyone. The moment I saw her, I knew I'd love her as my mother for the rest of my life."

"How can you decide something so serious in a moment?" Adia asks.

"Do you remember when you first knew you loved your parents?"

"No," Adia replies.

"It could have been at birth, or it could have been the first time they held your hand, or made you laugh. For you, love is always there. For me, I never knew what unconditional love felt like, not from a parent, not even from a girlfriend. Since I was twelve, people approached me because I could play basketball.

Sese cares for me because I'm Osei, her son, and not because I'm Osei Wharton, the famous basketball player."

"Why is she so easy to love? I find myself having strong emotions toward her, but I hate myself because of it," Adia says.

"Adia, why would you hate yourself?" Osei asks.

"I resented her for so long because my dad has always loved her. My mom knew it and made our lives miserable because of it, but it still feels like a betrayal to love her as much as I do. I find myself even needing her approval."

"I know this is hard for you. When your mother passed, she asked Asa and me to support you and your dad in any way we could. Your journey would be long and difficult. I didn't understand at the time, but listening to you, now I do. Loyalties are tough, especially when, on the days of your mom's passing, you had a potential stepbrother, more importantly, a potential stepmother. I was there when your mom asked Sese to look after you. She was sincere and serious."

"That's what is so disturbing. My mom was profoundly serious."

"Adia, she didn't want you to be alone. She wanted you to have someone who would advocate and navigate life on your behalf. She wanted you to start to see life and love as a right, not a privilege."

Asa takes Adia's hands, "You can always lean on me. I love you more than life."

"When and how did you two first meet?" Osei asks.

"I started liking her when we were gawky ninth graders. I constantly followed her around. If she joined the math club, I joined the math club." My older sister told me I needed to do everything I could to impress her, and the first thing she suggested was that I should shower regularly!"

Osei bursts into laughter until tears roll down his cheeks. Wiping his eyes, he says, "Oh man, don't tell me you were one of those kids."

"Yes, I was a walking pigpen."

Osei gathers himself. "Okay, so when did you know you loved Asa?"

"Since the first grade."

Asa looks at her in disbelief. "No Way."

"Why do you think I always bought extra snacks for school?"

Asa looks dumbfounded.

"Because I wanted to sit next to you. If you ask my dad, he'll tell you I knew how to spell your name before I could spell my own."

"Why didn't you ever tell me?"

"Because I didn't want to scare you away. Asa Hollander, I have always loved you. Osei told me he fell in love with Sienna the moment he saw her. I realized that's what happened to me. I fell in love with you the moment I saw you at Friends Seminary."

"I remember you bringing your dad's brownies to school and sharing them with me."

"I only shared them with you, and no one else."

"And we'll continue to share our love for an eternity. To my eternal love, my wife, Adia Marie Hollander."

"This is too sappy for me. Although I'm so happy for you, it's getting late. I have to drive to Philly tomorrow morning, so I'm going to turn in," Osei says.

Bruce and I quietly slip out of the room.

70

We Are Getting Married

Over the next few months, we all settle into our new normal. Osei's is thriving, and the Seventy-Sixers are leading their division. Bruce has found his stride at the University of Pennsylvania, and I've fully embraced the foundation. The girls are happy, their lives rooted in love and family. Adia and Asa have taken to Philly life but occasionally spend weekends in Manhattan.

Osei and I have breakfast in my office every morning when he's at home. Reflecting on everything that's transpired over the last few months, each moment is a reminder of how much has changed. The letter from his mother lies unread, waiting, patient and solemn, for the moment he feels ready to face the truth it holds.

Bruce, Millie, and I spend time at the Dakota, occasionally inviting the girls and their husbands over for dinner, games, or a movie.

On this particular evening, Osei, Adia, and Asa join us at the Dakota. Earlier today, Dee filmed an episode of her show here, and we're feasting on the leftovers: chicken cordon bleu, grilled asparagus, and a pasta salad with eggplant, tomatoes, and basil.

It has been a while since we were all together as a family. So, Bruce and I take this opportunity to announce our marriage to the kids.

"It's about time," Osei says.

"Have you set a date?" Adia asks.

"We were thinking about November, over the Thanksgiving holiday, when everyone will be together in Oregon," Bruce replies.

"We're planning on Thanksgiving Day, I chime in."

"I can't be there," Osei says. "We're playing the Knicks on Thanksgiving Day."

"If you can't be there, we'll postpone it until Christmas. We'll plan to get married in Manhattan and have the reception here," I say.

"That's so romantic. Manhattan is beautiful during the holidays," Adia says.

Bruce looks at me, smiling, "Christmas it is."

"Let's celebrate," Osei says, heading to the wine cellar and returning with two bottles of champagne.

Adia raises her glass. "I'd like to be the first to toast you. Thank you for loving and believing in each other. I wish you many years of happiness together."

With tears in his eyes, Bruce says, "Thank you, darling."

He walks over to where I'm sitting and kneels in front of me. "I can't count the number of times I have done this in my mind. Sienna, I have loved you all my life. I can't go another second without saying this. Without you, I'm lost. Will you marry me and be by my side forever?" He slide a rare blue diamond ring on my finger. I look into his eyes as tears stream down his face. "Yes, we'd be lost without each other." We kiss for what feels like an eternity, slow and thorough. The kids lose their minds.

"I don't know if this is the most romantic thing I've ever seen, or the sexiest," Osei says awkwardly.

"I'm confused too. I think you two need to get a room," Adia chimes in.

Asa walks over and takes my hand. "I have never seen a blue diamond before. It's beautiful."

The kids head off to the media room.

Still reeling from all the excitement, Bruce goes for a run in Central Park to let off some steam. I settle in on the kitchen nook with a glass of champagne, looking out at the park below.

My phone vibrates, it's Dee.

"Sese, thank you for letting me use your kitchen. The viewers are enjoying watching my show in real kitchens."

"Dee, hold on. I have another call coming in."

I switch over to Taylor.

"I'm so glad you called! I have something to tell you, and I wanted you to be the first to know."

"I'm all ears."

"Bruce and I are getting married," I blurt out.

"This is good news!" she screams.

"Can you help me with planning? I want to get married at the courthouse and have the reception here at the Dakota."

"Of course!"

"I'll call you back. I need to finish speaking with Dee."

"Dee, the Everything Chocolate Christmas party will be at the Dakota and will double as the wedding reception for me and Bruce.

Not responding. Instead, she asks, "Who was on the other line earlier?"

"It was Taylor."

"So, you had to tell her before you told me or anyone else about your wedding. Sese, you are shameless."

"I'm not. You were the second person I told."

"Whatever. Regardless, I'm over the moon happy for you. Please, please let me tell Rainey."

"Be my guest. I'm calling Gloria now to tell her and Jackson. Give Arjun my best. I love you."

Gloria answers, "Hello, gorgeous."

"Right back at you. I know we're all meeting for Thanksgiving in Oregon, but could you celebrate Christmas with us at the Dakota? Bruce and I are hosting the Everything Chocolate Dinner and using it as our wedding reception."

"Wait, what? You're what?"

"You heard me."

"Jackson, hurry, come here," she screams.

"Gloria, what's going on?" Jackson exclaims.

"Bruce and Sese are getting married."

"It's about time," he says, with a matter-of-fact tone.

"Jackson, I can't believe you. This is a big deal," Gloria says.

"It would be a bigger deal if they weren't getting married. Hello Sese. Tell your future husband-to-be to call me."

"Sese, excuse him, he's not a romantic. I want to hear everything. How did Bruce propose?"

I thought about the night Bruce proposed, and I decided I definitely couldn't share those details with her. Instead, I told her about the proposal earlier tonight in front of the kids. I snap a picture of the ring and text it to her, Taylor, Dee, and Rainey.

After the call, my mind drifts back to the night when Bruce actually proposed. We are in bed enjoying pizza night when he says, "Sese, we should make a baby."

"Make a baby? Are you crazy? We're too old for that."

"Speak for yourself. We're never too old to try. I'm a bit old-fashioned. If we're going to make a baby, we should be married."

I pulled his head to my chest, touched by his words.

"Sese, will you marry me? I want your heart," he says, kissing my breast. "And I want to share our love forever," he whispers.

He moves his hands between my thighs, gently parting them. "You're a gift, and I want to spend my life unwrapping you." Minutes later, we were fully committed to the baby-making mission.

Bruce walks into the kitchen after his run.
"What are you thinking about?" he asks.
"Making a baby."
He glances around. "Where are the kids?"
"Watching a movie."
"I'm going to shower, join me, and we can have another go at making a baby."
In the afternoon. Osei knocks on the bedroom door and does his usual thing, walks in, without an invitation.
"Hey, handsome, how was the movie?"
"I don't know, I nodded off. It was some chick flick that Adia wanted to watch."
Rainey calls, and I place her on speaker.
Hey Rainey, "What's up?"
"Hey, Auntie," Osei says.
"Sese, I'm upset. I had to hear about your engagement from Dee."
Before I can answer, she's off to the races, telling me I treat her differently from everyone else, and if it weren't for her, I never would have met Bruce. For the next five minutes, she's having a conversation all by herself.
I finally put an end to her ranting by asking, "Do you like the ring?"
She excitedly says, "I absolutely love it. Did Osei buy it? It looks like it cost a fortune."

"Auntie, Bruce bought it. I didn't know blue diamonds existed," Osei says.

Walking in, Bruce says, "Hello Rainey, I bought it, and it did cost a fortune, and she's worth every penny, and I intend on getting my money's worth."

"I'm happy for both of you. I'll see you both soon," Rainy says and hangs up.

"She's a handful," Bruce says,

Osei looks at him and asks, "Did you really date Auntie Rainey?"

"Yes, we went out a couple of times."

"Only a couple?" Osei asks.

"It would have been more, but there were two things which played against her."

"Which were?" Osei asks.

"One, she wouldn't stop talking long enough for me to kiss her, and second, I met Sese, and it was all over."

71

Kir Royale

In the days that follow, we return to Philly. The foundation is keeping me busy with speaking engagements, meeting city dignitaries, and CEOs of major companies, all to maintain and grow the foundation's visibility. Fundraising is a tremendous success, thanks to the incredible support from the community and our sponsors.

There's a knock at the door, and moments later, Chloe enters and settles into a chair.

"Sienna, you are getting married in two weeks."

Before she can finish, I cut her off, eyes wide. "Wait, did you say in two weeks?"

"Yes, in two weeks."

"Oh no! I haven't done a thing. I'm totally screwed."

"Actually," she says calmly. "Adia and I have taken care of everything."

"Taken care of what, exactly?"

She opens her iPad. "I just emailed you the *Everything Chocolate Christmas* menu Dee sent earlier today. I ordered the invitations from the same boutique in London, updated with your and Mr. LeBlanc's names, the date, and silver wedding bells. They went out last week to last year's thirty guests, plus twenty more, including foundation board members, Osei's manager, and reps from Nike. Adia and Taylor took care of the courthouse ceremony, the decorations, and your bouquet. All the details should be in your inbox shortly. Oh, and you've got a private fitting at Saks today at 3:30. Your schedule is clear, so you are good to go."

"Oh my God. When did you all find the time to do all this?"

"I knew you didn't have the time, so I asked Adia to help me. I hope you are okay with us butting in."

"I'm at a loss for words. I can't thank you enough."

"Oh, by the way, forty-five of the fifty people invited have RSVP'd."

I call Bruce with a hint of excitement and disbelief, "Do you realize we're getting married in two weeks?"

"What in two weeks?"

"You are not getting cold feet, are you?" I ask.

"Hell no, but we haven't made any plans."

"No, we haven't, but Adia and Chloe have," I say, telling him all that they had done.

"Wow," he says. "We'll do something nice for them. And don't worry about getting me a wedding band, we can figure that out later."

"I've had your wedding band for twenty years," I say softly. "I just made a minor adjustment, replacing the center diamond with a blue diamond.

"Twenty years? You bought a wedding band for me twenty years ago? And you still have it."

"It's a long story. There are a few parts that will probably bore you to tears."

"I'm not easily bored. I'll see you tonight. "

As I'm backing into a parking spot at Saks, my phone rings. It's Taylor.

"Sese, do you have a moment?"

"I always have time for you."

"Good. I'm at your house. I'll see you soon."

"Taylor, I can't come home now. I have an appointment at Saks to look at wedding dresses. I'm getting married in two weeks, and I don't have a dress."

"Don't worry. The appointment was canceled."

"Canceled!' I shout, my voice rising in disbelief. "Taylor, I need a wedding dress."

"Bye, Sese, I'll see you soon."

I sit there, so tightly my knuckles turn white, with equal parts fury and confusion swirling inside me. I'm so upset I can hardly breathe as I open the front door. Standing in the foyer, with tears in their eyes, are Taylor, Gloria, Dee, and Rainey. Each holding a champagne flute filled with Kir Royale. Taylor hugs me and says, "You silly girl, you didn't think we were going to let you pick out your wedding dress without us, did you?"

I glance into the living room and gasp. Three mannequins stand elegantly by the window, each draped in the most breathtaking wedding gowns I've ever seen. The fabrics shimmer in the light, delicate lace and satin whispering promises of a perfect day.

"Personally, I like the one in the middle," Gloria says.

"I like them all," Dee says.

I start slipping into the gowns, feeling the soft fabrics embrace me as I twirl in front of the mirror.

"Sese, you have always had the most perfect breasts," Rainey quips.

"I've always been partial to her ass," Taylor chimes in.

"You are both perverts," I say.

"You have a loving child without having had to give birth to him. No stretch marks or sagging breasts," Gloria says.

Rainey smirks at Gloria. "Please, yours came courtesy of a surgeon's scalpel."

Gloria lifts her top without hesitation, her voice low, almost daring. "True. But perfection has its price."

Rainey arches a brow, then unbuttons her blouse. "No need. Mine came with standard issues."

"Rainey." Gloria studies her for a moment, her expression shifting from challenge to administration. "Whoever did your work left nothing to improve."

"Can we focus on Sese's breasts and ass for now?" Dee says.

The first dress is beautiful with lace flowers on the bodice and a long train. I look in the mirror, running my hands down the fabric, smoothing it over my hips. Tilting my head, I study the Edwardian neckline and the seemingly endless train.

"I think this one is too formal for the courthouse ceremony and the reception afterward," I say.

They all nod in agreement. I slip into the second dress, my fingers tracing the delicate straps as I turn to see the full effect. The neckline plunges, and the open back reveals a daring expanse of skin, stopping just above my derriere.

"This one is too sexy. Bruce would take one look at you and drag you straight to the judge's chambers," Dee says.

The third dress is perfect. It has the right balance between sexy and elegance. The soft crepe fabric drapes beautifully off my shoulders, framing a low cowl neckline. The asymmetrical hemline adds a modern touch, hugging my waist and hips in all the right places. The open back is adorned with delicate streamers that fold seamlessly into fabric, cascading to the floor like whispers of silk.

"This is the one," Taylor exclaims, her eyes lighting up. "I love that it's cream, instead of white. Sese, it blends nicely with your skin tone."

72

In Front of Everyone We Love and Cherish

I call Bruce to let him know that the girls and I are on our way to the office. When we arrive, he and the guys are already there. Osei, Adia and Asa have bought food and drinks.

"Osei, when did you get home?" I ask.

"About an hour ago," he says.

"Congratulations, Osei, you had a very good road trip. A championship is in your future," Kelvin says.

Jackson taps his glass to get everyone's attention. "Sese, these next few days are for you and Bruce. With special attention paid to you. You've been the rock we've all leaned on, always there, especially for our women, never asking for anything in return. Sienna Katia Lewis, I salute you. And I know my good friend Bruce will always love you."

"Thank you," I say, with tears in my eyes. "I love you all, and more importantly, I've felt your love. I was going to do this privately, but I want everyone I love to be a part of it."

Cupping his wedding band in both my hands, I kneel before Bruce, my heart pounding.

"Bruce, my love, I have carried this ring with me for the past twenty years. From the moment we first met, I wanted to be your wife. You are my everything. So, in front of everyone we love and cherish, I'm asking you to marry me."

He takes my hand and says, "In front of everyone we love and cherish, I accept."

We kiss and kiss and kiss, until Osei says, "For everyone who thinks this is a romantic kiss, raise your hands. For everyone who thinks this is sexy as hell, raise your hands?"

Everyone raises their hands for the sexy as hell kiss.

"This is definitely another of their X-rated kisses," Adia says, her hands partially covering her face.

"I raise my glass to the couple who came up with pizza night, and I wish them a million more pizza nights," Gloria says.

With a confused look on his face, Osei says, "What is pizza night?"

Arjun smirks and replies, "It's not for the faint of heart."

73

Compliments of Your Son

Two days before the wedding, I'm in New York working with Dee and her team on preparations for the Everything Chocolate Dinner and my wedding reception, when I get a call from Osei.

"Sese, can you meet me at the Teterboro Private Airport. I'm flying to Oregon tonight, and I may not be back in time for the Everything Chocolate dinner and the wedding reception. I'm sorry."

"Osei, you must be here."

"Something important came up, and I have to fly to Nike's headquarters. I'll fill you in on the details when you get here."

"Sese, you're too upset to go alone. I'll ride with you to the airport," Dee says.

I was expecting Osei to be waiting for me in the lobby, but I'm told he's waiting on his plane.

"Dee, I can't believe him," I say, anxiously boarding the plane as anger builds inside of me. "I'll talk some sense into Osei. He can't leave tonight."

To my surprise, Gloria, Jackson, Arjun, Taylor, Rainey, and Bruce are on board. I turn to Dee, "What is going on? Where's Osei?"

He took off about ten minutes ago," Bruce says.

I start to cry, and tears well up in my eyes. "I wanted to see him before he left."

"Calm down, Sese, you'll see him when we land. We're all going to the same place," Bruce says.

Now I'm completely confused, my eyes move from face to face, searching for answers.

My voice trembles as I ask, "What do you mean?"

Gloria smiles. "Osei, the boys, Kelvin, Adia, Asa, Marie, her fiancé, Colin, and Eric, are on a plane in front of us."

"In front of us? Where are we going?"

"We're taking you on a trip. Compliments of your son," Bruce says,

"Dee, you should have been an actor. All the way here you complained about Osei, knowing I was being set up. Shame on all of you."

"You have no one but your son to blame for this," Bruce says.

The captain announces, "We've been cleared for takeoff. Please take your seats. Welcome aboard, Ms. Lewis."

We land two hours later to find a fleet of SUV's parked on the tarmac. Osei and the boys were playing outside, one of them.

I walk over and say, "Osei, when did you become such a convincing liar?"

He opens the door, smirking, and says, "A harmless lie now and then is okay."

Bruce grins. "Welcome to Virginia."

"Why are we back in Virginia?" I ask.

Osei grins and says, "For your wedding, of course. Virginia is for Lovers."

I look at Bruce, who smiles. "Like I said, compliments of your son."

The cars stop in front of the chapel at our alma mater. I follow Taylor and Gloria to the rear entrance, where they lead me to the chaplain's office. My breath catches when I see my wedding dress hanging from a hook on the wall, waiting for me.

Heart full, I turn to them. "Pinch me, is this really happening?"

"It was always your dream to get married here, so with Osei's help, we were able to make it come true. Sese, stop crying, I have to do your makeup," Gloria says.

Taylor helps me step into my wedding dress, guiding the fabric and smoothing every delicate fold into place. The soft crepe drapes naturally over my body. I glance in the mirror, as my heart races, as I take in the transformation.

Beside me, Taylor and Gloria slip into their dresses. A striking midnight blue, the fabric shimmered subtly under the soft light. Their gowns, a shorter yet equally stunning version of mine, mirror the grace and sophistication of the moment. Taylor fastened the final clasp on my gown, her eyes shining with emotion. A mixture of excitement and nervousness swirls inside me as it sinks in. I'm getting married. Osei stands in a well-tailored midnight blue tuxedo, calm and composed in front of the ornate doors, soon to open to friends, family, and, more importantly, Bruce.

"I'll be honored if you let me walk you down the aisle," he says.

I take his arm, and I look up at my beautiful child. "The honor is all mine."

The chapel doors open, and a sharp breath escapes me. Flowers are everywhere, cascading down the arches, draping over the pews, and filling the air with sweet fragrance. Massive orbs of roses hang from the ceiling, wisteria trailing like delicate waterfalls to the floor. The aisle is blanketed in rose petals, a breathtaking tapestry of every shade imaginable. It feels like stepping into a dream.

Sese, "Do you like everything?" Osei asks.

"Yes, this is absolutely spectacular. I couldn't ask for anything more."

As we walk down the aisle, the University choir begins singing "Ave Maria."

Standing at the altar are Bruce, his best man, Jackson, and my matron of honor, Taylor. I glance at Bruce and see the tears streaming down his face. Adia comes and stands next to me, and together she and Osei place my hand into Bruce's.

We both turn and face the Chaplain, as the soft murmur of our family and friends fades into the background.

Bruce leans over, saying, "What took us so long to get here?"

"Sometimes, the wrong train takes you to the right station."

He nods and says, "Amen."

Surprised, the Chaplain looks at us. "We haven't started the ceremony yet."

We both give him an apologetic smile.

The ceremony was quick, and before I knew it, Bruce and I were kissing. Arm in arm, we turn to greet the crowd, who clap and whistle enthusiastically.

As we walk down the aisle, Rachel Brown's Bumblebee is playing throughout the church. I look at Osei, and he shakes his head and points to Adia. She's singing along with the song. *Let's go back to the day we met. Just close your eyes and remember when you laughed so hard at all my jokes. Be mine, don't you wanna be mine, all mine. Be my bumblebee, my valentine, and I'll be yours, keep me, keep me, and I'll keep you with me. Everywhere we go so happy, that's for sure.*

Everyone is dancing to the funky reggae beat of the song.

At the end of the aisle, I throw my bouquet. Marie catches it and excitedly turns to Colin, who gives her a big kiss.

The reception is in a huge tent next to the church. Bruce and I head to the center table and sit down. I look at Bruce, "Did you know about this?"

"I knew we were getting married, but nothing about all of this. Are you okay with everything?"

"I couldn't be happier."

Osei walks to the center of the tent, where a wooden dance floor has been installed.

"I'm not going to bore you with a long toast, just a story. I recently asked Sese when she knew she loved Bruce. She told me it was the night he carried her on his back to campus while she drunkenly sang, 'Somewhere Over the Rainbow.' I asked Bruce the same question. He told me the same story. He knew it then, too, when she serenaded him with *Somewhere Over the Rainbow* while he carried her on his back. So, I relayed this story to one of my biggest fans, and she agreed to join us tonight and sing Bruce and Sese's love song. Family and friends, I give you a Grammy Award winner, and Philly's own Mrs. Patti LaBelle."

"Are you freaking kidding me?" Bruce says.

The soulful voice of Patti LaBelle rings out as she enters the dance floor singing, *"Somewhere over the Rainbow."*

Everyone goes wild. When she gets to the center of the dance floor, she beckons for me and Bruce to join her. He takes my hand, and we dance.

Bruce beckons for everyone to join us on the dance floor as Patti breaks out with a "New Attitude."

After dancing to "New Attitude," Osei asks Gloria, Dee, Taylor, Rainey, and me to come to the center of the dance floor, where Patti serenades us with "You are My Friend."

There isn't a dry eye in the place. Patti leaves us, and for the rest of the night, we drink and dance for what seems like an eternity.

Several hours later, Osei stops the music and says, "I hate to bring this party to an end, but it's time to leave."

The booing starts. Responding, he says, "We can stay and party until the crack of dawn, but we'll have to fly back to New York commercially, with a layover in D.C."

Everyone starts rushing to the waiting cars. It's 1:00 A.M. when we arrive at the Dakota, and we're too excited to sleep, so the party continues.

"Osei, I still can't believe Patti LaBelle sang at my wedding," I say.

"I wanted this day to be special. You deserve better than a simple courthouse wedding. I hope you don't mind me interfering with your plans."

"After the glorious day I had, I don't mind at all."

It's noon when Bruce and I finally get in bed, and before we doze off, we take a trip to Jupiter for the first time as a married couple.

74

The Warmth of Our Lives

The next morning, the apartment feels like Grand Central Station. Tomorrow is the Everything Chocolate Dinner. Dee, Arjun, and her crew are finishing the preparations. The food and the decorations are even more spectacular than last year.

Rhett calls. "Hello, Sese, we've just arrived at JFK, and we'll see you soon."

"Really, I didn't know you were coming!" My surprise melts instantly into a grin.

Osei takes my phone and says, "Hello Rhett, I've arranged a car for you and Min-Ah. The driver will be holding a card with your name on it. We'll see you soon," Osei says.

"Osei, what's going on?" I ask.

"I thought it would be nice if all the men you love were all in one place," he says.

"Thank you, but you know I love you the most."

"I know, we won't tell Bruce."

Rhett and Min-Ah step into the lobby of the Dakota, their eyes wide with amazement. "This is it, the legendary building!" Rhett exclaims, his voice filled with disbelief. Min-Ah's face lights up, her hands pressed to her chest. "I can't believe we're actually here," she says, brimming with excitement. They both stare around, taking in the historical charm of the place, the same walls that John Lennon once called home. "I've read about this place so many times," Min-Ah adds. "But seeing it in person… It's unreal!" Their awe is evident as we walk to the elevator.

As the elevator door closes, Rhett says, "We're walking in the footsteps of history."

Min-Ah and I settle in the media room to watch *Late Autumn,* a movie starring Hyun Bin and Tang Wei. We're joined by Adia and Chloe.

The movie ends, and Adia says, "I'm absolutely in love with Hyun Bin."

"Join the club," Min-Ah adds.

Rhett and Bruce go for a run in Central Park. When they return, we all settle in and Rhett tells us how he and Min-Ah first met; halfway through the story, Min-Ah interrupts him, saying, "Don't leave out the part about me calling the police on you."

"A minor detail," Rhett says.

"Wait, it's a detail we all want to hear," Osei says.

"I promise to tell you, but I don't want to relive that horrible memory right now."

"The most important thing to remember is you didn't give up on your feelings for Min-Ah," I say.

Rhett kisses Min-Ah and says, "I thank God every day you didn't give up on us."

The morning of the Everything Chocolate dinner, I wake to snow-blanketed streets. With at least twelve to eighteen inches expected to fall.

I pray that all the hard work for the Everything Chocolate dinner and our wedding reception won't be derailed by a snowstorm. Osei, back from the airport with his best friend, Mason, and Zoe, walks in covered in snow.

Shaking the snow off, Mason says, "What's cooking? This place smells like a gourmet restaurant."

Osei takes him by the shoulders and leads him to the kitchen, saying, "You'll feast on the best food you have ever had in your life tonight."

At four o'clock, there had not been a single cancellation due to the snow, and two hours later, the apartment was packed.

Over two feet of snow has accumulated outside, and the sweet chocolate is flowing inside.

Two other apartments on our floor are having Christmas parties too. With the doors open, guests flow freely between the units. At one point, there were at least a hundred people in our unit.

"Sese, this is the best party I've ever attended. The food is fantastic. Who would have thought chocolate and baby back ribs were a thing?" Osei says.

He points to a tall guy standing in the corner, devouring ribs. "That's Guillaume. He lives next door, and he says he's not leaving until all the baby back ribs are gone."

"I don't think anyone will be leaving anytime soon. I think we'll all be snowed in."

Bruce is across the room talking to Jackson and Eric, and I beckon him to come over.

"Here comes your husband," Osei says.

"I proudly say, can you repeat that?"

"Here comes your husband."

"Bruce, it looks like no one will be able to leave anytime soon. I'm trying to sort out the sleeping arrangements. Rainey, Dee, and Taylor all live a few blocks away, and they're willing to let some folks stay with them. I want Gloria and her crew, Rhett, Min-Ah, Mason, and Zoe to stay here."

Guillaume, who has finished stuffing his face with the baby back ribs, comes over and introduces himself to me and Bruce.

"I didn't mean to eavesdrop, but I've three empty bedrooms, and you are welcome to use them for your guests," he says.

"Thank you, Guillaume, we'll definitely take you up on your offer," Bruce says.

Now, Mark and his girlfriend, Ingrid, and the two Nike executives won't have to try to make it back to their hotels.

The party is still going strong at 2:00 A.M., and Bruce and I take refuge in the media room. I take his hand, and I twist his wedding band on his finger. "You are all mine."

"Yes, and from this moment on, my everything is for you," he replies.

He leans in for a kiss, and I pull away. There are other people in the media room.

"I can't believe you are being shy. We're a married couple."

Before I can answer, Osei appears, "Can you guys take a walk with me?"

I glance back at Bruce and say, "Sure, it's getting hot in here. I need some fresh air."

"You are such a coward," Bruce says.

"Sese, will you bring the letter from Vanessa? I'm ready to try to understand why she did what she did and forgive her for it."

I go into the bedroom to get the letter and change into warmer clothes. Osei and Bruce are waiting for me at the front door. Osei hands me my down jacket. Bruce, holding two thermoses, passes one to Osei and keeps the other one.

"Osei, your thermos is filled with hot chocolate, and ours is filled with hot whiskey, honey and lemon, better known as a hot toddy."

"I wonder if you can mix chocolate and scotch?" Osei asks.

"Of course, you can. It's called boozy hot chocolate," I say.

"Why am I not surprised?" he replies.

We make our way to Central Park and sit on a bench facing the Dakota.

Every apartment on our floor is lit with Christmas lights, and people are dancing in every window.

"It looks like Mason is having the time of his life," I say.

"Mason has never had a bad time. He's been the Yin to my Yang, my anti-depressant from the beginning."

I take the letter from my pocket and hand it to Osei.

"I don't think I can read it." He says softly. "Can either of you read it?"

I hand the letter to Bruce, and he starts to read it out loud.

My Dear Son,

I'm sorry I won't be by your side to see you grow into the exceptional man I know you'll become. I've been fighting depression and other mental illnesses all my life. My father has tried to help, but I can't trust him anymore. He and Phillip, your father, want to lock me away. I overheard a conversation Phillip had with my father. They were conspiring to put me away.

I won't be locked away again. I'd rather die than go through that again. I want to tell you I can fight this and live, but I'm not strong. I placed you in an orphanage because I don't trust my father to take care of you. He would send you away because of who he is and the public image he must maintain. He can't have a bastard for a grandson. I've always been an embarrassment to him. On the adoption papers, I lied and listed someone else as your biological parents, because I don't want my father to find you.

Osei says with tears in his eyes, "Why did she do this to us? We would have taken care of each other."

"Osei, please don't blame her. She was not well, and because of her illness, she didn't trust the people closest to her."

Bruce starts to read again.

I want you to grow up strong and not with the stigma of having a mentally unstable mother. The names on your birth certificate are Bruce LeBlanc and Sienna Lewis. When you find them, they will love and accept you. Bruce and Sienna are the couple I wish Phillip and I were. I do love your father, and I know he loves me, but our love is just… different. I'm sorry, I know what I'm doing will be the best thing for you in the long run. I love you, and I don't ask you to forgive me. I ask only that you understand. Signed Vanessa Henry.

"Now we know how your names got on my adoption papers," Osei says.

"Vanessa and I worked together in the Bursar's office, and she had access to everyone's personal information."

He stares at me, stunned. "Sese, why does everyone want to give you the responsibility of raising their children?"

"What matters, Osei, is you and I found each other, and I thank your mother for trusting your well-being to me, no matter the circumstances."

He opens his thermos, blows into the mouth of the container, and takes a drink. The rich aroma of the chocolate fills the air.

Bruce unscrews the top of his thermos, pours some scotch into it, and hands it to me. I take a sip, feeling warmth spread through me.

"Osei, I say softly, "now you know how you and I came to be."

He stands up, takes my hand, and smiles. "I'm truly blessed to have you in my life. But right now, I'm freezing. Let's go inside."

I look into my son's face. "Osei, from the moment we met, we warmed each other's souls."

As we cross the street, Adia and Asa wave from the window. We wave back, and together Bruce, Osei, and I step into the warmth of our lives.

The End

www.ingramcontent.com/pod-product-compliance
Lightning Source LLC
LaVergne TN
LVHW011941060526
838201LV00061B/4175